The Beauty of Summer

A Novel

The Beauty of Summer

A Novel

Louis N. Jones

Dove
Publishers

Note from the Author:

This is a book about intimacy. It is an uncomfortable and controversial subject not often discussed in Christian circles, although it is
on the hearts and minds of non-Christians all around the world. One of
my callings as a fiction writer and publisher is to merge creativity with
reality. As such, the story you are about to read is fiction, but it will
ring true with many a reader.

Though this is a Christian fiction book, we want to warn you that
it may not be for everyone. This book falls in the category commonly
called edgy Christian fiction. Because of the subject matter, and to
present the reality of the environment where this story takes place, this
book contains a few instances of frank language and subject matter
that may not be appropriate for all readers. This book contains characters that struggle to find intimacy, but often fall into lust and sex. It
contains scenarios that are real and raw, but still restrained and safe for
the average Christian reader. This is not a fairy tale, but a book about
real romantic relationships where the characters struggle with the
myriad of issues those types of relationships present. I pray that you
read and enjoy it as a real but redemptive urban Christian romance. If
you do enjoy it, I would like to hear from you. If you don't enjoy it, I
would like to hear from you as well.

Blessings

Louis N Jones
www.louisnjones.com

The Beauty of Summer

Published by Dove Christian Publishers
A division of Kingdom Christian Enterprises
P.O. Box 611
Bladensburg, MD 20710-0611
www.dovechristianpublishers.com

ISBN: 978-0-9975898-0-1

Other Novels by Louis N Jones

Prodigal in the City

The Colors Will Change

Adverse Possession

Contact with this author at:

www.louisnjones.com

PROLOGUE

Wednesday, 9:01 p.m., Richmond, Virginia

"Why can't we go to your place?"

The girl, fresh out of high school and ready for as much debauchery and rebellion as her five-foot-eight frame could muster, rolled down the passenger side window and flicked the still-smoldering remnant of a joint out onto the road.

Her date, five years her senior, remained silent and kept his eyes on the road. The motel was somewhere on Broad Street, but he wasn't sure if he was going in the right direction. He had just passed several blocks of government buildings that quickly made way for pricey townhomes. It didn't seem like the right neighborhood for a cut-rate motel. He decided to drive only five more blocks before he made a U-turn and headed northwest.

"There's a Holiday Inn. Why don't we stop there?" the girl urged.

Because the Super 8 is cheaper, the man thought. But he dared not say that aloud, even though he had long stopped trying to impress her. She was willing to be intimate with him, and that's all he cared about. "Be cool, Gracie. I'm sure the Super 8 is around here somewhere."

"Tim, y'know I'd rather go to your place," Gracie cooed.

"My roommate has the apartment tonight," Tim lied. His only roommate was a ten-year-old cat, and she was too old to care. He had no intention of allowing Gracie to see where he lived. He was planning for this rendezvous to be short-lived.

He was driving his brother's car. He drove it a few more blocks, then gave up and decided to go the other direction. He started to make a U-turn against the posted sign, noticed an RPD cruiser with two officers inside sitting across the street, and made a right instead. For some strange reason, the refrains from the Phil Collins/Philip Bailey song *Easy Lover* began playing in his head.

"You think we can get some snacks before we go to the room?" Gracie said.

"Girl, we just ate," Tim noted.

"I know. But I'm hungry."

"Need to stop smokin' so much of that stuff."

"Only had two joints today."

"That's enough."

Gracie ignored him. "There's got to be a 7-Eleven nearby. They have one every five blocks." She turned to him and said slyly, "There're other things in there you might need, too."

Tim looked at her briefly out of the side of his eye before he stopped at a red light. "Don't worry, girl. I got it covered."

He made another right turn and then drove a few blocks before the street ended, forcing him to turn right again. He approached the red traffic light at Broad Street and stopped. He turned to Gracie, checked her out, and reached for her. She giggled and playfully slapped his hand away.

"You're so thirsty," Gracie said.

"Can't help it. I have been waiting for you to turn eighteen for months."

"The light's green."

Tim signaled, then made a left turn and headed northwest up Broad Street. He had driven a few blocks before he tried reaching for her again.

"Tim, watch out!" Gracie's eyes widened in horror.

Gracie's shout was preceded only a second by a loud metallic thud. Tim looked up just in time to see a crumpled late model Acura rolling backwards across the intersection in front of him.

He cursed, then tried to slam on the brakes. But he was going forty miles per hour, so it was much too delayed a reaction. Both he and Gracie shielded their faces as they slammed into the Acura. The force of the impact drove Tim's car under the Acura, forcing the Acura to flip over on its side and land against the median strip dividing Broad Street. The bumper of Tim's car curled up, the hood sank, and the windshield shattered, sending crystalline shards bouncing off the deployed air bags. Tim's car stopped, its nose lodged against the bottom of the Acura, where it was quickly greeted by a spray of leaking transmission fluid. Tim and Gracie lay bloodied and unconscious, each leaning in opposite directions against the center pillars of the car.

Several pedestrians had seen the accident, and a few had started to dial 911 on their cell phones. Some of the men started to approach the vehicles to check on the occupants. The man who approached the Acura could see, through the shattered windshield, a woman, crumpled, bruised, and bloodied, lying on a bed of glass against the passenger side door, which was now flat against the sidewalk.

Unsure if the woman was dead or alive, he pulled out his cell phone and dialed 911. Once the dispatcher had told him a unit had already been deployed and on its way, he hung up the phone and looked carefully at the woman inside the car. Despite the blood and glass all around her face, he noticed that she was very beautiful.

He had been a Christian since his early teens, and so he did the only thing he knew how to do at that point. He prayed that if she was alive that the Lord would restore her broken body and lead her on the road to health. And, if she was dying, that she had made her peace with Christ.

But as of that moment, unbeknownst to him, she had not.

CHAPTER ONE

Six days before

Xavier's marriage proposals were getting more ornate as time went on.

Just two months before, on the fifteenth, Summer Maldonado came to work, sat at her desk, checked her emails, and found a new message from Xavier with a photo attached. The photo was taken of her on a recent romantic trip to the Bahamas. There she was, lying on Paradise Beach in a Caribbean blue one-piece, her perfectly manicured toes dug in the white sand, her natural long black hair pouring gracefully out of a wide-brimmed straw hat, her cinnamon-toned skin glistening in the mid-afternoon sun. The caption on the photo read: "You are the picture of perfection. Will you marry me?"

One month before, also on the fifteenth, a bouquet of fifteen red roses in a tall crystal vase was waiting on her desk upon her return from lunch. The note on the flowers read: "Will you marry me, and let our relationship blossom like the petals of a rose?" The note gave Summer a mile-wide smile. Her boyfriend was corny but thoughtful and sweet.

Summer would answer his last two proposals the same way she

answered the eleven previous ones, all tendered on the fifteenth of the month. She would never explicitly tell him no, but always, "Ask me again next month." Xavier would be persistent enough to ask her every month, like clockwork, on the fifteenth.

It was the fifteenth of the month again, and Xavier Williams had texted her earlier that morning to ask her to join him that evening at the Wild Ginger, an Asian restaurant on the western outskirts of Richmond. It was a Thursday night, but still the Wild Ginger would be almost impossible to get into without a reservation, so Summer knew Xavier had planned several days beforehand.

Thursday was casual day at Visual Notions, one of the leading video production companies in Richmond. But Summer, the marketing manager, had chosen not to dress down that day. She wore a simple purple sheath dress, professional enough for the job, but sexy and formfitting enough to make sure Xavier's eyes didn't stray, which they did from time to time. Just a few minutes after seven, she left the office, which was on the seventh floor of an office building in downtown Richmond. The restaurant was only a fifteen-minute drive away in moderate traffic, so she had plenty of time to get there before the 7:30 reservation.

During the drive, Summer switched on the built-in MP3 player and allowed Stevie Wonder's *Ribbon in the Sky* to drown out the faint street sounds that made it inside the tinted windows of her late model Acura. She had to brace herself to turn down yet another one of Xavier's proposals, and she hoped that the proposal would come at the latter part of the evening, so that it wouldn't dampen the majority of their date. She knew she would have to say yes to him one day, but right now, her mind was not in that space. Her excuse was that she was not ready to be a wife, and that was true, to an extent. But as loving and doting as her boyfriend was, there were some things about him that bothered her. But she had neither the willpower nor the bravery to tell him the truth about himself. So, month after month, she kept hoping he would change and that somehow the rarest of miracles would alight upon him like a feather on the shoulder, and he would transform into a

man that she would be comfortable marrying. Someone who was NOT like her father. Xavier did not yet seem inclined to come home drunk and beat her like her father beat her mother. But his controlling nature and his frequent drinking made him a likely candidate.

Summer hadn't seen Nestor Maldonado in thirty years. She assumed he was still somewhere in Brazil; Summer had no clue where, and she didn't wish to know. But his aura remained with her like a bad odor. He hadn't always been a drunken looser; he had actually been quite personable, engaging and sober when Susan Wright met him during a vacation to Rio. Enthralled with the idea of living in Brazil, and tired of her hardscrabble life in Atlanta, Susan, an African American janitor, married Nestor a year after meeting him. Summer was born in July a year later. Susan named her after her favorite song, "Summertime," from *Porgy and Bess*, the one sang by Ella Fitzgerald and Louis Armstrong. Most people in the states assumed, without asking, that she was named that way because she was born in the summer, not knowing that Brazilian summers began in December.

The marriage went well until Summer was four years old. Several days after her birthday, Nestor lost his job at the soft drink plant as a result of a layoff, and the hard drinks soon followed, with the beatings right on the heels of the drinking. By the time Summer was five years old, she had heard, and in some cases seen, her mother beaten at least twelve times during one of Nestor's drunken tirades. Finally, Susan got tired of it.

The fateful day of Summer's introduction to the United States came on September 8th, the day after Brazil's Independence Day, two months and three days after her fifth birthday. Nestor had come home late the night before, his breath reeking of Skol's, with whatever celebratory spirit he had engaged in long gone by the time he crossed the threshold of his house. Susan met him in the kitchen and accused him of cheating on her, an accusation based purely upon woman's intuition, but in this case, that was spot on. But for some reason, she never had the gall to confront him about it until then.

The argument in the bedroom became so loud that the words

spilled out onto the streets. Susan's words were spiced with Southern rage, and a deep Georgia accent that Susan had tried to conceal, but surged forth whenever she was angry.

You need to leave those bitches alone!

If you don't stop this, I'm gonna take Summer and leave!

A scream. Several crashes. A door slamming. Spewing of obscenities in Portuguese. Another door slam. Then, eerily quiet.

The next day, Summer and her mother were hitch-hiking their way to Galeão International Airport, headed to Atlanta with only two garbage bags of belongings and an open-ended plane ticket purchased months earlier by a cousin in Atlanta who mailed it to Susan to encourage her to leave the son-of-a-bitch.

Xavier had not yet deteriorated as drastically. But Summer could see the signs brewing. The drinking, for one. Xavier could knock them back with the best of them, and it was only Summer's interventions that prevented him on many occasions from tipping over the edge of drunkenness. Xavier also had a paternalistic bent that bothered Summer. Xavier, like Nestor, didn't believe in a woman working. It was why Susan quit her $20,000-a-year janitorial job and stayed at home to cook his meals and chase dust bunnies. Xavier also believed that the man was the head of the household and that the woman should obey. To Summer, it was elementary math: head of household = man controls woman; woman has no say, no options, no life. And there was no way Summer was going to quit her $95,000-a-year job for any man, no matter how much he was paid.

Nonetheless, Summer kept hoping that Xavier's love for her would lead him to believe that having a strong, capable, independent woman would prove to be his greatest asset. The drinking she could deal with, but there was no way she was going to marry a man who had every intention of relegating her to housewife.

Summer pulled into the shopping center where the restaurant was located. She found a parking spot near a nail salon, with only a two-minute walk to the front door of the restaurant. Summer's dress

was short-sleeved, and it was getting chilly out. She wished she had brought her shawl from the car with her. No worries. She would just send Xavier out to her car to get it.

The restaurant had clean, modern lines, decorated in mauves, grays, and browns, with a huge bar in one wing and a dining area in another, separated by the hostess station and a small waiting area. As she expected, the restaurant was packed, but she had no trouble finding Xavier in the crowd. He was already seated at a small table by himself at the far end of the restaurant, adjacent to a large window with a view of the parking lot. Summer headed to Xavier's table. She drew an admiring glance from a gentleman seated in the waiting area.

Xavier stood as she approached. He was six-foot-one, clean-shaven, with a full head of closely cropped hair and eyeglass frames that would set a full-time minimum wage employee back about two weeks' pay. His fair skin contrasted with his crisply tailored suit, which hung on a thin, not lanky but athletic, build.

Xavier looked just as handsome as the day she met him eighteen months before. Xavier held a plum position as the vice president of media relations at the city's gas utility. Summer had been trying to get the utility's video production contract, and her attempts brought her in frequent contact with Xavier. They had several business lunches together before Visual Notions won the contract. After the paperwork had been signed, the business lunches turned into dinners. Eventually, Xavier won Summer's heart as well, which was not an easy task. Summer had no lack of men who wanted to court her, but it was Xavier's earthy charisma, his passionate devotion, and his quiet manner that hooked her. He was drawn to her as a person, and not just for her body. And a man who could afford to book the executive suite at the Jefferson Hotel *just because* certainly was a plus.

"*Meu Amor*," Summer said to him as they embraced. They exchanged a simple peck on the lips, which, given the posh surroundings, was a great deal more sedate than how they would have kissed in private.

Xavier motioned Summer to the chair directly across from his.

That was odd. Usually they sat at ninety-degree angles to one another. Summer ignored his directive and parked in a chair directly to Xavier's right. She then checked him out in his suit. It looked like the one that she had bought him for his thirty-eighth birthday a few months ago. As her gaze moved up to his eyes, he was looking off into the distance.

Summer followed his gaze but saw that it led nowhere. "Are you alright?" she asked.

Xavier finally looked at her. "I'm fine."

"You look nice. Is that the suit I bought you?"

Xavier looked down at himself, seemingly surprised. "Yeah, I guess it is."

The waiter came over with a wine list. Xavier quickly waved him away. Again, *unusual*. Summer studied his body language. Xavier seemed tense. His arms were tight against his body; his hands clasped in his lap. His gaze wandered off to nowhere again.

Summer toyed with the white napkin on the table and tried to say something to ease the tension. She was usually the talkative one in the relationship, so she had no problem starting a conversation. "So, how was your day?"

"It was good. Yours?"

"Wonderful. I was excited about meeting you here."

"Ever been here before?"

"No. First time." Summer noticed that Xavier's gaze trailed off again. It seemed as if he was looking at the front door.

Summer asked a burning question. "Are you expecting someone? I mean, other than me?"

Xavier's eyes finally returned to her. "I have something I need to tell you."

Summer swallowed hard. There was no passion, no joy in his voice. She tried to play off the obvious implication in his voice by making jest. "What, you're breaking up with me?" She said it with a bat of her eyes and a bedroom voice.

Xavier was silent.

Summer waited for a laugh, a smile, an angry denial, anything that

would acknowledge the humor in what she had said. Instead, he just sat there, carefully avoiding her eyes. Summer drew back in her chair and said, "X, what's going on?"

"Summer, this is not easy for me to say."

Summer felt blood rushing from her face. There were only two reasons people made that statement: if someone had died, or if they were about to end a relationship. And Xavier's incessant staring at the front door give her a clue as to which one it was.

"X, don't tell me you're breaking up with me."

C'mon, X. Tell me no. Tell me I'm wrong. Stop my heart from beating so fast in my chest.

Finally, he looked at her. And his eyes told her the truth. *Dear Jesus.*

Summer drew back in her chair again. "X, please don't kid around with me."

"I'm serious."

Summer looked in his eyes and didn't see any hint of his normal jovial nature. But something didn't gel. Why would he invite her to a fancy restaurant just to break up with her before they served the wine? That was too callous for Xavier, so she knew this conversation had to be leading somewhere other than the termination of their fifteen-month relationship. "X, stop kidding with me. Let's talk real here."

"This is not a joke, Summer."

There were two things at that moment that convinced Summer that Xavier was not joking. The first was that he used her real name. Xavier never called her by her real name unless he was angry. Usually it was *honey* or *baby* or *sweetie* or *gorgeous* or some variation thereof.

But Summer was *really* convinced when she looked up in response to a shadow darkening their table. The person standing there was not a waiter.

Xavier stood. "Summer, you know Jada."

Summer looked up at Jada Hardy with the scorn of forty jilted women. Jada Hardy was the assistant to the president of Visual No-

tions. Her office was just ten paces away from Summer's. There she stood, fake auburn hair, fake nails, Hershey-bar-dark model-thin body, and enough chest that if someone tapped her gently on the head from behind, she would tip over forward. And for all she knew, *that* might be fake. Summer quickly dialed back her hard look, realizing that Jada had enough clout to get her fired with a bat of her eyelashes. Summer had liked Jada. Until now.

Jada tried to be cordial in a less-than-cordial situation. "Hi, Summer."

Summer looked down at the table. "Jada."

Jada walked over to Xavier's side of the table. Summer looked up just in time to see Jada plant a respectable kiss on Xavier's cheek. She then sat in the chair directly to Xavier's left. When Xavier sat back down, he looked over at Summer and saw a blaze in her eyes.

"Summer, I wanted to let you know that me and Jada have been seeing each other for a few months now."

Summer inhaled deeply. Her heart began to palpitate. The shock of that statement cut her deeply than anything she would have imagined, rendering her vocal cords inoperative. She focused her eyes on the table, fighting back tears, not wanting to give either of them the pleasure of seeing her cry.

At that moment, Summer realized the mistake she had made a few months before. Summer had invited Xavier to her office to have lunch, something she rarely did with her friends. She preferred to separate her business and personal interests as much as possible. After lunch, when Summer was walking Xavier to the door, Jada strolled past. In courtesy, Summer introduced Jada to Xavier, referring to him as "one of Visual Notions' clients." Not my *boyfriend*, or my *man*, or even my *friend*, but my *client*. The last thing you want to do is introduce your man to another gorgeous, buxom, clasping woman as nothing more than a business interest.

The waiter returned to the table, interrupting an awkward silence. Once he had given his welcoming spiel, he asked for their drink orders. Xavier politely sent him away once again, and then focused his

attention on the two lovely ladies sitting at his table.

Emboldened now that the worst of his silent confession was over, Xavier said, "Listen, I know the two of you have to work together. I was hoping we could come together, talk it out, and at least be civil to one another."

Summer knew the hidden meaning behind Xavier's words: this is my new girl. I'm going to be coming around the office quite a bit, nuzzling up to her, and I don't want you screwing things up.

Summer phased out Jada for a moment and focused her icy glare on Xavier. "You couldn't even give me the courtesy of breaking up with me without bringing your new girlfriend along, and you expect me to be civil?" Summer threw her hands up. "I don't even know why you're doing this."

"Why I'm doing what?"

"Why you're breaking up with me."

"You know why."

"Because—" Summer stopped, realizing that what she was about to say was too personal for Jada's ears, and frankly none of her business. She turned to Jada. "Could you excuse us for a moment?"

Jada cut her eyes at Xavier, seeking his permission. Xavier nodded. Jada cut a final glance at Summer before she stood and walked toward the bar on the other side of the restaurant.

Summer leaned in toward Xavier. "You're breaking up with me because I wouldn't marry you?"

"You know I'm looking for a relationship that is going somewhere, Summer. I've been asking you for your hand for months. I can't wait any longer."

Summer sighed. "You know I have issues with marriage—"

"Yeah, I know. And your daddy issues. Although I don't think you're against the idea of marriage as much as you are against the idea of marrying me."

Summer leaned back in her chair. She couldn't argue. Xavier was a fantastic boyfriend. But not every relationship was made to make the leap to marriage. From her perspective, there was so much that needed

to be worked out. Unfortunately, Xavier had lost patience. And with so many women around waiting to throw themselves at a handsome, high-paid stud such as Xavier, he no longer needed to be patient.

When they had started dating, Summer told him that she intended to be celibate until marriage. Her mother had raised her that way, according to her Christian principles. And Summer considered herself a Christian, even though she had not been to church in many months. But Xavier was the type of man who was used to wrinkling a woman's sheets within one to two weeks of the first date, so challenges greeted his relationship with Summer from the beginning. And Summer went into the relationship fully intending to make a decision about marrying Xavier within a few months. But then, the alcoholism and the controlling issues surfaced, and that was all she needed to hold off any possibility of a deeper relationship. Summer adored her mother, but she didn't want to become her by marrying a man that was potentially abusive. She saw how much it affected her mother, and she had no intention of following in those footsteps.

But now she sat there, quickly drowning in the hurt and pain of rejection. What was worse, he was cheating on her with a co-worker, a woman she respected and trusted. She fast-forwarded through her life and realized she was about to go through life once again without a man, lonely and depressed. Thirty-five years old, and no closer to having a successful relationship than she was at eighteen. Her entire life had been relationship-deprived, especially since moving to Richmond. The realization of losing the one person who seemed drawn to her was so frightening that her next words were a compromise against facing the ugliness of the next few months, perhaps years, of her life.

"X, I don't want to lose you. I could look more closely at this marriage thing. Please let's talk and work this out."

"Summer, I've already proposed to Jada, and she accepted."

Summer squeezed her eyes shut. This was unbelievable. The evening was just getting worse, and she could feel Xavier slipping out of her grasp. "You haven't known her that long."

"But we don't need to know each other for long to know that we

were meant for each other. When you feel that way, there's no sense waiting."

"You used to say that about us."

"What?"

"That we were meant for each other."

Xavier looked way. "Maybe I was mistaken."

That stung more than anything that Xavier had said. That their relationship was a sham, a *mistake*. She wasted fifteen months of her life on a mistake. They were hard, sharp words, but she didn't want to acknowledge them. She knew that Xavier was the man for her. She knew it now more than ever.

And with those thoughts, she was moving into the same dangerous territory and destructive co-dependent behavior that her mother had exhibited throughout a year of abuse; that sometimes it was better having a man in your life that abused you, than no man at all.

Summer's next words were abrupt and only half-hearted. "Okay, I'll marry you."

Xavier shook his head. "We had our chance, Summer. I'm going to be with Jada now." He looked toward the bar, hoping that he could meet eyes with Jada and summon her to return to the table.

Summer's eyes were moist with tears now, and as she blinked, they started to flow down her face. "How can you do this to me?" She made no effort to stop the flow, as they had begun to drip off her chin and onto the tablecloth. A few of the patrons noticed her tears and stole periodic glances, trying to figure out what was going on without appearing nosy.

Jada returned to the table, at which point Summer noticed that several of the patrons had noticed her crying. Flustered, Summer grabbed her purse, got up from the table, and without a word, headed for the door. One of the waiters saw her on the way out and asked if she was okay. She hurried past him without answering.

Then suddenly, just before she reached the front door, anger mingled with her sadness like a suitor cutting in on a dance. This woman, Jada, the one she trusted and respected for years, just stole her man

from her. There was no way she was going to do that without Summer making a bold statement about it.

Summer turned around and headed back into the restaurant. On a table near the door, three wine glasses, half-full with Merlot, were sitting there, left by departing patrons. Summer clutched her purse tighter between her left arm and her side, then grabbed two of the glasses. She marched toward Xavier's table. Xavier and his new girl-toy Jada were sitting next to each other, nuzzling close while reviewing the wine selection, so they didn't notice her approach. By the time they did, it was too late.

With the precision of a gunslinger, Summer hurled both the glasses forward, sending the wine out of the glasses and directly into Xavier and Jada's faces. They jumped up and screamed, and the room fell silent, as all eyes were now on them. Summer dropped the glasses on the table and marched toward the door. The glasses rolled off the table and crashed on the floor, creating the only sound in the room at that moment.

As Summer left, she couldn't help but notice that a few of the women, understanding her pain, had smiles on their faces.

* * *

Summer went home to her apartment in the Midlothian area of Richmond, just a ten-minute drive away from the restaurant. As she entered her apartment and tossed her purse on the couch, she regretted, for a moment, that she was not one of those sisters who would have cussed Xavier out within an inch of his life, and then keyed his BMW on the way out. But this hurt, *really* hurt. She couldn't believe that the man she loved did this to her. It was a type of grief that felt worse to her than a death of a loved one. And without hope, the grief was much more difficult to survive.

Summer's only hope was that Xavier would come to his senses, change his mind, and return to her with hat in hand and an apology.

Maybe once he saw how much he had hurt her, he would reconsider his decision to marry Jada. Maybe once again her phone would ring, or her doorbell would chime, and Xavier would be on the other end, realizing what a fool he was.

Summer looked out over the city through her patio door. She lived alone, which she hoped would only be a temporary situation since moving from Atlanta two years ago. Her mother, Susan, still lived in Atlanta, in a four-bedroom house owned by her cousin, the same cousin who gave them shelter after their retreat from Brazil. Over the years since returning to the States, Susan eked out a living at various janitorial jobs, as her lack of education would not allow her to do much else. Nonetheless, she pushed Summer to do well in school, always impressing upon her that an education was the key to getting anywhere in America, unlike Brazil, where many women tended to rely on their husbands. Summer was denied the pleasures of daily TV watching, as Susan wanted her to focus on her studies. It was not a struggle, as Summer loved to read and would devour any printed material she could find. Even the myriad of boys who called on Summer during her high school years could not get far as long as Susan was guardian of the gates.

Summer's devotion to her studies earned her several scholarships, which enabled her to attend Clark Atlanta University with barely an out-of-pocket investment. Susan was proud to be able to send her daughter to a college that had produced the likes of Ralph Abernathy, James Weldon Johnson, and other African Americans who broke down barriers of racial segregation. She had intended to major in history and become a teacher. However, after she spent some time volunteering at the college radio station, a college boyfriend told her the five-foot-ten-inch well-spoken beauty would be a great media personality. She decided to major, and eventually earn a degree, in journalism and communications. During her sophomore year, she became the fill-in host of a drive-time jazz program, replacing the regular host whenever he was away.

Summer continued to volunteer at the public radio station after she

graduated from Clark. Eventually, the station manager hired Summer to be the drive-time host of her jazz program. The program was appropriately named "Summertime," and the *Porgy and Bess* song became the theme of the show. Summer then used her newfound clout to get Susan hired as a production assistant, even though Susan had little experience in radio. Summer felt that the Lord was blessing her mother and her, and she was grateful to be in God's good graces.

However, several years later, the station began to lose funding, and cutbacks were necessary. Syndicated programming replaced Summer's program, and she was eventually fired due to a reduction in force. Susan retained her job at the station despite her inclination to quit in protest once Summer got fired. Summer urged her not to. She didn't want to see her mother return to wielding mops, buckets, brooms, and rags, and some days coming home too tired to eat.

It wasn't long before Summer's absence from the station was felt, and fans and local media began to inquire what had happened to her. Once word spread about her termination, media companies began to court her with offers. The most promising came from a local entrepreneur and TV producer, Mark Battman, who had assembled a team to look into the feasibility of starting a video production firm in the West End of Richmond. The West End was a burgeoning area with many new corporations, museums, and restaurants, all potential clients for Battman's new firm. Summer, with now over ten years' of radio experience, agreed to partner with Mark. Summer would lend credibility to Mark's firm and help him win clients in the greater Richmond area. With Mark's and Summer's experience, the newly created Visual Notions would win five clients even before the name plate was affixed to their rented suite in downtown Richmond.

Summer was heartbroken at having to leave her mother in Atlanta while she helped run this upstart firm in Richmond. It wasn't that she didn't have any other choices. But this was clearly the best one, an opportunity that was too good to pass up. She always planned to save enough money and buy a house, then send for her mother to come live with her in Richmond. She was still several thousand dollars away

from attaining that goal. Maintaining the upscale life in Richmond proved to be very expensive. With her apartment, weekly maid service, expensive restaurant meals, and the high taxes of living single and childless, she spent almost three-quarters of her monthly income. She had $20,000 in savings, not nearly enough for a down payment on the type of home where she could ensure that her mother had her space, and she would have hers.

Summer was too upset to eat. She pulled off her dress, left it on the floor near the patio door, and headed to bed. On the way, she picked up her purse, pulled out her iPhone, and cradled it in her hand on her way to the bedroom. In case Xavier changed his mind about her, she did not want to miss his call.

* * *

Summer would fall asleep for an hour, wake up for an hour, and then fall asleep again for an hour, *rinse, repeat,* until she finally awoke at seven in the morning. She thought about staying home, so she didn't have to deal with Jada. But she needed to work to keep her mind off Xavier. She showered, dressed, and then headed out.

When she arrived at work at eight, Jada hadn't arrived yet, which was a small blessing. Summer could sequester herself in her office, shut the door, pull the blinds to the large window facing the corridor, and hopefully not have to deal with her all day. She could use this day to catch up on paperwork.

At 9 a.m., there was a gentle tap at her office door. Summer hoped it wasn't Jada. "Come in."

Mark Battman walked in, opening the door until it hit the door stop and bounced back an inch. He was about an inch shorter than Summer, thin, with a five o'clock shadow. His hair was cut short on the sides and jagged on top, making him look a lot younger than his forty-five years. To Summer, he resembled a younger, skinnier Brad Pitt. Summer found him quite attractive, and might have flirted with

him a while back if he wasn't married with kids.

"Summer, may I see you for a moment?" Mark said. Although he phrased his statement as a question, Summer could tell by his tone that he wasn't asking.

"Okay." Summer dropped some papers she was holding and got up to follow Mark out the door. She was surprised when Mark turned left, rather than right, toward his office. She continued to follow Mark past the studio and into the empty general conference room. Mark motioned toward a chair, then closed the door. As Summer sat down, and before the door was completely closed, she could see Lenny Yates, the security guard, just outside the door.

The stark realization hit her at that moment. In less than five minutes, she would be out of a job. Jada had obviously told Mark about the dinner the night before and about Summer redecorating her face with a $200 bottle of Merlot. Jada had already stolen her man. Summer didn't think Jada would be as petty as to take her job, too.

Mark sat down two chairs away from Summer. He looked down at the table for a few seconds, collecting his thoughts, before he finally said, "Summer, Jada called me last night. Something about you assaulting her at dinner, and—"

"Mark, are you going to fire me?" Summer interrupted. "Because if so, get on with it. I don't need the foreplay before the screw."

Mark looked down at the table, unable to meet her eyes. "I'm sorry, Summer. You've been a great employee, but—"

Before he could finish his sentence, Summer was up and out the door, headed back to her office. Mark looked up and nodded to the security guard, who followed her.

Summer marched back into her office and grabbed her purse and jacket. They were the only personal items she regularly kept in her office. Lenny, the security guard, stood just outside the door.

"Miss Maldonado, what happened? Why'd you get fired?"

"Long story, Len," Summer said, leaving everything else in the office as it was and walking past him toward the elevator. She didn't bother to say anything to her fellow employees; this was embarrassing

enough without having to answer all their questions. When she reached the elevator, she saw that Lenny was not far behind. "Don't worry, Len. I'm not going to steal any paper clips or burn the office down."

"I know, Miss Maldonado. But I gotta do my job."

"At least you have one." When the elevator door opened, Summer and Lenny boarded it. Just after she pressed the lobby button and before the door closed, she saw Mark standing in the foyer, watching her leave.

"He's such a coward," Summer whispered to herself, though loudly enough for Lenny to hear.

"Don't worry, Miss Maldonado. You'll be alright. Just hang in there."

"Thanks, Len."

When the elevator arrived at the lobby floor, and they had disembarked, Lenny turned to her, nodded downward and said, "I gotta get that access card from you."

Summer reached down at her waist and snapped the access card from her belt. She handed it to Lenny, then secured her purse on her shoulder and headed for the exit.

"Good luck, Miss Maldonado," Lenny said as Summer passed the security desk.

"Thanks, Len. Take care."

As she walked out to the parking lot and toward her car, Summer had never felt so defeated in her life. She lost her man, she lost her job, and now she had lost what little self-respect she had left. As she climbed into her car, she knew that Lenny's statement, "you're gonna be alright," was an overused cliché.

She was *not* going to be alright.

* * *

Summer was lying on the couch staring at the ceiling when she heard her phone ring. Thinking it night be Xavier, she scrambled off

the couch and to the kitchen, where she had left her phone. Checking the caller ID, she saw the word: "Mãe." She was disappointed it wasn't Xavier, but she was always glad to hear from her mother, whom she spoke to at least twice a day.

She answered the call. "Olá, Mãe."

"Olá, dear. How are you?"

"I'm fine, Mãe."

"No, you're not."

Summer walked back to the couch, engaging the speakerphone. "What are you talking about?"

"You're not fine."

Summer wasn't sure if it was something in her voice that gave her away, or if her mother had developed some clairvoyant talent. "Why do you say that?"

"I called your job today to speak to you. They told me you no longer worked there. So, you either quit or you got fired, neither of which makes you *fine*."

"Why didn't you call me on my cell, Mãe?"

"I did. Earlier today. You didn't answer, so I called your job."

Summer remembered. Once she had arrived home, she paced the floor for an hour before lying on the couch. She dozed off for a couple of hours, and now it was well past two in the afternoon. She likely hadn't heard the phone ring while she was asleep.

Summer lay on the couch, holding the phone in her hand at arm's length from her lips. "I got fired."

"What happened? Why did they fire you?"

"I didn't ask the official reason. But the real reason was that I tossed a drink in the face of the president's assistant at dinner last night."

"Why did you do that?"

Summer sighed. She decided to tell her mother the whole story, knowing that Susan would interrogate her until she did. "X and I broke up last night. He invited me to this romantic Asian restaurant, just to break up with me. And he actually brought his new girlfriend with

him, the president's assistant. I was so hurt, shocked, embarrassed, and betrayed. I didn't know what to do. I just snapped, and I went back into the restaurant and tossed drinks in X's face and hers. Then I left."

"And they fired you for that? That didn't happen on the job."

"Doesn't matter, Mãe. It's considered assault on a fellow employee, even if it happened away from the job. It's against policy. And Mark didn't even want to get my side of the story. He'd made up his mind to fire me before he met with me. He even had a security guard waiting in case I acted like a drama queen."

"Wow."

"Wouldn't surprise me if Mark is doing Jada. A lot of people in the office think so."

"Isn't he married?"

"When has that ever made a difference, Mãe? You should know better."

Silence on the other end.

Summer gulped. "I'm sorry, Mãe. I shouldn't have said that."

After an awkward but silent few seconds, Susan spoke again. "Well, you're not fine. You're upset. I can hear it in your voice. Virginia is only a two-hour plane ride away. I'm coming up there.

"Mãe, you don't have to do that."

Susan knew her daughter well enough to know that those words meant: Mãe, you don't have to upend your life and inconvenience yourself and cancel your plans just to tend to me, but I would really like it if you would. "Yes, I do. Now the last-minute plane ticket is going to be steep, but I'm not going to let my daughter wallow in misery the whole weekend by herself."

Sumer didn't argue. "I'll cover the plane ticket, Mãe. Don't worry about that." Tears started to flow down her face.

"Okay. I'll be there before bedtime."

"Thanks, Mãe."

"See you later, dear."

News of her mother's visit strengthened Summer's resolve. With her mother coming, at least she had someone to talk to. She had failed

at making any friends, other than Xavier, since coming to Richmond. She couldn't figure out what it was about herself that made people not enjoy her company. Even when she was living in Atlanta, friends were few and far between.

She decided to tidy up the apartment. The maid was not due until tomorrow, but Summer wanted things to be neat and clean before her mother arrived later that evening.

* * *

Thinking that a jog around the community would clear her head, Summer put on her pink workout shorts, black activewear tank top, and running shoes, tied her hair into a ponytail, and started to do stretches in the foyer of her apartment to ready herself for her run. She knew going for a jog by herself was tactically risky in this neighborhood. She didn't have to worry about being attacked, but she did have to worry about men in the neighborhood seeing an attractive woman jogging by herself and using that as an opportunity to try out whatever come-on lines they had conceived. When she first moved into the neighborhood, that was an attractive and welcome prospect. Now, she didn't want to *think* about men.

When she went outside, it was 6:05 p.m. The sun was low in the sky, and the air was at sixty-eight degrees, ten degrees cooler than it had been most of the day. Summer took a deep breath and then started her jog. She would start at her apartment building door and then circle three times around the neighborhood. That would give her a two-mile run.

As she jogged, Summer noted the differences between this community and the community she had left in Atlanta. This neighborhood, called Crestlane, was a gated community of corporate professionals and mid- to high-level government workers. Here, most people stayed in their apartments except to travel to and from places outside of the community. It was quiet, and not many people were around except

for fellow joggers and some male service workers, who were prone to stopping whatever they were doing and ogling her as she jogged past.

The neighborhood where her mother lived in Atlanta was a mix of low to middle-income persons, a community decidedly blue-collar. It was a community of mostly detached single-family homes, with a couple of apartment buildings on the outskirts of the neighborhood. Susan's cousin Cicely owned a home in the community since the sixties. Given the opportunity, she would fete visitors with the tale of how the neighborhood was upscale until the late eighties. In the early nineties, people who were making money moved out to neighborhoods such as Lithonia or Druid Hills, leaving only low-income workers who could not afford to move. Despite white-collar flight and an escalating crime rate, Cicely stayed in her home. She would rather live there than in one of those boring upper-class communities, where people didn't know their neighbors. *Something about struggling together creates community,* she would say. As a result, everyone in the neighborhood knew everyone else in the neighborhood, kids would come outside to play with other neighborhood kids, mothers would exchange anecdotes and gossip on the sidewalk outside their homes, and men would tinker with their cars and catch up with other men on the latest with the Falcons or who was the cutest dime piece in the neighborhood. It wasn't a perfect neighborhood by any stretch of the imagination, but there was *life*. Living in Crestlane for two years, Summer understood the dichotomy on a greater level. Compared to her old neighborhood in Atlanta, Crestlane was about as dry as a Peruvian desert.

On her second jogging pass, Summer stopped at the gate booth. She did not recognize the Puerto Rican woman sitting there.

Summer spoke to draw the woman's attention away from her cell phone. "Hi."

"Hi," the woman said, setting her phone on the desk. "What can I do for you?"

"My name is Summer Maldonado. I'm in Apartment 323B. I'm expecting my mother sometime this evening, maybe as late as 10 p.m. I just wanted to make sure she was let in without a problem."

The woman grabbed a clipboard with forms from somewhere down out of Summer's sight. "'Your mother's name?"

"Susan Maldonado."

The woman started writing. "Okay. I'll see to it, Miss Maldonado."

"Are you new here?"

"No, I'm temporary. I actually work at Alliance, across town."

"What happened to the regular gate attendant?"

The woman continued to write. "She quit."

"Why?"

"Something about she didn't pass some certification. So, rather than wait for them to fire her, she quit. That was dumb though."

"Why?"

"You quit, you don't get unemployment."

"So, are they looking for someone to replace her?"

"I think so. You interested?"

"Maybe."

"You'll have to check with the Crestlane office."

"Okay. Thanks." Summer started her jog again, intending to go around the community one more time before she stopped, took a bath, and started preparing dinner.

* * *

It was 8 p.m., and Summer had just spent the last full twenty-four hours without Xavier. She had hoped that cooking would help keep her mind off him, but even as she took the herb-crusted roasted chicken out of the oven, she could not stop thinking about him and hoping that he would call, stop by, text, tweet, Facebook, email, *anything*. She kept hope alive by imagining that *Miss Thing* Jada would set him off in some way, forcing him to abandon his marriage plans and come running back to her. Maybe he would realize that God never intended him to be with a woman whose bosom was made in a factory in Singapore.

How horrible a girlfriend must I have been for Xavier to date someone else while we were still together, and then propose to her? The words he spoke stuck in Summer's mind, like a kernel of popcorn between the teeth. A mistake. Was their relationship a mistake? Was there nothing redeeming in their entire fifteen months together for their relationship to be classified as nothing more than a mistake? It didn't seem like a mistake during their first date, when he drove her to York-town; they ate a fancy steak dinner, and then they strolled on the beach by the York River, talking for hours.

It didn't seem that way on Christmas Day, when Xavier invited Summer and Susan to his mother and father's house in Petersburg. There, they sat among Xavier's two brothers and three sisters, along with assorted in-laws, aunts, uncles, cousins, nieces, and nephews, all buzzing about and making Summer feel as if she was part of the family.

It didn't seem that way during the many days they sat cuddled on Summer's couch, binge-watching old TV comedies and kissing like teenagers during every commercial.

It didn't seem that way on her birthday, when he feted her with yellow roses, and then an evening of scrumptious Caribbean food and live jazz at a club in the West End of Richmond. Even after the club, they went to his apartment, put on Cannonball Adderley's *Dancing in the Dark*, and danced until Summer felt as if she was floating out of her body. That night, more than any other, was the most tempting for her, for she was sure she would have violated her Christian principles and made love to him if he had pressed her. But he didn't. Instead, rather than drive her home, he set her up in his spare bedroom, while he went to his. In hindsight, Summer thought she should have gone into his bedroom and given herself to him. Maybe then, he would still be with her.

No, it was not a mistake, Summer thought. A good relationship cannot be made into a mistake just because another woman comes along. Xavier was not perfect, but he was the man for her. She knew that now. Without him, she had nothing. With him, she had everything

she needed. And there was no way she was going to allow that wench Jada to take her man. Not without a fight.

Summer placed the chicken on the counter, and then placed fresh green beans inside of a frying pan with some olive oil. She had to come up with a way to get Xavier back. But whatever her plans, she could not share them with her mother. Her mother had raised her to be proud, strong, and independent. Not a blubbering idiot begging for her man back. But Summer was not as strong as her mother hoped she was. She was weak. She knew it. Weak and flawed. She needed and wanted Xavier. Without him, she could no longer live.

CHAPTER TWO

My heart
Is sad and lonely
For you I sigh
For you dear only
Why haven't you
Seen it?
I'm all for you
Body and soul

Sarah Vaughan had just finished singing that stanza of lyrics on the song *Body and Soul* when Susan knocked on Summer's front door. Summer grabbed the remote, turned down the volume on the stereo, and rushed to the door.

"Mãe!" Summer squealed, embracing her mother as soon as she opened the door. Susan dropped the carry-on bags she was holding and returned the hug. She was almost the spitting image of her daughter, with barely a line on her face to tell her sixty years, and auburn and black hair as bountiful as someone half her age. The years, and Cicely's home cooking, had taken a toll on her figure, for she was no longer as svelte as she was back in the days when she was courting for a husband, and she was easily nine inches shorter than Summer. But she was not so chubby that she could not draw a man's eye, even at her age.

"Come in, Mãe," Summer said, grabbing her mother's bags. Once they were both inside, Summer carried the bags into her spare bedroom, and then came back out. "How was your trip?"

"It was good," Susan said, looking around the apartment. "You've done some more decorating since the last time I was here."

"Just picked up a few things." Summer moved toward the kitchen. "You hungry? I made dinner."

"Honey, I should have called and told you not to do that." Susan sat on the couch and studied the photo of Xavier and Summer that was still sitting prominently on the coffee table. "I had to eat during my stopover. With my sugar and all."

Summer's voice came from the kitchen. "Are you taking your insulin?"

"Yes, I am." The scent of rosemary and thyme reached Susan's nose. "Something smells good."

"It's the roasted chicken you love so much."

"Well, I gotta have some of that right out of the oven. So, make me a small plate. I'll work it down."

Once they had sat down at the table to eat and made small talk, Susan broached the subject *du jour*. "So, how are you doing?"

"I think about him a lot," Summer said sullenly.

"That's gonna happen, child. You loved him. That doesn't go away with the flick of a switch." Susan set her fork down and reared back in her chair. "You were only five at the time, but I had the hardest

time when I left your father. I loved him, and I missed him, and it took every bit of strength in me not to call him and ask if we could come back home."

"How did you handle that?"

"Found another boyfriend." Susan had met Summer's eyes for only a moment before she started eating again.

Now Summer stopped eating. "Mãe, you never told me you had another man. And I never met or saw him."

"Girl, don't be so naïve. You know who I'm talking about."

Summer shot her a frown of confusion. "Who?"

Susan just looked at her.

"Oh." Summer suddenly felt dumb for not guessing what her devotedly Christian mother was talking about. She returned to her eating. "I just never heard you refer to Him in that way."

"Well, he is. All that adoration, that devotion, that attention that I once gave to Nestor, I gave to Jesus. And Jesus loves me in a way that Nestor never could. It's real, everlasting, Godly love. That how I got through. And that's how you can make it through."

"I haven't been to church in so long." Summer started playing with the last of the green beans that were on her plate. "The last time I went was when I was back in Atlanta."

"Maybe you should find yourself a nice pastor and a church here in Richmond. I'm sure Bishop Asherton down in Atlanta can give you some references."

Summer dropped her fork on the plate with a pronounced *clink*. She stood up and walked over to the glass patio door, which yielded a view of a patchwork of darkness cut in with squares of light from surrounding apartments. Summer remembered the first time she went to church with her mother in Atlanta. She was just six years old. The loudness, the screaming of the preachers from the pulpit, the people falling out under the Spirit in the aisles frightened her. It was very different from some of the more sedate Catholic churches in Brazil. She attended church with her mother almost every Sunday after that, and eventually got used to the tone of the service, but also became indif-

ferent to it, the whole church thing. By the time she turned fourteen, she had spent so much time in church and had been sheltered from so many things, that she began to wonder about the world outside of church. The schools she attended, the lives she saw on TV, all presented to her a world that seemed more liberating and more fun and compelling than the church routine. To her, church was only popular with church people. Elsewhere, people had fun, made money, and lived happy lives, without daily devotion to God and church.

Summer turned back to her mother and found Susan still eating, seemingly unaffected by Summer's tepid reaction to her church remark. Susan was used to her daughter's attitude about church and God, which had been festering since long before she started attending college, and became worse once Summer met her first college boyfriend, a young man who was anything but Christian. Susan, rightly or wrongly, took some of the blame for that. Susan strived to make sure that Summer was not a carbon copy of herself, an uneducated woman scraping together a few dollars in order to survive. In doing so, Susan lamented that she may have pushed Summer into a world where the object of worship was money and opulence, and God was only needed to cleanse one's conscience periodically. Then, she spent most of the past ten years trying to back-pedal Summer away from it. It was like getting a person addicted to drugs, and then encouraging them to go to detox.

Susan was undaunted. "Let me make that call for you." Susan intended to make it no matter what her daughter's answer.

Summer sighed heavily, which answered Susan's question more than any words could. Summer walked to the table, grabbed her plate with three green beans still left on it, and headed to the kitchen. "Mãe, I don't think I need a preacher right now, okay? I have some money saved up, so I'll be okay financially for a month or two." She returned to the dining table and took Susan's empty plate away. "And this situation with X and Jada is going to blow over. Once he realizes that situation is not going to work out, he'll come running back to me."

Susan wiped her mouth with her napkin and then said, "You want

another woman's sloppy seconds?"

Susan heard a *clank* from the kitchen that made her jump. Summer returned immediately after to the dining room and burned a ferocious look in her mother's eyes.

"Excuse me, Jada is taking *my* sloppy seconds, okay? X is—" she pointed to herself "—*my* man." Summer angrily grabbed the empty glasses from the table and headed back into the kitchen.

"He can't be yours if he doesn't want to be," Susan retorted, getting up from the table.

Summer returned to the dining room. "Mãe, I love you, and I'm glad you're here. But if you can't be my cheerleader, at least don't root for the opposing team."

Susan let out a breath of laughter and smiled. "You're so cute with your metaphors." She kissed Summer lightly on the cheek. "I'm just trying to help."

Susan's warm affection deflated her quickly. "I know, Mãe." She watched as Susan headed for the spare bedroom. *But I don't need your help*, Summer thought as Susan disappeared into the room. *I have this all taken care of.*

* * *

Four days later, Summer returned to Visual Notions for a debrief before she got her final paycheck. When she walked into the lobby of the office building, Lenny and another security guard were stationed at the front desk.

"Good morning, Miss Maldonado," Lenny greeted with an out-of-place chirpiness, as if Summer had not been fired just days before.

"Good morning, Lenny," Summer replied drolly. "I'm here to see Sherry."

"Yes, ma'am." Lenny pushed a sign-in book toward her. "Just put today's date, the time, your—"

Summer cut him off. "Yeah, uh, Lenny, I know the routine." She

signed in and then handed the pen back to Lenny.

"Alright. I'll call Sherry and let her know that you're here."

"Thanks, Lenny."

While Lenny picked up the phone at the desk, Summer looked around. She hadn't been away from the office that long since her first day of work; she never even took a vacation. Four days away seemed like weeks, and it felt weird to be there, and to be wearing jeans, a tank top, and thong sandals to the office. Even on casual days, she had never dressed down this much.

Lenny hung up the phone and said to Summer, "Miss Sherry will be right down."

"Thanks again, Lenny." Summer had at least five minutes before Sherry made it from the seventh floor to the lobby, so she decided to talk to Lenny about an idea that had been brewing for a couple of days. "Lenny, are you interested in looking into other employment?"

Lenny looked back to see where the other security guard was. The other guard was busy typing something on the computer. Confident that the guard was not actively ear-hustling, Lenny said, "Yeah, I'm interested in other opportunities."

"I have a job you may be interested in. It's a full-time guard position. I think it pays more than what you are being paid here."

"But you don't *know* what I'm being paid here."

"Is it more than sixteen dollars per hour?"

Lenny drew back slightly, his face registering surprise. "No. Not even close."

"So, you're interested?"

"What are we talking about here?"

"There's a position open at the complex where I live. It's at the front gate. I've already spoken to the hiring people, and they've agreed to give you an interview, if you're interested. With a good word from me, I'd say you have a ninety percent chance of getting the job."

"Where's the job at?"

"It's the Crestlane. It's only about a fifteen-minute drive from here." Summer started to rout through her purse. "Are you interested?"

"Yeah!" Lenny said enthusiastically.

"Okay." Summer produced a card from her purse and set it on the front desk counter so that Lenny could see it clearly. "This is the name and number of the recruitment officer. Call her and tell her that you spoke to me and that you're interested in the gate attendant position at the Crestlane."

Lenny turned over the card and jotted the information on the back. "Man, this is five dollars more an hour than what I'm making here."

Summer smiled. "Well, you've always been so nice to me while I was working here, so when I heard about it, I thought about you."

"Appreciate that so much, Miss Maldonado."

"Summer?"

The voice came from behind her. Summer turned and saw Sherry standing near the elevator. "Hi, Sherry." Summer then turned back to Lenny and said "good luck" before she accompanied Sherry on the elevator.

Lenny stared at the card for a few seconds before his fellow security guard chimed in with a comment. "If I had a chance to see that fine spicy filly come and go every day, I'd take that job too, raise or no raise."

Lenny turned to him. "You heard that?"

"Yeah."

"Yeah, well, I ain't thinking about all that. I'm thinking about how this job is gonna help me take better care of my son."

"I hear you."

"Do me a solid, man. Keep this close until whatever happens, happens."

"No problem, man. I got you."

They shook hands, and then Lenny said, "I'm going on break."

"Handle your business."

Lenny held the card and headed out the door toward his car, intending to do just that.

* * *

Summer was grateful that the human resources wing was on the opposite side of the floor from Jada and the marketing team's offices. She had no desire to run into Jada, or Mark, or anyone else, for that matter. She just wanted to get her final check and disappear.

Sherry escorted Summer into the HR conference room and directed her to a chair directly opposite the table from where Sherry had set up a laptop and some forms. Once they both sat down, Sherry said, "Summer, I know this is a bit awkward for you, so I'll try to make this as quick as possible. But you know it's standard practice for us to do a debrief of terminated employees, so please bear with us. Now, you don't have to answer any question if you don't want to."

Midway through Sherry's spiel, Summer had the most brilliant of ideas. She kept staring at the laptop, studying it, barely hearing anything Sherry said after the word *terminated*.

"Can we proceed?" Sherry said.

Summer hadn't heard Sherry's question. She was following the direction of the network cable, making sure it was plugged into the wall network port.

"Summer?"

Summer looked up. "Yes?"

"Can we proceed with the questions?"

"Sure," Summer answered, trying to think of a way to get Sherry out of the room for five minutes.

"First of all, do you know and understand the reason you were terminated?"

"Well, uh, Mark was going to tell me, but I didn't let him. I just walked out on him."

Sherry took a heavy breath. "Well, let me tell you the reason. You were terminated for violating section twelve dash four of our code of conduct, which forbids assaulting another employee. The policy does not qualify where that assault takes place. Do you have any questions about that?"

"No," Summer muttered.

"Do you agree with the reasons you were terminated?"

What difference does it make now? I'm fired, were the words going through Summer's mind. Instead, she said, "I take responsibility for my actions." Summer knew that that statement was legally inconclusive, but that an HR neophyte like Sherry would likely take it to mean everything she had hoped.

"Okay, let's move on." Sherry started punching something in the laptop, and Summer observed closely. "According to the property list, you still have some property belonging to the company."

"What property?" Summer asked.

"A laptop, according to this."

"Oh, no. The laptop is in the hutch behind my desk."

"Okay, but the hutch is locked. Do you have the key?"

Summer's eyes averted to the left. That was her opportunity. She reached in her purse, pulled out a set of keys, and then disengaged two from the key ring. She handed them to Sherry and said, "These are the keys."

"Good." Sherry stood.

Good sign so far, Summer thought.

"I'll be right back," Sherry said.

Bingo!

Summer waited until Sherry walked out the door and headed around the corner to the administrative wing. She had only about four minutes before Sherry would return. She jumped up, gently shut the conference room door and locked it from inside. She drew the blinds on the windows and hurried to the laptop. Without sitting in the chair, she pulled up an extra tab on Internet Explorer and typed in the web address for the company's employee information system. She knew it was likely that her access to this system was disabled, but she still knew Mark's credentials. She used them to log in.

She quickly pulled a scrap piece of paper from her purse and used Sherry's pen to write down the information. Then, she closed the tab on Internet Explorer, leaving the original HR debrief collection form visible on the laptop. She rushed to the blinds, opened them again, then gently unlocked and opened the door to the conference room. She

was back in her seat for two minutes before Sherry returned.

"Okay, we got the laptop. So it looks like you're clear on the property list," Sherry said, sitting down at her laptop, totally unaware that Summer had just been there. "So let's move on."

"Gladly," Summer said. She would leave Visual Notions not only with her last paycheck, but also the home address and telephone number for Jada Hardy.

* * *

The sounds of Minnie Riperton's *Loving You* chirped out of Jada's cell phone; she had made the song her ringtone for Xavier after he sung it to her one evening at dinner. Vaguely aware that Summer was somewhere in the building, she shut the door of her office, sat behind her desk, and answered the call. "Hey, lover."

Xavier's voice came over the speakerphone, which Jada kept at a low volume that only she could hear. "Girl, I miss you so much."

"How's the conference?"

"Boring, except when we took a tour of the city. Got to see Beale Street. The Zoo. The place where King was shot. Got to be here for two more days. Never knew they could come up with four days of stuff to present about natural gas."

"Would you have been griping like this with Summer?"

"She wasn't giving me none. You are."

"Well, I'll call you tonight, and I can walk you through pretending I'm there."

"I'd like that."

"Summer's in the building somewhere. I think she's in HR."

"You think it was a good idea getting her fired?"

"She threw a drink in my face. I couldn't let that go. And besides, there was no way she was gonna let me off the hook for dating you. She's vindictive like that. It's better that she's not here."

"You can be so nasty sometimes."

"And that's what you like about me."

"Gotta go. I look forward to your call tonight."

"Talk to you then."

Jada ended the call. *Two more days in Memphis*, she thought. She looked toward Mark's office. *When the cat's away, the mouse will play.*

* * *

It was Tuesday evening, and Susan was still at Summer's apartment. She had decided to stay until Friday so that she could get the cheapest flight back to Atlanta. Susan was nothing if not frugal, even when her daughter was paying for it.

Susan's extended stay was no problem for Summer. She enjoyed the company, although there were times when her mother would wear out her welcome by insisting that her daughter come to pray with her, or by urging her to come and listen to a scripture she was reading, or by imploring her to watch a deep Southern evangelist rail on for half an hour about Jesus and how he saves, heals, and delivers. Summer knew that her mother was strategizing to bring the church to her, since Summer hadn't gone to church in years.

One of her mother's favorite evangelists was scheduled to come on the gospel channel in about fifteen minutes, so Summer thought this was a good time to slip out of the apartment and work the second phase of her plan to get Xavier back. She showered and dressed in black spandex capris, a gold colored sateen tank top, and matching high heel ankle strap sandals. She grabbed her phone, the keys to her mother's rental car, and her purse from the coffee table and headed back to her mother's room, where Susan retired just after dinner.

Summer knocked on the door. "Mãe?"

"Come on in, dear," came Susan's voice from the other side of the door.

Summer did not open the door, but said, "I'm going to step out for a few. I'll be back shortly."

"Okay."

"I'm going to take your car and put some gas in it, okay?"

"That's fine."

Summer walked toward the front door, grateful that her mother did not ask where she was going, or the real reason she needed the rental car.

* * *

The GPS in the rental car led Summer to West Grace Street, a cobblestone street lined by sugar maples and well-kept narrow and deep row houses. Jada's house was beige brick, with red brick stairs leading to a mahogany door. Summer drove further up the street, through an alley and around to the rear of Jada's house. There was no vehicle in the back driveway, and there appeared to be no lights on in the house. She drove back around front and parked on the side of the street opposite the house. She turned off the ignition and the lights.

Summer knew it was tactically risky. If Jada spotted her there, she could accuse Summer of stalking her, although the risk was minimized because Jada would not recognize the car. Even worse, she would lose the chance to win Xavier back. She had to be careful. She'd only planned to be there just long enough to observe the house and the neighborhood and plan for her next step. And she knew her mother was likely expecting her back shortly. Her ultimate plan would have to wait until her mother was back in Atlanta.

Summer took her iPhone out of her purse, loaded the camera app, turned off the flash, and started taking photos of the house. Then she sat and observed the goings-on, which weren't many. The street was fairly quiet. She saw one man walking his Border Collie. Another car rolled up the street and turned the corner. A woman came out of her house, grabbed children's toys that were sitting outside, and went back inside. She scoffed at the sight of the college-age couple who walked down the street, their hands in each other's back pockets.

She returned her attention to the house, observing details that might be helpful. There was a two- or three-foot walkway between the east wall of Jada's house and the house next door. When Summer looked closely, she saw that the walkway extended all the way to the rear of the house and ended near the back alley. The small front lawn was well-manicured, with a wreath of ivies surrounding it. The porch roof was supported in front by ornate ironwork columns. *Doesn't seem the type of house belonging to a floozy like Jada*, Summer thought.

Her thoughts were interrupted by a knock on her driver's side window. Summer jumped and turned. The woman there waved and smiled and then motioned for Summer to roll her window down.

Summer engaged the ignition switch and rolled down the window. "May I help you?"

"Actually, I was going to ask you that question. You've been sitting here for a while, so I was wondering if there was something I could help *you* with?"

Summer shot her a look of annoyance. *Who is this white woman to be getting all in my business?* Nonetheless, she acquiesced because if this suspicious woman were to call the police, it would ruin her plans.

"I'm waiting for a friend," Summer finally said.

"What friend?" the woman responded.

Boy, this woman is nosy, she thought. But she had to be careful how she answered. A woman this inquisitive probably knew everyone on the block. If she lied, the woman might assume Summer was up to some malfeasance and call the police.

"Jada Hardy," Summer finally answered. "She lives in that beige house over there."

"Oh, okay." The answer seemed to satisfy the woman.

Summer started some questions of her own. "Are you a friend of hers?"

"Oh, no." The woman shook her hands in front of her, brushing off any possible association. "I wouldn't say that I'm a friend."

Summer thought quickly. This woman already knows what she looks like, and that she was there to see Jada. If the woman wanted to

give Jada a heads up, she could, and her plans would be toast. Maybe she could turn things around by getting this woman on her side.

"To be honest, I'm not one either. At least not anymore," Summer said.

"Why do you say that?"

"Because I think my husband is cheating on me with her."

"Oh, you poor dear."

"That's why I'm here. I'm not trying to confront Jada. But I need to get some evidence, so I can confront my husband."

The woman leaned in closer. "Well, she does seem to have a lot of men coming over."

"Does she live alone?"

"Oh, no. There's a disabled woman that I think is her sister. Other than her, nobody. Well, except for a male friend that comes around from time to time. But I don't think he lives there."

"Tell me about him."

"He's a black guy, real ritzy looking. Drives a BMW. He was over there almost constantly over the weekend. Before that, I would see him there occasionally. Is that your husband?"

Summer felt a tinge of sadness come over her. "No."

"Well, he's not been the only man I've seen over there. Even my husband goes over there to talk to her sometimes. But trust me, he's not going over there just to talk about current events."

"Your husband's cheating on you with *her*?"

"Oh, no. He just goes over there and talks with her in the yard. He knows better than to go inside. I think she's just a little eye candy, something for him to look at. And she's got a *lot* to look at, if you know what I mean."

"You let your husband do that?"

"I'm his wife, not his jailer. He can look, as long as he comes home to me."

"Nice you can trust your man like that."

"You're such a pretty, sweet girl. I don't understand why your husband needs to cheat on you."

"Can you do me a huge favor?"

"Anything, hon."

"Could you call me if you happen to notice a white man over there who drives a tan Lexus, Georgia license plates?"

"Is that your husband?"

Summer gave her a half-smile and lied. "Yes."

"Such a shame. I'll keep an eye out."

"Thank you." Summer jotted her cell phone number on a notepad she kept in her car. She handed the sheet to the woman. "If you see him, call me. Day or night. No matter what time."

"Sure." The woman looked at the paper. "But what's your name?"

"Er, uh, Angela Battman. And your name?"

"Phoebe. Phoebe Carlson. That's my house over there." She pointed to a mauve colored row house surrounded by sugar maples.

"Thanks, Phoebe. And please don't share this with anyone. Absolutely no one. And as far as you are concerned, I was never here."

"Well, I hope you catch him, darling. Nothing makes me angrier than a cheating man."

Good, thought Summer. That's what I am counting on.

* * *

As the owner and chief operating officer of a vibrant and profitable video production company, Mark Battman did not leave his office until after 8 p.m. most nights. It also gave him convenient opportunities for trysts with Jada Hardy in his office. Their torrid affair had been going on for over a year, with Mark's wife none the wiser. However, the relationship had not escaped the notice of some members of the staff. While no one had ever caught them displaying any affection, Mark and Jada's degree of friendliness to one another was a tip-off that they had more going on than producing videos.

But now Mark was having second thoughts. He had only heard about Jada and Xavier's engagement the night that Jada called him on

his cell to complain about Summer's behavior at the restaurant. The betrayal was setting in—he had hoped that if things soured between him and his wife, Jada could become his main squeeze. Now, even though Jada shared him with Mark's wife for more than a year, Mark felt uncomfortable sharing Jada with Xavier. It made things more challenging, as he not only had to hide the relationship from Angela, but Jada had to hide it from Xavier.

It was another reason he had to fire Summer. Mark knew how headstrong Summer could be, and that she would not give up on her relationship with Xavier easily. That would make for a very uncomfortable working relationship with Summer. And with Summer's heightened sensibility to Jada's betrayal, Summer might inadvertently discover the relationship between Jada and him. It was a big mess he had to clean up, and quickly.

While Summer was on West Grace Street staking out Jada's house, Jada and Mark were still at the office, patiently waiting for the last over-dedicated employee to leave. Once the employee had left, Jada sashayed into Mark's office, her short, tight spandex skirt swishing against her hips. It was her intent to have a quick one with Mark before she headed home to call Xavier.

Mark, however, was not in the mood. Seated behind his desk, he said, "I don't want to do this, Jada."

Jada parked her hands on her hips and cocked her head to the side. "Say what?"

Mark repeated himself, more slowly. "I don't want to do this."

Jada rolled her eyes at him and looked away.

Mark looked down at his desk. "You know what, I don't think we should do this anymore."

"What do you mean?"

"I think we should stop seeing each other."

Jada turned her back to him, knowing that he would take one look at her curvaceous figure and quickly change his mind. One of Jada's strengths, for which Mark hired her, was that she was a consummate saleswoman and a hottie to boot. She knew how to close the deal with

whatever assets were available. She knew how to turn a no into a yes. And although Mark was having second thoughts, Jada knew exactly what to do to get him on board again. And she knew Mark could not resist when she started flaunting her figure.

The tactic worked, to an extent. Mark knew he could not continue the relationship. But he saw no harm in having one last tryst with her, just for the road.

But Jada had longer range plans. As long as Mark remained captivated by her, he would give her whatever she wanted: power, position, a raise whenever she asked. That was why she slept with him. It had very little to do with sex—she could get that from almost any man she met. It was all about strategy.

Jada continued to face away from him, but lifted her arms in such a way that her skirt started to ride slightly up her hips, something she knew Mark would notice. "Are you sure about that? You sure you want to give all this up?"

Mark was vaguely aware he was warring between the pleasures of the flesh and his logic. He didn't want to give up Jada, but things were getting too messy for his tastes. "Yeah, I think we should take a break."

Jada turned back to him, searching his eyes. Although Mark was not one to jest, she had to make sure he was not joking about this. When it was clear that he was serious, Jada said, "Tell you what. Let's go down to Alan's and get a drink. We'll talk about it."

Mark shook his head. "You know we agreed not to hook up in public."

Jada scoffed. "It's just two colleagues going for drinks after a hard day's work. What's the big deal?"

"People are not going to see it that way. We can't assume we're the only ones who know what's going on."

"Okay, then let's go to my place. Karen is on some kinda overnight church trip, so she won't be back until tomorrow. It's a great night. We can get some drinks, hang out in the backyard with some great weed."

Mark felt ashamed that he was so weak-willed. An evening with Jada at her home sounded too good to pass up. He had been invited there before, but only when her older sister Karen was away for some reason.

He had never met Karen, but Mark remembered Jada telling him a little about her. She was what Jada called a church girl, heavily devout, and could barely exist a day without the word "Jesus" coming out of her mouth in a way that was not blasphemous. Karen had been living with Jada for about a year, right after an accidental fire totaled her home of twenty years. To escape the fire, Karen jumped out of a second story window and nearly obliterated her right hip. Since their parents were in Detroit, and Jada knew her parents would not have the room to house Karen nor the time to look after her while she recuperated, Jada agreed to move Karen into her home until she was better.

Jada, knowing Karen with her Christian sensibilities would have an issue with her bringing Mark or any other man to her home, avoided bringing Mark around when Karen was at home, opting to have her trysts with him in the office, or in some cases, in hotel rooms. But now, with Karen away for the evening, Jada could bring Mark to her home and be as uninhibited as she wanted.

There was one problem. "What about my wife?" Mark asked.

"What about her?"

"C'mon, Jada. The last time I was over your house, I didn't get out until after midnight. Do you realize how hard I had to work to convince my wife that I was not cheating on her?"

"Tell her you were having drinks with a client. You do it all the time."

"Yeah, and at some point my wife is going to get suspicious and stop believing it." Mark rose to his feet and grabbed his jacket from the back of his chair. "We can hang out one last time. But after this, Jada, we gotta go our separate ways. Personally, that is."

"Okay," Jada said, not believing one word of it. She knew that once she worked her magic on him that evening, he would change his mind.

***

Once Summer had arrived home, she managed to coax her mother out of the spare bedroom and into the living room to watch TV with her. Susan, who never knew a TV program she couldn't fall asleep on, barely lasted thirty minutes into an episode of *Scandal* before she was out.

Summer's cell phone rang, waking Susan. Summer looked at the ID, hoping it was Xavier. It wasn't. In fact, she didn't recognize the number at all. Nonetheless, she answered the call.

The voice on the other end was unfamiliar for a moment, until the caller identified herself. "Hi, Mrs. Battman. This is Phoebe Carlson, the woman you met on Grace Street."

Summer glanced over at Susan, whose eyes were alternating between watching the TV and watching her. She stood and walked over to her patio door, opening it. "Yes, Mrs. Carlson?"

"You asked me to call you if I saw a tan Lexus? Well, my husband and I were just returning from visiting my daughter's house, and we saw the car parked in front of the house. It had Georgia license plates, like you said."

Summer walked out onto her balcony, smiling and shaking her head. *She knew it.* To her, this was evidence enough that Mark and Jada saw each other. But she knew it would not be enough evidence for anyone else. They could claim they had dinner, and then got busy on a work project. They could come up with any number of excuses. So, merely witnessing the car would not be enough. Summer had to go to the next phase of her plan, the scariest one of all.

"Thank you so much, Mrs. Carlson," Summer said, closing the patio door behind her so that Susan would not hear her next words. "I'm going to head right over there. Could you keep an eye out and let me know if you see anything else before I get there?"

"Well. It's kind of hard to see anything from my house, with the trees, and all. I can see the car, but that's about it."

"Just call me if the car leaves before I get there."

"How long will you be?"

"About fifteen minutes."

"Okay, I'll stay downstairs until you arrive. But if it is much longer, I really need to go to bed soon. And I won't be able to see anything from my bedroom."

"I understand. I'll be there right away. Thanks again."

"You're welcome, Mrs. Battman."

Summer hung up the call, then looked out over the courtyard of her apartment complex. A huge fountain shot water in the air almost as high as her third-floor apartment. Summer always marveled at the engineering of the fountain so that water never splashed beyond the borders of the fountain, even when it was breezy outside. The soothing sounds of the water spray lulled her to sleep on many nights.

She had only a few minutes to think. Now that Mark was at Jada's place, how would she get evidence that this was anything but a casual visit? Short of seeing them step outside for maybe a goodbye kiss or an exceedingly intimate hug, she had no idea how she would do it. And she didn't relish the idea of staking out Jada's place like a cop on the prowl.

She decided to go anyway, hoping that an opportunity would present itself. She walked inside the apartment, grabbed her purse, stuffed her cell phone into it, and rummaged around for her car keys, ignoring the incessant stare of her mother.

"What are you doing?" Susan finally asked.

"I have to step out for a moment."

"Step out where?"

"Just have to step out."

"Summer, where is it you have to go at eleven at night?"

"Out."

"Where?"

"Mãe, I'm not fourteen years old anymore. You don't have to interrogate me. Let's just say that I'm going out, and I don't want to tell you where. Can you accept that?"

Susan gave an intense but sad look at her daughter. She realized

she could not control Summer's decisions, although she wished otherwise. She only nodded and said, "At least tell me that *wherever* you are going, you'll be safe."

"I will, Mãe." Summer went over to her mother, planted on her cheek a *no hard feelings I still love you* kiss, found her car keys, and then headed out the door.

Susan looked at the door for a few minutes, then closed her eyes and spoke to the only other person in the room now.

"Lord, I don't know what's going on with my daughter. But please protect her and keep her. Show her your heart, Lord, and make her fall in love with you again. In the name of Jesus."

Susan then went back into her bedroom, knowing that she could either read or sleep. And sleep was out of the question.

***

Xavier sat awake in his hotel room waiting for Jada to call. It was now past eleven, and he had not heard from her since their mid-afternoon conversation. He thought about calling her, but didn't want to appear as if he was checking up on her. Besides, Jada never specified exactly *when* she would call.

He lay back on the plush king-size bed and allowed his thoughts to drift to Summer for a moment. Distressed as he was that Summer had acted so childishly at their last meeting, he understood fully why she acted that way. It was not the most tactful of break-ups, and having Jada there only exacerbated the tension. In hindsight, he would have done it somewhere public, yet in a place without so concentrated a density of people, like a park.

Xavier never had any problem getting girlfriends, and most of them would do whatever he asked. Summer was different. At first, he thought it was because she was born in Brazil, but after a few months of dating, he realized it was because she was raised in the church. Xavier himself had been raised in church, but slowly drifted away once he was firmly into adulthood and no longer cared as much what

his parents thought if he didn't go to church five times a week. But with Summer, there seemed to be a struggle within, as if part of her wanted to be free of any religious restraints, yet another part wanted to cling to the safety of those beliefs.

He remembered the first time he asked if he could make love to her, although his request was more implicit than he intended. He was in Washington, D.C. meeting with executives from a gas association. It was only two months after they had started dating. He called her in Richmond and asked her to drive to D.C. to join him for dinner, and then ride back with him the next day. Summer agreed, driving two hours to Washington, D.C. in a one-way rental car, and then meeting Xavier at Phillips Restaurant on the Southeast waterfront. They had a romantic dinner while looking out at the view of the Potomac River. He was certain that dinner at a beautiful restaurant with a romantic view would stoke her fires. After the waiter had collected their dishes, Xavier asked her to join him in his hotel room.

Summer cheerfully avoided answering the question, making idle chat with Xavier until the restaurant's 9 p.m. closing time. Just before they left, she told Xavier that she was a Christian, and she did not believe in sharing a hotel room with a man unless they were married. As Xavier had no experience arguing a woman out of her religious convictions, he nodded, said he understood, paid the check, and had Summer follow him in his car to his hotel nearby. He paid $250 for a separate room for Summer for the night, chit-chatted with her in the lobby bar over glasses of Cîroc, and then saw her to her room at 11:30 p.m., after which he headed to his. He lay in his hotel room hoping that Summer would dial him up and ask him to come calling to her room. That never happened. During the drive back to Richmond the next day, Xavier knew he had to marry this girl if he wanted any intimate relationship with her.

So he started proposing to her. Every month, he asked. And every month, her answer was, "Ask me again next month." Finally, seeing that Summer had no intention to marry him, it was so easy to entertain Jada's interest, as she had been flirting with him since the day that

Summer introduced them.

Xavier hated to break Summer's heart. But he knew Summer would have to work out a lot of issues before she would be ready for marriage. Throughout their relationship, Summer seemed intent on projecting her father's sins onto him. While Xavier certainly knew his way around a bar, he doubted he would ever descend to the level that Nestor Maldonado had. And beating a woman—absolutely not.

But Xavier could not wait for Summer to resolve her issues. He yearned for her, intimately. He could no longer handle observing her hourglass figure, experiencing her seemingly effortless sexiness, and taking in her scent of sweet jasmine, without aching to touch her. Summer was beautiful, even more so than Jada, he thought. But Jada was ready to give him her all. Summer wanted to hold it until God said otherwise. And Xavier thought that was not fair, to him or to any other man, to experience such loveliness, and only be able to engage her with three of his senses, but not the other two.

Nonetheless, he missed Summer. There was something special about her. It had only been five days since their break-up, and he pined for her again. He thought it may have been the loneliness of the hotel room and played it off as such. But still, he could not stop thinking about her, even as he waited patiently for Jada's phone call.

***

As Summer made the turn onto West Grace Street, she slowed down, made a U-turn and slipped into a parking space about five doors down from Jada's house, on the opposite side of the street. She didn't want to get any closer in case Jada or Mark were standing outside or looking out the window. They might notice her car, which both of them knew very well.

She pulled her cell phone out of her purse and enabled the camera app. Then she stuffed her purse under the driver's seat and thought about what she would do next. She wasn't certain. She could sit there and wait until they came out, hoping to catch them in some uncompro-

mising position. But she had no idea how long that would be. Or, she could walk around the house and hope that undrawn blinds or open curtains would give her a view of something going on inside. As she thought further, she decided that walking around the house would be the best and quickest option, but also the riskier one.

She got out of the car, leaving the doors unlocked in case she had to make a quick getaway. This community didn't seem like the type where thieves were trolling to steal cars, so she felt safe leaving her keys in the ignition, at least for a few minutes. She walked quietly up the sidewalk, keeping her eyes fixed on Jada's house. As she approached, she slowed down further, studying the windows and the front door. There was a light on in the living room, but she saw no other obvious activity in the house. Summer halted as she contemplated her next step. Then, she walked up the first group of brick stairs to the front yard of the home, headed to the right, and slowly walked along the passageway between Jada's house and the house next door. Mild palpitations accompanied her walk.

She continued along the passageway, looking up at the windows. The narrowness of the passageway made it impossible for her to see inside, or for anyone inside to see anything outside, as her head was below the level of the first-floor windows. Where the house ended, a wooden plank fence began, about six feet high, surrounding the entire backyard. Summer was five foot ten, but was sure that anyone looking out of one of the rear second-story windows would be able to see her despite the cover of the fence. She crouched down and walked slowly and carefully toward the outer right corner of the fence. Then suddenly, she heard it.

She stopped, trying to determine what she had heard. The din of nearby traffic on Monument Street made it difficult to ascertain. It almost sounded like a breath, or a grunt, but could have been any other obscure sound. But what made it especially interesting was that Summer was almost sure it came from Jada's backyard.

She started again, creeping around to the back. There was a gate, with enough of a gap between the gate post and the gate that she could

crouch down to almost grass-level and see inside without being detected. As she knelt down on the concrete, she could feel the coolness of it through her jeans. She then allowed her entire body to lie on the alley concrete outside the gate, and positioned her head so that she could look through the gap in the gate.

What she saw shocked, disgusted, and delighted her at the same time.

Summer pulled her phone out of her jeans pocket and made sure she activated the camera. She knew she could not get a decent photo through the gap of the gate, but what she saw was so incriminating, she had to risk discovery in order to get a good shot.

She carefully stood to her feet and drew close to the gate. She held the phone high over the gate, watching the image on the screen. Her hands were jittery, and she hoped she didn't drop the phone. When she was satisfied, she pressed the button. The flash seemed to light up the entire block.

"What the—" Summer heard the male voice coming from the backyard.

Summer pulled the phone close to her and ran like she was being chased by hounds. She scurried along the passageway, figuring she was safe for a moment, because it would take both Mark and Jada a minute to put their clothes on and chase her. Once she had cleared the passageway, she ran across the yard, jumped down to the sidewalk, and dashed to her car, looking back to make sure no one was following her. She jumped in her car, started the ignition, and quickly pulled out of the parking space. As she turned the corner, she looked into the rear view mirror and thought she saw a shirtless male figure just appearing in the yard, looking in her direction.

***

Summer pulled over at a 7-Eleven to collect her nerves and calm her racing heart. She hadn't run like that since high school, but fortunately, her regular workouts enabled her to make the sprint. She did

not get out of the car, but checked the photo on her phone once again. The image was clear enough to make out Mark's face, but the other woman, her back to the camera, could be anyone. However, the long fake auburn hair and the dark skin was a dead giveaway to anyone who knew her. And Xavier knew her well.

Summer pounded the air with her fist, letting out a "Yes!" with each punch. If this photo weren't enough to get her back together with Xavier, then nothing would. She backed up her phone to her cloud service, not wanting to take any chances. She then pulled her purse from under her seat, stuffed the phone into it, and headed for home. She would make the call to Xavier first thing tomorrow morning.

***

"Who the hell was that?" Jada said as Mark walked back into the house wearing nothing but a pair of khaki chinos and a pair of now soil-stained socks. While Mark was in the front yard, Jada had time to slip on her clothes and come into the house.

"I don't know," Mark told her. He started pacing, in obvious distress. "Why would anyone want to take a picture of us?" He looked at Jada, hoping she had answers.

Jada remained silent, turning things over in her head. Finally, she spoke. "There are three people who might want to do that."

"Who?" Mark asked.

"One is Xavier. And I don't think it was him. The second one is your wife. And according to you, she doesn't have a clue."

"So, who is the third person?"

"Summer Maldonado."

Mark laughed. "C'mon, Jada. You're reaching. How would she know where you lived? And how would she know we were doing what we were doing, and the time we were doing it?"

"You hired her, Mark. You know how crafty she can be. Besides, of those three, she's lost the most. Xavier still has me. You still have your wife. But Summer's lost everything."

Mark reached for his shirt, which hung over the back of an arm-chair in the living room. "I knew I should have ended this at the office."

"Shoulda woulda coulda." Jada walked to her living room window and looked out, parting the blinds only slightly. "We can go over this all night. The question is, what are we going to do about Summer?"

"I'd say we just wait it out. See what happens. We don't know for sure if that was Summer. If it was, she'll make her intentions known."

"Shouldn't we at least call the police? That was an invasion of privacy."

Mark laughed. "Invasion of privacy? We were in the backyard. *What* invasion of privacy?"

"There is a fence around the backyard. Nobody should have seen anything."

"I don't want to bring anyone else into this. It's embarrassing enough. I shouldn't be here, and yet you want me to put it on official record?" Mark slipped on his shirt and tucked it in his pants. Walking through the kitchen and out the back door into the backyard, he retrieved his shoes and put them on. Jada followed him.

"So, you're leaving?" Jada said.

"Yeah. It's best I go home."

"So, what about us?"

Mark gave her a sad, though determined look. "We're done. I can't take any more risks." He walked past her into the living room, grabbed his keys, and without another word, stormed out the front door.

Jada shook her head while looking at the door. *Such a weak man*, she thought. *And a weak man will always come back*. She locked up downstairs, and then walked up to her bedroom to call Xavier.

***

Susan had told Summer that she wanted to stay in Richmond until

Friday when the plane tickets were cheaper, and that was not a lie. But it was a convenient excuse for the real reason she wanted to stay: she had been praying, and the Lord had placed a heavy urging on her heart not to leave. Not long after settling into her daughter's apartment, she knew why.

Summer tried to act as if nothing was wrong, but that was clearly not the case. Susan noticed how skittish she seemed sometimes, as if she was trying to hide something. A few times, Susan caught Summer in the living room, just sitting, seemingly in a daze, no TV, no computer, no book, nothing. Just staring off into empty air. Other times, Susan would walk by Summer's bedroom and hear her inside crying. Summer had made no mention of trying to find another job, and Susan had observed how Summer's appetite appeared diminished of late. Summer made no effort to get rid of the various photos of her and Xavier scattered around the apartment. Even her appearance began to deteriorate. Summer had started to blow off her weekly salon appointments. Lately, her long dark bountiful hair was wrapped in a scarf.

However, when Susan woke up the next morning and found her daughter in the kitchen, Summer's countenance seemed to have changed. Summer had changed into a fresh, light, and airy linen outfit, had a smile on her face, and was preparing breakfast.

"Bom dia, Mãe," Summer chirped. She poured her mother a cup of coffee, strong and black, then added milk that she had boiled on the stove.

"My, my." Susan sat at the breakfast nook, stirred her coffee, and noticed all the breakfast items which Summer had prepared, fresh papaya, watermelon, and cheese bread. To appease her mother's Southern taste buds, she had fried some bacon and prepared a small pot of grits.

Sipping her coffee, Susan said, "What brought all this on? Most mornings, I'm lucky to see you even get up out of bed."

"It's a good day, Mãe." Summer prepared her mother a plate of bacon, grits, and papaya, while she settled for cheese bread, watermelon, and bacon.

Not wanting to let the line of conversation drop, Susan pressed. "So, what makes this such a good day?"

Summer had taken two slices of watermelon before she bothered to answer the question. "I think things are going to work out for X and me."

"Why do you say that?"

"Just a feeling."

"And what if they don't?"

"They will."

Susan cast her eyes down and started eating her grits, giving her some time to think. She began to wonder if Summer was delusional. Xavier had not contacted her since their break-up, and her calls and texts to him—at least seven a day—were neither answered nor returned. Susan surmised that maybe that was where she had run off to last night. Maybe she had some clandestine meeting with Xavier, which, for some reason, she didn't want to tell her mother about.

"Does this have anything to do with where you went last night?" Susan pressed.

Summer looked annoyed. "Ma—"

Susan threw her hands up. "Sorry. Just asking." She returned to eating, content to remain silent on the subject.

Summer relented a bit, realizing that her mother was likely the only friend she had in the world right now. "I found out that Jada, the girl that Xavier cheated on me with, is sleeping with my former boss."

"Really?"

"Yes."

"How do you know?"

"I *know*."

Susan nodded, knowing that was all she was going to get, and surprised she got *that* much.

"So," Summer continued, "when X hears about it, he'll leave her, and come back to me."

Susan merely looked at Summer but did not nod nor affirm her comment. Summer had always blamed Jada for being the principal

factor in her break-up with Xavier. But Susan had been around long enough to know better. Jada was *not* the problem, and getting rid of Jada would not resolve whatever issues caused their break-up. So, she knew already that Summer was dealing with this the wrong way, and she dreaded her daughter getting her heart broken again.

"Honey, maybe we should just talk to a pastor about this, to make sure you're making the right decisions here."

Summer finished the last of her cheese bread. She heard what her mother had said. She did not answer her mother nor acknowledge that Susan had made the suggestion. All she knew was that she wanted Xavier back. And there was no way she was going to ask a pastor for advice, when she knew he would likely not give a ringing endorsement for her to hook up with a man who was engaged to another woman and likely had been sleeping with her.

Susan read the look in her daughter's face and repeated her suggestion. "Summer, we need to do this." Sometimes she wished she had the verve and spitfire to counteract Summer's headstrong attitude, but knew that was not in her personality. Maybe a man of the cloth could find other ways to get through to her.

Summer sipped her black coffee and remained quiet.

Seeing that she had upset her daughter, Susan let the matter drop. They finished their breakfast in silence, and then Susan moved to the living room, where she turned on a morning gospel program. Summer scoffed, collected the dishes, and then headed to the kitchen.

Summer loaded the dirty dishes into her dishwasher, thinking that she didn't need a preacher getting into her business. *Mãe will see. I'll get X back, and all will be well.* She started to hash out mentally the remaining step of her plan. She could take the pictures to Jada and demand that she break up with Xavier over the threat of having the pictures released to the public. As ambitious as Jada was, Summer knew that having pictures of Jada all over the Internet was the one thing that Jada did not need. But there was a problem with that approach. If Jada broke up with Xavier, he would grieve her. And that was not an option.

Her only remaining option was to show the pictures directly to

Xavier, knowing that he would immediately break up with Jada, and then she would be there to soothe and comfort him. She would have to risk Xavier's being angry at her for going through the trouble to obtain the pictures.

Summer decided she would go with the last option. Once she arranged the dishes in the dishwasher, she picked up her phone from the counter and called her salon. She would try to get an emergency appointment that day and be ready to go to Xavier's office and ask him to meet her that night.

And if she and Xavier got back together, and he wanted to spend the night with her, this time she would not say no.

***

Xavier, with a single rolling suitcase in tow, exited the Richmond International Airport terminal and strolled across Federal Road to the valet parking booth. Once they had retrieved his car, he drove out of the parking lot and onto Route 60 toward downtown Richmond.

Just after he got off the plane, his office had sent him a message. Summer had stopped by the office looking for him, and wanted to see him immediately regarding his new girlfriend. Xavier texted Summer and agreed to meet her at a pizza joint in Bon Air, close to his home.

Xavier had to admit he was curious. He was more than a little bothered by the fact that Jada did not call him until after midnight, and even then, she seemed distressed and did not want to talk long. And he had tried to call Jada several times today, but the calls went straight to voicemail. He wondered if there was some connection between Jada's distant behavior and Summer's request to meet with him. He hoped that Summer hadn't confronted her in some way.

He also had to admit that he missed Summer. He looked forward to seeing her, but could only hope that they remain friends. He had no intention of getting back together with Summer, and intended to honor his commitment to Jada fully.

Buford Road Pizza was a tiny, white stucco, hole-in-the-wall with a four-stool bar and barely enough room inside to move around. It was one of those places that no one would dare to venture if they were not already familiar with it. But Xavier thought they had the best pizza in town. Its old town charm reminded him of childhood summers at his grandparents' house in Albany, where they had liquor bottles and old antiques on almost every shelf of the basement. He also had a sizeable tab at Buford, which he paid dutifully and promptly ever month. Xavier had brought Summer there before. She loved the pizza but hated the ambiance. Which was perfect in order to demonstrate that he had no romantic intentions in meeting her.

Xavier arrived a few minutes before Summer, so he sat outside in one of the wrought iron chairs that were long due for a paint job. He felt a little strange sitting there in a Brioni suit, at a place where the highest standard of dress was usually jeans and a T-shirt.

The owner's son, Antonio, popped out of the door and greeted Xavier as if they had been pals for years. They made small talk and dished about sports before Antonio walked back inside with instructions to make a small pepperoni pie for Xavier and his expected guest.

Summer pulled up a few minutes later in her Acura. Xavier watched her as she got out. The first thing he saw was her stunning legs, shiny and naked up to the hem of her several-inches-above-the-knee orange and yellow dress. He looked away quickly. He wanted to check her out, but knew he was not strong enough to ogle her for long. The breeze brought the scent of Chanel to him shortly before she approached.

Summer sat down in the chair across from him, crossing her legs alluringly the moment he cast his gaze back upon her. As the sun was low in the sky, her large sunglasses served a fashionable rather than practical purpose. She didn't bother to greet him formally, but asked, "How was your trip?"

Xavier was not in the mood for small talk. He wanted to find out what Summer had to say, and then get out of there as quickly as possible. This girl was on a mission. He knew it, and he was not too sure

he could hold up against her flirtations.

"It was good," Xavier said. "What do you have to tell me?"

Summer took a deep breath. "I have proof in my car of what I'm about to tell you. It's going to be painful, but I felt you needed to know. I'm going to tell you, but hopefully you'll believe me, and I can spare you the additional hurt of seeing my proof."

Antonio came outside with the piping hot pizza and set it on the table. He nodded at Summer, then said to Xavier, "Holler at me before you leave, playa'."

"I will." Xavier looked at Summer and extended his hand toward the pizza. "Have some?"

Summer shook her head. As Xavier started to eat a slice, Summer heard some chatter from the kitchen, and the words *that ain't the girl he normally be with!*

"So, what did you want to tell me?" Xavier repeated.

Summer took another deep breath. "Jada's cheating on you."

Xavier barely looked up from the pizza. "Cheating on me with who?"

"With Mark Battman, her boss."

Xavier finished half a slice, then placed the rest on the plate and looked piercingly into Summer's sunglasses. "I know."

Summer managed a confused frown. "You know what?"

"I know."

"What?"

"I know that Jada's sleeping with Mark Battman."

"How did you … ?" Summer suddenly had a thought. Jada knew she was busted, and she was trying to get ahead of things with Xavier. "Oh, Jada must have called you last night or today to tell you."

"No. I've known since the day you and I broke up."

Summer's eyes went wide, and her mouth parted slightly to accommodate her breathing.

Xavier explained. "Right after we wiped the wine off our faces, Jada told me she occasionally slept with Mark. She said she didn't love him, but it was just a relationship to help her advance her career."

"Wow." Summer removed her sunglasses and set them on the table. "I would never have guessed you already knew."

"Yeah, I knew."

"So, what happened? You broke up with her, right?"

"No. We're still together. Still planning to get married."

That statement was like a haymaker to the gut. Summer thought about any possible way she could have misinterpreted what Xavier had just said, because Xavier could not be *that* stupid. "You're kidding me."

"No."

"But she cheated on you."

"I told you I know."

"She cheated on you *last night*!"

"Well, I didn't know about last night, but yeah, I know she's sleeping with Mark."

"And you're okay with that?" Summer's voice had started to travel.

"I'm fine with it."

Summer stood up. "Are you a fool, or what?"

Xavier stood up as well. "It's called an open relationship. My mom and dad had that kind of relationship."

"You never told me that!" Summer said angrily.

"Well, I didn't think it was any of your business what my parents' sexual practices were."

"It was my business what *yours* were!"

"I've never had one before this. This is the first."

"I don't believe this." Summer turned her back and took a few steps away, running her hand through her hair and massaging her scalp. She wanted to scream, and might have if Xavier had not asked his next question.

"What is it to you anyway? You and I are not together anymore."

Summer kept her back turned to him. She massaged her forehead. Her entire plan had crashed and burned. Slowly, she said, "I don't understand how you can let your future wife sleep around with another

man."

Xavier walked closer to her, as he did not want his explanation heard by everyone within earshot. "Let me say this. Most marriages end in divorce. Of those divorces, most were because of cheating. If you go into a marriage knowing that your wife is going to cheat, it no longer becomes a reason to divorce. And we already beat the odds."

Summer turned, looking at him incredulously, but saying nothing.

"Summer, you've seen Jada," Xavier continued. "The girl is freakin' hot. If I marry her, I'm at home every day sweating bullets because I'm afraid some other guy is going to snap her up. And monogamy doesn't work anymore. It hasn't worked in a long time. That was for the 17th century. It's not for these times. We live in a sex saturated society."

Summer continued to glare at him.

"Jada goes out and cheats, but she comes home to me," Xavier explained. "I'm her main man. And I'm okay with that."

Summer was appalled with how sick Xavier sounded. And she was even more appalled that she was still in love with him and still wanted him.

Xavier took his wallet from his jacket pocket. "Is there anything else you wanted to tell me? Because I need to go and see Jada."

Struggling with the realization that Xavier was quickly slipping from her grasp, Summer moved closer to him until their breaths mingled. Xavier could clearly smell her Chanel, the scent of seduction.

"X, listen," Summer purred.

Xavier could not look her in the eyes.

"X, I love you. I still do. And I am willing to forget everything that happened before today. And most importantly, I am willing to go home with you right now and give myself to you. If you'll have me. I can be everything that you need. You don't need Jada."

Nothing in all of Xavier's education had taught him how to resist such a blatant come-on. But he knew that Summer did not mean what she was saying, and would likely regret it later, and he had no intent of going there with her.

"Summer, I—"

Summer moved in and silenced him with a hungry kiss. She moved her hand to the back of his neck and began massaging him there. Xavier pulled away.

"I can't do this, Summer."

"Yes, you can." She started toward him again.

Xavier stepped back. "No!" His voice was forceful and loud. Summer drew back in surprise. He had never raised his voice like that to her.

"I will *not* have you, Summer. We're done."

Summer felt tears right at the edges of her eyes, and she tried to suppress a quivering of her lips. She quickly turned her back to him, and then, suddenly, without saying another word, marched toward her car, got in, started the ignition, and sped off down Buford Road.

Xavier walked back to the table just as Antonio was coming outside.

"Don't look like it worked out too good, bro," Antonio said to Xavier.

"No, it didn't. At least not for her."

"Put this in a box, man?"

"Yeah. I'm taking the pizza to go."

"Your girl's shades over here, too, bro."

As Antonio walked back inside with the barely eaten pizza, Xavier grabbed the sunglasses and examined them. These were the ones he had bought her during a trip to the mall several months ago. He slipped them into his jacket pocket, knowing that those sunglasses were the only part of Summer he would likely get to keep.

* * *

The bar in downtown Richmond was formally called *the Lager Lobby*, but all the workaday types who frequented the bar's happy hour knew the owner and called it *Alan's* after him. When Summer

walked in, it was well past eight. A few of the patrons recognized her from Visual Notions, but they had never seen her dressed so alluringly. A few of the guys ogled her, trying to decide if they wanted to go up to talk to her, and if so, the best approach.

Summer sat at the bar, planting her high-heeled feet firmly on the ledge just a few inches off the floor. The bartender tonight was a college-age girl Summer did not recognize, which was fine with her because she was in no mood for conversation. "Cognac," she said to the bartender. The girl nodded and reached for a bottle of Hennessey, which was Xavier's frequent spirit of choice.

Summer never drank until she arrived in Richmond. Even when she was working at the jazz radio station, hanging around with hard-smoking and hard-drinking musicians, she always steered clear of booze. But when she started working at Visual Notions, where almost everyone in the office hung out with each other at happy hour and most business deals were secured over wine and spirits, Summer succumbed to social pressure and started to drink occasionally. She started with wine and beer, then moved to harder drinks. Even so, she never got drunk.

Now, with a combination of embarrassment, failure, betrayal, and rejection swirling around inside her, Summer couldn't cope—the pain was much too great and her heart literally ached inside her. She couldn't stop thinking about Xavier, and that bothered her now, because she knew she could never have him. Having lost all hope, she went into despair. She was drawn to the booze, hoping it would help keep the images of Xavier out of her head.

She downed the first shot of cognac quickly, then asked for another, then another. After downing the third shot, she asked the bartender for the entire bottle. The bartender refused, even after Summer offered her $40 just to put in her pocket. Summer asked for another shot. Again, the bartender refused. A beautiful woman, alone, in a bar, getting drunk, was never a good scene. She asked Summer for permission to call someone to pick her up. Summer refused. At least two guys in the bar offered their assistance in taking her home. The bartender

shooed them away and offered to call her a cab. Again, Summer refused. She didn't think she was that intoxicated that she couldn't drive ten minutes away to her home.

Summer stumbled out of the bar about forty-five minutes after she entered. Feeling dizzy, she made her way to her car and got inside. The alcohol was starting to take effect now, and she was beginning to get sick. Having never been drunk before, she had no idea how the alcohol would work on her system. She wanted to get home quickly before she passed out in the middle of downtown Richmond.

She started the car and pulled out of the parking lot. Turning right, she approached the intersection at Broad Street. Observing the green light, she proceeded across the intersection and made a left turn toward home. Her muscles started to relax, and she had trouble controlling the steering wheel, which caused her to swerve side to side as she drove up Broad Street. She observed a green light at the next intersection and kept driving, accelerating up to thirty miles per hour as she nosed into the intersection.

But the traffic light was not green.

Another car, coming from the passenger's side, shot into the intersection just as Summer's car was entering. A two-second tire screech was heard before the car slammed into Summer's car at the A-frame between the engine and the passenger compartment. Summer's car twirled in a 180-degree spin, careened to the left across the median strip, and rolled backwards into the path of another car approaching at forty miles per hour from the opposite side of Broad Street. The approaching car skidded, but also slammed into the driver's side of Summer's car, forcing it to flip over on its right side against the flower box on the median strip. Summer, not wearing her seat belt, was thrown about the car. She felt a spinning sensation in her head, and then the crushing of metal against her skin before she blacked out, and her crumpled body landed against the broken glass of the passenger window.

***

Susan felt led to pray for her daughter, and she always obeyed those urgings. Her daughter had told her, before leaving to meet with Xavier, that she would likely be coming home very late, but never bothered to tell Susan where she was going or what she was doing. That was strange, because Summer was normally very open with her mother about her comings and goings.

Susan stayed awake until after 10 p.m. Figuring that her daughter would not make it back home before her bedtime, she took her final shot of insulin for the day and then headed back to her bedroom. It was Wednesday night, and Susan was scheduled to be on a plane back to Atlanta on Friday morning. She knew two things as she climbed under the covers of the bed: one, that she would have to find a reason not to get on that plane on Friday; and two, that her daughter needed some serious help if she was trying to get back together with a man who was unfaithful to her.

As she closed her eyes and tried but failed to sleep, Susan's cell phone chirped out the chorus of *Shackles* by Mary Mary, her daughter's ringtone. She reached for the phone and answered. "Hey, hon."

"Miss Maldonado?"

The female voice she heard was not her daughter's. "Who's this?"

"This is Jackie Styles. I'm a nurse at VCU Medical Center. Is Summer Maldonado your daughter?"

Oh, God, no, please don't tell me she's dead. Susan sat up in the bed. "Yes, I am. Is she okay?"

"She was involved in a serious car accident, ma'am. She's in surgery now. She was banged up pretty bad, but we think she's going to be okay. It might be good if you could come to be with her. Are you able to make travel arrangements to get to Richmond?"

"Oh, I'm already in Richmond." Susan had climbed out of bed and was juggling the phone from hand to hand as she tried to get some clothes on. "What's the address of the hospital?"

The nurse told her.

"Okay, I'll be right there. Thanks for calling."

Jesus, Jesus, Jesus, please keep my daughter, Susan prayed aloud

as she frantically slipped her shoes on. She was glad she went against her daughter's wishes and called her bishop in Atlanta to get the telephone number of a respected pastor in Richmond. She planned to call him as soon as she got to the hospital and found out her daughter's condition.

She had her excuse to cancel her plane ticket back to Atlanta. There was no way she could go back there now.

CHAPTER THREE

By the time Susan got to the hospital and made her way to the surgery floor, Summer was out of surgery and in the recovery room. Dr. Pratt walked out to meet Susan, who by now was trembling with worry.

"Doctor, how is she?"

"Miss Maldonado, she is out of surgery. She's still under anesthesia, so she's not awake yet. She had a dislocated shoulder, which we had to fix, and several bumps, scratches, and bruises. But she's lucky to be alive."

"Luck had nothing to do with it," Susan told the doctor. "She's *blessed* to be alive."

"I'm sure that's true."

"What happened? How did the accident occur?"

"You'll have to talk to the police about that. A couple of officers are around here somewhere."

"Can I see her?"

"Of course. I'll let you know when it is okay to go in. I believe the police have requested to see her when she wakes up, so you may have to step out of the room while they talk to her."

Looking over Dr. Pratt's shoulder, Susan saw two uniformed officers. Nodding toward them, Susan said, "Are those the officers?"

Turning, Dr. Pratt said, "Yes. Let me introduce you."

Dr. Pratt led Susan over to the officers. "Officers, this is Susan Maldonado, Summer's mother." While they met and greeted, Dr. Pratt quietly slipped away.

"What happened, officers?" Susan asked.

"Your daughter was in a three-car accident," the male officer reported. "We believe she was drunk at the time of the accident. Her car was completely totaled."

"No. My daughter does not drink and drive."

The male officer looked briefly at his female partner, then said to Susan, "We have at least half a dozen witnesses that saw your daughter's car run the red light full speed at 6th and Broad. The EMTs that responded to the scene said she reeked of alcohol. She's lucky to be alive. Her car was completely flipped on its side, and she was not wearing a seat belt. If she had been ejected from the car at the same time the car flipped … ." The officer paused, certain he did not need to complete his sentence.

"Lord." Susan looked down, trying to process the news she had heard. After a moment, she looked up and asked, "What about the people in the other cars? No one is dead, are they?"

"Thankfully, no," the male officer said. "There was one lady driving one vehicle. She got a few contusions and scrapes, but she's okay. Then, there was a young man and a young lady in another car. The lady has a concussion, and the man a fractured wrist and some cuts and scrapes. We found marijuana in their vehicle, so they'll likely be arrested for that. You should know that your daughter is also likely to be arrested on a DUI charge, and be cited for not wearing a seat belt."

Susan looked stressed. "Will she go to jail?"

"That's up to the courts. My advice: get her a good attorney."

With all the questions that were asked and answered between Susan and the police, one question remained unanswered for Susan. Why would Summer, who was never much of a drinker, get drunk? She wanted to blame Xavier, who was known for tipping back a few, for his bad influence. But she knew that Summer was to blame, for she had chosen a lifestyle that put her in touch with all the wrong people.

When Susan had finished talking to the police, she called Pastor Gillen, who was referred to her by her bishop in Atlanta. She would have to apologize for calling at such a late hour. But she knew her daughter needed to come back to God, and she need a good shepherd in her life to help lead the way.

***

It wasn't until early the next morning when Summer opened her eyes. At first, all she saw was a blurry haze. But after she had blinked her eyes a few times, objects started to come into focus—the tiles in the ceiling, the rods holding the curtains around her bed, a flat-screen TV mounted on a stand high on the far wall. She tried to turn her head to the left, but couldn't because of a neck brace she was wearing. Then, the pain registered, searing throughout her entire body, and she cried out.

Her mother was there, napping in a chair next to her bed. When she heard Summer cry out, she quickly jumped to her feet and stood over her daughter's bed so that Summer could see her.

"Mãe." Summer croaked.

"Yes, hon, I'm here. What's the matter?"

"It hurts."

Susan called for the nurse. When the nurse arrived, she greeted Summer, took a few vital signs, and then increased the dosage of her morphine drip. Susan sat and rubbed her daughter's hand until she was comfortable. She brushed the hair out of Summer's eyes, making sure she did not touch the bandage on her forehead, which covered a bruise.

"Feeling better, hon," Susan asked.

Summer nodded.

"You want to tell me what happened?"

Summer asked for a cup of water. Susan poured a cup and then helped Summer drink it. Once she had finished drinking, Summer explained all that had happened, from her meeting with Xavier to her trip to the bar, to her getting in her car and driving off. However, she could not remember anything after crossing the intersection. The tears gently started to flow from her eyes. Susan wiped her face with a tissue.

"I still love him, Mãe," Summer said to her. "With everything that he has done to me, I still love him."

"I know you do." Susan patted Summer's hand. "It's not easy to break those emotional connections. But in this case, I think you need to. I think you need to move on. This man almost cost you your life."

"No, Mãe. It wasn't X. It was me. It was all my doing."

Susan nodded. "I'm glad to hear you say that. You're right. It *was* your doing. But my point is, it was your focus on him that made you do what you did. And you should never be that obsessed over a man that you completely lose your mind like that. You are too beautiful and too strong for that."

Summer responded, "I'm not strong. My whole life is a string of failed relationships, first with my boyfriend in college, and now with X. And I really thought X was the one. Or as close as I could get, anyway."

A knock on the hospital room door drew Susan's attention. Standing there were the two police officers that she had talked with the night before. The female stepped forward and said, "Good morning, Miss Maldonado. If you'd excuse us, we'd like to speak with your daughter for a few minutes."

Susan nodded, then looked at Summer. "Honey, do you want me to call an attorney before you speak with them?"

"No," was Summer's response. She knew that she would likely face arrest for the accident, and she had settled her mind on that. She had accompanied Xavier to court a few months before after his arrest

for drunk driving. The judge gave him nothing more than a fine and a suspension of his license. She could live with that. She had no desire to grapple with lawyers and extended court cases.

"Are you sure?"

"I'm sure."

"Okay. I'll be back in a few, okay?"

Summer nodded as best she could, then looked at the officer who stood at the foot of her bed. The top of the officer's head almost directly aligned with the bottom of the TV on the wall. The other officer shut the door after Susan had left, and then stood beside it, making sure no one else entered.

"How are you feeling, Miss Maldonado?"

"I've been better."

"I'll bet." The female officer stepped around to the side of the bed, where Summer could still see her without having to turn her head. "Do you know why you're here?"

Summer nodded.

"Want to tell me what happened?"

Summer relayed the same story she told her mother, except leaving out the part about visiting X. That was none of their business.

After Summer had finished, the officer said, "You could have been killed. How many drinks did you have?"

"Three. Maybe four."

"And you were at the bar for how long?"

"I don't remember. Maybe an hour."

"Are you aware three other people were injured in the accident?"

Summer's face sunk. "No, I wasn't. How are they?"

"Some bumps, bruises, and scrapes. They're going to be popping pills and taking the bus for a while, but otherwise, nothing major."

The officer nodded and looked back at her partner, who didn't seem to have any follow-up questions. To them this was open and shut. There was no need to flog Summer with more questions. They had more pressing matters to attend to. When the results of the blood test came back, using the blood sample that a nurse had taken the night

before and turned over to the police, they would have all they needed.

"Miss Maldonado, let me tell you what's going to happen from here," the female officer said. "When the doctor clears you for release, you'll be placed in the custody of the Richmond Police Department. You will be charged with driving under the influence and destruction of property. You may or may not be held in jail prior to your arraignment. You are not to leave this hospital until a Richmond police officer escorts you out. Do you understand everything I am telling you?"

The mention of jail scared Summer, but nonetheless, she answered, "Yes."

"Thank you, Miss Maldonado. You get well. We'll be in touch."

Susan came back inside almost immediately after they left. "What happened? What did they say? What did they want?"

"I might go to jail when I leave here, Mãe." Summer stared at the ceiling, realizing her life had just gone from bad to worse.

"Oh, Jesus." Susan sat down and held her daughter's hand again. "You need a lawyer. You really should not have spoken to the police without one here."

"Wouldn't have made any difference." Summer lay, tired and dejected, feeling drowsy as the medicine worked on her pain receptors. "I got drunk. I hurt three people. There's no walking away from that." She tried to wrap her mind around the prospect of going to jail, even for one day. But as much as that frightened her, it frightened her even more that she would have to face the rest of her life without Xavier.

***

The next few hours brought Summer a whirlwind of activity. She was wheeled to one room for x-rays, to another for a CT scan. Nurses buzzed in and out, checking vital signs, making sure she was comfortable, checking the sling on her left arm where she had dislocated her shoulder. One came in and removed the neck brace. The doctor came in afterwards, telling her that everything looked okay and that

she would be released in a matter of hours. All the while, a uniformed police officer stood nearby, making sure that Summer didn't leave the hospital. To her, that was the most humiliating part of the entire experience—having a cop watch her like she was a dangerous criminal.

After she had napped for a couple of hours, she awoke to find her mother outside the room conversing with a man she hadn't yet met. He didn't look like a doctor, nor one of the nurses, although he wore a black suit and a grey fedora. She continued to look at them until they noticed that she was awake. They turned to walk into the room. Summer noticed that the man was wearing a clerical collar. Perhaps he was the hospital chaplain, she thought.

"How are you feeling, hon," Susan asked, pouring her a glass of water.

"A little better," Summer responded, taking the glass from her mother. Before she brought it to her lips, she asked, "Who's this?"

"This is the pastor I was telling you I was going to have my bishop in Atlanta contact. This is Pastor Gillen. Pastor, this is my daughter, Summer."

Pastor Gillen removed his hat, revealing a clean-shaven head. He was light, ruggedly handsome, and distinguished looking, like someone at city hall or within the walls of Congress. He held his hat in one hand, his leather-bound Bible in the other. His scent was just at the edge of detectability, pleasing, not overpowering, something more elegant than a drug-store brand of cologne. "Nice to meet you, Summer. I hear you've had a pretty rough couple of days."

That was the understatement of the year, Summer thought. She nodded politely. A few days ago, she might have been completely upset that her mother did not honor her wishes not to speak with a pastor. But now that she was facing jail time, she was sufficiently terrified, so she was more receptive to speaking with a man of God. The accident had shifted her perspective a little. Maybe she needed to get back into the church, back into a true relationship with God. None of her other relationships worked for her, so she might as well try this one.

"You want to tell me about it?" Pastor Gillen asked.

Summer shook her head. She didn't mind talking, but she was not going to pour her heart out to him. Not just yet.

"Well, Summer, your mother tells me that you're no stranger to the Lord, that at one point in your life you had a relationship with him. But I want you to know that although you've left God, God has not left you. Jesus yearns for you. He misses you. He wants his beloved to come back home. Now, I'm not here to pressure you, or to make you do something you don't want to do. But I wanted to let you know that I'm available to you, if you need to talk, or if you need anything."

"Thank you," Summer said softly.

Pastor Gillen looked at Susan, trying to gauge her response to her daughter's indifference. After a couple of seconds, he turned back to Summer.

"I understand you're going to be charged when you are released."

"Yes."

"DUI?"

"Yes. And destruction of property."

"Hmm. I have some contacts at the Commonwealth attorney's office. I can't make any promises, but I'll see what I can do. In the meantime, an attorney might be a good idea."

"I told her that," Susan chimed in.

"I can see what I can do about that, too, if you'd like," Pastor Gillen offered.

Summer was thinking about her money situation. She had lost her job, and an attorney would not be free. Xavier's DUI attorney had cost him $4,000. Summer had $20,000 in the bank, but since she was facing DUI charges, a criminal record would hinder any search for employment. She needed as much of that money as possible to live on, without throwing it away on a high-priced attorney.

But the word *jail* kept popping in her head, and suddenly spending $4,000 on an attorney to reclaim her freedom sounded like a good investment. She still had Xavier's attorney's number on her cell phone.

"I have someone I can call, but thanks anyway," Summer said.

"Well, can I at least pray for you?"

"Sure." Summer figured it would help, or it wouldn't. But either way, it wouldn't hurt.

Pastor Gillen came around to the right side of Summer's bed, where he could hold her right hand. He placed his hat and Bible gently on the bed, then grasped Susan's hand. Just as Pastor Gillen closed his eyes and looked as if he was about to pray, he opened them again.

"You know, Summer, I wasn't going to bring this up right now, but your mother did fill me in on everything that had happened with you, even the situation with your boyfriend."

Summer cut her eyes over at her mother, giving her a snide look that let her know that she did not approve of her revealing so much of her personal life to a stranger, even if it was a pastor.

Pastor Gillen continued. "I will say this. A woman who desires something from a man that she hasn't already received from God will be frustrated, confused, and disappointed." Pastor Gillen let the comment sink in, then he began to pray.

They prayed for almost ten minutes. And as Pastor Gillen said the words, Lord, the doctors here are giving her treatment for her injuries on the outside. Lord, let the balm of your holy spirit heal her injuries on the inside, Summer began to feel a lightness within that was not the morphine. She was beginning to feel peace and hope, almost as if an unseen and compassionate hand came into the room and soothed all of her heartaches. During that ten minutes, for the first time in the past week, Summer felt like she wanted to live instead of die.

CHAPTER FOUR

Two weeks later

From the moment that Summer left from the hospital, things started looking up for her. As the police had warned, Summer was taken to the police station immediately upon release from the hospital, but her lawyer bonded her out immediately after booking, and waived her appearance at arraignment. Summer was delighted that she could go home without spending any time in jail. Her lawyer indicated that he would arrange for a plea agreement with the attorney for the Commonwealth where she would agree to a ban on driving for a year and a fine of $5,000, but no jail time.

The next day after her release, Summer began looking up scriptures provided to her by Pastor Gillen. As she studied the scriptures, she found that she liked reading the Bible, more so than when she was a child, when it was difficult to understand and challenging to relate to. Now, with all of her struggles, it seemed as if every scripture was talking directly to her. They brought her peace and fulfillment at a greater level than she had enjoyed since moving to Richmond.

Susan took a leave of absence from her job and agreed to remain with Summer until after her DUI trial. Susan would often study the

Scriptures with Summer and join her daughter in prayer. They attended Pastor Gillen's church together. She had even begun to notice that Summer was no longer averse to her Christian programming choices, and on many occasions, even sat to watch them with her.

Despite her willingness to try to return wholeheartedly to her Christian roots, Summer still thought about Xavier on occasion, and still hoped that he would change his mind about her. But it was no longer something that she counted on, and she was ready to face life without him. She had often wondered why she was so attached to Xavier, even to the point of almost destroying her life. But one Sunday, a sermon by Pastor Gillen gave her more insight into why Xavier had such a hold on her. Summer was sure the sermon was not designed specifically for her, yet it answered many of her questions. She bought the recorded CD of the sermon, ripped it to the new smartphone—her old one was destroyed in the accident—and listened to it again as she was jogging around her apartment complex.

In Revelation 4:10–11, it reads, *"The four and twenty elders fall down before him that sat on the throne, and worship him that liveth for ever and ever, and cast their crowns before the throne, saying, Thou art worthy, O Lord, to receive glory and honour and power: for thou hast created all things, and for thy pleasure they are and were created."*

We were created to worship God. We were created as worshippers. And we can go without worship no more than we can go without food or water. The problem is what we are worshipping. Oftentimes we take the worship that is due to God and give it to other things. Some of us worship money. Others of us worship power and prestige. To some of us, our job is the object of our worship. Often, we even worship ourselves. And since we were created to worship, and it is in our spiritual DNA to worship, if the object of our worship dies, we die along with it, because we can no longer survive without worship being a part of our lives. So, when that which we worship goes away or dies, we die along with it. Unless, of course, we decide to worship something else.

It made perfect sense to her. Summer was worshipping Xavier.

Her devotion to him was unrelenting. She yearned to see him every minute of the day. He gave her almost everything she needed: companionship, love, encouragement, affection, a shoulder to cry on, and a partner with whom to laugh. He doted on her often, treating her like a queen. Xavier became her God, her object of devout adoration. He was her everything, and apart from him, nothing else mattered. When he was suddenly torn from her, she felt the slow creep of death come upon her. And she faced a strange juxtaposition. In trying to get Xavier back, she was trying to survive. But in the process of trying to survive, she was dying to the destiny that God desired for her.

She sought more insight when she sat down with Pastor Gillen during one of his counseling sessions.

"Pastor, you made a comment, while I was in the hospital, that a woman who desires something from a man that she is not already receiving from God, will wind up confused, frustrated, and disappointed."

"Yes."

"Well. What about sex? I want sex from a man. I can't have sex with God."

"No, you cannot. But the act of sex is a part of intimacy, physical and spiritual intimacy. You cannot be intimate with God in the way that you are intimate with a man. But, you can be intimate with God."

"How?"

"Through worship and praise. The act of worship, which includes prayer, establishes intimacy with God. Similarly, the act of lovemaking establishes intimacy with your husband. But you must understand, God will sustain you in intimacy with him until a man comes along. Our relationship with Jesus, collectively as part of the church, is the model for our relationship with a wife or husband. Without a relationship with Jesus, we cannot expect to be a good and holy husband or wife. Without the establishment of intimacy through worshipping God, our intimacy with our spouses will not be complete, nor will it bring us fulfillment."

"I know Xavier was like a God to me."

"He was."

"But if he was, why couldn't I marry him?"

"For the same reasons many people, though they may worship God, often do not fully move into His will and purpose for their lives. In some cases, there is fear. In other cases, there is something about themselves that they find so precious that they are not ready to give it up in God's service. Like the rich young ruler in the Bible, who had obeyed God from the time he was a child, but could not give up his riches once Jesus requested he do so. In your case, I think it's a little of both."

"I understand the fear part. But what was I not willing to give up to marry Xavier?"

"You weren't willing to give up your independence. In every marriage, you have to give up something in order to function as one. And since Xavier wanted a traditional marriage, my guess is that you weren't ready to be a humble, submissive wife."

Summer realized that Pastor Gillen was exactly right. It even spoke to her relationship with God. Though she had worshipped God throughout her teen years, something changed once she went to college, and she became fully immersed in a world in which God was not a priority. Eventually, in order to adapt, Summer cast away almost every aspect of her relationship with God—leaving only infrequent, incidental prayers and her virginity as the gradually cooling embers of her Christianity. She worshipped God in this sense, but was not willing to let go of her attachment to a Godless world.

She realized that in order to have a successful relationship, her devotion to Xavier, or to any other man, could not take precedence over her devotion to God.

***

A week later, once her doctor had cleared her to be out of the sling and given her the okay for physical activity, Summer went out for one

of her evening jogs. She had no intention of stopping at the front gate house, but what she saw made her slow her pace, and then stop completely. "Lenny?"

Lenny Yates, the security guard at her old office building, was sitting in the gate house reading the newspaper. When Summer called his name, he looked up, then waved. "Miss Maldonado! Surprise!"

A beaming Summer walked closer to the gate house and pulled the earphones out of her ear. "You got the job?"

"I did. I just started yesterday."

"That's good to hear. Congratulations!"

"Thanks." Lenny moved to the entrance of the gate house. "This is gonna be good for me. I can do some things for my son I wasn't able to do before. I mean, the hours aren't the best. I'm working the evening shift. But I guess that's what they do to the new guy, huh?"

"How old's your son?"

"He's four. Little dude's the love of my life."

"Well, I'm glad it all worked out for you."

"Miss Maldonado, I want to thank you for letting me know about this opportunity and putting in a good word for me. You have no idea how good this is for me. If there's anything I can do for you, you got it."

Summer smiled. "Well, to start, you can stop calling me 'Miss Maldonado.' You can call me Summer."

"Okay, Summer. I can do that."

"Great. Congratulations again."

"Thanks."

Summer replaced the earphones on her ear and jogged away. Lenny watched her as she left. Security tended to be a boring job, but the sight of Summer Maldonado completely made his day. He smiled, then went back into the gate house to finish reading his training manual.

***

After a long, stressful day at work, Xavier decided to go home early. His apartment was located in a former Broad Street office building that still looked, on the outside, to be the home of a local or state municipality. Only those who ventured inside knew any different, and rents were sufficiently high enough to keep out anyone who was not decidedly white-collar and very well-paid.

The two bedroom apartment, on the fifth floor, gave him a great view of downtown Richmond. His apartment was sparsely decorated, allowing the bamboo floors, the sky blue walls, the granite countertops, and the natural light flowing in through uncovered windows to provide most of the ambiance. His custom-made furniture was by an Italian designer, which was his excuse to pay almost $40,000 to furnish his apartment, even though the furniture looked no different than something you could get down the street at Haverty's.

Xavier came home just long enough to change into his jogging shorts and a tank top, swap his cell phone for his iPod, and head back outside. Most days, he would jog over to the Arthur Ashe Center or Parker Field, circle them, and then head back home. But this time, he would jog up to Joseph Bryan Park, nearly doubling his normal two-mile-a-day jog. The longer jog gave him time to think. He hadn't heard from Summer in three weeks, which was not unusual given that he had unceremoniously kicked Summer out of his life. But what bothered him were the recent reports that Summer had been in an accident, and that the accident had happened not long after his meeting with her at Buford's. He was wracked with guilt that the accident might have been connected to him, and he was worried that Summer might be critically injured, if not dead.

He had been trying to reach her on her cell phone, to no avail. Calls to the hospitals yielded no information. Visits to her apartment were out of the question. He knew that if Summer was hurt, Susan Maldonado was likely in town. There was no way he wanted to have a confrontation with Susan. He remembered a moment shortly after he started dating Summer. Susan approached him and said, "If you hurt my daughter, I'm gonna hurt you." Xavier knew she was not joking.

He jogged along the road adjacent to Joseph Bryan Park and found a footbridge that crossed a pond. He crossed over the bridge, made his way deeper into the park, and found a grove of violets. He stopped there, thinking it would be the perfect place to do something he hadn't done in months, since his mother contracted a viral infection that he thought would take her life. He remembered the words, uttered many times in his childhood, long since abandoned. He wasn't certain he still believed them, but in desperation, people grasp for any hope they can find.

God, in the name of Jesus, let Summer still be alive. Let her be okay.

***

Xavier came back to his apartment to find Jada sitting on the couch in the living room with a scowl that could have boiled water. She had just left work and let herself in to Xavier's apartment with keys that he had given her after he broke up with Summer.

"Hey, my love." Normally, Xavier would have greeted Jada with a hug and kiss, but since he was sweaty from the jog, he decided to head straight to the kitchen. Jada followed him.

Once Xavier had grabbed a bottle of water from the refrigerator, he turned and saw Jada there, glaring at him with contempt. "You okay?" he asked, confused.

Jada's response was sharp and immediate. "Why are you still calling Summer?"

"What do you mean?" He took a sip of his water. His question was a delaying tactic. He knew what she meant.

"You've been calling Summer."

"How do you know that?"

"I checked your work cell phone while you were out jogging. Over the past four days, there are twenty calls to her cell number."

Xavier's eyebrows furrowed. He couldn't believe that a woman

who had the audacity to sleep around with her boss would be checking up on him by examining his cell phone. "Yeah, I've been trying to reach her."

"Why?"

"I heard she was in an accident. I've been calling to see if she is okay."

Jada's voice calmed. "An accident?"

"Yeah. I heard she was in a really bad car accident off Broad Street, not far from Alan's. They said her car flipped on its side. I've been trying to call her, but all I get is her voice mail."

"How'd you hear?"

"From your boyfriend Mark. Alan called him and told him after a couple of cops came to the bar investigating the accident. Alan didn't know that Summer was no longer working at Visual."

"Well, I'm sure she's okay. If not, we would have heard something."

"Now, here's a question for you. Why are you checking my phone?"

Jada shrugged. "I don't know. I was here; your phone was on the table. I just got curious."

It was a quick, convenient lie. Jada had noticed a change in Xavier's demeanor ever since his last conversation with Summer at the pizza place. He had become quieter, more withdrawn. He no longer had the same lust for her in his eyes. His lovemaking was not as passionate as it once was. Jada knew Summer had something to do with it, so she would periodically check his phone when she had the opportunity, just to make sure he was not trying to contact her again.

"Hmm," Xavier responded. He would accept that explanation in order to avoid an argument. But he did not believe it. Not by a long shot.

Jada quickly skipped the subject. "Are we still going to dinner?"

Xavier reluctantly said, "Yeah. Just let me clean up." He set his half-drank bottle of water on the kitchen counter and walked out toward his bedroom.

In his bedroom, he got undressed and then pulled fresh underwear from his bureau, pushing aside the framed photos of him and Summer hidden in the bureau out of respect for Jada. He pulled one out and gazed at it. This one was taken at the Virginia State Fair, which they attended one year with one of his brothers, his wife, and their children. They were cuddled together on the Ferris wheel, which Summer got on only after about thirty minutes of prodding because she was afraid of heights. Nonetheless, she had so much fun that the photos show no signs she was petrified every time the wheel circled to the top.

Summer's accident justified Xavier's many calls to her. But even if the accident had never happened, he still would have called her. He dreaded the way their final conversation occurred. The way she tore away in distress after he told her he no longer wanted her made his heart sink. He never intended to hurt her. And it gnawed at him further that the accident happened just a couple of hours after their conversation at the pizza joint. Even worse, she was drunk when the accident happened, which Xavier never explained to Jada.

The unanswered question was: why were his calls to Summer continually going to voice mail? Did she change her number to avoid contact with him? He had an urgent need to know. Even if he heard she was okay, but never spoke to her, that would ease his mind quite a bit.

He went into his bathroom and prepared to step into the shower, hoping that the relaxing water would help him to think clearly about his next step with Summer.

***

The next day, Xavier was so assaulted with worry that he was determined to get some answers. He would take his chances on encountering Susan.

After work, Xavier rolled up to the front gate of Summer's apartment complex. He pulled into a parking space adjacent to the gate house and got out of his car. Lenny walked out of the gate house to

meet him.

"Can I help you?" Lenny said.

"Yeah, I'm here to see Summer Maldonado," Xavier told him.

"Your name?"

"Just say X. She'll know who it is."

Lenny nodded, then headed back into the gate house. On a computer, he pulled up Summer's name, then punched a button that automatically dialed Summer's telephone. After a few rings with no answer, Lenny walked back out where Xavier was standing.

"Don't think she's home, man."

"Can you leave a message for her?"

"Sure can."

"Just tell her that X stopped by, and to call me."

"You got it."

"Do you know her?"

"Yeah. She got me this job. Matter of fact, you look kinda familiar to me."

"Really?"

"Yeah. I used to do security on East Leigh. Maybe I saw you over there, or something."

"Well, I do business with a company on East Leigh, called Visual Notions."

"Maybe that's where I saw you."

"Well, have you seen Summer at all?"

"Yeah. Saw her just yesterday. She was out jogging."

That calmed Xavier's mind. At least she was alive and hopefully well.

"Thanks. If you see her again, please have her call me."

"No problem. Will do."

Xavier climbed back into his car and drove off. Hearing that Summer was alive took a great load off his mind. But it didn't completely liberate him, as he still needed to talk to her, to see her, to hug her and tell her he was sorry for what had happened. But he had no idea when he would ever get that opportunity.

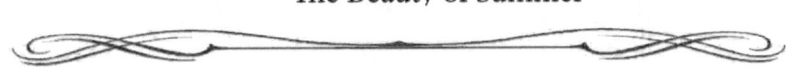
***

Summer and her mother arrived home about two hours later. Susan pulled her rental car up to the gate. Lenny held up his hand to stop her as she was passing through.

"Some guy named X was here to see you," Lenny told Summer.

Summer cut eyes over to her mother, who sat in the driver's seat expressionless. She then looked back at Lenny. "When did he come by?"

"About two hours ago. He said he wanted you to call him, but he left no number."

"Okay. Thanks, Lenny." Susan continued to drive through the gate and into Summer's parking space.

Susan and Summer headed upstairs, their hands full of groceries. Susan finally said, "So, are you going to call him?"

Summer thought about it for a moment and then said, "Yeah, I am. I'm curious to know what he has to say."

"So am I," Susan said as they headed into her apartment. "But Summer, you've come so far. Don't turn back now. That man has caused you too much pain."

That was easier said than done. Xavier still had a charismatic hold on her, and it would be very easy for her to fall under his spell if she weren't well-fortified. She left her mother to tend to the groceries, and then went into her bedroom, kneeled by the side of the bed, and asked the Lord for guidance.

***

"Hello."

"Hi, X."

Xavier was lying on the couch watching TV. He sat up and looked at his watch: 9:30 p.m. Jada was not due from the hairdresser for another thirty minutes. He switched the phone to his left ear. "Hey,

Summer. I've been trying to reach you."

"I'm no longer using my old number. This is my new one."

"How are you? I heard you were in an accident."

"Yeah." Summer explained all that had happened with the accident and her ensuing court case.

"Wow. Well, I'm glad you're alright now. I was really worried something awful had happened."

"How are things with you and Jada?"

"Things are good. She wants me to move in with her in about a month. Her sister's supposed to be moving out."

"Hmm. Is she still seeing Mark?"

"Mark shut that down after you took those pictures. He's still afraid you're going to blackmail him somehow." Xavier grabbed a still-cool beer from the coffee table and took a swig.

"I don't want anything from Mark, and I have no interest in working there again."

"Are you working anywhere else now?"

"No. Just taking a break. Weighing my options."

"Hmm."

There was silence on the line for about a minute before Xavier finally said, "I miss you, Summer."

Summer sighed. "I miss you, too."

"That's a good thing, right?"

"But I'm learning to miss you a lot less each day."

"Wow. That's cold."

"But, it's true. I'm getting my life together with God. My mother and I have started to go to church again. I'm building my relationship with Jesus, and the more I get to know him, the less I miss you. Eventually, I won't miss you at all."

"I knew there was a church girl in there somewhere."

"Yep. And she's coming out in all her glory, praising God in all of His."

"We can still be friends, right?"

"We can."

"And I can still call you from time to time?"

"You can call me anytime."

"That sounds good. You know, I prayed for you."

"*You* prayed?" Summer asked incredulously.

"I was worried. I couldn't get in touch with you. I didn't know what else to do."

"Maybe that's God's way of telling you that you need Him more than you think."

"Maybe it's God's way of telling me I need *you* more than I thought."

"I'm sorry. I'm not willing to become God to you. Just like I'm no longer willing to allow you to be God to me."

"Was I really that?"

"You were my everything, X."

"I'm sorry I hurt you."

"I accept that, X, but if you are really sorry, you will give your heart to Jesus."

"Maybe I do need to go back to church."

"That would be a good start."

They talked for another ten minutes. Each of them was glad there were no longer any hostilities or hard feelings between them. But Xavier still held a special place in Summer's heart, adorned with memories of their times together and love which, although tempered, still burned with the smallest of flames.

CHAPTER FIVE

One month later

Things continued to progress well for Summer. The judge accepted her plea agreement at a hearing held two weeks earlier, resulting in a $5,000 fine, and a suspension of her license for one year, but no jail time, for which Summer was extremely grateful. Summer called Xavier to tell him the good news, and he congratulated her and offered to take her out to dinner to celebrate. Summer turned down the offer, feeling that they were not in a place in their friendship where they could start hanging out again. She wasn't certain if they would ever be in that place. Now, her focus was on her relationship with Jesus, and she needed no distractions. And Xavier, no matter what his intentions, would be a big one.

She joined Pastor Gillen's church and signed up to work in the church's media ministry. She helped produce the church's Sunday video screen presentations and handled public service announcements and commercials for the church. The existing members of the ministry were a bit jealous that Summer was allowed to join so soon and was given so much responsibility. But Summer's radio and media experience and her willingness to volunteer was something that Pastor Gillen

could not turn away. He turned her loose and watched her ply the full extent of her skills. Summer brought such a professional polish to the ministry, with her clear and strong radio voice and her bag of tricks she had learned from Visual Notions. Pastor Gillen couldn't help but think that God had brought Summer to him especially for this purpose.

Pastor Gillen also knew that Summer was in need of money, as all but $5,000 of Summer's savings was depleted. Summer had started to look for work, but found it difficult because of her DUI conviction and lack of reliable transportation. Pastor Gillen could afford to pay her only a small stipend for her services to the media ministry, but he yearned to pay her much more.

When Summer's savings fell down to $1,500, she felt the pangs of desperation. If she didn't get a job soon, she would lose her apartment, and possibly end up homeless. She always had the option of moving back down to Atlanta with her mother, but Summer wanted to make it on her own. She had no clue how she would do that without a job. Mark Battman had called all of the contacts she had developed while at Visual Notions and had her blacklisted, so she could not depend on those relationships for leads. She would hate to be forced to work a mid-level job and downgrade herself to a mediocre apartment community.

However, there was one contact that Summer had not approached about a job, and she hated to do it. The last thing she wanted to do was go, hat-in-hand, to Xavier and ask him to help her find a job. It would be the last thing that her mother and her pastor wanted her to do, but right now, he *was* the last resort. She had sensed that Xavier regretted breaking up with her and was trying to work his way back into her good graces somehow. If Xavier helped her find a job, she would be indebted to him. And knowing Xavier, he would request, as payment for the debt, another chance at her heart.

Try as she might, she could not think of any other option. It was either Xavier or going back to scouring newspapers, cold-calling human resources departments, and hopping on the GRTC to go to countless interviews that led nowhere. Her $2,000 rent payment was loom-

ing. This fact alone resigned her to calling a man that, at one point, she thought she would never see again.

Summer prayed for strength. Then, she waited until her mother stepped into the bathroom for an evening shower. When she heard the water running and the slight squeak of the shower door, she slipped out to her balcony to call Xavier.

"Hey, X," she said when he answered.

"Hey."

"I need a favor."

"Anything."

"I need a job, and I need one quick."

"Are you suggesting I hire you at the gas company?"

"I'll take anything."

"I'll look into that. On one condition."

"What's that?"

"You have to go to dinner with me."

Summer laughed at his persistence. "I don't think that's a good idea, X."

"Why not? You get a free meal, some great company, and maybe a job out of it. What's the downside? We have dinner, we talk, then you go to your home, and I go to mine."

"And what would be the agenda, other than getting me a job?"

"You're always about business, Summer. We don't need an agenda in order to go to dinner together."

"Okay, but I'm agreeing to this only on the condition that you understand this is not a date."

"Understood."

"Then, I'll accept."

"Great. How about Mezzanine, Thursday, 7 p.m.? I'll make reservations."

"Uh, uh, not Mezzanine."

"Why not?"

"That was where we had our first date."

"And you enjoyed it. I thought maybe you'd enjoy it again."

"No expectations?'

"No expectations."

Summer gave in. Xavier's tastes in restaurant always leaned toward eclectic, cozy, and romantic, so anything he chose would have likely been the same. "Okay. But again, this is not a date, nor will it lead to one. I prefer to look at it as a job interview."

"I got you. See you on Thursday. Do you want me to pick you up?"

"I'll take a taxi. Thanks."

Summer ended the call, then walked back into the apartment and looked at herself in the full-length mirror affixed to the door of her coat closet. She desperately needed her hair done before Thursday, but knew she couldn't afford the $150 it would cost her at a salon. And using plastic was not an option—she had learned long ago not to depend on credit. At least—and she was proud of this—all of her credit card balances were zero.

She would ask her mother to try to style her hair. And she hoped that her mother wouldn't bother to ask why, although she knew better than to cling to that hope.

***

Thursday

The taxi pulled up at Mezzanine just a few minutes before seven. Summer stepped out, tipped the driver, and then immediately heard Xavier's voice call her name as the taxi driver left. She looked and saw that Xavier had secured a table on the patio in the front of the restaurant.

He stood when she approached. Summer quickly noticed how handsome he looked in his trademark black suit, crème-colored silk tie, and black oxfords that shone like mirrors. She made up her mind

she would not compliment him or let on that she noticed how good he looked. Summer had chosen a simple black dress with a tweed blazer, an elegant yet professional look, with her hair pulled in a bun and a string of pearls around her neck.

Summer rejected Xavier's efforts to hug her, settling for a hand-shake before she headed to her seat. Xavier pulled out her chair, and when she sat, he unfastened his jacket and took a seat.

"I'm glad you agreed to have dinner with me." Xavier studied her face. He saw only one sign of the injuries she had suffered in the accident. The scar from the gash on her forehead was still visible, but, fortunately, had faded quite a bit. "You look great."

"Thank you." Summer wanted to return the compliment. But she thought *you look good enough to eat* might not be appropriate uttered aloud.

They sat in silence for about a minute, neither knowing how to break the ice. Finally, the waiter came over, and they placed their drink orders. Xavier ordered water out of respect to Summer, although he had a craving for champagne. Summer ordered a ginger ale.

"So, how's things with you and Jada?" Summer started. "Did you guys move in together yet?"

"Yeah, we did. About a week ago."

"Is she comfortable with me being here with you, assuming she even knows about it?"

"Not exactly," Xavier said, taking a sip of his water. "But I told her it was a simple business dinner."

"So, let's get on with business. You said you were going to look into a job for me."

Xavier sighed, but he played along. He would get the business out of the way first, and then hopefully she would be excited enough about it that he could share his heart. "Well, I'm afraid I could not work out a job at my company. There are some budget issues we are dealing with now. But, I do know of another opportunity."

"What is it?"

"There is a new, upstart TV station going on the air within the next

couple of days here in Richmond. It's going to be on one of the digital subchannels. It supposed to feature mostly syndicated stuff, but they are going to have a local news block from 7 a.m. to 9 a.m., and another evening news block from 10 to 11:30. Seems like they're trying to give the FOX affiliates a run for their money."

"I heard about that." Summer leaned forward with interest.

"Well, they're hiring on-air talent for their newscasts. Anchors, reporters, you name it. I thought you might be interested in becoming a reporter."

Summer leaned back as she mulled over the idea. "X, I don't know. I mean, I did some reporting at the radio station, but I've never done anything on TV. They want people with a lot of experience in this market."

"Like I said, it's a young station. They don't have a lot of money, so they can't afford that kind of talent. But that means they are willing to take chances on people that have the aptitude for this. And if there's anyone that has the aptitude to be a reporter, you do. You have a great voice. You're very photogenic. And all they need to do is see those photos you took of Jada and Mark to know you are a great investigator."

Summer laughed, then said, "It takes more than that."

"Like what?"

"You have to know how to write. You have to have a nose for great news stories, a keen knowledge of current events."

"All of which you have."

"I don't know."

"You like Maya, right?"

"Yes."

"What's that quote from *I Know Why The Caged Bird Sings*? 'Can't Do is like Don't Care. Neither of them have a home.'"

Summer was glad that Xavier believed in her more than she did. "How much does it pay?"

"Depends on the contract you sign." Xavier reached in his shirt pocket, removed a business card, and laid it on the table in front of

Summer. "That's the agent that's handling recruitment for the station. He's a good friend of mine. I already told him you might be calling him. Once you do, he'll interview you, and if he likes you, he'll sign you with his agency, get you a resume, video reel, and headshot, and get it in the hands of the GM at the station. I think the GM's someone from the Atlanta market, so you might know him."

"Who?"

"Scott Iverson."

Summer brightened. "I know Scott. He graduated two years ahead of me."

"I thought Clark Atlanta was an all-black school."

"They had a few white people there. Not many. But they stuck out, and almost everybody knew Scott Iverson."

"Well, there you go. Now you got two connections."

The waiter came and took their orders. Afterwards, Summer said, "X, I really appreciate this."

"Well, just because we're not dating anymore, doesn't mean I'm gonna let you resort to begging for a bed down on Grace Street." Xavier took a moment to pause for effect, and then said, "Speaking of begging … "

"Don't go there, X."

"Summer, I can't stop thinking about you. And I know you think about me, too."

"You think about me, yet you live with, sleep with, and marry Jada."

Xavier leaned forward. "Why can't we have our own thing?"

Summer scoffed. "I don't want to be your jump-off girl, X. If you want me, it's you and me ONLY. And I'm not interested in being with a man that would cheapen me by asking me to be a party to his open marriage arrangement."

"As I recall, a few weeks ago, you were down with this. Why are you throwing shade now?"

"Because I know Christ now, X. I know it's only been a few weeks, but I'm a different girl now. And you need to respect that."

Summer stood and prepared herself to leave.

"Where you going?" Xavier said, standing as well.

"I'm leaving."

"But they haven't even brought the food out yet. At least stay and have dinner. No more discussions along those lines. I promise."

Summer relented and took her seat again. They sat in silence until the waiter brought out the food. Summer said a blessing over the food, and they began to eat.

Xavier stole periodic glances at her as she ate. Plenty of women get religion when they get their hearts broken, he thought. After a while, they get tired of staying at home alone with God and need someone to touch, to touch them. Xavier was willing to wait for that moment to come. In the meantime, he would have to get to know the new Summer better before he made any more attempts at winning her heart again.

"So," Xavier finally said. "Tell me about your church."

***

Xavier pulled his car up to the driveway adjacent to the gate house of Summer's apartment complex but did not turn in the driveway. Summer climbed out of the passenger seat. Xavier bid her goodbye before he drove off. Summer began her short walk to the gate. As she walked past the gate house, she noticed Lenny inside watching TV. Lenny waved at her.

Summer heard something familiar in the TV program he was watching and went over to the door of the gate house. "Hey, Lenny. What are you watching?"

Lenny greeted her, then said, "This preacher I like to watch."

Summer also watched for a moment. "My mother likes to watch him, too."

"Yeah? I like the way he teaches the Word. He explains it in a way you can understand and relate to."

"Do you go to church?"

"Yep. Never miss a Sunday. When I got the job here, I told them I could work every day except Saturday and Sunday. Saturday's for my son, and Sunday's for *the* Son."

"Yeah. I just recently started going back myself."

"It's a good thing to do. Keeps your head right. Kinda tough out there these days, so you need someone greater than yourself, y'know? What church you go to?"

"Heritage Church of Richmond. What about you?"

"Revival Word of God Church. Hey, you ought to come with me this Sunday. It's Friends and Family Day. I guess I can consider you a friend, so you should come."

Summer was more touched than she expected to be. No one had invited her to church in the two years she had been in Richmond. No one had invited her anywhere, except to a bar or to their bed. "Can I bring my mom?"

"You can bring anybody you want. We ain't gonna turn nobody away."

Summer reached in her purse for her phone. She punched a few buttons, then said, "What's your church's address?"

Lenny gave it to her, along with the service time.

"Where is that?" Summer asked.

"Over in Church Hill, right there close to where 95 and 64 split."

"Okay, well, maybe I'll see you there."

"Maybe?" Lenny shook his head. "C'mon, Miss Summer. You gotta give me more than that. Seeing you come in the place on Sunday will be the highlight of my day. You can't deny me that."

Summer smiled. "Okay, I promise I'll be there."

"That's what's up."

Summer waved and headed out the door. "See you, Lenny."

"See you, Miss Summer."

Lenny watched her as she left. At Visual Notions, Summer always seemed rather *bougie* and standoffish to him, just like a few of the people he had met since taking over the job at Summer's apartment

complex. But Summer helping him to get this job caused him to see her in a new light. Although she still seemed rather sophisticated and haughty, she wasn't as uppity as he had first thought.

But of course, he would reserve final judgment until he saw whether Summer would show up at his church, smack in the middle of northern Church Hill, arguably one of the roughest neighborhoods in Richmond.

***

The next few days came and brought another whirlwind of activity for Summer. She called the agent, and he requested to see her right away, as the station was preparing to go into its final round of interviews for on-air talent. Summer took a taxi and interviewed with the agent before he decided to represent her. He set up appointments for her to get head shots, and then arranged for her to return to record a video reel consisting of compilations from on-camera work she had done with Visual Notions. It was Wednesday, and the agent estimated he could get a package over to Scott Iverson by Friday.

Summer had been thinking about the dinner conversation she had with Xavier after she had threatened to leave the restaurant the other night. Xavier had asked her about her church, but seemed somewhat disinterested as Summer went on about the wonderful people she was meeting, and her role on the media ministry, and how she was growing in the word of God. There had been an immediate change in his countenance, from lustful persistence to patient tolerance, as if he was listening only to try to endear himself to her. And Summer knew that Xavier was not at all interested in church, despite his pretense. Not once during their time together had the two of them attended church together, not even on Easter.

Pastor Gillen had encouraged her to preach the word to others, no matter the circumstances in which they may hear it. *What is important is that they hear the Word, and God will add to it as He sees fit*, he had

told her. Summer hoped that everything she said to Xavier about her church and her newfound life in Christ would resonate in some way, and that her friendship with Xavier would lead him into his relationship with God.

She had also been pushing her mother to return to Atlanta. Susan had taken a leave of absence from her job to stay with Summer, but Summer was concerned that Susan would lose her job if she didn't return home soon. As Summer was well-recovered from her accident and her soul and spirit flourished under the watchful ministry of Pastor Gillen, Susan agreed to head back to Atlanta that Friday. Summer did not reveal to Susan that she was almost out of money, or Susan would have stayed longer. Susan drove to the airport with her daughter, returned the rental car, and gave her daughter an emotional hug goodbye before she boarded the flight back to Atlanta.

The money situation was perilous. Summer was now down to $800. Rent day was still approaching, and Summer knew that if she were to get the job at the TV station, she wouldn't see a check for at least three weeks after she started work. She needed money within the next week, or she was in serious trouble.

Pondering her options, she found two. Once again, Xavier's name popped in her mind. A $5,000 loan from Xavier would solve many of her financial problems, at least for a month. The other option, as devious as it was, would keep her from reaching out to Xavier again. But it was so morally dubious that Summer had to wrangle with it in her mind for a day before she made her decision. She decided to go with the second option, even though it was also illegal.

It would involve the photos she had taken of Mark and Jada. She was glad she had not erased them, as she had been tempted to do, but kept them in a file in her cloud service. Barring any last-minute influxes of money to her almost dry checking account, Summer would set her plan into motion on Monday morning.

CHAPTER SIX

It was 11:15 a.m. at Revival Word of God Church, and the praise and worship part of the service was already underway. The church building was no bigger than the other detached homes in the surrounding neighborhood, and in fact looked as if it might have been a house itself in a former life. Only the steeple at the point of the gable and a handmade marquee on the yard at the front of the church set it apart from any other house in the community. Directly across the street was a series of four two-story brick apartment buildings, parallel to each other, plain, long, and rectangular, with gabled roofs. They were separated by crumbling concrete walkways leading from the main sidewalk, with about six feet of withering grass on either side of the walkways. Men, women, and children lingered about on the grass and on the front stoops of the apartment buildings. Flapping in the breeze were a few white sheets hanging on a clothesline in front of one of the apartments. Someone was blasting a song by the Wu Tang Clan out of the bedroom window. Despite its explicit lyrics, and the fact that impressionable children were present, several people bounced their heads to the music, their own form of worship counteracting what was going on directly across the street.

Inside the church, two columns of oak-colored pews, separated by a center aisle, held about sixty worshippers, all of them African

American, most either younger than fifteen or older than forty, dressed in finery that some of them would not have the opportunity to wear anywhere else. Gaudily decorated wide-brimmed church hats sat atop heads of ladies who were sixty-plus. The older men wore respectable suits; the younger men sported their form of dress: a fresh pair of jeans and a button-down shirt with some fashionable urban design on the front. Some of the younger ladies, who didn't want to go through the trouble of maintaining two separate wardrobes, wore the same provocative outfits to church as they did to the nightclub. This often prompted the older ladies to frown and decry the lack of decorum from the younger ladies, while many of the younger men, and some of the older ones, feasted their eyes.

Window air conditioners buzzed in two of the windows alongside the outer walls of the church, but the sounds of jubilant celebration obliterated the din from the air conditioners. For these worshippers, Sundays were a time to forget about problems and sing, clap hands, and, in some cases, dance to the tune of modern gospel standards being performed live by the choir and worship team to a grateful, joyous crowd. Everyone was on his feet doing *something*, except for a few stalwarts who thought it appropriate to remain seated and not display such emotion.

Lenny Yates was not one of the stalwarts. He joined the rest of the crowd singing and clapping hands, often prodding his son, Leonard Jr., who stood beside him and could barely see above the tops of the pews. They both wore identical tan suits. Lenny made sure his head was clean-shaven to counteract the male-patterned baldness that was starting to appear in his late thirties, but still left a slight goatee, with no mustache.

He would occasionally look back at the front door to check to see if Summer had arrived. There was no sign of her. Just as the praise and worship service, which normally lasted about forty-five minutes, was beginning to make way for the testimony service, Lenny was beginning to think that Summer would not show up. *It was okay, though*, he thought. At least his son was there. He got to attend his church with

Lenny Jr. every other Sunday. The other Sundays, Lenny Jr. was at his mother's house, under a self-made visitation arrangement with the woman that at one time he was going to marry.

Soon, the singing and clapping stopped temporarily, and a deacon came to the pulpit to facilitate the testimony service, an opportunity for church members to stand, sing their favorite hymn, gospel, or praise song, frequently off-key, and then tell a brief story of how the Lord had been good to them.

"Anybody got a burning testimony they want to share with the saints?" the deacon asked.

One woman stood and started singing, "O the Blood of Jesus" as off-key as humanly possible, and no one cared. The congregants chimed in, singing two verses before the woman continued with her testimony.

"First giving honor to God, who is the head of my life and to Jesus Christ, his Son. I honor the pastor of this church, to all the elders and ministers, to the deacons and to the mothers of the church and the missionaries, members, saints, and friends. I thank God that I'm saved, sanctified and filled with the precious Holy Ghost. The other day … "

Midway through the woman's longer-than-usual testimony, the sanctuary door creaked open. Lenny heard it and looked back. Standing there, being attended to by two white adorned ushers, was Summer Maldonado, her statuesque frame towering at least half a foot above the tallest usher. Lenny's heart warmed in his chest.

After the woman had finished her testimony, an usher led Summer to a seat across the aisle and one row behind where Lenny sat. Before she sat down, Summer quickly scanned the crowd and spotted Lenny, who was looking back at her. She waved and smiled. Lenny waved back.

A few curious eyes wandered over to Lenny, and then back to Summer, with many wondering who this girl was and what connection she had to Lenny.

After the testimony service came a selection by the choir, then the offering, then another selection, and then the celebratory mes-

sage. Pastor Malachi approached the pulpit, his round bespectacled face showing little wrinkles to reveal his sixty-eight years on earth, although his completely gray goatee provided a clue. He was scheduled to retire from the pulpit the following year, with his son, who sat behind him, taking over the leadership of the church. The congregation showed their respect by standing and clapping when Pastor Malachi approached the pulpit. The preacher quickly redirected their honor and adoration to God, shouting, "Praise the name of Jesus" several times until the crowd was almost in a frenzy.

Lenny stood up and joined them, clapping his hands and saying "Thank you, Jesus" in gratitude for the blessings the Lord had brought into his life, especially the job that Summer had worked out for him. He couldn't help but to look back at her again. He had seen her in hard-edged business suits countless times. But her purple silk three-piece suit made her look especially radiant, more down-to-earth and prettier than he had ever seen her.

Pastor Malachi started his opening remarks, which lasted for almost a half hour, then started to read from his text for the day.

"Hebrews 11:6 reads, 'But without faith it is impossible to please Him, for he who comes to God must believe that He is, and that He is a rewarder of those who diligently seek Him.' We've looked at the scripture before, but I want to focus on the word *seek*."

A few *amens* came forth.

"Most people, when they read this scripture, focus on the word *rewarder*. That's what excites them about this scripture. That's the landing point. God is a rewarder. And he truly is a rewarder."

More *amens*.

"But if the word *rewarder* was not there, this scripture probably wouldn't be one of the most oft-quoted scriptures in the Bible. If I was to remove the word *rewarder*, and read the scripture another way, it would probably read, 'But without faith it is impossible to please Him, for he who comes to God must believe that He is, and must diligently seek Him.' Now if we read the scripture in that way, without the *rewarder* part, it becomes about our pleasing God, but the word *reward-*

er implies God pleasing us. And while we cannot and should not alter scripture, we should understand that the emphasis here is not on God pleasing *us*, but on us pleasing *God*."

Several *amens*.

"For to understand this scripture, we have to draw the conclusion that God does not exist to please us. We exist to please God."

Several louder *amens* and a *come on, preacher* rang in the air. Summer sat, listening attentively, but not saying anything. She was not the *amen and hallelujah* type of girl. She occasionally looked over at Lenny and noticed he was the exact opposite, *amen*-ing and *hallelujah*-ing almost every time the preacher took a breath.

"To seek God is not to search for something that is lost. For God can never be lost. He is everywhere. He is omnipresent. There is nowhere in the universe where we can go that God's hand is not present. But when we seek God, we seek His holiness. We seek His presence. We seek His knowledge. We seek His truth. Every day for us is a seeking process, where we go into God and look to know something of Him that we did not know before. And God is so vast, that no one can ever hope to say, 'I know God.' There is always more, more, more to know."

Yes, Lord!

Preach it, pastor!

"And God's promise is, for those who would diligently seek Him—that is, those who do it earnestly, consistently, with effort—God will reward."

Hallelujah!

Praise God!

"But for those of us who love God and want to please Him, we seek not because of the reward, but in spite of the reward. Even if our lives seem as though God ain't doing nothin' for us, our faith dictates that we continue to seek Him. We look for so many rewards on the outside—cars, homes, a handsome man or a *fine* woman ... ."

The congregation laughed at his emphasis on the word *fine*.

" … like First Lady Malachi down there."

The congregation laughed and shouted their approval of his compliment with *go ahead, preacher* and *tell it, man of God*! First Lady Malachi, seated in the front row, a beautiful silver-haired woman, began to blush. For a darker-skinned woman such as First Lady Malachi, the evidence of the blushing was never in the skin color, but in the way she turned her head slightly down, rolled her eyes, smiled, and toyed slightly with her hair.

"But often the rewards are on the inside. Knowing God helps us to know ourselves, and realize the things that are in us that are contrary and displeasing to God. The reward, saints, is that we become better people, better saints, holy, more pleasing in His sight. Even when it seems like God is doing nothin', He is changing us within. *Often the things we want God to reward, God holds back because He is doing something in us.*"

That statement struck Summer and prompted intense thought. Were Summer's job and financial problems signs that God was working in her? *Surely God wants me to find a job, doesn't he?*

"But if you hang in there, God will show up in a way you would never have imagined."

I know that's right, preacher!

"Now I'm gonna have my own testimony service. Brother Yates, if you don't mind, why don't you stand up and tell the people about how the Lord blessed you the other day."

Lenny stood, looked straight at the preacher, cleared his throat, and said, "Well, y'all know I was working security downtown. I was grateful for the job, y'know, and I ain't had no complaints. But it wasn't payin' me enough to make ends meet. Y'all know how that is."

Several *amens* were his response.

"So, I had an opportunity to get another job at an apartment complex across town. I want y'all to know that I applied, and last week, I got the job!"

The congregants erupted in applause.

"And it's paying me a lot more than what I was being paid at my

old job!"

The clapping was stronger now, punctuated by *hallelujahs* and *praise God.*

"I praise God, because it was a long time coming. I thought God was gonna keep me in that old job forever. But in His time, he reached down and blessed me. I just had to keep my mind on Him, and never give up."

Amen!

Hallelujah!

Lenny looked directly at Summer for a second, then turned back to the pastor. "Sometimes the Lord sends people in your life at the right season. Although the Lord blessed me, I would not have had this new job if it wasn't for this lady. She told me about it and put in a good word for me. They respected her recommendation so much that they hired me the same day of the interview. So, I invited her here today, and I just wanted to acknowledge her. This is Summer Maldonado." He motioned for Summer to stand.

Summer reluctantly stood to her feet and smiled as the congregants clapped. Those near her shook her hand, and one lady hugged her. She then faced Lenny with a look that said *I'm going to get you for this*.

Lenny saw the look but continued anyway. "And not taking anything away from the First Lady, but talk about a *fine woman*!"

The congregation laughed and clapped again. Summer blushed, gave Lenny a look of feigned shock, and quickly took her seat. She appreciated the acknowledgment, but would have to remember to gently and kindly give him the blues about it.

***

Service was over three and a half hours later. Long services like this were one of the reasons Summer no longer went to church. When things started getting very busy in her life, she could no longer commit

herself to such large chunks of time on a weekend. Nonetheless, she was glad she came, and felt quite inspired by the time the service was over.

Summer stood near the aisle and waited for Lenny. Several congregants gave her handshakes and hugs on their way out. Eventually, Lenny made his way over to her, after being delayed by all the people who wanted to personally congratulate him on his new job.

"Summer, I'm glad you could make it," said Lenny, approaching her. In deference to the custom of the church, they exchanged a short church hug, where their chests and pelvis did not touch.

"I'm glad I could come," Summer responded. "I enjoyed the service, and I thank you for the acknowledgment."

"No problem. You saved my life."

"But you could have left out that other part, though."

"What? The part about you bein' fine? Well, that was the truth. You *are* fine."

Summer blushed again. "Well, I appreciate the compliment. But you didn't have to say that in front of the church."

"It ain't that serious." Lenny pointed to his son, standing on his left. "Summer, this is my son, Lenny Jr."

Summer knelt down and took Lenny Jr. into her embrace. Nice to meet you. You look just like your daddy."

"Thank you, Miss Summer" Lenny Jr. politely said.

Summer stood. "He's so adorable and well-mannered."

"Yeah. That's my little man. Hey, what are you doing after church?"

"Nothing really."

"How 'bout you come with us to get something to eat? I always take Lenny out for dinner on Sundays. It's his reward for putting up with my cooking the other six days of the week."

Summer hesitated. "Well, I don't really have a car right now."

Lenny's eyebrows furrowed. "Where's your Acura? In the shop?"

"Something like that."

"How'd you get here?"

"Took a cab. That's why I was a little late."

"Well. That ain't no problem. I got a car. I can take you back home after we eat. Pastor always says, 'If they get here on the bus, you make sure they go home in a car.'"

"Okay. That sounds like a plan."

"And, just so you know, my car is kinda beat up. Ain't that fancy."

"That's okay. I'm sure your other car is a Jaguar."

"Real funny. Hey, lemme say goodbye to a couple of people, and then we'll go."

"Cool."

Summer watched as he walked back toward the front of the church with his son in tow. Lenny Jr. seemed completely happy and at-ease with his father, and the boy was obviously well cared for. Summer admired a man who could raise his child by himself and do it so well. That spoke volumes about his commitment and his character. It would be good having a friend like that in her life.

Lenny and his son returned just three minutes later. He said, "The one thing about a service this long. If you wasn't hungry when you came in, you'll surely be hungry on your way out."

Summer agreed. "Yeah, I'm starved."

Lenny motioned toward the front door. "Well, let's go eat. How's Olive Garden sound?"

***

Summer had spent most of the fifteen-minute trip to the Olive Garden talking with Lenny Jr., who was especially verbose about his new bicycle, his school and summer camp, his friends, his mother, the latest episode of *The Fairly OddParents*. She noticed that Lenny was not particularly talkative, which she attributed to his discomfort over the condition of his vehicle, a 1990 Sentra with carpet worn to the metal, and worn and torn car seat covers covering even more worn and torn seats. Summer was glad there was no cigarette odor in the car,

which meant that Lenny either did not smoke or chose not to smoke in the car.

They arrived at the restaurant, which was teeming with the after-church crowd. They waited about fifteen minutes for a table before a hostess showed them to their seats. Lenny Jr. sat directly beside his dad and Summer directly across from them. Lenny Jr. busied himself with an electronic video while Lenny and Summer talked.

"Sorry about the car," Lenny said, looking away. "I know it's not what you're used to."

"And what am I used to?" Summer said, almost laughing.

"Girl like you is used to Mercedes, Lexus, y'know, nice cars."

"Well, you don't know this, but I spent thirteen years struggling in Atlanta, me and my mom. In thirteen years, I've been in my fair share of beat up cars. My first car out of college was an old Plymouth. It had no A/C, no heat, no shocks. It was an ugly pink; it sounded like a roomful of Harley Davidsons, and it went only fifty miles per hour downhill. None of my friends wanted to be caught dead in that car. So, yours is nothing compared to that."

"Atlanta, huh? Is that where you were born?"

"No. I was born in Brazil. I was there for five years before I moved to Atlanta."

Lenny snapped his right fingers. "See, I knew there was something exotic about you."

"Really?"

"Yeah. I knew it was something. I guessed Dominican Republic, Jamaica, maybe Trinidad. I just didn't know what. Can you speak Spanish?"

"No. The language of my country is Portuguese."

"Tell me something in Portuguese."

Summer laughed, then said, "Eu estou muito contente de conhecê-lo."

"Okay, what does that mean?"

"I'll tell you later."

Lenny gently slapped the table. "C'mon. You can't leave me han-

gin' like that."

"I'll tell you later."

"Summer, c'mon."

"Nope. Later."

"When later?"

"After dinner."

The waiter came and took their orders. Afterwards, Lenny continued the conversation.

"So what about after the thirteen years in Atlanta?"

"Went to college, did some interning at a radio station, then worked there after I graduated. I had my own radio show for about nine years."

"Wow. What kind of show?"

"Drive-time jazz."

"Meet anybody famous?"

"Oh, yeah. I interviewed Herbie, Wynton, Miller, so many to name. I did an interview with Etta right around the time that the movie about her came out. But my favorite is Nancy Wilson, and I love me some old Nat King Cole. You like jazz?"

"I'm kinda gettin' into it more. Didn't used to. I'm told jazz don't really appeal to you 'til you of a certain age. And I guess I'm that age."

"What kind of music do you like?"

"Oh, gospel, definitely. Some kinds, not all. I don't like the real repetitive stuff. A little neo-soul on occasion. I like classical."

"Classical? Where did you grow up?"

"Mosby. Not far from the church. Then I moved to my aunt's house in Hampton for a bit."

"How does a guy born in Mosby Court get into classical music?"

"Probably trying to redefine myself, broaden my horizons. Just 'cause you in the hood don't mean the hood gotta be in you. They say it's hard to break out of the hood, but I think it even harder to break out mentally, in your mind. Leave them hood thoughts behind and move on to bigger, better stuff. Started checking out some classical stuff, and found that I liked it."

"Well, I'll have to take you to a jazz concert someday. You might like it."

"I'm gonna hold you to that."

"Do that. It'll have to wait until after I find a job, though."

"Speaking of which, I heard some rumors about how you lost your job at Notions."

"Really? What rumors?"

"I heard you beat Jada Hardy like she stole something. And she did—your man."

"Not exactly true."

"What happened?"

Summer hesitated, not sure how much of this personal side of her she was ready to reveal to Lenny.

Lenny sensed her hesitation and said, "I mean, I asked because you don't seem like a violent person, and I don't want that image of you in my head if it isn't true."

"Well, the truth is I threw a drink in her face. I didn't hit her."

"Because she stole your boyfriend?"

"My, you're nosy."

"I mean, it's not like it's a big secret she stole your man. Before I left, I saw him and her coming in and out together several times. That same guy that came over to your apartment looking for you the other day."

Summer reached for a glass of water on the table. "If you don't mind, I'd rather not talk about that."

"Still a little raw, huh?"

Summer nodded while taking a sip of water.

"I understand. Truth be told, if he's hangin' around with Jada, you gotta question his judgment. She's a straight up gold digger. She'll sleep with anybody who's got a halfway decent paycheck. He was a lot better off with you. So, his loss. He kicks a girl like you to the curb, he deserves what he gets. So, you'll be alright. Like the pastor said today, *'often the things we want God to reward, God holds back because He is doing something in us.'*"

Summer was struck. That was the same statement that caused her to think earlier.

Lenny continued. "I think, like the pastor said, God wants us to seek His face. And then, the rewards will come. In his time. Could be now, could be years from now. But they will come."

Summer looked down and started cleaning her fingernails, which didn't need cleaning. *God will bless in His time. But what if I need it in my time?* She started to think about her rent situation, and what she planned to do the next day to resolve it. Everything in her soul and spirit was telling her what she was about to do was immoral, but somehow, assurances from God weren't enough. She was so used to doing things her way, and when the pressure was on, she couldn't help but take the reins. If God could bless her before 8 a.m. the next morning, she would gladly accept and acquiesce. Otherwise, she had to take action.

Summer cleared her mind of these thoughts momentarily and tried to steer Lenny off his soapbox. "How are things going with the new job?"

***

Lenny pulled up to the gate house of Summer's apartment complex. He put the car in park, turned to Summer and said, "you never told me what that Portuguese statement was."

Summer smiled, gathered her purse, and then stepped out of Lenny's car. She then leaned in and said, "Thank you for dinner. Next time, it's my treat."

"When is the next time?" Lenny asked.

Summer said goodbye to Lenny Jr. in the back seat, and then started to walk toward the gate. She turned back and said, "I'll see you at the gate house sometime and let you know."

Lenny shook his head. "You're a beguiling woman, Summer."

Summer looked back one more time and smiled before she disap-

peared into her apartment

***

Twenty-four minutes later, Lenny was home at his apartment just a few blocks away from his church, and not far from the Mosby Court neighborhood where he grew up. He parked on the street in front of his building, then got out of the car and went around to the passenger side to unbuckle his sleeping son from the seatbelt and take him out of the car. With his free hand, he reached for his Bible. He immediately noticed something sticking out of it that was not there when he left church.

Once he had gotten upstairs to his second-floor apartment and put his son to bed for a nap, he retrieved the Bible and pulled from it what looked to be a napkin from the restaurant. Written on it was, "804-555-7645. Call me. Summer."

He smiled. He hadn't asked for her phone number, yet, she had given it voluntarily, which made it all the more special. It seemed as if he was quickly building a great friendship with Summer, and that encouraged him immensely. He set the note on his living room coffee table and made a mental note to call her later. But right now, he had to do some things to get his son ready for the next day, and he could not be distracted by anything or anyone, not even his new friend.

***

At around 10 p.m. that night, right after Lenny had put Lenny Jr. to bed for the night, he picked up his cell phone and called Summer. As the phone rang, he was worried that Summer would not recognize the number and would likely let the call go to voicemail, since it was so late.

His concerns were unwarranted. Summer answered after four rings. "Hello."

"Hey, Summer."

"Hey, Lenny. I see you got my gift."

It touched Lenny that Summer recognized his voice. "Yeah, I got it. Nice to put it in the Bible. If I never read my Bible, I would probably have never found that note."

"Yep."

"So, you wanna tell me what that thing was you said in Portuguese?"

"I said, 'I'm very glad to know you.'"

Lenny nodded, smiling. "I'm glad to know you, too."

"But you called me too late. I was getting ready for bed. I got something important to take care of tomorrow."

"Yeah. I probably have to get to bed, too. I like to be up before my son gets up. Sorry I called you so late. I had some things to take care of to get him ready for his camp tomorrow."

"You're a great father."

"Thanks, Summer."

"Call me tomorrow."

"Sure. Hey Summer?"

"Yes?"

"Can we pray together real quick?"

"Sure."

"Father, in the name of Jesus, I pray that you give us a good night sleep tonight. Lord, let us be better servants tomorrow than we were today, and anoint us to say the right things and make the right decisions. I pray for Summer, that you will continue to fill her heart with your presence, and touch her in her areas of need."

Summer, deeply touched by the short prayer, returned the favor. "Lord, I pray that you will continue to increase Lenny, both in his knowledge of you and in everything that He needs from you. Lord, bless his relationship with his son, and make it so that his son always continues to be a joy to him. In Jesus' name."

They both said amen together.

When Lenny got off the phone, he uttered another quick prayer.

"Lord, thank you for drawing Summer and me together. I don't know what you are doing, but Lord, add your blessings to it. In Jesus' name."

Summer did not utter another prayer, but thought about the one that Lenny had offered. *Anoint us to say the right things and make the right decisions.* She truly hoped some invisible power would come upon her to give her strength enough to cancel her plans for the next day. But until that happened, it was full speed ahead.

She pressed ahead with her exhaustive bedtime routine: hair in curlers; wrap hair in scarf; brush teeth; change into nightgown, which, despite living alone, was a habit she never dropped from her days of living among six family members in Atlanta; call mother to check in on her; remove lipstick, which, along with occasional eye shadow, was the only makeup she ever wore.

At around 11:30, she called it a night, knowing that the next day would be interesting indeed.

***

Xavier was beginning to miss his old apartment. Moving in with Jada meant giving up the freedoms he once enjoyed—to come and go as he pleased, to leave the TV on all night, to leave his shoes where he wanted, to spend his weekend days as he wanted rather than to have to plan around Jada. It was all gone. At least Summer would give him his space whenever he needed, but Jada was determined to smother him until he could no longer draw a breath. It didn't help that Jada wanted to ensure that Xavier had no contact with Summer.

It was Sunday, and Xavier had planned to sleep in, but Jada woke him at 7 a.m. because she was making breakfast and needed him to run to the store for bacon. At noon she insisted that he go shopping with her, an odyssey that took almost four hours, not including the thirty-minute stop for lunch at Panera Bread and a fifteen-minute catch-up chat with a college girlfriend she hadn't seen in years. Then it was over to Jackson Ward to visit a beauty supply shop she preferred, then

over to Horsepen Road for sushi, and then, finally, home almost twelve hours after he had awakened. There was no rest for Xavier that day.

The natural reward for him hanging out with her all day was sex, but even that wasn't as exhilarating to Xavier as it used to be. It was beginning to annoy him that Jada was still sleeping with Mark Battman, despite her assurances that Mark had discontinued the relationship. Now that he was living with Jada, he was beginning to see and experience what Jada would be like as a wife, even though the nuptials had not occurred and were still several months away. He thought he would be accepting of an open marriage, but found himself increasingly uncomfortable with Jada's late night dalliances with Mark. Although Jada said her relationship with Mark was strictly for professional reasons, Xavier wondered if Jada was getting something physically and emotionally from Mark that she wasn't getting from him. And that bothered him and fueled his jealousy. Since he was no longer with Summer, he needed that emotional connection with Jada, but Jada seemed to have a deeper relationship with Mark than with him. It was only when Jada left him alone at 8 p.m. that he had time to think and realize that Jada's arrangement with Mark did not work for him.

While Jada was in the basement ironing clothes for work, Xavier came down to the basement to again broach the subject of her relationship with Mark.

"I thought you were resting," Jada said as Xavier walked down the stairs to the laundry area.

"I was." Xavier was shirtless, which always helped to soften Jada's resolve a bit. "I wanted to talk to you."

"About what?"

"You and Mark."

Jada sighed, said nothing and continued to iron.

"I need you to break it off with Mark."

"I thought we had talked about this."

"We had. And I decided I'm not comfortable with the arrangement."

"That's something you should have decided before we hooked up.

Mark was around long before you were."

Xavier drew closer to her. "I don't think you get me. This is not a request. I need you to break it off with Mark."

Jada stopped ironing and searched Xavier's eyes, finding a seriousness she had never seen. "What about you and Summer?"

"What about me and Summer?"

"When are you gonna break it off with her?"

"I'm not with her."

Maybe not physically. But you are in your heart. You're in love with that bitch, and you know it."

Mark's jaws tightened at that remark. "Don't call her a bitch."

"Why is it okay for you to hang out with Summer, and I can't hang out with Mark?"

"I'm not sleeping with Summer."

"Oh, but you want to. It bugs you that she's the only girl in your tired-ass life that never gave you none. But if she pulls up on you and offers you some, you're going to take it. Tell me I'm wrong."

He couldn't.

Jada returned to her ironing. "Why are you with me anyway?"

"Why are you with *me*? My money? Tryin' to get your mortgage paid? Houses over here in the West End ain't cheap."

"I don't need your money."

"Then why?"

Jada stopped ironing and pondered the question longer than Xavier would have liked. "Lust. Just lust. I thought lust was love. I was wrong."

"So are you saying you don't love me?"

"I loved the idea of you. Strong, black man with a great job, great family. I'd hear how good you were with Summer, how you guys went to some of the nicest places together. Summer seemed really happy with you. I couldn't have that with Mark. I wanted that with you. But was it love? I don't think so."

The remark stung Xavier, but it was not surprising. He wasn't sure he loved her either, but he knew he loved Summer. To him, Summer

was like a grocery store where you bought most of your food, but Jada was like that store that had the few items your regular grocery store didn't carry. His relationship with Jada was just one of convenience. He had also fallen in lust and thought it was love.

Xavier looked down dejectedly at the sea-blue carpet. "So, what are we doing?"

Jada also looked down. "I don't know."

"How did we agree to get married if we don't love each other?"

Jada looked upward, then said, "We made each other feel good. We were caught up in that feeling."

They stood in silence for almost three minutes before Xavier said, "I have a question to ask you. Please answer it honestly."

Jada nodded.

"If Mark wasn't married, and he was available, who would be here right now? Me or him?"

Jada continued her downward look for a long few seconds, then looked up at Xavier with a sad, silent face.

The silence was all the answer Xavier needed. Without another word he turned and headed back up the stairs, with Jada looking after him.

CHAPTER SEVEN

As was his usual routine, Mark Battman walked into his office at 8 a.m., set down his leather bag, turned on his computer, then went out to the lounge to make a cup of coffee. When he stepped out of the lounge and into the hallway, he saw Summer Maldonado headed from the elevator foyer down the hallway in his direction. He stopped, waited until she was just a few feet away from him, then said, "Summer. What are you doing here?"

"I need to talk to you," Summer said with an urgency that suggested this was not going to be a cordial chat.

"How did you get up here without an escort?"

"The security downstairs is a joke. A tight skirt and a smile, and they'll break down like stale saltines."

"Well, I'm not sure I feel comfortable meeting with you without a rep from HR present," Mark said, walking back toward his office. As Summer followed him, he said, "Do you mind if I call someone from HR?"

"It's up to you. Not sure if you want HR to see what I have to show you."

Just then, Mark remembered. *The infamous photo*. Mark had not heard anything about it in months, so he thought maybe he had dodged a bullet and Summer decided to let the matter drop. But no, here she

was, playing her trump card.

"Let's go into my office."

Summer followed Mark down the hallway and past the cubicles and offices of Visual Notions. It was still early yet, and most of the staff had not arrived. When Summer passed by her old office, she peered in, noticing no one was inside, but hesitated just long enough to notice the nameplate on the wall outside the door. *Jada Hardy*. She scoffed. *I can't believe he gave that slut my office*, she thought.

When they reached his office, Mark stepped aside and allowed Summer to enter. She walked in, sat down in front of his desk, and immediately opened her purse to retrieve her cell phone. Mark shut the door, then quickly walked over behind his desk, but remained standing until Summer had her cell phone in her hand.

Summer pressed a few buttons, then held up the phone so that Mark could see the screen. There, in all its glory, was the photo that Summer had snapped of Mark and Jada that night at Jada's house.

Mark looked at it for a few seconds, then turned away in shame. He took a seat and then stared at the far wall, thinking of how a few minutes of pleasure gave Summer the power to destroy his marriage and his career.

His phone rang. Mark pulled his phone from his pocket, looked at the caller ID, decided not to answer, pressed a few buttons and set the phone on the desk. Still looking away from Summer, he asked, "So, what are you going to do with that?"

"I don't know," Summer said, stuffing the phone back in her purse. "I have several options."

Mark turned to hear what those options were, but Summer was not talking. She just sat there, giving him the blankest of expressions.

"I could have you arrested for that, you know," Mark said, hoping to scare her into submission. "Invasion of privacy. Trespassing."

"Maybe. But you have to prove I took the photo, and you have to prove I have the photo. Good luck with either of those. Besides, legally, it's kind of hard to argue you had an expectation of privacy when you're boffing Jada in the backyard."

"So, what do you want?"

"It's not what I want. It's what you are willing to give."

Mark smiled, not a smile of amusement, but a kind of sly, defeated smile, as if he had just lost a playful bet. Summer was extorting him without legally extorting him. He knew Summer had that kind of cunning. He just never thought he'd be on the other side of it. Nonetheless, he'd play along. He couldn't afford for his wife to find out about Jada. If she did, she would divorce him and walk away with half of his company and most of his dignity.

"So, do you want your job back? Is that what this is about?"

Summer shook her head. "Mark, I would never work for you again. If you kick your best employee to the curb just to save face with your mistress, I'm not sure you're the type of person I want to work for."

"So, what then? Money?"

Summer said nothing, giving him the blank expression again.

"Okay, how's 5,000 dollars?"

Summer started to rise. "Gotta go, Mark. I want to get out of here before Jada comes in. I might lose my decorum around her."

"Okay, ten thousand."

Blank stare.

"Fifteen thousand dollars. Summer, that's two months of salary."

Summer appeared to mull it over for appearance's sake only. Fifteen thousand was actually double what she'd hoped to get. "Tell you what, Mark. Since you're giving me $15,000 of your own free will, why don't you make the check payable to me, with a cashier's check, and include with it a letter, addressed to me, saying something like, 'Thank you for the years you have spent with this company. In appreciation, we have decided to give you a severance check of $15,000. The check is enclosed with this letter.' Then, you sign it, and hold it for me. I'll come and pick it up. Have Jada type it, just for kicks."

"So, what happens with the photo?"

"Nothing. I erase it."

"No trace?"

"No trace."

"Okay, Summer. I'm doing this. But if that picture gets out, for any reason, I'm coming after you, Summer. I'll sue you for everything you have and ever will have."

Right now, that's not much, Summer thought. She reached for a Post-It note on his desk, and a pen, and scribbled her new phone number. "Call me when it is ready, but no more than two days."

"You know, you're way too pretty to be this shrewd."

Summer was reminded of scripture she had once read: *I am sending you out like sheep among wolves. Therefore be as shrewd as snakes and as innocent as doves.* She knew it was a far cry to use that scripture to justify what she was doing now. But she couldn't help but feel complimented.

"I'll look to hear from you soon." Summer turned and headed out of the office. As she walked down the hallway, she looked into Jada's office again and noticed that she was now inside. When Jada saw Summer walk by, she quickly got up and went to the door, opening it just as Summer had reached the elevator foyer. She watched until Summer had boarded the elevator, then hurried into Mark's office, where Mark sat rubbing the tension and stress in his shoulders.

"What was that all about?" Jada asked. "What was Summer doing here?"

Mark sidestepped the question. "Go down the hall to accounting. If Harry is in, tell him I need to see him right away."

***

Summer should have felt an overwhelming sense of relief; after all, she would have a $15,000 check coming within the next two days, money that would allow her to pay her rent for a few months until a job came through. But instead, Summer felt a foreboding conflict. She knew it was wrong when she did it; yet now that it was over and she was successful, she felt an even stronger pang of guilt. She would later

learn that it was the Holy Spirit, convicting her heart, causing her great dissatisfaction. It would be the one time in her life where getting a lot of money would make her feel absolutely horrible.

But then there were those stresses in her life that weighed upon her, and she wondered whether she would rather be stressed out or feel guilty. She had already received a letter from her insurance company reporting that they planned to pay for the replacement of her car, but that they would not pay for her medical expenses, and the medical expenses and property damage of the two people whom she injured in the accident. Now, their insurance companies were coming after her for the money. Having $15,000 made her feel that much safer.

Summer decided to eat a bowl of fruit and then spend the rest of the day lounging in her bedroom with daytime TV to mitigate the loneliness of her apartment. At 5 p.m., after a quick nap, she slipped on her spandex active wear and went outside for her routine jog. As usual, she jogged around the community a few times before she ended her jog with a brisk walk toward the front gate house. As expected, Lenny had begun his shift, and was standing at the booth, but as she approached, Lenny's face was glum, and he didn't offer his usual smile.

"Hey, Lenny," Summer began. "Are you okay?"

"Not really."

"What's wrong?"

"Stuff goin' on, that's all."

"You want to tell me about it." Summer patted Lenny gently on the shoulder, a move that was more flirty than comforting.

Lenny turned, looked at her for a second, and then turned his gaze back to the ground. "My baby momma got locked up."

"Oh, no. What happened?"

"She was at the mall yesterday with some girlfriends. They said she slipped a watch in her purse without paying for it."

"Oh, no. That's too bad."

"Yeah."

"Are you close to her?"

"Not really. We broke up about a year ago. She wasn't really

able to take care of Lenny Jr., so that's why I got him. But she's been struggling, just like me. I would tell her to have faith in God, and He will provide. Just like He did for me. But she was so stubborn and so strong-willed. She always did things on her own, rather than putting it in God's hands. And that's what has hurt her, because when you take things out of God's hands, and put them in yours, you're putting them in less capable hands. I hope she knows that now."

Those words struck a familiar chord with Summer. Lenny wasn't just describing the mother of his son. He was unwittingly describing *her*. And that caused the guilt pangs to intensify, almost to the point where she could think of nothing else.

"So, what's going to happen to her?" Summer inquired.

"She's gonna be locked up for a year, if the charges stick," Lenny said. "And Lord knows I don't want to be taking my son to Fluvanna to see his mother every other week. I don't want him exposed to that."

"What's Fluvanna?"

"A prison. About an hour from here. Way out in the boonies. She was locked up there before for the same kind of stuff."

"That's unfortunate."

"Please pray for her. Her name is Trinee."

"Sure. Anything else I can do?"

"Nothing I can think of. From here, it's up to God and the law-yers."

Summer patted his shoulder again. "Well, you can count on me to pray." She sighed. "Well, I'd better let you get back to work. I don't want you to be fired for fraternizing."

"No doubt."

"Call me tomorrow on your lunch break."

"I will."

Lenny watched her as she left. He was really starting to like Summer. She seemed humble, sweet, blade sharp, and lonesome. But most of all, *saved.* And it didn't escape his notice, as she jogged away, that she had a very nice body. He wanted to get to know her better, mostly because he was growing fond of her.

He remembered Pastor Malachi's admonition just after he had broken up with Trinee.

Son, just because they look good don't mean they are good for you. Men are visual creatures, so they may act on something that looks good to them. But a man of God has an extra dimension to consider. A man of God is stimulated by a woman that is spiritually attractive. And for a true man of God, the spiritual attractiveness is the essential element that makes a physically attractive woman someone for him to consider.

He had made that crucial mistake with Trinee. Outwardly, she was pretty, but inwardly, she was a train wreck. Pastor Malachi wanted to make sure that if Lenny thought about dating again, he had the right perspective. Lenny had a few opportunities to go on dates during the year after he broke up with Trinee, but found the women so spiritually bankrupt that he thought it best to just focus on his son and wait until God had brought the right woman along.

Now, he was beginning to wonder if Summer was that woman. A year ago, he wouldn't have believed it. Summer seemed way out of his league. But now, this woman had grown on him *big time*. Now he knew that anything was possible with God.

***

Xavier was seated by himself at a table in his company's cafeteria when his cell phone started ringing. He checked the caller ID, then pressed a button to answer. "Hey, Gene."

"What's going on, X. Hey, buddy, I know you're busy, but I got some good news for you. Got a few minutes?"

"If you don't mind me chewing my chicken sandwich in your ear, yeah."

"Not a problem. I got a call from Scott Iverson just a few minutes ago. That girl that you referred to me?"

"Yeah."

"Scott wants to sign her."

"Seriously?"

"Yeah, man. Since you kind of hinted that you were her ex-boy-friend and you wanted to get back together with her, I thought I'd let you know first, so you can tell her."

"Summer may not like you telling me her business. She's proud like that. You're her agent. You should tell her."

"C'mon, man. This girl's about to be a reporter in one of the top fifty markets in the United States. She's going to be very excited about that. You literally saved her life. She might be very grateful. *Very grateful*. You really want to pass that up?"

Xavier dropped his sandwich on the plate and picked up the phone. He had placed it on speakerphone so that he could finish eating. He looked around to see if anyone had heard the remark. Fortunately, everyone appeared busy with their own lunches and lunch partners to have heard his phone, and gladly the din in the cafeteria made it less noticeable.

Xavier put the phone to his ear. "Gene, Summer's a church girl now. She's not going there. Trust me."

"Hey, man, I heard some of those church girls can be the biggest freaks. They got all that sexual frustration packed inside of them, and no way to let it out. When it does come out, *boom*! You want to be there when it happens, bro. When she hears she's got this job, she's gonna want to celebrate right then and there."

Xavier mulled it over, and figured he had nothing to lose by telling her. "Okay, man, give me the rundown."

"Okay, so, I gotta call Scott back so we can make an appointment to go over the contract. It's for ninety days. Just a trial. They'll give her a few assignments. If she works out, they'll negotiate a standard three-year contract. I'm gonna go for $15,000 for the three-month trial. I don't think I'll get much more than that."

"Fifteen thousand? Before taxes? She was being paid that *after* taxes at Visual."

"Yeah, but keep in mind that Iverson's got a young station, and

Summer ain't exactly Lesley Stahl. She had the radio gig in Atlanta, sure, and she looks great, but can she deliver a story under budget and on time? He's taking a chance here, but if it works out, he'll have a hell of a reporter."

"All right. I'll talk to her."

"Call me back when you do, let me know when she can meet with Scott."

"Will do."

"How's things with Jada?"

"Taking a break from that for a while. I've moved back into my apartment. Good thing I held on to it."

"Clears the road for you and Summer."

"Let's hope."

"Good luck, bro."

"Thanks."

Xavier was glad for Summer, even though she would be taking a pay cut. But it was better than nothing. He thought it would be good to personally deliver the message to Summer. He made plans to do so at 6 p.m., as soon as he left the office.

***

Xavier pulled his car up to the front gate house shortly after 6:30 p.m., finding Lenny on duty. Xavier rolled down the window. Lenny came out to meet him.

"How you doing?" Lenny greeted. "You're the same guy that came by here before, right? X, you said your name was?"

"Yeah. I'm here to see Summer."

Lenny hesitated a little longer than he should have, studying him, observing the Italian cut of his suit, the supple leather of his BMW, the Tag Heuer on his wrist. *So this is what she likes—pretty boys with money*, Lenny thought. "I need to call up, get authorization to let you through."

Xavier looked at him, his eyebrows furrowed slightly. "Okay."

Lenny returned to the gate house, closed the door, and dialed Summer on his cell phone. When she answered, he said, "You got a visitor."

"Who?"

"X."

Lenny then heard a breath. It was not the sharp intake of breath that indicated a pleasant surprise, but a quick exhale that indicated an unwelcome one. Summer had still not shared with him her prior relationship with Xavier and how that led to her accident, but Lenny could guess that the two were not on good terms. "Want me to get rid of him?"

"No. Send him up."

That answer disappointed Lenny, and he wasn't sure why. After all, he was only Summer's friend. And it wasn't as if Summer would have any interest in a guy who was living paycheck to paycheck, when she could be with a guy that wore $2,000 watches. Lenny was lucky to be able to afford a $25 Timex. Lenny knew he had no dog in that fight. The mere sight of Xavier zapped him of every bit of faith.

Lenny pressed the button to open the front gate. He then looked at Xavier, providing him no further instructions as he would with most visitors, as he was sure that Xavier knew exactly where to go.

"Thanks," Xavier said, driving through the gate.

Lenny didn't bother to respond, as he normally would have. Lenny didn't like this guy. He cheated on a wonderful woman like Summer. Whatever direction Summer took, he hoped she didn't succumb to his charms.

He opened the gate house door and made a mental note to call Summer in a few minutes to check on her.

***

Summer had not been expecting anyone to come over, especially

Xavier. She thought about refusing to receive him; however, she didn't want to be discourteous to someone whom she still considered a friend.

She had just showered and was wearing nothing but her panties. She pulled on a pair of jeans and a T-shirt, checked her hair, and went to the door just as Xavier was starting to knock.

She opened the door slightly, just enough so that they could see one another, but not enough for Xavier to walk in. *God, he looks great in that suit*, she thought. "Hey, X. What's up?"

"I have some good news for you. Can I come in?"

Summer opened the door wider and motioned him inside. She closed the door and walked immediately to her easy chair in the living room. Sitting down, she pointed Xavier to the couch. Once he was seated, she said, "Okay, what's the good news?"

Xavier did not delay. "I spoke to your agent today. You got the job at the station."

Summer brought her hands to cover her mouth and screamed for joy. She took her hands away and said, "Seriously?"

"Yep. You and Gene still have to work out the contract, but you're going to be a reporter in Richmond, my dear."

Her whole body went into celebration—a feet stamping, hand twirling smile as wide as a football field celebration. Xavier enjoyed her celebration, glad to be able to witness what was likely the first real smile on her face in months.

"Oh, God, I can't believe it!" Summer screamed, then stood and starting walking around. "God is so good."

Xavier smiled and stood. "Hey, don't forget *I* had something to do with it, too."

Summer turned to him. "Thank you so much, X."

"No problem." Xavier held out his arms. "So, give me some love."

Summer went to him and let him draw her into his embrace. The moment their bodies touched, something stirred within them. Summer had always enjoyed his hugs. He held her close, emanating warmth,

passion, and love. She lingered, letting him hold her tight, one hand on her lower back, the other on her upper back. Her loneliness pummeling her resolve, causing it to evanesce, and her body responding, relaxing in his arms. She felt safe, she felt secure. In his arms, for that brief moment, she had no cares, no worries.

The ringing of her cell phone brought her back to her senses, and she quickly and effortlessly broke away from the embrace and picked up her phone from the coffee table. She looked at the caller ID, noticed it was Lenny, and denied the call, sending it to voice mail. She then put the phone back on the table and took a few steps away from Xavier, ashamed that she had allowed herself to get caught up. Xavier started to draw closer to her, but Summer held up her hand, motioning him to stop. She sat on the couch, and looked up at him as he regarded her with yearning in his eyes.

"I'm sorry," Summer said in a muted voice. "I shouldn't have … let you … hug me like that."

Xavier slowly backed away in frustration. He sat on the end of the couch opposite of where Summer sat. After a long, awkward silence, he asked. "Who was that on the phone?"

"The security guard from downstairs. Probably wanted to make sure you got to the apartment okay."

"I doubt it."

"Why do you say that?"

"He seemed … annoyed by me when I came to the gate. No, it wasn't annoyance. It was jealousy."

Summer scoffed and turned away.

"Oh, yeah. That's what it was. You got something going on with your security guard friend. That's why you brought him over here from East Leigh."

Summer frowned at him. "You are so crude."

"Tell me I'm wrong."

Summer's response was immediate. "You're wrong. He's just a friend."

"*He's just a friend.* If I had a nickel—"

"Well, it's true." Summer glared defiantly at a far wall.

Xavier sensed that Summer was getting annoyed, so he let the matter drop. After a few minutes of silence, he said, "Y'know, I've moved back into my own apartment. I'm no longer living with Jada."

Still looking away, Summer said, "Really?"

"Yeah."

"Did you break up?"

"You can say that."

"It isn't what I say. It's what *you* say."

"Yeah, we broke up."

"So, why are you telling me?"

"C'mon, Summer. You're a smart girl. You know why I'm telling you."

"And you're a smart man, so you know it won't make any difference."

"Well, maybe I'm dumb, because when we were hugging, it didn't seem that way. It seemed, for a moment, like we were feeling each other again. I felt it. I know you felt it. What you felt was my love, my care, my concern for you. That's why Jada and I broke up. She knew she could never compete with my love for you."

Summer turned her head to look at him, the defiance on her face slowly melting away.

"You're a diamond, Summer. A precious diamond. I know that now. You're worth so much. You're priceless. And I was a fool to give up a precious diamond for a fake."

Summer looked in his eyes, which were sober and pleading. He was feeling the pain of being without her, and that broke down every wall she had cast around her heart.

"It takes a lot to find a diamond, and a person who finds one never gives it up easily," Xavier said. "I will do whatever it takes to get my diamond back. I'll go to church. I'll do whatever to work out our marriage differences. I'll do anything, because I am madly in love with you, Summer. And I want the chance to prove that to you."

They sat there for another two minutes, silent, Summer pondering

his words, Xavier trying to think of more to say to convince her. Coming up empty, Xavier stood and headed for the door. Summer watched him, unsure if she wanted him to leave, but certain that if he stayed, she might do something she would later regret.

"You should call Gene tomorrow, work out the contract. Congratulations again." Xavier open the door, and then turned and said, "If the security guard is successful at getting with you, make sure you let him know how lucky he is." With a hint of melancholy, Xavier stepped out and shut the door behind him.

Summer hung her head and sighed deeply. Maybe this was a sign that God was pulling her life back together. She had a high-profile job. She had $15,000 coming, and Xavier finally realized the error of his ways. Several weeks before, she had prayed for this.

But for some reason, although it was great in her mind, it rang hollow in her heart.

***

Lenny was standing near the gate house when Xavier came rolling around the corner and through the exit gate. Xavier and Lenny looked blankly at each other as Xavier pulled out of the driveway and made a left turn onto the street.

Lenny grabbed his cell phone and dialed Summer. After three rings, she answered.

"Hey, Lenny."

"Hey Summer. You alright?"

"Yeah. Sorry I didn't take your call earlier. We were having a deep conversation."

"Anything you want to share?"

"Not really. But I have some great news."

"Really? What?"

"I got a job!"

Lenny was ecstatic. "Oh, wow, praise the Lord. That's great, Sum-

mer. I knew the Lord wouldn't keep you out of work for long. Where will you be working?"

"At a TV station, WIDN."

"Really? That's great. Never heard of WIDN, though."

"Well, not a lot of people have. They've been simulcasting network stuff the past three months, but they are going to go independent and start with some local news and lifestyle programming in a few days. And I am going to be one of their reporters." She sang the last sentence.

"What? You mean, I'll have the privilege of knowing a TV reporter?"

"Yes, you will! And I feel like celebrating."

"How?"

"When's your lunch break?"

"In about two hours."

"Why don't you come up to my apartment on your lunch break? I'll cook something, and I can tell you all about my new job."

The sound of a car skidding went off in Lenny's head. "Uh, I'd like to do that, Sum, but there's this rule about fraternizing with the tenants during shifts. They were very clear about it."

"OK, well, how about lunch tomorrow? My treat."

"Sure. Where?"

"Tillie's. Near the old job. About one o'clock."

"I'm there."

***

He knew Tillie's was pricey, but informal. Nonetheless, Lenny dispensed with his usual jeans and T-shirt and wore slacks, a button down shirt, and dress shoes to fit in with the workaday crowd at Tillie's and to impress Summer. He had arrived a few minutes early to scope out the scene. The restaurant itself resembled a diner, with large booths directly across a thin corridor from the serving counter

and stools. It wasn't large, but at forty-five minutes past noon, it was packed. Lenny was lucky to get one of the last booths available.

Lenny was completely pumped that Summer had asked him to lunch, and even more encouraged that Xavier's visit the night before had been so brief. He hoped this would be an opportunity to get to know her better before *pretty boy* sank his hooks into her.

While waiting for Summer, Lenny thought about Summer's request for him to come to her apartment. To him, that meant that Summer had become comfortable enough with him to invite him into her personal space, and that was heartening. But Lenny had lied about the fraternization rule—there was no such thing. But there was no way he was going to spend time in a gorgeous woman's apartment at 8:30 in the evening, even though he was certain Summer's intentions were pure. He was a Christian, but he was also a man, and he didn't trust himself in that situation. His pastor had warned him long ago about this. *Some people say that if you don't want to get wet, don't dive in the ocean. But I say if you don't want to get wet, don't get nowhere near the ocean, 'cause you might fall in.*

Lenny felt as if he had spent most of his life in compromising situations. He was born and grew up in Richmond's historic Jackson Ward neighborhood, in the housing projects on the north side of Interstate 95. He spent most of his formative years living in a cramped three-bedroom apartment with his mother, father, and Aunt Etta, who was his mother's only sibling. Aunt Etta was born in North Carolina, but grew up in Jackson Ward during the late '40s and early '50s. She would frequently regale Lenny with stories of vibrant African American life and culture in the neighborhood, about the teeming nightlife and entertainment venues that would host the likes of Ella Fitzgerald, Duke Ellington, and Count Basie. She would try to help him see that the poverty, violence, and hopelessness that he saw when looking out his window was a far cry from the way things used to be for African Americans in the neighborhood. *Son*, she would say to him, *the government caused all this, by coming into our neighborhood and messing things up. First, they tried to break our backs during slavery. Then,*

when slavery went away, they tried to disenfranchise us with Jim Crow. Then, when Jim Crow went away, they started messing with our good neighborhoods, tearing down stuff and building all these projects. Know what projects are? They the government's way of sticking all the po' black folk in one place so that white folks don't have to deal with them in their communities.

Despite Aunt Etta's efforts to mold and shape him, ghetto life remained a pervasive reality. When he was six years old, Aunt Etta moved out to live with her boyfriend, who was a shipping dock worker in Portsmouth. The move crushed Lenny, and he missed her deeply. But Aunt Etta's absence also changed his mother. While his father was on travel working as a track mechanic for CSX lines, his mother would frequently invite men from the neighborhood into her home. She would send Lenny outside to play, saying that she needed to have a conversation with these men, and Lenny was too young to know any better.

One day, after school, he climbed the stairs to his apartment floor and heard his mother, his father, and another man yelling, even though he was several yards down the hallway from his apartment. A trusted neighbor stepped out of her apartment and told Lenny to step into her apartment, where he spent the rest of the afternoon playing with her son, Terrance, who was Lenny's age. Lenny would later hear the sirens of police cars and ambulances, but that was nothing unusual for this neighborhood. When 9 p.m. came, just about the time Lenny was starting to get homesick, his mother showed up at the apartment, picked him up, and took him back to their apartment. Lenny noticed that some of the furniture in the living room that was there that morning was no longer present. His mother hustled him into his bedroom, got him ready for bed, and then told him that his father would be away working for a long time, and would not be home for a while.

Lenny wouldn't learn the truth until three years later. When he was eight years old, his mother took him for a visit to his Aunt Etta's, after which she left to get some cigarettes. She never returned, abandoning Lenny to live with Aunt Etta. When Lenny was nine, Aunt Etta

told him the truth: his mother had been sleeping with a man from the neighborhood. His father caught them together and was so angry he strangled the man to death. He was convicted and sent to prison, and shortly after, inmates avenging the death of their friend stabbed him to death in the shower. Due to *strike one you're out* laws, his mother was evicted from her apartment shortly after she had abandoned Lenny, and was never heard from again.

When Lenny was ten, and smack in the middle of his puberty years, he met Trinee Frazier and quickly started to refer to her as his *girlfriend,* even though he had no idea what that meant. Once he turned fourteen and started high school, he found out there were three things you didn't want to be: a punk, a gay man, and a virgin; a boy who was not voraciously interested in girls was often considered to be one or all three. He was of the age where his peers' opinion of him mattered greatly, and he began, through subtle touches and gestures, to test how willing Trinee would be to allow him intimate access to her. During an overnight camping trip sponsored by Aunt Etta's church, he had sex with Trinee for the first time, but it was so awkward and unfulfilling that Lenny made no more attempts until several years later. Once Trinee dropped out of Virginia Commonwealth University, she started inviting him to her apartment. He came without hesitation or remorse, and hoped not to leave until the next morning. Lenny Jr. was conceived out of one of their many passionate late-night encounters. Though Lenny Jr. was the love and joy of his life, Lenny had no intent to have another child in that way. If he was intimate again with another woman, he wanted it to be with his wife.

That was easier said than done. He started going to church and ex-perienced salvation when Lenny Jr. was three years old. Shortly after, he cut off his sexual activity with Trinee, which prompted their break-up and his eventual move out of her apartment. Several times during the next year, Trinee had tried to tempt Lenny, usually by showing up at his apartment wearing some form of undress. Each time, Lenny turned her down, which he found a lot more challenging than turning down a second pork chop at dinner. Every part of his flesh wanted to

be intimate with Trinee again. But the more he got to know Jesus, the more he began to see that Trinee would not make a suitable wife for him. She was too fast, too racy, and had no moral direction.

Lenny snapped out of his thoughts just as Summer walked in the restaurant. She was a few minutes early, wearing a purple skirt and a white blouse. She easily found the booth where Lenny was sitting. He rose, and they embraced. This time, it wasn't a church hug, but not as close, nor as long, as her hug with Xavier. Her warmth, softness, and perfume struck fire within Lenny.

"Congratulations again on your new job," Lenny said as they sat.

"Thank you!" Summer said almost musically. "I just came from the contract review."

"Really?"

"Yeah. I was so excited about this job that I called my agent last night right after I talked to you. He called the station manager and set up an appointment for this morning. It's a done deal."

"So, tell me about it. What exactly will you be doing?"

Summer tossed her hair, then leaned forward. "I'm going to be a lifestyles and entertainment reporter. No political stuff, no murder scenes, which is good, because I don't do blood."

"Don't blame you."

"The pay is not as good as I would have hoped. But it's better than nothing. I'll have to cut back on some things, but I can make it work."

"Do you get paid more than me?"

"Yes, I do."

"Good. I would have been upset if the job you helped me get was paying more than the job you got. When do you start?"

"Actually, in a couple of days. They want to put me on an assignment right away."

"Really? What?"

"They want me to go to Martha's Vineyard to cover an African American film festival. There's a director from Richmond who's participating. I don't know all the details yet. They'll give them to me when I go in."

"Wow. Wish I could go with you."

"I wish you could, too, but the company's paying for it, so it's not like I can bring guests. Besides, you and I still have to pull together a date for a jazz concert."

The waitress came to take their orders. Lenny noticed that Summer ordered only a garden salad and a glass of water.

"Wow, you eat like a bird," Lenny commented.

"I know. I've never really eaten that much. I definitely didn't get that from my mother. She eats likes crazy."

"Well, it works for you. You definitely look good."

Summer tried, unsuccessfully, to push back a smile.

Lenny continued. "I'm surprised you don't have umpteen men trying to get your number." That was less a compliment than a fishing effort from Lenny. He hoped she responded to it, eased his concerns. *Why was an unmarried woman Summer's age, as beautiful as she is, still single? Maybe she's got too many issues. Maybe she's nuts. Maybe she doesn't care for men.*

To his surprise, Summer spoke to it. "Can I ask you a few questions?"

"Sure."

"First of all, how do you know I *don't* have umpteen men asking for my number?"

"I don't know. I kinda thought you don't have a lot of prospects. I mean, you're hanging out with me, a broke, busted, and disgusted unmarried father. Surely there would be better men for you to hang out with if they were available."

"What makes you think that?"

"Think what?"

"That there would be better men for me to hang out with?"

"'Cause you're fine."

"Why is it that men always think that a beautiful woman has to be bombarded by men?"

Lenny swallowed, then said, "Well, I can't speak for all men, but men are visual. We like to be around beautiful women."

"Is that why you're here with me? Is that why you invited me to church?"

"I would have invited you to church no matter how you looked. But I have to admit, I do find you attractive."

"At least you're honest."

"But it doesn't stop there. I want to get to know you better. And I guess I'm wondering why a woman like yourself isn't married yet."

Summer leaned back and gazed out the window at their booth. She was quiet but pensive, wondering how much of herself she should reveal to Lenny. Finally, she said, "You may be surprised to know that I've had only two boyfriends my entire life. There was one in college. And there was X."

"Only two?"

"Just two. My boyfriend in college got frustrated because I wouldn't spend the night with him in his hotel room during spring break, so he hooked up with some other girl. So, that relationship ended. I didn't have another one until I met Xavier almost two years ago. X wanted me to spend the night with him, too, but I wouldn't, so he started proposing to me. He would propose to me every month, and every month, I would tell him to ask me again the next month."

"Why?"

"My mother was abused when I was a child in Brazil. My father beat her sometimes until she was black and blue, especially when he was drunk. That's why we left Brazil when I was five. Now X can be a hard drinker, too, and I just kept having these visions of X beating me just like my father beat my mother. My distant cousin Cicely, who we stayed with in Atlanta, was also abused by her boyfriend. So I grew up knowing the red flags of abuse. And there was no way I was going to let that happen to me."

Lenny let her words sink in. Never would he have thought Summer would have such a violent past. He continued to listen, compassion in his eyes.

"Marriage scares me, Lenny. I couldn't say yes to him, because I was afraid of what would happen. Now, if he's violent, I can go back

to my own apartment and never see him again. I have my own life, and control of it. But being married is different. You give up that control. I would be under my husband's domain, and that's scary to me. I may be black, but I'm also a Latina. And for Latinas, marriage and family are very important. I don't want to be forty years old and still looking for a husband. But I'm fearful of what that means. So, most of the guys who approach me, I just push them away, because I'm afraid of that level of closeness and intimacy with a guy. I think that's mostly why I don't have sex with them. Not so much because I'm Christian, but because that would take me to another level of closeness, and that scares me. I think the only reason I'm with X is because we got to know each other professionally before we got personal, and I saw some potential in him. I guess I'm just another screwed-up girl."

"No." Lenny reached over and placed his hand on hers. "Don't say that about yourself. It ain't true. Just because you're afraid of marriage? With what you've been through, I wouldn't blame you for being afraid. Marriage is a big step. I think a lot of people rush into it before they know what it means. But you shouldn't rush into marrying a guy just because he wants to have sex with you, or because your culture says you should be married by a certain age. Take your time, girl. And any man that's with you should understand that and be willing to wait for you, if you're worth it."

Summer began twirling her straw in the water that the waitress had just brought to the table. "No one thinks I'm worth it."

"I think you're worth it."

"Wish I had a dime for every guy that said that before they found out the booty was on lockdown."

"I'm not that guy."

"The only reason you're here is because of my looks."

"No, I said I'm here because I find you attractive. That isn't just on the outside. That's on the inside, too."

"Yeah, sure," Summer said doubtfully. "Is that one of your pickup lines?"

"Look, Summer, I've known since my first days working on East

Leigh that you were a fox. All the fellas used to say it. They used to check you out like crazy when you walked by. Some of them probably stepped to you, didn't they?"

"Almost all of them."

"But not me."

"Not you."

"Wanna know why?"

"Why?"

"Because I'm looking for something deeper. Not just a pretty face, although that's nice. And if you hadn't come back to get your check that day, I probably would have never seen you again. But you reached out to me. That said something to me about you. You got a good heart, girl. You let the Lord use you to bless me. And then, I found out you knew the Lord, and you came to my church. You weren't the same ice princess I used to know at East Leigh. That told me that there was a woman that could be just as beautiful on the inside as she was on the outside. And that's why I'm here."

Summer, whose head was hung down through most of their talk so far, looked up at Lenny.

Lenny leaned back. "Pastor used to tell this story. Ever heard of the Bradford Pear?"

"The what?"

"Bradford Pear?"

"Like a pair of twins?"

"Naw. Like a pear tree."

"No."

"Well, the Bradford Pear is one of the prettiest trees you'll ever see. Nice white flowers. Gives good shade. Problem is, if you get near the tree, it smells like old gym socks."

Summer laughed. "Oh, no."

"Yeah. Pastor says that's how some girls are. They look good to the eyes. But once you get close to them, they start to smell something awful. Then he went into scripture. I don't remember the exact verse, but it was something like how we are the sweet aroma of Christ."

"Hold on." Summer went into her purse and pulled out her phone. She pressed a few buttons to come up with a Bible app on her phone, and then scrolled and pressed some more until she was ready to report what she had found. "It's in Second Corinthians 2:15. 'For we are to God the aroma of Christ among those who are being saved and those who are perishing.'"

"That's the one." Lenny nodded. "So, Miss Summer, if I got closer to you and found you was smelling like stinky feet, we wouldn't have much of a relationship. I'd have hit the bricks a long time ago. Just like I did with Trinee."

"I thought you said she broke up with you."

"She did, but she tried to get back together with me. I wasn't having it."

"How's her court case coming along?"

"She got out today on a 3,000 dollar bond. That's good, 'cause she watches my son while I'm at work. My aunt watches him sometimes, but she's getting up in years, and she lives all the way out in Hampton."

"What about your parents?"

"My dad's dead, and my mom dropped me off at my aunt in Hampton when I was eight years old and never came back. No one knows where she is."

"I'm sorry to hear that."

"It's okay. I've turned it over to God. But I still wonder where she is and what she is doing."

"Well, if you're ever in a bind, I could watch your son for you."

Lenny shook his head. "I couldn't impose."

"And I wouldn't offer if it were an imposition."

"Sum, you're about to start a new job. You don't have time for this."

"I can work it out."

"And what do you know about kids? Do you have any?"

"No, I don't. But I babysat all the time while I was in Atlanta."

"Sum, I don't ... "

Summer interrupted him with a stern look. "Lenny?"

"Yes?"

"When I offer to do you a favor, here's how you answer: 'thank you so much, Summer. I really appreciate it.' And then you shut up."

Lenny threw his head back and laughed. After looking at her fondly for a few seconds, he acquiesced. "Okay, Sum. I thank you, and I do appreciate it."

"You're welcome."

"See? I told you. You have a great heart. I see the Lord using you mightily."

"Well, you might change your mind about that when you hear what I have to tell you next."

The waitress brought their meals to the table. Lenny had ordered a Reuben with a side of fries, which, after saying the blessing, he tore into while Summer enjoyed her garden salad. After the waitress had ensured they were fine for the time being and left, Lenny followed up on Summer's comment.

"What do you mean I might change my mind?"

"Well, I caught Mark Battman in a very compromising position with a woman who is not his wife, and I have pictures to prove it. I went into his office yesterday morning, showed him the pictures, and basically extorted 15,000 dollars in exchange for not releasing the pictures. I'm actually supposed to pick up the money by today."

"Hmm." Lenny stopped eating for a moment as his thoughts halted all activity. "Back in the day, I'd have told you that you deserve that money. Mark had no business firing you. But if you didn't work for that money, earn that money, or it wasn't given to you of his own free will, taking that money is stealing. And you don't want to stop the flow of God's blessings by doing that, do you?"

Summer conjured a weak justification, a last ditch and futile effort to assuage the guilt that had come on her since leaving Mark's office the previous day. "The money would really help me."

"I know it would. But God is our refuge and strength, a very present help in times of trouble."

Summer began to gaze out the window again. It would take a lot of faith to give up $15,000. She wasn't sure she had that much faith.

"By the way, Summer, I didn't change my mind about you."

Summer turned her gaze toward him, becoming more enamored with him by the minute.

"If you didn't have a great heart, you wouldn't have told me that. The heart that confesses cleanses the soul."

Summer nodded. "I never would have thought you were this way, Lenny. I thought you were as ghetto as the rest of those security guards at East Leigh."

"Hey, I'm from the ghetto," Lenny said, chomping down the last of his French fries. "But it took a lot to get the ghetto out of me. And it's still a work in progress. God ain't finished with me yet."

"Hmm." Summer saw an opportunity to know more about this man who had fallen gracefully into her life. "What is God still working on?" Summer's eyes went left when she asked the question, but when Lenny delayed answering, she returned her gaze back to him.

"Couple of things," Lenny said. "One, I'm a financial wreck. My credit is shot. I owe almost every bill collector in Richmond. I over-stepped my bounds when I started taking care of Lenny Jr., but I'm hoping this job helps out some. And I know I need to make some better decisions, and God is working with me on that."

Lenny's confession had Summer thinking about the many radio shows she had hosted where the guest was a lifestyle expert, and about the advice they gave for women who were dating men with bad credit. *Run for the hills*, they would say. But there was nothing about Lenny that made her want to run. His honesty only endeared her more to him.

"What's the second thing?" Summer asked, hoping that it wasn't anything too bad.

"I have a weakness for pretty women," Lenny said.

"Hmm." *This could be the dealbreaker*, Summer thought. "Would you say you are a womanizer?"

"Lord, no. I've only had one real girlfriend in my life to date, and that was Trinee. And I never cheated on her. Now, if I'm attached to

someone, I know how to appreciate another woman's beauty, and keep it moving. But when I'm single and unattached, like I am right now …
"

Summer waited for him to finish his statement.

" … I get weak in the knees."

"Even with me?"

"Especially with you."

Summer laughed under her breath. His subtle flirting at the beginning of their lunch had become more pronounced now, and she wasn't the least offended. In fact, she liked it. A lot. But she still had unresolved feelings for Xavier, and she didn't want to hurt Lenny by leading him in a direction that she could not follow.

Summer and Lenny talked until 3 p.m., after which Summer rode with Lenny to Lenny Jr.'s school to pick him up, and then to Trinee's apartment to drop him off, before they drove back to Summer's apartment complex. Once parked, they got out of Lenny's car and walked side-by-side toward the gate house. Lenny had his uniform draped over his shoulder, ready to start his shift.

"I enjoyed lunch with you today, Summer," Lenny said as they walked.

"So did I," Summer said. "And you know, the invitation to dinner is still open. My apartment. On your break. And don't tell me about any fraternization rule. I've lived here for two years. There's no such thing."

Lenny smiled, then stopped and turned to her once they were almost at the gate house. "Truth is I don't think it's a good idea for me to come up to your apartment."

Summer laughed. "What do you think is going to happen? Your break is only thirty minutes. You eat, you go back to work."

Lenny was unwavering. "Just a rule I have."

"A rule?"

"Yep. Like I told you, I got a weakness."

Summer nodded. "Okay. I'll bring you out a plate."

"You better."

They resumed their walk toward the gate house. When they arrived, Lenny waved at the guard on duty to let him know he had arrived, and then turned again to Summer.

"Y'know, since you're inviting me to your apartment for dinner, do I get the privilege of introducing you to my friends, my church, and my family as my new lady?"

Summer blushed again, but never took her eyes off him. "You can introduce me as your friend."

"Friend, as in girlfriend, or … ?"

"Lenny," Summer drew closer to him, "I'm not ready for the boyfriend–girlfriend thing right now. I'm really screwed up, and you're too nice a guy to sit around waiting until I get all my issues ironed out. I'd rather just be friends for now. *Good* friends, but just friends."

Lenny felt as if he could peer into her eyes and see straight into her soul. Beyond her stoic resistance, Lenny could see the sadness that she could not enter into a deeper relationship with him. All he wanted to do was reach out and hug her, but due to the heat he felt when they hugged at the restaurant, he thought it best to refrain.

"I understand, Summer." Lenny reached for her hand and held it in both of his. "Promise me one thing."

"What?"

"When you get everything squared away, that I'll be the first person you call."

"Promise." Summer reached out her arms and drew him in. The hug was close, but brief, one of those types of hugs that he hated to start, but didn't want to end.

"I'll let you get to work." Summer turned toward her apartment. "Call me on your break."

"I will."

Lenny walked into the gatehouse. The security guard sat there looking at him with a sly smile. "What?" he said to the guard.

"I saw you over there doin' your thing with shorty, man," the guard said. "If you want some extra time, I can cover for you."

"No need."

"How'd you manage to pull that, man?" the guard asked. "Lot of these honeys up in here are waiting for Denzel Washington to fall out the sky."

"It's not like that. We're just friends," Lenny responded, bristling at the disappointment that churned within him the moment he said those words.

CHAPTER EIGHT

Summer walked into her apartment, dropped her purse on the floor, and flopped on the couch before going deep into thought. *Why am I so afraid? Why am I so screwed up?*

It was a question that Summer had contemplated for many years. She had few memories of her childhood; the only ones that remained were hearing her mother's screams in Brazil whenever her father beat her. Her one pleasant memory was seeing Ipanema Beach for the first time. Her memories of early adolescent years were more plentiful, but none of her memories included much of a social life. From grade school through college, she had few friends, especially compared with others around her. At first she thought it was her mother's sheltering and devout gospel mongering that caused her to have few friends outside of the church. But even throughout her years at Clark Atlanta, during which she largely discarded any hint of a connection to church and spiritual life in order to be more popular, she never had much of a social calendar, which made her feel like a pariah on campus.

The nagging question was: why? Why was it that the only people who were drawn to her were men who were interested in sex? What was it about her that made people not enjoy her company? Summer had been told all her life that she was pretty. But that wasn't enough to make up for the ugliness that she felt turned people away from her.

One day after a shift at the college radio station, Summer came home and asked her mother what was wrong with her that she didn't have more social relationships. Summer vividly remembered Susan's response. *Don't worry about that. The people that God wants in your life, God will put there, and they will be drawn to you.* To Summer, that was all well and good. But why was she the only one who never received invitations to parties, never got unexpected and impromptu calls from friends asking to hang out, and never had chat sessions with girlfriends that lasted into the wee morning hours? Why was God punishing her with loneliness, but blessing everyone else?

***

Two days later, on her first day at WIDN, Summer walked into the office of Scott Iverson, the general manager. Summer had known Scott since college. Scott had curly blond hair and a thick body that could have used fewer hamburgers and a lot more Pilates. Scott's office was on the second floor of a small office building on a cul-de-sac. It was bright, airy, and sparse, decorated with little other than a desk, a chair, and two guest chairs at the front of the desk.

"Summer!" Scott stepped from behind his desk, approached her and shook her hand as she walked inside. "Welcome aboard."

"Thanks." Summer moved to a guest chair and set her beige leather attaché next to it before she sat down.

"How's your first day been so far?"

"Very busy. I've been non-stop since six this morning."

"Welcome to broadcast news," Scott said matter-of-factly. "You haven't seen anything. It's slow today. Wait'll a big local story hits. So, Pete introduced you to everyone, gave you an overview of the programs?"

"Yes, he did."

"Sorry we weren't able to get your desk ready just yet. We got you in here pretty fast and we weren't able to make all the preparations

we needed to. Hopefully, we'll have it together by the time you get back. Are you still assigned to that Martha's Vineyard thing? The film festival?"

"Yes."

"What's the local connection there?"

"A city councilwoman who ran for mayor two years ago and lost, she decided to pursue her dream and go into the film business. So, her documentary about Church Hill is premiering at the festival. And based on early reviews, it's great and could get national distribution."

"Sounds interesting. Are you ready for this?"

"Yes, sir. My flight leaves in five hours, and my cameraman's going to meet me there after he covers a live shot for the six o'clock news."

"Hmm." Scott stood up, came around and sat on the corner of the desk facing Summer. "I'm going to be honest with you about something. There are some people at this station who thought it was a bad idea for me to hire you."

Summer's face sunk a bit. "Why?"

"Well, you've taken a much-coveted job as an entertainment reporter. You get to travel around, meet celebrities, go to movies and concerts. A lot of people wanted that job. Plus, you have no real experience nor pedigree in TV news."

"Neither do most of your reporters. Most of them are interns from Fox and CBS. And my radio—"

"Yeah, your radio experience and the fact that I knew of you at my alma mater are the only reasons you're here." Scott gave her a serious look. "My point is that there are people here waiting for you to fail. Don't give them that satisfaction. Now, you may answer to the news directors and the EPs, but you represent me, because I brought you in here."

"Yes, sir."

"You do your absolute best, you work hard, you go above and beyond, and we'll be signing you to a permanent contract in ninety days."

"I'll do my best."

"Good." Scott stood and pulled an envelope from his desk. "Now I know you have to get some things done before your flight, so I won't hold you. Here's the advance you asked me for."

"Thanks so much." Summer took the envelope, opened it and examined the $2,000 check. "This will help a lot."

"Glad to help. We don't want to have a homeless reporter. We need you to report the news, not make it."

"Thanks, Scott." Summer stood, and they shook hands again before she left the office.

The $2,000 check, and the $15,000 Summer picked up from Mark the day before, gave her enough money to soothe her mounting fears. It wasn't enough to cover the $5,000 the hospital was charging her for her stay, or the $55,000 the insurance companies were trying to collect for the injuries to the other parties in the accident. But it allowed her to maintain her current lifestyle until more money came in from her job and she could afford to hire an attorney to fight the insurance companies. It was all the more reason why she needed this story to shine like none other. She needed Scott Iverson to know she was the real deal.

***

Summer convinced Lenny to take her to the airport ninety minutes before his shift. He was grateful for the opportunity—he had been thinking about her for the past two days, but unable to see her often because she had been busy making preparations for her new job and the trip to Martha's Vineyard. While on the way to the airport, Lenny updated her on what was going on in his life.

"Y'know, I had a long talk with Trinee yesterday," Lenny started. "This latest arrest has got her thinking that maybe she should turn her life around, and she really wants to try to be a better mother to Lenny Jr. So, she's gonna go to church with me this Sunday."

Summer voice was more excited than she was. "Really?"

"Yeah. I think she's finally getting tired of hitting rock bottom."

Summer started checking her fingernails and said nothing.

"Doesn't mean we're getting back together, or anything," Lenny added.

"Well, you're a single man, so you can date whoever you want."

"Clearly, we *both* know that's not true."

Summer twisted her lips. His remark was true. *Snide*, but true. This gave her the opportunity to try to clear up any hard feelings since she told him she was not interested in a boyfriend–girlfriend relationship. The feelings were not overt, but subtle, such as his emphasizing that they were *just friends* whenever he had an opportunity. She felt his mention of Trinee's interest in going to church was retaliation for Summer's rejecting his advances. *I tell him I just want to be friends, and now he's suddenly into Trinee again.* She needed to address what seemed to be a widening gulf between them, and to apologize for leading him on by inviting him to her apartment.

"Lenny, I'm sorry if I led you to think that we were going to be anything but friends," she said. "I love you, but I think you misconstrued that as *being in love* with you. And I'm not."

"'Cause you're in love with Xavier, right?" Lenny asked.

Summer sighed. "I tried to work him out of my system. But then he kept popping in my life, and he's been so contrite lately. I know he still loves me. And he realizes he made a mistake. He's even willing to go to church with me."

"Sounds like both our exes are more alike than we know."

After riding in silence for a few minutes, Lenny said, "Whatever you do, Summer, I hope it is what the Lord wants for you above what you want for yourself. I hope you maintain that perspective."

"And you the same."

They arrived at the airport and pulled in front of the main terminal. Summer grabbed her purse, got out of the car, and retrieved a single suitcase from the back seat. She then walked around to the driver's side of the car and knelt down so that her face was on the same level as Lenny's.

"I know one thing the Lord does not want," Summer said. "He does not want us to have hard feelings over this."

"Oh, I don't have any hard feelings. I admit I was disappointed, but my jaws ain't gonna be tight forever. I know how to keep things where they need to be."

"I'll call you when I get settled." Summer leaned in and kissed him on the cheek before she headed to the terminal. She gave him one final wave before she disappeared inside.

Once she checked her bag and retrieved her boarding pass, Summer pulled out her cell phone and typed a reminder to call Lenny when she got to her hotel.

She made another note to call Xavier.

***

By 6 p.m., the Cessna aircraft carrying Summer and three other passengers landed at Martha's Vineyard Airport, where a taxi was waiting to take her to the hotel. While riding in the taxi heading for the town of Oak Bluffs, Summer observed her surroundings, noticing at first only tree groves, some of them fencing off farmland, others providing a wall of privacy for mansions occupied by celebrities and the elite. The sun was low in the sky, and it would be dark soon, but Summer hoped to see as much as she could before nightfall.

After about a twenty-minute drive, the trees made way for early 19th-century homes, and eventually, narrower streets lined with cottage-sized shops. She smelled the salt in the air and knew she was near the water. The taxi pulled into the parking lot of a huge Victorian style house that Summer had thought was a commercial hotel, but resembled a huge bed-and-breakfast. That was okay with Summer, as she liked facilities that were cozier and resembled the comforts of home. To her, it was better than staying in swanky hotels like the ones she and Xavier had visited during their vacations.

Summer checked in and immediately headed up to her room. Her

camerawoman, Meg, would be arriving at eight and staying in a nearby hotel. They planned to meet up and walk to one of the restaurants in downtown Oak Bluffs. Before then, Summer had a lot of work to do.

The room was modest and homey, like a country cottage, with sky blue paneling, a window air conditioner, and Queen Anne furniture. Her window offered a view of the nearby beach. She would have to be sure to avoid being so distracted by the view that she couldn't get her work done.

She unpacked her Macbook, switched it on, and checked her itinerary. The film she was covering would not premiere until 5 p.m. the next day, but she and Meg would have to get establishment shots of various places around the vineyard, and then do teasers in front of the theater and on the beach. She was scheduled to conduct her interview with the producer/director, Sheila Nathan, shortly before the premiere of the film. She would have to work on her scripts, and review the clips of the film provided by the production company.

She also needed to brush up on the background of Nathan, a former Richmond city councilwoman. Elected for two terms in the Sixth District, Nathan ran for mayor of Richmond, but lost to the incumbent largely because of her lack of political experience. Nathan mostly agreed with her critics' assessment of her lack of experience, so she retired from politics and decided to pursue a career based on her love of film. Being a film producer and director was the best way to combine her love of film with her socially conscious political stance. Her film about the history of Richmond neighborhood Church Hill, particularly the Mosby Court and Fairmont areas, was her best way to get her voice out nationally and advocate for more resources for these distressed communities. Summer's interview with Nathan would be the major part of her report, and she needed to make sure she prepared challenging and thought-provoking questions.

By the time she finished with her work, showered, and changed into blue jeans and a linen blouse, it was 8:30 p.m. The sky had transformed to a deep orange and blue hue, with moonlight diffusing through the clouds. There was still a fair amount of traffic headed to

and from the downtown areas, and there was quite a bit of meeting and greeting on the porch in front of the hotel and in the verandas scattered around the rear yard. Summer dialed Meg and found that the camerawoman had already arrived and was checking into her hotel room a few blocks away. She figured that before Meg got settled, she would have time to make two phone calls.

She called Lenny first, finding him at work. He didn't have much time to talk, so she asked him to call her on his lunch break, which she knew would be around 10:30 p.m., at which time she would have returned to her room.

She then called Xavier. He answered midway through the second ring.

"Summer. Finally decided to call me, huh?"

"It hasn't been that long."

"It's been two days. That's a lifetime."

"I'm in Martha's Vineyard."

"So I hear."

"How did you know?"

"Talked to your agent today. He told me."

"Checking up on me?"

"Actually no. He called me, and it came up in conversation. In fact, I made up my mind I wasn't going to call you. The next move was up to you."

"Feel like doing something crazy?"

Xavier detected a slyness, a disinhibition in her voice, unlike the reservedness and caution with which she had spoken to him since their -break-up. "Like what?"

"Take a day off tomorrow, fly to the Vineyard, have lunch with me."

Summer heard Xavier laughing on the phone, but she didn't get the joke. "What's so funny?"

"You want me to come to Martha's Vineyard? Tomorrow?"

"Yeah."

He laughed again, then said, "Okay, let me get this straight. You

want me to spend a thousand dollars or more on a last-minute ticket, to have lunch with you, when I can have lunch with you for free right here in Richmond when you return. What's the return on investment?"

"You get to spend the day with the newest, sexiest reporter on the airwaves, on the island, at the beach. It'll be like a mini-vacation."

"So does this mean you're feeling me again?"

"We can talk about that at lunch."

The mystery of that statement intrigued Xavier, but also discouraged him. He needed a sure thing. *Hey, X. Come spend the day and the night with me. I promise you won't regret it.* Something along those lines, as that was as blunt as he could expect her to be. Absent such an assurance, Xavier was not excited about plunking down that much money for a day of conversation and dashed hopes for the night.

"That's a rather expensive lunch, Summer."

"You can afford it."

"That's not the issue. The issue is do I *want* to afford it?"

The quaint romanticism of this town got Summer feeling friskier than she should have been. "Tell you what. Tomorrow, we'll have lunch. Then, I'll be at the film festival from about four until around seven. After that, Meg and I are going to lay out the piece, do some edits, and then send the file to the station. We should be done at around ten. After that, I'm all yours."

"Really?"

"Yes."

"Will I need to book myself a hotel room?"

Summer hesitated, pondering briefly how her answer to that question would affect her soul as well as her body. But her flesh spoke—in fact, yelled—louder and more persuasively than any reasoning or moral conviction.

"Summer?"

"Yes, X?"

"Will I need to get a room?"

"No."

"Am I staying the night?"

"Yes."

"I'll be on the next available flight. Where are you staying?"

"Tell you what. Meet me at a restaurant called The Galleon. It's a seafood place in downtown Oak Bluffs. The staff at my hotel recommend it highly. If you can get there by one o'clock tomorrow, that'd be great. Make sure you rent a car. I'll need a ride to the festival."

"Sounds like a plan. See you there."

Summer ended the call and then lay back on the bed. Things were finally coming together for her. This seemed as if it would be a great job, and she would have Xavier to boot.

This felt good to her. She had been thinking about Lenny, and discovered that his financial problems bothered her more than she had initially let on. She would be going through her own financial struggles as a result of her debts to the hospital and to the insurance companies. She didn't need a man in her life that was going through the same things. Xavier not only had it all together financially, but she believed that he had turned things around and would be a great boyfriend to her again. After all, she loved Xavier, and didn't want to lose him if she didn't have to.

She relaxed and smiled, feeling a thousand weights lifted off her shoulders.

***

Lenny decided to take the ninety-minute drive down to Hampton to visit with his aunt Etta, whom he hadn't seen in almost two months.

During the next two years that Lenny lived in his aunt Etta's house, she had to work hard to ensure that Lenny's self-esteem was not irreparably damaged by the abandonment of his mother and his father's life sentence for murder just two years before. She quickly got Lenny involved in church and other civic activities, and made sure he didn't have much time at home to sulk and think about his troubles.

Lenny pulled into the driveway of Aunt Etta's house, a small

house with white siding, a cross gable roof and wood lattice shielding the porch area. The quiet neighborhood had many such neatly kept homes, set off about ten yards from the sidewalk, sparsely decorated with trees.

Aunt Etta sat in the living room so that she could see anyone who approached her front door through the window, without having to look far away from her TV. When she saw Lenny approaching, she got up out of her chair and walked over to the door with a quickness that belied her sixty-eight years.

"Leonard!" Etta whipped open the door and took Lenny into her embrace. "This is a surprise."

"How you doin', Auntie?"

"I'm alright, for an old lady." She stepped aside as he walked inside the house.

Lenny looked around. The place hadn't changed much since he moved out thirteen years before. Aunt Etta was a transplant from the rural areas of North Carolina north of Rocky Mount, and her house held a deep Southern charm, from the dark oak paneling on the walls, to the odor of bacon and fried apples still lingering in the air from breakfast, to the framed photos of almost every family member Aunt Etta ever knew existed. The most modern item in her living room was a Zenith nineteen-inch TV circa 2000, and it was perched solidly on top of a console TV, circa 1950, that had burned out ten years before.

"Want somethin' to eat?" Aunt Etta offered.

"Naw. I won't be staying too long," Lenny responded, sitting on the couch. "I gotta work tonight. You know I got a new job?"

"Yeah, I heard about that." Aunt Etta resumed her favorite seat near the window.

"How'd you hear that?"

"You know Angela told me." Angela, Trinee's mother, had moved from Hampton to Richmond after her daughter's second incarceration, hoping that her presence would help to stabilize her daughter. It didn't. "You makin' more money?"

"Oh, yeah."

"That's good. Glad to hear that, 'cause I know how much you was strugglin' with takin' care o' Junior. Angela told me somethin' else, too."

"What?"

"You got a new lady friend. Angela said she looked out the window when you dropped Junior off the other day, and she saw you had a pretty girl in the car."

Lenny looked to the floor. He would have loved to tell Aunt Etta that Summer was his girlfriend. Aunt Etta always wanted him to have a good girl, but was disappointed in the direction of Trinee's life, and had tried to convince him not to move to Richmond to be with her. *Plenty of good girls here in Hampton. You don't need to be runnin' around with that fast tail girl,* she would say.

"She's just a friend, Auntie," Lenny told her.

"Is she single?"

Lenny thought about Xavier. "Not quite."

"What you mean not quite?"

"She's interested in this other dude."

"Why is she riding around with you?"

"I thought at one point she was interested in me."

"Maybe she still is, if that's the woman the Lord has for you."

"I don't know about all that, Auntie." Lenny shifted in his seat. "I mean, this other guy is straight ballin'. Expensive suits. Drives a BMW. I can't compete with that. This girl is way too bougie to be hangin' around with me. Couple of days ago, she acted like she was feelin' me. Then I told her about my many credit problems. Now, all of a sudden, she just wants to be friends."

Aunt Etta came to her feet. "Lemme tell you somethin'. Don't you sit there on my couch puttin' yourself down. You a good man. Them credit agencies don't define you. You just as good as that man that got money. You came up in the church. You know the Lord. You ain't perfect, but neither is he. Don't you get ghetto syndrome and start thinkin' you gotta scrape the bottom of the barrel to find a woman. What does this woman do for a livin'?"

Lenny swallowed. "She used to be a marketing manager. Now she's a TV reporter."

"And are you interested in her?"

"I can't stop thinking about her."

"Then, you needs to pray about it. Don't you give up just because that other man get a heavier check than you. God's pockets are deeper than both of you."

"I've been praying about it. Almost every other hour."

"Then you gotta have faith. If that's the woman for you, she'll be yours. But if not, the Lord will have another one prettier and better than her."

It was difficult for Lenny to imagine a woman more beautiful than Summer. And try as he might to have his aunt's strong and simple faith, the reality was that many women select men on the basis of their finances. He had heard a preacher once say that if a man wasn't making at least $70,000 a year, then he wasn't marriage material. If that were true, then Lenny probably wouldn't be marriage material until the Lord came calling him home. He knew there was no way he could afford to take care of himself, Lenny Jr., and Summer on his salary, especially since Summer, based on her style, seemed rather high maintenance. To him, it had nothing to do with putting himself down. He simply couldn't afford Summer.

"Why don't you invite her on the Fourth?" Aunt Etta said, referring to the annual family cookout on the Fourth of July. "Your uncle Deno's having it over here this year, instead of at his place. He said he wants as much of the family to show up as possible. Can you make it?"

"I think so. That's Trinee's holiday with Junior." Lenny's thoughts turned to Trinee. "Auntie, y'know Trinee's been talking about going to church with me."

Aunt Etta snorted. "Really? Why is she all of a sudden interested in church?"

"I think this last stint in jail turned her around."

Aunt Etta sat back down. "I don't think it got nothin' to do with jail."

"What do you mean?"

"You know Trinee's been trying to get back together with you for the longest time. All of a sudden, you show up at her house with a pretty woman in your car, and now she's interested in goin' to church. *Hmph.*"

"I don't know, Auntie. I think it may be genuine."

"Well, I hope so. But it depends on why she doin' it. If she doin' it 'cause she recognize she need to change her life for herself, then that's good. But if she doin' it to get back together with you, then guess what'll happen when she finally gets you?" Aunt Etta paused for effect, then said, "Y'know, before my dear husband passed, he used to say that some girls going to church was like puttin' on a hair weave. It'll make you look real good, but you know it ain't real."

"I thought that you, of all people, would be excited about someone going to church, no matter what the reason."

"And I am. I'm not sayin' she shouldn't go. But I'm sayin', you need to be careful. If she's real, it'll show, in time." Aunt Etta headed toward the kitchen. "Lemme make you some lunch before you head back. Ain't no sense in making that trip on an empty stomach."

Lenny smiled. He had hoped she would make him something to eat, but didn't want to impose by asking.

He sat back on the couch. His visit to Aunt Etta's should have brought him some clarity about his situation, but now he was more confused than ever. But he did agree that inviting her to the cookout was a good idea. Maybe some time around Aunt Etta would soften Summer's resolve a bit.

***

Summer sat on a bench outside the Galleon restaurant on Circuit Avenue in downtown Oak Bluffs. She looked at her watch. Noon. Still another hour until Xavier arrived.

She had taken care of the preliminaries for her story. All she

needed now was the interview, then a few reaction shots of people exiting the screening. Until then, she just wanted to relax, enjoy Xavier's company, and set the stage for later that night.

Summer was ready. She yearned so much for a man's touch, and the hug from Xavier the other night reminded her of how much she had missed it. She was prepared to go all the way with Xavier, and the Vineyard, with its ageless beauty and ambiance, was the perfect place to enjoy that experience.

In the few days since Xavier had come to her apartment, she had time to think. Somehow, it didn't seem fair that fully enjoying her relationship with Xavier meant sacrificing her connection with God. Why couldn't she enjoy both?

Pastor Gillen had led her through many scriptures outlining what a proper Christian dating relationship should look like, but it all seemed rather archaic to her. The command that sex was only for the marriage bed seemed harsh for those who were in their mid-thirties and weren't anywhere close to marriage. Summer wondered how, without sex, anyone could sustain themselves in a society that in many ways resembled the ancient Corinth of Apostle Paul's time? After all, America seemed to have three major gods, and none of them named Jesus. The god of money, the god of power, and the god of sex. And the god of sex seemed to be just as strong as it was in the days of Corinth, where fornication and debauchery were an integral element in religious rites and pagan celebrations.

Though Summer had chosen until now not to have sex, the influence of it was pervasive. It was everywhere—in TV shows, in movies, in books, on the Internet, in music. There were restaurants with scantily-clad women as waitresses. The government was now endorsing same-sex marriage. There were porn stars who claimed to be Christian and thanked God for their careers. Sex seemed to be the ultimate act of worship, a sought-after spiritual experience. The worship of Jesus often came second, or third, or fourth, even in the hearts and minds of those who claimed to love him.

Summer tried to justify her feelings by telling herself her heart

was good. She wasn't going to be intimate with Xavier just to enjoy the act. She wanted to be closer to him, to engage with the man she planned to marry one day. She wasn't throwing her body all around town, being a slut, having sex with random men. How could God be angry with that? She knew Xavier was the man that God wanted her to be with, especially since he indicated his desire to go to church with her. How could God be displeased with her giving herself to the man whom He gave to her?

Summer sat quietly and watched the people walk by. Some of them were obviously tourists, as the summer season swelled the island with vacationers. Others lived there, or frequently visited, and they walked with familiarity, knowing some shopkeepers by name, and they didn't browse the souvenirs, and they didn't look with wonder and awe at almost everything around them. Most of them were white, but the presence of a few black islanders made Summer a bit more comfortable. She was glad not to be the only black person in the town. She would later learn that Oak Bluffs had the greatest percentage of blacks than any other town in Martha's Vineyard, which made it an appropriate setting for the African American Film Festival she would be visiting in a few hours.

Summer noticed a yellow Jeep Wrangler pulling into one of the angled parking spaces on the opposite side of Circuit Avenue. She paid it no mind, focusing on the people walking along the Avenue. It wasn't until she saw a tall figure looming at her left that she turned.

She jumped up quickly. "X!" She wrapped her arms around him, holding him close. Xavier responded by pulling her in, his hands slightly below her waistline. He then pulled back slightly, looking in her eyes, seeing the longing there. He moved in and slowly, gently placed his lips on hers. They kissed for a little over ten seconds before Summer tapped him gently on his back, reminding him of where he was. Summer wasn't sure how the islanders would react to their public display of affection. Most of them paid no attention.

Xavier released her, but continued to hold her hand. "Good to see you, Summer. Shame it's costing me almost 1,200 bucks, though."

"Don't worry. I'll make it worth your while." Summer led Xavier into the restaurant and informed the hostess of her reservation. Galleon had the typical seafaring décor, and the dining area was small and cramped, with tables less than six feet away from one another. The place was packed, because it had a reputation as the best seafood restaurant in a town teeming with seafood.

Just before they were seated, Summer ran her eyes up and down his body. His knee-length khaki shorts, beige T-shirt, and deck shoes made him fit in with almost every other tourist on the island. "You look great. But I never figured you were a Jeep kind of guy."

"It was the only thing they had available to rent," Xavier explained. "Either that, or I had to take the bus."

"I can't believe you were crazy enough to do this."

"I'd do anything for you. You know that."

"It's good to see you."

"It's better to see *you*."

"Ever been to the Vineyard before?"

"Can't say that I have. I've been to Nantucket, though. Family friend invited us there once for the Fourth of July weekend."

"Where is it?"

"Farther out in the ocean, maybe a good fifteen miles from here. It's an island, just like this one. Kinda feels the same." Eager to dispense with small talk, Xavier leaned forward. "So, let's talk real here."

"Okay."

Xavier reached across the table and held her hand. "It looks like we're getting back together. Am I mistaken?"

"We may have been physically apart, but my heart was never far from you, X." Summer gently squeezed his hand. "No, you're not mistaken."

"We've said and done some pretty dumb things, both you and I, but it looks like we're back on track."

"Can I ask you a question?" Summer request was not so much permission to ask, as it was a warning that her question would not be run-of-the-mill.

"Sure you can."

"Did you mean what you said when you said you would start going to church with me?"

Xavier released her hand and leaned back. "Summer, I haven't been to church in twelve years, except weddings, funerals, and rummage sales. I'm not gonna lie to you. It's not my cup of tea."

Summer frowned slightly. "But you promised me."

"And I'll keep my promise. I'm just saying, it's going to be hard for me at first."

"Xavier, if you're doing this just for—"

Xavier held up his hand, interrupting her. "I'm doing this now for you. Eventually, I hope I will be doing it because it is best for us. I know that your faith teaches you that it is wrong to marry an unbeliever. Well, I'm not an unbeliever. I believe in God. I've believed for a long time. I just don't follow Him like most Christians."

"What do you mean when you say you believe?"

That was a question that threw Xavier off guard, and he wasn't sure how to answer it. "Um, I believe there is a God, and I believe He helps us, that He's protecting us."

Summer nodded. That was a good start. She could work with that. She didn't want to get into a heavy theological discussion with Xavier, so she decided that she would talk about their planned evening together.

Summer suddenly heard the first few bars of Dave Brubeck's *Take Five*, recognizing it as Xavier's ring tone on his personal phone. Xavier pulled the phone from his pants pocket, checked it, then hit a button and slipped the phone back into his pocket.

"Who was that?" Summer asked.

"Work calling. They can't handle these emergency days off."

"So, why don't you call them back? I can wait."

"No. I'm not going to handle work while I'm here with you. Whatever's going on can wait until I get back. It isn't every day that I'm in Martha's Vineyard with the most amazing girl in the world."

Summer smiled, a wide one that drew a smile from Xavier. "I

hope I can continue to make you smile like that."

The waitress, who looked at least sixty years of age, made small talk and then took their orders. Summer and Xavier took the waitress's recommendations and ordered wild salmon for her, and wild striped bass for him.

The waitress had barely left the table before Summer heard *Take Five* again. Xavier again reached into his pocket, checked the caller ID, and then silenced his phone without answering.

"Why don't you just take the call?" Summer said, smiling. "It's okay. I did kinda drag you away from your job at the last minute, so handle your business."

"Okay." Xavier stood. "I'll be right back." Clutching his phone tightly, he left the table and headed toward the exit.

Summer's eyebrows furrowed. It was strange that Xavier left the table to call the office. He had never done that before. It caused Summer to think further, and she realized another weird fact: Xavier almost never accepted business calls on his personal phone. She guessed he could have left his business phone in the car or at home, but she doubted it. *Perhaps I'm being too cynical*, she thought.

When Xavier returned to the table a few minutes later, Summer noticed that his visage had changed. The casual observer might not have noticed, but Summer recognized it immediately. His perturbation showed in the slight crease in his brow, the diminished confidence with which he walked, and the way he avoided directly looking at her for more than five seconds. His cell phone was no longer in his hand.

"That was Joe at the office," Xavier explained. "He's covering a meeting for me and wanted to know where my notes were."

"Hmm." Summer wanted to believe him, but she could not get past his leaving the table to make a phone call. He had never done that in front of her, and it was strange that he would start now. "Why did he call you on your personal phone? Where's your work phone?"

"Probably in the car," Xavier answered, shrugging. "Anyway, uh—"

"Why did you need to leave the table to make your call? You

never did that before." Summer pressed. She realized she was getting into tricky territory interrogating Xavier, but she hoped he would have some answers that would settle her mind. But until she got answers, the questions would be eating away at her.

Xavier's eyes shifted back and forth before he answered. "I was pretty sure I'd have to ball this guy out for calling me on my personal phone on my day off, and I didn't want to do it in the restaurant and embarrass us in front of all these people."

Xavier was either an expert liar or he was telling the truth, and Summer wasn't yet sure which. "I thought you didn't give your office your personal phone number. You told me that once. That's why you always carry your work phone. So, why would they suddenly know your personal phone?"

Xavier took a drink of water before he answered. "I'm sure my assistant has my personal number. She probably gave it to Joe."

"But why? Where's your work phone?"

Xavier looked at her steadily for a few seconds before he said, "Summer, I know you're a reporter, and you're trained to ask questions. But I'm not one of your stories."

"No, you're not." Summer lowered her voice. "But you're the man I'm about to give my heart and my body to, and I need to know if I can trust you."

Xavier frowned. "So, you think I'm lying?"

Summer extended her hand, palm raised upward. "Give me your phone."

"What?"

"Give me your phone."

Xavier scoffed. "So now you want to check up on me?"

"An honest man would be giving me that phone without hesitation."

"So you think I'm dishonest?" Xavier said the words as if the concept was as far away from him as the next galaxy.

Summer pulled back her hand. "You know what my pastor once told me? He said that in any relationship, no matter how close the

people are to one another and how much they trust one another, some-times things are going to be vague and unclear. And one party will need clarity and will ask questions so that she gets that clarity. Now, a husband who cares about his wife, loves her, and is being truthful and honest with her, will want her to have that clarity, without being defen-sive, or without making her feel that she is wrong for needing clarity. Do you see what I'm saying? One of the things I learned in journalism is this: if you want to know if someone is telling the truth, ask him a lot of questions. Even repeat some of the questions, but ask them in a different way. An honest person will never mind answering any of your questions, and will rarely contradict himself. But a liar will avoid answering, or give incomplete answers, or be very uncomfortable in answering or giving up information to prove himself."

"There's nothing unclear here, Summer. I got a call from work. I didn't want to get loud in the restaurant. That's it."

"Fine." Summer extended her hand again. "Give me your phone. If the call history says your job called, all this is squashed, and I will owe you a big time apology."

"Okay, y'know what? No, I'm not gonna give you my phone. And you know why? Because I don't want to set a precedent where you start checking on everything I say and everything I do. There's sup-posed to be trust in a relationship, Summer."

Summer leaned back. His refusal struck her deeply. She didn't consider herself the smartest woman in the world, but she knew when a man was lying. Dealing with the men in her old Atlanta neighbor-hood, in college, and Mark Battman, she had had enough practice with men who embellish the truth. She gathered her purse and stood. The waitress had not yet brought their food to the table.

"Where are you going?" Xavier asked, still seated.

"I'm leaving." Summer had no idea where she would go, and she would have to take the bus or a taxi to the theater. But she knew she didn't want to stay with Xavier.

"Why?"

"Because you are a liar." Summer said the words so sharply that

the couple at the next table peered at them awkwardly.

Xavier stood. "Summer, c'mon. I'm not lying to you."

"That was Jada, wasn't it?"

"No, it wasn't."

"Prove it."

They both stood, glaring at each other. They had now drawn the attention of patrons at three other tables.

"Let's go outside." Xavier fished in his pocket for some money for a tip for the waitress.

"No. You either prove it now, or I leave here, alone."

"Summer, this is crazy. I paid 1,200 to come here."

"Consider that the cost of your lies, because it'll be a cold day in hell before you get any of this—" she slapped her behind "—tonight!" Summer marched toward the exit.

Xavier dropped a few bucks on the table and tried to chase Summer. However, his foot got caught between the leg of his chair and the chair behind him. He went down, seeing the edge of his neighbor's table coming up at him fast before his world turned dark.

Summer turned when she heard a thud, a crash, and then screams. She saw Xavier lying on the restaurant floor, his leg still caught between two chairs, blood draining down his forehead from a gash somewhere on the side of his head. "Oh, Jesus!" She ran to him, knelt down, tried to stir him, but there was no response.

Having heard the screams, the manager ran over quickly, then ordered the waitress standing behind him to call 911. The waitress ran quickly to the rear of the restaurant. The manager then held out his hand to stop Summer, who had just removed her phone from her purse and was about to dial 911 herself.

"Let us call from a landline," the manager said calmly. "They'll arrive quicker that way."

A man in his mid-fifties walked over from another table and regarded a distressed Summer, who was about to reach for Xavier and cradle him in his arms. "Don't move him," he said to Summer. "I'm a doctor." He knelt down closer to Xavier, shooing Summer back a

few inches so that he could get closer. "Anyone have a flashlight?" he yelled.

Within a few seconds, a woman had whipped out her cell phone and activated a sharp white light. She handed the phone to the doctor, who leaned close to check for breathing, and then gently pulled open Xavier's eyelids and shone the light into them. The doctor nodded confidently, then gave the phone back to the woman.

"Is he going to be okay?" Summer asked.

The doctor stood. "Well, he's not going to die, if that's what you mean. Beyond that, I can't say. He'll need to go to the hospital, get checked out for skull fracture, neuropathy, get a CT. His pupils were round and reactive, so I doubt there's any brain damage. It may be a serious injury, or he may have just gotten his bell rung. Hard to say." He looked up at the manager. "Get me a couple of plastic bags."

The manager turned and hurried away toward the kitchen. When he returned a minute later, he had two plastic bags in his hands. The doctor took the bags, then grabbed a clean napkin from a nearby table. He wrapped his hand in one bag, then gripped the napkin with it and applied it to Xavier's wound, giving it firm pressure. "Got to stop this bleeding."

Summer looked on, helpless, gravely concerned, and wracked with guilt. *I tried to leave suddenly. I made him chase me. This is all my fault. Lord, I hope this is not serious.*

Blind hope made way for earnest prayer. Summer closed her eyes and spoke to the Lord for the first time since Xavier declared his love for her in her apartment. She didn't care who was looking. She needed the Lord now more than ever.

When she opened her eyes after saying a short prayer, she heard the whine of an ambulance. The manager worked on clearing an aisle so that the EMTs could bring a stretcher into the restaurant. The doctor continued to apply pressure to the wound, while Summer walked to the other side of him and started to rifle through Xavier's pockets. She felt the need to explain. "I need to drive his car to the hospital," she said to the doctor, who accepted her explanation with a nod, checked the

napkin, and then continued to apply pressure.

Summer pulled Xavier's wallet, car keys, and cell phone from his pockets. She stuffed the wallet and car keys in her purse, but hesitated with the phone. She could not resist the urge to check the cell phone to see who had called him earlier. Unfortunately, the phone was locked. She checked his pockets again for another cell phone. None.

Frustrated, she stepped to the side to allow the EMTs to approach Xavier. The doctor identified himself, then gave a rundown of his findings to the EMTs. He then used the other plastic bag to help remove the bloody napkin and the first bag, then stuffed the napkin and the first bag into it, twisted it shut, and handed it to an EMT as he stepped away from Xavier.

Both Summer and the doctor stood by and watched as the EMTs examined Xavier, then fitted him with a neck collar and loaded him onto a stretcher with a vacuum mattress. While the EMTs strapped Xavier to the mattress, Summer turned to the doctor.

"Thank you for your help," she said, shaking the doctor's hand.

"My pleasure," the doctor responded. "Glad I could help."

Summer followed the EMTs out the door. On the way out, she grabbed the $25 that Xavier had left on the table, added to it another $180 from her purse, then handed it to the manager and said, "Here, this should cover my meal and the meal for the doctor and his party. Keep whatever's left."

The manager nodded his head in acknowledgment and watched as Summer and the EMTs left the restaurant.

***

Summer felt she had no other choice but to drive Xavier's rented Jeep to the hospital, despite the fact she had a suspended license. She drove carefully, so as not to arouse the suspicion of police. On a hunch, she looked in the glove compartment. She found Xavier's work cell phone there. She shook her head, left the cell phone there, and

closed the glove compartment.

When she arrived at the hospital, she faced a long wait as the doctors and nurses worked on Xavier in the treatment room. She sat alone inside of a plush, modern waiting room with huge windows that offered a picturesque view of the greenery just beyond the hospital grounds. She checked her watch. It was 2:30 p.m. She had just ninety minutes until her interview with Sheila Nathan, the subject of her story. She pulled her cell phone out of her purse and checked it. She saw that there were several missed calls from Meg, the camerawoman, as well as from the assignment desk. She hadn't heard the phone ring, a fact that she quickly blamed on the poor cell phone reception on several areas of the island.

Summer dialed Meg first. "Meg, you called me?"

"Yeah. Have you heard what's going on?"

"What do you mean?"

"The assignment desk has been trying to reach you. They're going to move your story up to the six o'clock newscast."

Summer was shocked into a few seconds of silence. It was her understanding that the story would air the next morning. "Uh, why are they changing it?"

"I think they need a filler for the C block. Plus, a couple of the syndicated entertainment shows are also covering the festival tonight."

"Meg, that's only three and a half hours from now. We don't have enough time."

"Sure we do. If you get back to the hotel now, we can work out most of the edits. Then, when you do the interview with Nathan, we can work in that footage and then get the file to the station."

"Meg, that's cutting it pretty close. The EP's going to want to see the piece by 5:30. Maybe by the time the graphics people get done with it, it'll be just ready to air by the C block."

"I know, but we've been trying to reach you for two hours."

Summer sighed and started pacing the floor. "Meg, I'm not sure I can make it. My boyfriend's in the hospital."

"What happened?"

"We were having lunch, and he stood up, slipped and hit his head on the table. I'm at the hospital now."

"Your boyfriend's here at the Vineyard? Did you come with him?"

Summer didn't feel like explaining. "Long story."

"Do you think you'll be able to make it by four o'clock with Nathan?"

"I don't know. I'm waiting to hear from the doctor."

"Summer, if you don't get the interview with Nathan, your entire story is no good. And the festival starts at five, so you won't have another opportunity with her."

Summer thought quickly. "Why don't you handle the interview?"

There was a short silence on the line before Meg answered, "You're kidding me, right?"

"No. I'll give you the questions. Just ask them and record her answering. I'll do the VOs later. We did this all the time in radio. When I get freed up from the hospital, we'll work on the final editing."

"Nathan's not going to want to talk to a camerawoman."

"What would she care? There's no other station following this story. She's getting free publicity. What's she going to do? Turn it down?"

"She was expecting you, is all. Not me."

"Meg, please handle this for me. I'll owe you big time."

"You bet you will."

Once Summer had finished talking to Meg, she dialed the station and told them the story would be ready by 5:30. She hoped that she was telling the truth. It all depended on when the doctors would report on Xavier's condition, and when she would be able to see him.

She sat down and stuffed her phone back into her purse. She noticed a red light rapidly blinking on Xavier's phone, meaning that his phone was receiving a call in silent mode. Curiosity got the best of her, and she pulled his phone out of her purse and checked who was calling. What she saw did not surprise or shock her, but it would completely change her approach with Xavier.

The phone listed the name of the caller as "Sweetie." But the

photo attached to the name was clearly that of Jada Hardy.

CHAPTER NINE

Jada huffed angrily as she ended yet another unanswered phone call. Frustrated, she sat on the couch in the lounge at Visual Notions and tried to calm herself down before she headed back to her office. She had been trying to reach Xavier for the last two hours. Xavier had told her that morning that he would be going out of town for an important business trip and would not be able to be reached by phone. But Jada's contacts at the gas company quickly confirmed that was not true. Xavier had taken a day off, but it had nothing to do with the company.

Jada wondered if she had made a big mistake. She knew she would never be able to compete with Xavier's love for Summer. Nonetheless, she agreed to allow him to come over to her house two nights ago and let him cry on her shoulder about Summer's indifference toward him, after which she allowed him to spend the night with her. When they woke up the next morning, Xavier told Jada he could no longer deal with being in limbo, and wanted to resume his relationship with her.

Jada wanted to believe this, especially since her self-esteem could not handle being rejected by two men in the course of one month. Mark had finally dumped her two days earlier after his wife found out about their affair. Jada guessed that a disgruntled employee whom

Mark had fired for stealing decided to get payback by calling his wife and urging her to pay an unexpected visit to Mark in the office some night after seven. She did, catching Jada and Mark in the act. She moved out of the house the next day, leaving Mark wondering if his marriage was over.

Now, Xavier was lying about being on a business trip, and refusing to answer her calls. She knew in her gut that Xavier was with Summer. That woman had been the bane of her existence ever since she started to date Xavier. Jada wasn't in love with Xavier, nor was she that jealous of Summer. But Jada Hardy had an agenda, and Summer was just getting in the way. A gold digger to the core, Jada was determined not to lose. Now that Mark was no longer in the picture, Xavier was her only meal ticket now.

She walked back to her office, greeting several employees along the way. She knew what she had to do to stop Summer in her tracks. All she needed to do was get access to Mark's cell phone.

***

It was a little after 4 p.m. when Summer was allowed to see Xavier. The doctor explained that his head injury was only scalp level, that there was no spinal cord injury or damage to the skull or the brain, much to Summer's relief.

When she walked into the ER treatment room, Xavier was sitting alone on the side of the exam table, still wearing his original clothes, except for his shirt, which had been replaced by a hospital T-shirt. A gauze bandage was wrapped around his head, and his eyes were bloodshot.

"How do you feel?" Summer asked as she walked in the room.

"Hell of a headache," Xavier said. "Just waiting for the doc to get me a prescription, and I'm out of here."

Summer found a chair in a corner of the room and settled herself into it. "I'm sorry about what happened."

"Why are you sorry? I just got clumsy, is all."

"Yeah, trying to run after me."

"Don't put this on you. It's not your fault." Xavier placed his hand on the back of his head, almost as if trying to soothe a pain back there. "The doc tells me you got my wallet and stuff."

"Yeah." Summer reached into her purse. "Didn't want anything to go missing. And I drove your car over here." She produced his keys, cell phone, and wallet and handed them to him. Xavier stuffed his keys and wallet in his pocket, but hesitated with his cell phone as if he was about to check his calls. When he saw Summer studying him, he slipped the phone into his side pocket.

"Yes, she called," Summer blurted out, staring at him blankly. "Several times."

Xavier tittered awkwardly, then said, "So, you checked my phone, huh?"

Summer continued a nonresponsive stare.

Xavier shook his head in disgust, as if Summer's violation of his privacy trumped his lie about Jada calling him repeatedly over the past two hours. "I can't believe you did that."

"I can't believe you're still messing with Jada."

"Well, what do you expect?" Xavier said sharply. "I hadn't heard from you. I thought we were done. I got back together with Jada because it was clear you wanted nothing to do with me."

Summer would not accept any more excuses. "X, I love you. I really do. But I can't trust you, and that's big with me. What you've shown me is that you can be in love with me—madly in love with me, according to you—and yet go off and sleep with another woman. What kind of man does that? I can't live my life always wondering if you're out there being intimate with another woman. I need a man with integrity. I need a man I can trust. And you're not that man."

"I *am* in love with you."

"I believe that. I believe there is something emotional, even sexual that draws you to me. But you're not ready for a commitment that requires you to be faithful to me, that gives you no option to go off with

another woman when things get rough."

Summer left enough time for him to respond. When he didn't, she stood up. "I booked you a room at the Sunview Hotel. I programmed the directions in your GPS."

Xavier avoided her eyes. "So, it's like that? I almost get killed, and you're just going to leave me be?"

"I'm supposed to be doing an interview right now, but I stayed here with you," Summer snapped. "What more do you want me to do?"

"You can realize that I love you, and I don't love Jada."

"I love you, too. But unfortunately, that doesn't fix everything." Summer turned toward the exit.

"Where are you going?"

"I have a story due to the station in about ninety minutes."

"Let me drive you."

"Actually, I'd rather you didn't. I'll take the bus." Summer moved closer to the exit before she turned to him. "I'm glad you're okay. I really am. And I'll check in on you. But I can't see you anymore."

Summer left without another word, leaving Xavier in the room with his thoughts and regrets. Once again, he would have to figure out how to win Summer back. But unlike before, he had no clue how to go about doing it.

***

Buses in Oak Bluffs ran about an hour apart, so Summer did not arrive at her hotel room until 5:15 p.m., nowhere near enough time to finish the edits and get the story to the station by 5:30 p.m. She called the assignment editor and ashamedly told him that the story would not be arriving for the six o'clock newscast, but that she would surely have it ready by the eleven o'clock. She blamed the over-zealous producer that decided to move her story up twelve hours before it was due.

By the time she and Meg finished with the edits, it was 8 p.m.

After she had uploaded the digital footage and the raw footage to the station's control room using her wireless hotspot, Meg called it a night and headed back to her room. Summer was finally left alone to think about Xavier. She wondered if telling him she didn't want to see him anymore was a little too harsh, even though it was a flat-out lie. She knew it was a lie when she said it, but she wanted to set a standard and force Xavier to realize that he couldn't keep crossing the line with her. Jada should never have been in the picture anyway, so why was he still dealing with her? Or was she responsible because she cast him away and into Jada's arms? She could have reciprocated immediately when Xavier poured out his heart in her apartment that night. She could have responded, given him some indication as to where her heart was leaning. Since she did not do that, he didn't want to risk being alone, so he dialed up Jada again.

No, no, no, that was not her cross to bear. It was not her fault that Xavier had strayed back to Jada. No, if Xavier loved her—really, really loved her—he would not have resumed a relationship with the woman who had split them apart in the first place.

She ate one of the two slices of veggie-pepperoni pizza left over from her editing session with Meg, then lay down on the bed, having no intention to go to sleep yet, but dozing off anyway until sometime after 10 p.m. She wanted to stay awake to see if her story made it on the C block of the eleven o'clock broadcast, which she would watch through a live stream on her laptop. But Summer was so weary that she finally gave in, pulling off all her clothes and climbing into bed. Her flight back to Boston was leaving at 10 a.m., so she had plenty of time to rest before calling it quits on her first journalistic foray to the Vineyard.

***

Summer and Meg were back at WIDN by 11:30 the next morning, a Friday. Prior to leaving the Vineyard, she called Xavier to make sure

he was okay. She made sure she called while at the airport, just before her flight, so she would have a ready excuse to keep the call short in case Xavier tried to sweet-talk his way back into her good graces. But he seemed angry, as if sometime during the night, he realized he had spent almost $1,500 and had only a couple of glasses of water, a knot on the head, and a lonely hotel bed to show for it.

Summer came in through the rear staff entrance of WIDN and made her way to the basement newsroom. The room was huge, with a maze of half-height cubicles manned by reporters and producers, and glass-enclosed offices around the perimeter. Flat-screen TVs hung in various places around the newsroom, tuned mostly to station programming, but some tuned to competing stations. A four-sided digital clock hung in the center of the room, providing local time to all four corners of the room, much like the monitors that hang from the ceiling at stadium events.

Summer's desk was in a far corner of the room, on the opposite corner from the hallway that led to the studio and the control room. When she approached her desk, she noticed that the name tag of the previous occupant had been removed from her cube, but her name tag had yet to be affixed. She opened an empty file drawer and put her purse and laptop inside. As she closed it, she noticed the note on her desk:

Need to see you. Pete.

Peter Haag was one of three assistant news directors at WIDN. Scott had hired him away from the executive producer position at another local station, mostly by promising Pete that he would have more control over the content of daily newscasts. Pete was the one who had shown Summer around the station on her first day, and gave her a very thorough orientation on the operations of the newsroom. Pete seemed like a competent, professional journalist from whom Summer could learn a lot. But when she walked into his office and noticed his taut expression, she immediately knew something was not right.

"Hey, Pete." Summer greeted nervously. "You wanted to see me?"

Pete, bespectacled, with salt and pepper hair and a gray suit that

hung much too loosely on his rangy body, motioned Summer to the chair in front of his desk. He closed the door to his office and sat at his desk. "I understand you had some problems with the story."

Summer sighed hard. "Yes. I had a friend join me for lunch. He got in an accident, and we weren't able to get the story in by the six o'clock."

"Hmm. But my concern is not that the story was late. My concern is the quality of the story."

"What do you mean?"

"Well, I don't want to mince words here, but the story was ... well, terrible."

The word *terrible* stole her breath. *Couldn't he have been a little more tactful?* A few seconds went by before she responded. "I don't understand."

"Well, the questions weren't engaging, the voice overs were a bit passive, and the editing seemed a bit rushed. Bottom line is, we didn't air the piece."

Summer avoided Pete's steely glare. "Sorry to hear that."

"Well, so am I. And to be honest, I was ready to chalk that up to newbie inexperience. But then, we have another issue."

"Which is?"

"Did you try to extort $15,000 from your previous employer?"

If Pete's calling her piece terrible was a haymaker, this one was a sucker punch. During the ensuing ten seconds of silence, Summer wondered how Pete had found out about her deal with Mark. Was it a reference call to Mark that revealed it? She knew it would be of no benefit to her to deny it. "Well, it wasn't exactly extortion ... ."

Pete punched a few keys on his computer keyboard and then turned up the volume on his desktop speakers. Then, Summer heard the exchange between Mark and herself with unmistakable clarity. As she listened, she wished she had given the $15,000 check back to Mark. Maybe he wouldn't have exposed her like this.

Pete torturously played the recording until it was done. He then glared at Summer and said, "I know you finessed it so that you won't

have any legal liability. But Mark Battman is threatening to release this recording to the media and to the police."

Summer frowned. If Mark was going that far, he either told his wife about his affair with Jada, or she found out some other way. In any event, her leverage over Mark was history, and he had turned the tables. "What does he want to keep that from happening?"

"He wants two things." Pete reached down below his desk and re-moved a file. "One, he wants his $15,000 returned to him. And two—" Pete removed a page from the file and pushed it across the desk to Summer.

Summer took the paper and perused it for a few seconds before she said, "You're suspending me?"

"Yes, indefinitely." Pete's voice became more monotone and detached the more he spoke. "This still needs to be reviewed by legal, but if I were you, I'd make other plans for employment."

That was clearly the punch that put Summer flat on her back, out cold, dead to the world. "Pete, I'll return the money. I promise. But please don't do this. What's the basis for this?"

"It's a violation of the morals clause in your contract. If Mark releases that recording, it could be embarrassing to this station and detrimental to our brand."

Summer went ballistic. "Embarrassing? Detrimental? How? No station is going to care about that tape. It's not news. That tape doesn't prove much, and nobody in this town knows that much about me to even care whether I did it or not. Mark's bluffing. He's just using you to get me fired. I'll gladly return the money. But this is not worth firing me for."

Pete delivered his next sentence with the stoicism of an image hewn in stone. "That might be true, if you were a halfway decent reporter." Pete stood, but remained behind his desk. "There are many great reporters who want your job. We can't take a risk on someone who mixes business with pleasure and then throws together a story and expects us to put it on the air."

Pride and desperation battled within Summer, each vying to take

her over and direct her thoughts and actions. Pride eventually won, directing her to remain quiet and still so that she could leave that room with some dignity intact. But she knew this was not over. She still had a card to play.

"Does Scott know about this?"

"Scott was the one who signed off on it."

Summer looked at the bottom of the Notice of Suspension. Sure enough, Scott Iverson's signature was there. *He couldn't even suspend me himself. He had to get Pete to do his dirty work.*

Pete nodded toward the paper. "I need you to sign that. And I'll need your access card and all the equipment you've been issued."

Summer angrily grabbed a pen from a mug labeled *Do It* that served as a makeshift pen holder. She signed at the bottom of the page, then pushed the document back toward Pete.

Pete examined the document, then said, "The advance that Scott gave you? We've stopped payment on it. So don't bother cashing it."

Summer stood and headed back into the newsroom. The reporters and producers working on the 5 p.m. newscast were so focused, they had no idea what was going on. Once at her desk, she removed her access card from her purse and the laptop from her desk drawer and handed them to Pete. Without another word, she turned and headed for the exit, trying to maintain her professional demeanor.

Once she cleared the building, she turned right and walked down a few doors to the office park deli. The deli was quite crowded, so no one noticed her as she slipped past them and headed straight for the women's restroom. Fortunately, no one was in there, so she quickly retreated to a stall. She locked the door, dropped her purse on the floor, and allowed her steadily brewing emotions to have their way. The pangs of disappointment, fear, and anguish came together, grew within her, and overwhelmed her, forcing her to double over in the stall and sob, eventually migrating to a full-blown wail that could be heard well beyond the bathroom doors.

***

Sunday morning

It was rare for Lenny to arrive at church late, but Trinee had not been ready when he went to pick her up, so he had to wait for her. That was one of the things that annoyed him about Trinee when they were dating: she never did anything on time.

There was not a cloud in the sky, no discernable breeze, and the ninety-two degree air was stagnant and thick. Lenny eschewed his normal suit and tie, opting instead for a polyester sateen dress shirt, black slacks, and black oxfords. He dressed Lenny Jr. in a similar outfit. He wished he had more input into what Trinee decided to wear. The halter top, formfitting, leopard print spandex mini dress that she wore was more suitable for a night of club hopping, not a church. The only thing that made the outfit slightly more respectable was the crocheted shawl she had draped over her shoulders. Lenny did not protest, as he knew that Trinee was not a regular churchgoer, and her outfit was likely the classiest one she owned.

A few heads turned when Lenny, Trinee, and Lenny Jr. got their programs from the ushers and were directed to a seat near the middle of the sanctuary. They wondered about the petite, dark-complexioned girl with rainbow-colored hair and two studs in her lower lip and several on each ear. *Is she Lenny's girlfriend? Whatever happened to that very pretty girl that came to church with him weeks earlier? She looked like a nice girl. Don't know about this one.*

Pastor Malachi took to the pulpit about ninety minutes later, delivering a sermon entitled *When God seems to have left you alone*, taking his text from Lamentations 3:31–32: *"For men are not cast off by the Lord forever. Though he brings grief, he will show compassion, so great is his unfailing love."* His preaching was simple, yet profound and poetic, his voice perfectly orchestrated between thunderous highs that sent the worshippers into a praise frenzy, to lows that engendered contemplation and deep reflection. To this crowd, the style of preaching was just as important as the message, and they responded exuberantly to both.

When he had finished with the sermon, Pastor Malachi issued an altar call, which he did after most sermons. A few people trickled to the front, standing in front of the pulpit, ready to receive whatever blessing was available to them. One teenager was going off to college in a few weeks and wanted the Lord's blessing on his trip and his studies. A middle-aged woman wanted prayer for her wayward children who had been consumed by the streets. A young woman wanted prayer for a new job. And, without any prodding on Lenny's part, Trinee left her seat and approached the altar. She whispered in the pastor's ear two prayer requests: that the Lord would bless her with the right mind to stay out of prison and be a good mother to her son; and that the Lord would, as the pastor had quoted during his sermon, restore what the devil had stolen from her.

She never mentioned what she wanted God to restore, but she was specifically referring to Lenny.

***

Lenny kept his usual routine of taking his son to dinner on Sundays, and allowed Trinee to tag along. He chose Portland's, a restaurant on East Broad Street that served American cuisine. He liked the place because it was small and obscure and wouldn't have the after-church crowd like most of the chains. It had a robust kid's meal, and Lenny Jr. had raved about it on a previous visit.

They were seated at a booth near the rear of the restaurant. Now that she was no longer in church, Trinee removed her shawl, revealing a significant amount of cleavage. Lenny looked at her for a second before shame forced him to turn his eyes away. There was a time when Lenny would have gawked at her like a sightseeing tourist. Now, the dichotomy between enjoying the view and knowing that his eyes shouldn't dwell created such awkwardness that Lenny didn't know how to respond.

"You okay?" Trinee said, dropping her shawl on the bench next to

her.

"Why did you wear that to church?" Lenny asked, trying hard to look in her eyes.

"You said that the pastor didn't like women wearing pants to church. This is the only halfway decent dress I got."

"So, you thought it was a good option to wear your bust-out, thigh-baring, man-magnet dress?"

"Jesus said come as you are, right?"

"Actually, Jesus never said that. But even if he did, that's not what he meant."

"Your pastor wasn't complaining."

"Not then and there, no. But later, the next time I see him, he's gonna tell me—" Lenny tried his best to imitate his pastor's Southern drawl "—'Now, son, I know you ain't got no control over this. But if you gonna be bringing that young lady to church with you, you need to teach her how to dress proper.'"

"There was girls in that church with shorter dresses on than mine, so don't front."

"Maybe so. But you ain't them. And if you're serious about changing your life for the Lord, then you need to think about that."

Trinee skipped the subject. "I hear your auntie's having a cookout on Wednesday."

"Yeah, she is."

"Are you going?"

"I was thinking about it."

"Going alone?"

"Not if you let me take Junior."

"Other than Junior?"

Lenny knew what she was implying. But he had already decided to take his aunt's advice and invite Summer to the cookout, if he could reach her. He had called Summer on Friday afternoon and got nothing but her voice mail. When he arrived at work that day, he checked the gate security log and saw that Summer's access card had been used to open the gate shortly after 3 p.m. So, he knew she had arrived home

safely from the Vineyard. He figured she was busy with her newfound career, so he avoided blowing up her phone.

But now he was getting worried. He hadn't spoken to Summer since that Wednesday night after she had arrived at her hotel room in the Vineyard. Judging by the few weeks he had known her, it seemed uncharacteristic for her not to call for so long.

But that was not the immediate problem at hand. How would he tell Trinee that he had decided to take Summer to the cookout instead of her? He surmised that either now or later Trinee would find out about his decision to take Summer, so he might as well tell her now.

"I *am* taking someone, yes," Lenny confessed.

"Is it that girl you brought to my house the other day?"

"Yes. Summer is her name."

Trinee leaned back and gave Lenny a look as if to say you're giving up all this ghetto fabulousness to hook up with the bourgeois uptown chick. "So, are you dating her?"

"No. We're just friends."

"So, why are you going to take your friend to the cookout, and not the mother of your son?"

"C'mon, Trinee. It's not like nobody's going to invite you. I'm sure your mother will extend you an invitation."

"It's not the same."

"Not the same as what? You and I are just friends, and I'm not ready for that to move into another level yet."

"Even though I've changed? I went to church with you. I even came up for prayer and stood in front of the altar, with all those people looking at me."

"Yeah. With that outfit on, I was hoping you didn't fall out under the Spirit. Because if you did, something else would have fallen out."

"Well, I said *I* changed. My wardrobe still needs some work."

"Here's the real, Trinee," Lenny said. "Just because you start something, don't mean you're gonna finish it. You just started to make some changes in your life. Doesn't mean you're gonna stick with it."

"So, you have no confidence in me?"

"It's not that I don't have confidence. It's that I don't want to make a commitment to being anything but friends until you have reached a certain place in your life."

"You know what? I think that's a crock of—" Trinee cut herself off, not wanting to curse while her son was at the table. "I think you like this girl, and you're just stringing me along until you see what's up with her. You always did like them Barbie doll types."

Trinee had limited book smarts, but she could be quite perceptive at times. She was right. Lenny couldn't deny it, not with God as his witness. But to spare her feelings and maintain as much harmony as possible, Lenny dared not admit it. He opted to stare humbly at a corner of the restaurant and remain silent.

"That's okay." Trinee reached over and pinched Lenny Jr.'s cheek. "Junior still loves me, don't you Junior?"

Lenny Jr. smiled, which was the best response anyone would get out of him, as the coloring book and crayons that the waitress had given him completely consumed his attention.

Trinee leaned back in her seat and met Lenny's silence with her own. In the space of a few seconds of silence, she made up her mind to meet this Summer chick. She needed to let Summer know that if she planned on pushing up on Lenny and taking him off the market, Trinee would unleash the full force of her indignation.

It was a meeting that Trinee knew would not be cordial.

***

They ate quickly and made small talk before Lenny drove Trinee back to her mother's apartment. Once he had dropped off Trinee, Lenny decided to head to Summer's apartment complex to see if anyone had heard from her.

Lenny stopped at a red traffic light, then leaned back and spoke to his son. "Before we go home, Daddy's gonna pay a visit to Auntie Summer, okay?"

The bright smile on his son's face surprised Lenny. Junior had only spent one afternoon with Summer, and already he was in love with her.

When Lenny arrived, he pulled into one of the parking spaces adjacent to the gate house. "Wait in the car. I'll be right back," he told Lenny Jr. He rolled down all of the windows, then got out of the car and headed to the gate house. The weekend attendant, a short, stocky guy who, when seated, could barely see over the window sill of the gatehouse, was typing something on the computer when Lenny approached.

"Hey, Andy."

"Hey, Len," Andy responded. "What you doin' here on your day off?"

"You know a girl named Summer Maldonado? Lives here?"

"Don't know the name."

"Tall black girl. Long black hair. Great body. Sorta exotic looking."

"Man, you just described half the girls in this joint."

"Okay, can you check the gate logs from yesterday and today and tell me if her name shows up?"

Andy hunched over the computer and punched in quite a few keystrokes. Finally, he looked up and said, "Summer Maldonado, right?"

"Yeah."

"Naw, she ain't showin' up."

"Check the visitors log."

"Nothin' showing up there, either."

"Okay. Look up her apartment number for me."

"You not getting' me in any trouble here, are you?"

"No. I just want to check in on her. I see her a lot during my shift, but I haven't seen her lately. Just want to make sure she's alright."

Andy typed a few keystrokes. "Spell her last name for me."

Lenny spelled it.

Another few keystrokes, and Andy had the information. "She's in building B. Apartment 323."

"Thanks, man. You mind keeping me off the visitor's log? I don't want the bosses to start asking questions."

"Not a problem. Just so you know, you now owe me a favor."

"Got your back, bro. My son's in the car. Could you keep an eye on him for me? I'll be just a few minutes."

"You got it."

"Thanks again."

Lenny walked through the pedestrian entrance and toward Building B. When he reached the lobby, he pulled out his cell phone and dialed Summer. Again, the call went straight to voicemail. He took the stairs two at a time until he got to the third floor. Summer's apartment was down the hall, the next to the last unit before the hallway ended. He put his ear to the door before he knocked, but heard nothing. He then began to knock, his first knock a gentle one, then the subsequent ones becoming progressively louder until, by the fourth round, he was sure he would draw the attention of a neighbor. Still, no answer at the door.

Lenny headed back down to the lobby and walked down a short corridor toward the rear of the building. He looked through the glass door of the exercise room, but saw only a hulking, muscular man doing crunches on a workbench. Lenny continued out the rear door and into the courtyard, where he noticed two people, one reading a book, and the other playing with her toddler near the fountain. Since the two people seemed preoccupied, he walked further into the courtyard, turned, and looked up at the third floor at Summer's balcony. He noticed that the blinds had been drawn at the balcony door, as well as all the windows. To Lenny, it looked as if Summer was not at home. Though the log showed she had arrived home Friday afternoon, the log did not keep track of exits.

Lenny gave up and walked back through Building B to the gate house. Andy was standing outside the gate house, leaning on the wall, smoking a cigarette.

"Thanks for your help, man," Lenny said, heading toward his car. "Hey listen, could you continue to check the gate logs and let me know

if Summer's name shows up?"

"No problem," Andy responded, tufts of smoke pouring from his mouth as he spoke. "Your number in the computer?"

"Yeah. Thanks again." Lenny got into his car and looked back at Lenny Jr. "How you doin', Buddy?"

"Good," Lenny Jr. responded. "Did you see Miss Summer? Is she gonna come with us?"

"Naw, man. She's not home." Lenny said those words, convinced that they were true. But it didn't ease his worry, and he knew he wouldn't be able to rest easy until he knew what was going on with Summer.

CHAPTER TEN

Jada had fallen asleep watching an old movie on a retro TV channel when the sound of her doorbell awakened her. It rang over and over, as if someone was constantly pressing it. Jada climbed out of her bed, wearing nothing but her panties, went to the bedroom window, cracked the blinds slightly, and looked down.

Xavier. And he did not look happy.

So he wouldn't break her doorbell from the constant pressing, she cracked the window, yelled "I'm coming," and then padded downstairs. She unlocked and opened the door wide, hiding behind it as Xavier stormed in carrying enough heat to melt copper. She closed the door, and he saw her, then quickly looked away. "Go get some clothes on," he demanded.

Jada frowned. *That was new*. Usually by now, Xavier would be pouncing on her like a puma in heat. Nonetheless, without complaint, she complied, heading up the stairs, then came back down a few minutes later wearing a robe. She moved to the couch and sat down, hoping that Xavier would sit down as well.

He didn't.

"Let me tell you a true story," Xavier started, his glare never wavering from her eyes. "Yesterday, I got a call from an agent friend of mine. He happens to be Summer's agent. He tells me that he found

The Beauty of Summer

out that Summer was placed on suspension pending termination. When I asked him why, he said he had no idea. He's been trying to reach Summer since Friday, but has not been successful. So, he asked me if I knew anything, and I told him no. He said he would look further into it. When he called me back this afternoon, he told me that Summer had gotten suspended because Mark Battman, your boss, sent a tape to WIDN that records Summer extorting a large amount of money from Mark in exchange for not releasing those tapes of you and him getting busy in your backyard."

Jada looked away.

"So, I have a few questions for you."

Jada looked back at him, her defensive attitude switched on overdrive.

"How did Mark Battman know that Summer worked at WIDN?" Xavier asked.

Jada shrugged. "I dunno. Maybe Summer told him."

"Why would Summer tell him that? I didn't tell him. The agent didn't tell him. And Mark doesn't have any contacts at WIDN, so there's no reason anyone there would have told him. She hasn't been on the air yet. You're the only other person who would have known *anything* about Summer's job. And the only reason *you* know is because I told you."

"Well, X, I don't know how Mark knew," Jada said dismissively. "And what's the big deal anyway? Summer's a TV reporter, so everybody in town would have known she worked for WIDN."

"Second question. We all know that Mark's wife found out about you and him. Why would he risk further embarrassment by contacting a media outlet and telling them he was being extorted because he was sleeping with you? Why would he do that, given that he has a career and reputation to protect?"

"I don't know," Jada said calmly. "That's something you should ask *him*."

"I did. And you know what he told me. He had nothing to do with sending that recording to WIDN."

"How do you know he's telling you the truth?"

Xavier sidestepped the question. "WIDN would not have taken action against Summer until they verified the source of the recording. So, they likely called Mark. Except, when he was on leave last week to straighten out his home situation, you would have been the one receiving his calls. They said they spoke with a man who they thought was Mark. So tell me? Who did you get to pretend he was Mark? Some other guy in the office you're screwing?"

"You know what?" Jada stood. "You are completely out of your mind."

"Well, I'm sure Mark will get the truth once he returns to the office. But I have just one more question. Why did you do it? Why did you get Summer fired?"

Jada was defiant. "Like I said, I have no idea what you are talking about," she lied.

Xavier nodded. Her stoic exterior didn't fool him. He knew that he had said enough to wreck her confidence completely. "You know, that was a very underhanded, evil thing you did. And I don't want to be with a woman who would do something like that."

"So, you're breaking up with me again? You'll be back, just like you came back before. You know why? Because you're weak." Jada started to walk toward the kitchen.

"You're right." Xavier followed her. "I *am* weak. But now, I'm gonna be strong." He turned and headed for the door, but turned again and said, "And, by the way, when my company's contract with Visual Notions expires at the end of June, you can forget about me renewing it. I'm done with the *both* of you."

Jada yelled a curse word at him.

Xavier left Jada's house and got into his car. He tried once again to dial Summer, but the call went straight to voicemail. He sighed in frustration, finally accepting the fact that maybe Summer meant what she said, that she no longer wanted to see him again. It meant that he would have to face the coming days without a woman in his life.

And that scared him more than anything.

***

By the time Lenny arrived at work at 4 p.m. on Monday after-noon, he was a bit groggy. After putting Lenny Jr. to bed the night before, he tried to call Summer several times between 8 p.m. and 10 p.m., with no answer. He left an urgent message with his last call before heading to bed. *Summer, please call me, send me an email, text me, or something. Let me know you're okay. That's all I want to know.*

In between calls, he had plenty of time to think about anything he might have done to offend Summer. The last he spoke with her was last Wednesday night after she had arrived at the Vineyard. He had told her he didn't have much time to talk. He wondered if Summer interpreted that as hard feelings around her telling him she was not interested in being his girlfriend. What if she had decided to make things easier by cutting off all contact with him? Or maybe Xavier had won her heart, and she had cut off all contact to avoid making Xavier jealous.

Whatever it was, Lenny wished he knew. A good night's rest was elusive the night before, as Lenny was up every two hours checking his cell phone to see if Summer had called, emailed, or texted. Finally, that morning, he left her another message: *Summer, I've tried to call you for several days now, and you have not answered. I don't know what I did to make you avoid my calls, but I just need to know if you're okay. If I don't hear from you by the time I leave my shift tonight, I'm going to call the police and have them check in on you. If you get this, please call me.*

As a last ditch effort before his shift, he drove to WIDN. As he entered the reception area, he noticed large framed head shots of the on-air talent at the station. Summer's photo was not among them.

The receptionist greeted him warmly. "Welcome to WIDN. How can I assist you?"

"Yeah, I'm here to see Summer Maldonado," Lenny said.

With barely a blink, the receptionist responded, "I'm sorry. Miss Maldonado no longer works here."

The news shocked Lenny into a brief silence. Once he remembered that he had told that lie at East Leigh on behalf of wives who no longer wanted to have any contact with their husbands, he maintained his composure. "Are you sure?"

"Yes, I am."

"But she just started working here."

"She doesn't anymore."

"Is there a supervisor or someone that I could talk to?"

The receptionist's warm smile faded sharply. "Sir, it's our policy at WIDN not to discuss personnel matters with persons not employed with our company. No one will be able to give you any information about her."

"Well, can't you at least try?"

"No, sir." She moved slightly to the left.

Lenny knew that move well. She was edging closer to the panic button under her desk. One press of that button, and three security guards would pop out from behind closed doors, pick him up, and toss him out on the street like a rancid bucket of water.

Lenny nodded and smiled to set the receptionist at ease. *I'm not some crazed, angry black man ready to set this place off.* "I'm a friend of hers, and I haven't heard from her in a few days. I'm just concerned. Can you give me any information at all?"

"I'm afraid I have no other information, sir."

Lenny nodded. "Thank you." He turned and left, much to the relief of the receptionist.

As Lenny got back into his car, he was comforted, in a sense. Whatever was going on with Summer was not about him. Summer was very excited about the job, and there was no way she would have lost it unless something serious had occurred. But what was so serious? He drove away with more questions than he arrived with.

Once he arrived at work, he checked the gate log, then stood outside the gate house, hoping that Summer would come jogging by at her usual time. When she did not, he sat disconsolately in the gate house, hoping that he didn't have to face another night worrying about what

had happened to Summer. He wondered if he should just call the police and let them track her down. But he decided to wait until the end of his shift, to give her one last opportunity to contact him.

At 11:45 p.m., the attendant that worked the midnight-to-eight shift walked in, and Lenny still had not heard from Summer. He asked his fellow gate attendant to cover him for fifteen minutes while he went to check on her.

Before going up the stairs of Building B, he walked through the rear door and into the courtyard. He walked to the opposite side of the fountain, where he could get a good vantage point to see Summer's third-floor balcony door. He wasn't certain, but he thought the balcony door blinds had been opened slightly since he had observed them the day before. There were still no lights evident in the apartment.

Lenny went back inside Building B and walked up the stairs to the third floor. As he ascended the stairs, he observed how quiet it was, which meant that either everyone had gone to bed, or the walls in this building were solidly built to keep inside noises inside. This was different than the building where he lived. Whenever he climbed the stairs of his apartment building late at night, the potpourri of sounds from TVs, crying babies, women arguing with their significant others, and other noises came pouring through the walls so freely that there might as well have not been any walls at all.

The quietness of Building B would make his knocking more pronounced, and increased the likelihood that the neighbors would notice, but Lenny no longer cared about that. Even if he had to kick the door in, he was going to find out what had happened to his friend. *Tonight*.

Lenny pounded on Summer's door as if he were a cop demanding entry. After his second round of pounding and a try of the doorknob, he heard a click at the neighbor's door across the hall. When he turned, the door opened, and a short man with wispy blonde hair, a black T-shirt, and pajama pants stood peering out of the eight-inch opening.

"I don't think she's home," the man said. That was his diplomatic way of saying *quit banging on doors at midnight, you jerk. People are trying to sleep.*

"Do you know the woman that lives here?" Lenny asked.

"I've spoken to her on occasion. Can't say that I know her."

"Have you seen her lately?"

"Not since last week."

"Has anyone else been here to visit, knocking on the door, or anything?"

"Not that I know of." The eight-inch opening in the doorway now decreased to six inches.

"Okay. Thank you, sir."

The door shut quickly, followed by another click.

Lenny turned to look at Summer's door. He thought to pound again, but he didn't want to lose his job because a neighbor complained about noise. Instead, he pulled out his cell phone and prepared to dial the police.

Then, he heard another click. Only this time, it came from Summer's door.

Lenny hung up the phone, stuffed it in his pocket, and waited. The door cracked open a few inches, not nearly enough for Lenny to see anyone amid the darkness inside.

"Lenny, I'm okay," came a rattling, hoarse voice from behind the door.

Lenny walked closer to the door. "Summer, I need to see you." He noticed that the security chain was on the door. "Please let me in."

"It's late, Lenny."

"I know. And I'm sorry. But I need to see you."

"I don't want you to see me like this."

"I don't care about that, Summer. Let me in."

"No."

"Summer, please."

"Just go home, Lenny."

"No, I'm not going home. I'm not gonna lose another night's sleep worrying about you. Either you let me in, or I'm gonna harass you every day and every night until I see you." Lenny stood and waited.

After a few seconds, the door closed, the chain rattled, and then

the door opened again, wider this time. Lenny stepped forward, pushed open the door just enough for him to slip inside, and then shut the door behind him. He searched in the darkness for Summer. He found her walking toward the couch, wearing a long white terry cloth bathrobe and no shoes. Her hair was tousled and matted as if it hadn't been combed or styled for days. She moved with a slow gait, as if every muscle in her body was on fire. After she had laid on the couch, Lenny looked around the apartment. There were no lights on anywhere, nor any TVs, but Lenny could still make out a few things in the glow coming from the streetlights outside and diffusing through the white plastic blinds hanging over the balcony door. He had never been in her apartment before, so he had no way of knowing if the unwashed dishes on the kitchen table, or the papers scattered on the floor, or the empty blue bottles of vodka on the cocktail table, were normal for her. But dirty apartment or no, *this* Summer, the one he was looking at now, was *not* normal.

"Summer, what's going on with you?" Lenny asked, stepping off the foyer and into the living room. He walked over to the couch, where she was laying, her face toward the rear of the couch. He sat on the edge of the couch, reached over, and gently laid his hand on her shoulder. "C'mon, Summer," he said softly. "Talk to me."

Summer did not stir.

Lenny gently squeezed her shoulder. "Summer, I'm your friend. You can talk to me."

Without turning, Summer quietly said, "You shouldn't be my friend."

"Why not?"

"Because I'm all messed up." The treble of her voice was muted by the couch cushion.

"How are you messed up?"

That question brought no response from Summer. Lenny removed his hand from her shoulder and repeated the question. "How are you messed up? Because I can guarantee you, there's not a lot you can tell me that's gonna make me stop being your friend."

Summer still did not respond. Lenny got up, walked over to the balcony, and parted the blinds so that more light from outside flowed inside. He looked again at the vodka bottles on the table. He had no idea Summer was a drinker. She didn't seem that way. If anyone ever asked him what a drinker seemed like, he wouldn't be able to answer. There was just something about Summer that didn't fit the profile of a hard drinker. The empty bottles sat on the table without any shot glasses nearby. That meant she drank the vodka straight from the bottle. *Hard drinker indeed.*

Lenny walked over to the love seat directly across from the couch and sat down. He knew she had lost her job, but didn't know if the job was the catalyst for her odd behavior, or a casualty of it. But he had to get to the bottom of this, because he wasn't sure what would happen if he walked out that front door.

Lenny tried again. "Summer, I heard you lost your job."

"How did you know that?" Summer responded, quietly, without moving.

"I went to your job looking for you, and they told me."

"It's not the only thing I lost."

"What else?"

"My self-respect, my dignity, the only man I ever loved. And everything else I ever worked for."

Lenny decided to focus on her statement, *the only man I ever loved.* "You mean Xavier, right? What happened?"

"He's still sleeping with Jada."

"Well, it seems like that's a loss of *their* dignity. Not yours."

"There's something else you don't know about me."

"What's that?"

"I'm a drunk."

Lenny looked again at the empty vodka bottles. "People have a drink sometimes when they are going through something. Doesn't necessarily make you a drunk."

Summer turned to face him. There was a noticeable sheen on her skin, paleness in her eyes, and puffiness under them. "Remember when

I told you my car was in the shop? The day I went to your church?"

"Yeah."

"Well, that was a lie. My car is totaled because I drove drunk, got in an accident, and almost killed myself. In fact, I *should* have died. I'm a drunk. Just like my father."

Lenny drooped his head slightly. He had no idea his near-perfect Summer was that flawed. But even as she lie there, drowning in misery with 90 proof coming out of her pores, Lenny was attracted to her more than ever. This issue, this flaw, made her relatable, more human. No longer was she this unattainable trophy woman that was the prize of princes. She was no different than any other person he grew up with in Mosby Court.

Lenny leaned forward. "No, you shouldn't have died. God put you here for a purpose. You have a part in God's plan."

"I don't pray anymore," Summer revealed, looking upward. "God doesn't hear me. My life is a wreck, and God doesn't care."

"I don't think that's true, Summer. You know, Pastor Malachi preached a sermon yesterday out of Lamentations 3:31–32. What he was saying is that people leave the church when they go through grief, heartache, stuff like that, because it seems like the Lord isn't there. It looks like God kicked them to the curb, and they can't handle that. People pray for years for a husband or wife with no answer. They ask God to help their money situation, but they're still struggling. They might say, 'What's the use of praying?' Pastor said that many people walk around just like the people in Jerusalem after it was destroyed. People grieved, and they ain't have no hope that it would ever be restored. Jerusalem was destroyed 'cause of the people's sin. But if you were to ask anybody in captivity if they ever believed that God would rescue them, the answer was no, 'cause they believed that God caused the destruction in the first place.

"But once the people repented and had faith in God again, God restored them. They had to reject Babylon's way and culture and return to God. And I think that's what you have to do. Whatever it is that you need in life, Summer, you can't do it your way. It's gotta be God's

way. Then, he will restore you."

Summer looked away again. Lenny got up, walked over to the couch, sat on the edge again, and grabbed her hand. It felt warm and limp. "I want to pray for you, Summer, if that's okay," Lenny said, looking for an answer from her. Receiving none, he tugged gently on her hand. "Come on, get up."

Summer slowly rose, swinging her leg around until she was seated next to Lenny. She pulled her robe tight and hung her head, her hair almost completely shielding her face. Lenny reached over and pulled her hair to the side. Then he clasped her hands and started to pray:

"Lord, I thank you for bringing Summer into my life. During the few days I've known her, she's been such a joy to me, but I know you created her to be a special joy to you, and not only that, but to have joy in her own life. I don't know what plans you have for her, but I do know you have plans, and that she is not an accident waiting to happen. Lord, help her to see the error of her own way. Touch her with your spirit, so that she can walk in your light. Lord, let her know that your love is unfailing, and it is great, and that she will not be in Babylon for long. At the appropriate time, you will show up in her life. Father, you've loved her since she was a child. You loved her even when her own father didn't. You loved her through the pain, the abuse, the drunkenness. You loved her, and you brought her out. You love her now. And you will always love her. As the word of God says, 'What shall separate us from the love of Christ?'"

Lenny paused as he noticed a slight tremble in her hands. As he looked up, he saw a stream of tears, cleansing tears, flowing from her eyes. He continued, reciting the scripture in Romans 8:35–39 he had read, and studied, and found comfort in many more times than he could count.

"'Shall tribulation, or distress, or persecution, or famine, or nakedness, or peril, or sword? As it is written, For thy sake we are killed all the day long; we are accounted as sheep for the slaughter. Nay, in all these things we are more than conquerors through him that loved us. For I am persuaded, that neither death, nor life, nor angels, nor princi-

palies, nor powers, nor things present, nor things to come, nor height, nor depth, nor any other creature, shall be able to separate us from the love of God, which is in Christ Jesus our Lord.'"

The tears flowed more profusely now, and Summer started to sob, her entire body trembling. Lenny wrapped his arm around her and drew her to him, her face pressed against his shoulder. And there, she cried, for almost ten minutes, with Lenny brushing her hair occasionally, telling her it would be alright, although he wasn't exactly sure how.

***

It was one in the morning, and Lenny was still holding Summer, sitting there in the dark, although she had long since stopped crying. His presence was a comfort to her, a nonjudgmental companion to help salve her pain. She held on to him like a frightened child, and truth be told, she was more frightened than any child could ever be.

Lenny noted that it was well past the time for him to return home so that he could relieve Trinee, who was watching Lenny Jr. while he was at work. He hoped Trinee was asleep and didn't notice his lateness, but it was more likely that Trinee was up watching Fallon or Letterman, as she was a classic night owl.

Lenny gently tapped Summer on the shoulder. She turned her head up to look at him, her face only inches from his. Her vulnerability, her sweetness, her yearning for love, comfort, and affection was pasted clearly on her face. She had a look of passion and desire in her eyes, like she wanted to kiss him.

And she *did* want to kiss him.

And Lenny wanted to kiss her.

As he was preparing to succumb to the tranquil, tempting moment, thoughts popped in his head of his son, of the many sermons that his pastor had preached, of the embarrassment, guilt, and defeat he would suffer if he allowed this moment to take its due course.

He had to get out of there. And quick.

"I gotta go," Lenny whispered, shifting so that he could take his arm from around her.

Summer resisted, pressing into him. "No. I want you to stay," she breathed.

"Summer, I can't."

"Please. Don't leave me. Nothing's going to happen. I promise."

"I have to go be with my son."

Summer sighed. "Can you come back?"

"When?"

"Tonight."

"No, not tonight. I can check on you tomorrow morning after I take my son to his day camp."

Summer sighed again and loosened her hold.

Lenny took his arm from around her and stood up. "You need to get some sleep."

"I've been sleeping for three days."

Lenny reached down, grabbed Summer's hand and gingerly pulled her to her feet. He then placed his other hand on her waist and guided her toward the bedroom. "I want you to go in there, lie down, and I'll be back tomorrow morning."

"You promise?"

"I promise. You mind if I take your keys?"

"They're around here somewhere."

"Okay. I'll find them."

Summer padded into her room and shut the door. Lenny returned to the living room, turned on a lamp and started to look around for her keys. He found them on the kitchen counter. He then dialed Trinee on his cell phone, telling her he got delayed at his job and that he would be there in fifteen minutes. It wasn't exactly a lie. But he didn't tell Trinee that Summer was the reason for the delay, and that she lived in the complex where he worked. And as far as he was concerned, Trinee didn't need to know.

***

Lenny returned to Summer's apartment at 8:30 the next morning after he had dropped off Lenny Jr. at day camp at his church. The recently-hired woman on duty at the gate house thought Lenny was there just to visit the security office. Lenny saw no need to enlighten her as to the true nature of his visit.

He used Summer's keys to access the apartment. The daylight coming in through the balcony blinds cast a bright gray haze over the apartment. He dropped the keys on the cocktail table, then walked back to Summer's room. He knocked gently and called her name. When he got no response, he opened the door and peered inside. Summer was lying on her back, under the sateen sheets. He heard her breathing, and knew she was in too deep a sleep to disturb her.

He closed the door and walked back to the living room, where he started to tidy up. He removed the papers off the floor and piled them neatly on an end table. There were clothes spilling out of a suitcase near the foyer. Lenny folded them neatly and stacked them back inside the suitcase. He took the vodka bottles and threw them away along with the empty food containers, and dumped the trash in the hallway trash chute. He gathered the dirty dishes on the cocktail and dining tables and took them to the kitchen sink, where he hand-washed each of them, dried them, and put them away.

Lenny looked in the refrigerator and found eggs, half-and-half, and turkey sausage. He fried up the sausage while preparing the eggs for cooking. Once the eggs were just about ready for cooking, Lenny heard a door open and close. Shortly after, Summer walked into the kitchen, wearing the same bathrobe she had worn earlier that morning.

"You came back," Summer said with a look of surprise.

"Of course I did," Lenny said, heating a frying pan. "Why wouldn't I?"

Summer sat on a stool at the breakfast bar. "I thought maybe I'd scared you away."

"Nothing about you scares me, Summer. How are you feeling?"

"I have a huge headache."

"Got any aspirin, or anything?"

"No."

"I can go and get you some."

"I just think I need to eat something."

"Well, I got you covered." Lenny cooked the eggs and made some toast and jam while Summer watched. He prepared two plates and said a prayer before they started to eat at the breakfast bar.

Lenny broke a short silence when he said, "I tidied up the place a bit. Hope you don't mind."

Summer shook her head, more embarrassed than grateful.

As she dug in, Lenny asked her, "When's the last time you had something to eat?"

"I tried to eat on Saturday, but I couldn't hold anything down. So, not since then. This is good. Never knew you were such a good cook."

"I can do breakfast. Lunch and dinner leave much to be desired. Just ask my son." Lenny shifted in his seat, then said, "And when did you polish off those two vodka bottles I saw?"

"One on Friday night, and the other on Saturday."

"How'd you lose your job?"

"Remember the $15,000 I got from my old boss?"

"Yeah."

"Well, I still have it."

"I thought you were gonna give that back."

"I was. But I never got around to it. So, anyway, my old boss recorded our conversation, and he sent the tape to my new boss. My new boss decided they didn't want someone working for them who had extorted money from their old boss, so they suspended me."

"Suspended? Not fired?"

"In this business, a suspension is just a way of getting you out the door until they can complete the paperwork to fire you. It's a done deal."

"Well, you'll get another job."

Summer looked up from her plate at him. "Really? You think someone will want to hire a drunk extortionist?"

Lenny sighed. "I really wish you would stop calling yourself those

names. There is much more to you than that."

"You talk like you've known me for several years, but you've only been my friend for a few weeks. How do you know that?"

"Well, I know you're a woman of great compassion," Lenny answered without hesitating. "You're a strong woman, although you often don't use your strength. You're not very outgoing. But above all, you are a woman of God. But you're held captive by Babylon. And God wants you to come out. Am I wrong about any of that?"

Summer looked at him blankly but did not respond.

"And I think there's a lot more that'll come out, once I get to know the real Summer."

Summer looked down at her food for a moment, stirring the last of her eggs, then looked back up at Lenny. "Can I ask you a question?"

"Sure."

"Do you think everyone is basically evil?"

"I don't catch your reference," Lenny said. He did, but the question caught him off guard, so the statement was designed to delay his response, give him time to think.

"I was taught growing up that everyone is basically evil," Summer said. "My mom would always quote this scripture out of Romans chapter three. There is no one righteous, no one good, something like that. So, if the opposite of evil is good, and there is no one good, then that means that everyone is evil. The only way we can be made righteous or good is through Jesus Christ, through loving him, serving him, and obeying him. Well, I haven't been loving him. I haven't been serving him, and I haven't been obeying him. I know that. So, how can you call me a woman of God? How can you say I'm strong, and I have compassion? I'm none of those things. I'm a wretch, just like everybody else. Martin Luther King once said 'The ultimate measure of a man is not where he stands in moments of comfort and convenience, but where he stands at times of challenge and controversy.' Well, Lenny, I've really been challenged the past few months. I've never dealt with heartbreak until Xavier broke up with me. I've never lost a job before. So, those were my challenges. And how did I respond?

I almost killed three people, including myself. I extorted money from my former boss. And to top it all, I was actually willing to sleep with a man who cheated on me. Does that sound like a woman of God to you?"

"Maybe not." Lenny pondered her words carefully, wondering if he had spoken too presumptuously. He let the silence drift between them until his thoughts were clear. "But if people are basically evil, then how could they ever choose good? How would God ever be attractive to them? There has to be some goodness in them in order to be drawn to him. I think God created us to respond to his love, no matter how bad we may become. He gave us the capacity to be good, even if we don't always do it. And when I say woman of God, I'm not saying it based on what you are doing. I'm saying it based on who God created you to be. If God created me to be a man, I am still a man, even if I try to act like a woman. My actions don't change God's reality. And I think one of the worse perversions in the world is when a person's actions don't match up to who they really are.

"Y'know, I read that scripture you were talking about, in Romans 3. It talks about our spiritual condition. Yeah, spiritually I think we are nothing without Christ. But I think our souls, our will, has the capacity for good. That's why people can do many charitable and wonderful things, yet not even know or acknowledge God."

Summer nodded. "They do good things, but in the eyes of God, they are still sinners?"

"I think sinning in terms of our actions is one thing. But sin, in terms of separation from God, is the main thing. Think about it this way. What does a woman want from her man more than anything?"

Summer barely had to think about the question. "Intimacy."

"Intimacy?"

"Yeah. I mean, I guess, speaking for myself, I want a close connection with that man. I want to know that I'm his one and only. I want to have deep conversations that draw us together. I want to walk down the street hand-in-hand with him. I want him to hold me at night. I want to know that I am the most precious thing in the world to him."

"Okay. So, you've just described what God wants out of us. In-timacy. I think the greatest sin is not having intimacy with God. You know, husbands and wives can live with each other, share the house-hold, raise the kids, do many good things for each other, yet not be very close to each other. I mean—and I'm gonna be very blunt here—there are couples that have been married for many years, live together, and yet only have sex with each other three or four times a year when they are capable of being together more times than that. Now, some-thing is definitely wrong with that."

"I agree."

"That dynamic exists with couples. But it also exists between us and God. We can do many good things, but are still sinners because we don't have intimacy with God. I think that's what Romans 3 was saying. But if we establish intimacy with God, our actions are going to follow. Pastor Malachi always says the best way to change your ac-tions is to change your relationships."

"Hmm." Summer went back to eating her eggs.

"So, if you want me to take back what I said, I'm not," Lenny said. "You need to establish that close relationship with God, above Xavier or anybody else."

"That's what my pastor said to me," Summer said, finishing her eggs.

"Well, there you go." Lenny grabbed for Summer's empty plate and utensils and turned to place them in the sink. "Do you want some-thing else to eat?"

"No, I'm fine, thank you. That was so good."

"Glad you enjoyed it."

Summer watched Lenny as he began to wash the dishes. She had begun to grow even fonder of Lenny since her date with him at Tillie's. He was a man of great wisdom and integrity. There were many men that would have taken advantage of her the night before, but he did not. That earned him her respect and her trust, although she was cer-tain he had some chink in his armor that Summer had not discovered yet. To her, he seemed *too* perfect.

But Xavier had charisma, panache, and swagger. He walked among and rubbed elbows with the elite, and had connections too numerous for her to count. He was the type of successful man that, by society's mores and standards, she should have on her arm. But she neither admired him nor respected him, although she was madly in love with him. And that confused and frustrated her.

When Lenny turned back around to retrieve the remaining dishes, Summer averted her eyes, acting as if she wasn't checking him out for the past two minutes. Lenny drew her eyes back to him with a question. "What are you doing tomorrow?"

Summer said ashamedly, "Nothing."

"Want to come to a family cookout with me?"

"Why do you want to take *me*?"

Lenny gazed at her pointedly. "It should be no secret that I care for you. A lot. And I just didn't want you to spend the Fourth of July at home by yourself. Especially since your name is Summer."

"Why don't you take Trinee?"

"Because I want to take you."

"Will she be there?"

"Probably."

"Then I'll pass. I don't want to cause any trouble."

Lenny reached for her hand and held it with such affection that it soothed her. "Look, I want you to go with me. And if you don't go, *I'm* not going."

"Why? Why would you push your family to the side for me?"

"Goes to show you how much I care about you."

Summer took her free hand and placed it on top of his, sandwiching it between hers. "I can't let you skip your family cookout."

"Then, the answer is yes?"

Summer flipped his hand so that the palm was facing upward. She looked at his hands, strong and calloused, yet they touched her with such tenderness. She delayed before answering, "Yes, I'll go with you."

Lenny smiled. "Cool."

Summer regarded him for a few seconds before she realized she was gently caressing his hand. She released his hand and looked away sheepishly. Lenny smiled and went back to doing the dishes.

When Lenny's back turned to her, Summer's gaze returned to him. She figured the cookout would be fun, something she definitely needed. And it might be good to see Lenny in his natural element, around his family. If Lenny's family was anything like hers, they would be no good at keeping secrets.

Summer made a mental note to call her hairstylist and her manicurist for a last-minute appointment. She wanted to look extra nice in order to make a good impression on Lenny's family, but mostly because she was horrified that Lenny saw her this way, and she wanted to make up for it.

CHAPTER ELEVEN

By noon on the Fourth of July, the blazing sun was high in the sky, with no clouds to obstruct its brilliance nor temper its fervor. Lenny expected Interstate 64 to be jam-packed with vehicles headed to Virginia Beach, so he wanted to depart three hours before the 3 p.m. cookout start time. He spent most of that morning shopping for new clothes to wear, as this would be the first time he would be seeing some of his relatives since last July 4th. He also wanted to impress Summer with his style choices, from his chino baseball hat, to his khaki shorts, to his fresh white Adidas sneakers. Even had on new underwear. He rented a Toyota Corolla the day before so that Summer could ride to the cookout with him in style. He tuned the satellite radio to a jazz station, something he knew Summer would like.

At the arranged pick-up time, he pulled the Corolla in a visitor's parking space near the gate house and texted Summer on his cell phone to let her know that he was outside. After a few minutes of waiting, he finally saw Summer walking toward the gate.

His jaw immediately dropped.

Summer wore a tight multicolored, bold pattern vest top and a pair of jean cut-off shorts that was just two inches of inseam away from being panties. Her hair was salon fresh, cascading in shiny black waves to her shoulders, and she sported a wide pair of D&G sunglasses and

sandals. As she walked to his car, he could scarcely take his eyes off her; she looked more beautiful than he had ever seen her.

Summer climbed in the car and said, "Whew, it's hot out there."

It's even hotter in here, Lenny thought, his eyes moving to her legs, long and model sleek. His thought came out vocally as, "You look nice."

"Thanks." Summer tossed her hair. "You look nice, too." It was the first time she had seen him in casual attire. *It works on him*, she thought. She looked in the back seat. "Where's your son?"

"He's with his mama. We usually alternate holidays, just like we do weekends."

"Are they coming to the cookout?"

"Far as I know."

"I'm still a little nervous about that."

Lenny sighed as he pulled the car out of the parking space. "I told you there's no need to be. Trinee and I are not together, and we haven't been in a while. There's no need for her to start kirkin' out over you. It'll be cool."

"I hope so."

They had light conversation on the way to Hampton, alternated with long moments of silence while they enjoyed the jazz playing on the radio. As expected, they hit traffic, but still made it to Hampton within two hours, about an hour early for the cookout.

When Lenny pulled into his aunt's driveway, he immediately recognized the 1981 Chevy conversion van parked ahead of him. "Uncle Deno's here."

"Who's he?" Summer asked.

Since they had an hour before the cookout, Lenny laid it out for her. Fifty-four-year-old Uncle Deno was Aunt Etta's only sibling. A former Marine who served two tours in Lebanon during the Lebanese Civil War, he was only in his twenties when a bomb destroyed his barracks, killing almost everyone in his company. He came home to the supportive arms of his family, grateful to be alive. He would show his gratitude by giving selflessly to his extended family, committing to do

so for as long as he lived. His Fourth of July cookouts, held every year for the past ten years, served as part of the outworking of his commitment. Uncle Deno would accept no donations of food, money, or anything else. He paid for it all out of his pocket, as he was handsomely paid from his job as an upscale restaurant chef. Despite several family members urging him to accept money, he would do no such thing.

Everyone in the family, including Lenny, looked forward to Uncle Deno's cookouts. He would host them at various family homes around Virginia. But it made no difference where they were located; family members would make the trip to be there. It was practically the only time family members who had not been in touch with each other could catch up. Given the varying interests of his family, it was the closest thing they had to a tradition.

Lenny rolled down his window. "Hear that?"

"What?"

"The music."

Summer listened. "Yeah."

"Know who that is?"

"Yeah. Ray Charles. *I Got a Woman*."

"How you know about that?"

"Lenny, honey, I was a radio host for several years."

"Oh, yeah. Well, anyway, Uncle Deno's probably in the backyard, playing music, getting stuff together. He does not—will not—play anything at his cookouts that came out later than 1980. Uncle Deno is straight old school."

Summer smiled. "That's not a bad thing."

"No, it's not. But some of the young bucks keep goin' to him and saying, 'why don't you play some Usher, some Beyonce?' He always says, 'I'm not gonna play that junk. That ain't real music.' And he loves Frankie Beverly and Maze. Honestly, he's gonna play *Happy Feelin's* at least three times before the first round of burgers get done."

Summer laughed.

"You ready to go in?"

"I guess." She let out a trembling breath. "I don't know why I'm

so nervous."

"Because you want my family to like you. And they will. They will love you. Trust me. Especially Aunt Etta." Lenny got out of the car and walked around to the passenger side to let Summer out. They walked the cobblestone pathway along the left side of the house toward the backyard. Once they had passed the house, they could see Aunt Etta in the backyard, wiping down a table for food.

Aunt Etta, wearing jeans, flat shoes, and a simple red blouse, saw them walking toward her, beamed, and stopped what she was doing to meet them halfway. She hugged Lenny first. "Good to see you, dear. Glad you could make it."

"Wouldn't miss this for anything, Auntie," Lenny said.

While Lenny greeted Aunt Etta, Summer looked around the yard. It was vast, perfectly green, surrounded with a chain-link fence, and treelined, with umbrella tables and citronella oil Tiki torches interspersed with the trees around the perimeter. The grill was closer to the house and large enough to cook twenty hamburgers at a time. It had been prepared with charcoal and wood, but had not yet been lit. Another table held a turntable with an amplifier, speakers, and a milk crate full of LPs. *Definitely old school*, Summer thought.

Aunt Etta came to her next. "Is this Summer?"

Summer barely had time to say *yes* before Aunt Etta embraced her. It was a warm, lingering hug, like those shared between close friends who had not seen each other in a while. When Aunt Etta ended the hug, she said, "It's so nice to meet you."

"Nice to meet you, too," Summer responded.

Aunt Etta looked her up and down. "Lenny, you never told me she was *this* gorgeous."

Summer blushed. "Thanks, ma'am."

"Now, don't you go callin' me ma'am," Aunt Etta retorted. "I ain't your mama, your boss, nor your queen. You can call me Etta, or if you want, you can call me Aunt Etta. That's what everybody else calls me, whether I'm they aunt or not."

"Aunt Etta sounds good," Summer replied, smiling.

"Can you cook, dear?"

"I do okay."

"Come on in the kitchen with me, help me make these baked beans."

And that was it. Lenny knew that once Aunt Etta drew someone into her kitchen, it would be an hour before he saw them again. He chuckled as Aunt Etta and Summer headed into the house via the back door. He walked to a cooler near the house, dug around in the ice past the bottled beers for a canned ginger ale, and sat down at one of the tables along the fence. He had never discussed with Aunt Etta what she would talk to Summer about in that kitchen, but he hoped that she would say something to sway Summer to look at him as more than a friend. And with Xavier out of the picture, at least for now, this was the best chance to win her heart.

He couldn't deny nor resist what was going on inside him. It had happened with Trinee. It was now happening with Summer. It was confirmed that night when he held her in his arms. His feelings for Summer were off the charts. He could no longer see her as just a friend.

He harkened to remember the advice that Pastor Malachi gave him for finding the right girl. Son, fallin' in love don't mean the girl is right for you. You can fall in love with anybody. Fallin' in love is based on feelings, how that girl makes you feel, how much you got in common, how attractive she is, and how much sex appeal she got. But you can fall in love with a woman that may not be the right girl for you, which is why you gotta have some non-negotiable standards for the type of woman you want. Problem is, when a man falls in love, most of them standards go out the window. But you gotta know what kind of woman you want, and if she don't meet them standards, she ain't for you, no matter how you feel, no matter how much you're in love. For a worldly man, fallin' in love is enough. But for a Christian man, there's a lot more.

Lenny thought about what he wanted in a woman. In addition to being physically attractive, she had to be a Christian woman committed to God and church. She could not be an ardent feminist to the point

where she would not allow him to assert his role as a man. She had to be a non-smoker. She had to be a woman who was upwardly mobile, with goals and aspirations of her own that they could partner together to help meet. She had to desire children, at least two. And she had to be a woman with a very limited sexual history; Lenny didn't think he could date a woman who had been with seven or more men before him. She had to be intelligent, compassionate, a lover of justice, someone who would periodically challenge his thinking and help him grow in certain areas.

Lenny didn't see a lot of that in Trinee. Sure, she was cute. But Trinee smoked like a chimney, drank like a fish, and seemed to have no aspirations other than getting paid and getting pregnant. And Lenny wasn't sure that getting pregnant wasn't a part of her strategy to get paid, as he'd heard about women who have babies just to collect child support. And as far as her sexual history, Lenny did not believe for one second that Trinee had been a sexual teetotaler since their break-up. He couldn't prove it, but he was sure that whenever Lenny Jr. was not at her home on the weekends, she would work that spandex mini-dress to full effect on other men.

Lenny wanted to make himself as pure as possible for the woman he would eventually marry, which was why he stayed celibate since breaking up with Trinee. He kept busy in the church to avoid those moments of boredom where he would be tempted to go gallivanting for a companion for the night. The more he thought about his past conversations with Summer, he realized that Summer met his standards, as far as he knew. But then there was the matter of her relationship with Xavier. Was her heart still tied to him? Had he fallen in love with a woman who could never reciprocate his feelings?

His thoughts were interrupted when Uncle Deno and his wife walked into the backyard carrying loads of Farm Fresh bags. The moment Uncle Deno saw Lenny, he laid the bags down in the yard and met Lenny halfway. They embraced, and Uncle Deno kissed him on the cheek.

"How you doin' man?" Uncle Deno said, talking out of the corner

of his mouth. He was the closest thing that Lenny had to a father while growing up in Aunt Etta's house. He was strong, built like a linebacker, with a bald head and graying goatee. He had eyes that could convey the love and concern of a granddad, and yet give a hard stare that would back you down if you were ever in a fight with him. His tough demeanor aside, his yellow Hawaiian shirt and white knee-length shorts softened him a bit.

When they parted from the embrace, Lenny looked past Uncle Deno and waved at his wife, Marlie, who had started to pick up the bags left on the lawn. Marlie had married Uncle Deno in 1984, when Lenny was too young to understand the furor over a black man marrying a white woman, but old enough to know that his Aunt Marlie was a lot different than his other relatives.

"How you doin' man?" Deno asked again, his voice deep and calming. "Heard you got a new job."

"Yeah. Making a lot more money than I was before. Can't complain."

"That a new car you got out front?"

"Naw. It's a rental."

"Might be able to afford a new one after a while, huh?"

"That's my hope."

Deno put an arm around Lenny and led him toward the grill. "So, tell me man, who's the *fine* honey in there with your aunt? I saw her through the kitchen window when I was coming back to the yard."

Lenny frowned. "C'mon, unc. How can you disrespect Marlie like that?"

"Disrespect how? 'Cause I said she's fine?"

"Yeah. You know a lot of women don't play that."

"Lemme tell you somethin', young'un. Ain't nothin' wrong with noticing that a woman looks good. Long as you leave it there."

"But you're only supposed to have eyes for your wife."

"And I do. To me, Marlie is the most beautiful woman in the world. But she ain't the *only* beautiful woman in the world. That's the difference."

"I thought you were checkin' her out."

"Man, I ain't interested in that girl. I'm just wonderin' who she is. That girl is too young for me anyway. I'll be sixty years old in a couple of months."

"Ain't no strange thing to see an old head mixin' it up with a tenderoni," Lenny laughed. "Look at Michael Douglas and Catherine Zeta Jones."

"You got the money them Hollywood folk got, you can do that," Deno said, laughing. "When it comes to romance, age don't mean a thing when you got a million bucks. Besides, I loves Marlie. I ain't tryin' to mess that up. Woman been there for me since before I was in the foxholes with bullets whizzing over my head." Deno reached for the lighter fluid and sprayed it liberally over the charcoal and wood in the grill. "So, who is she?"

"She's a friend of mine."

"Girlfriend?"

"Just a friend."

"That the way you want it?"

"That's the way *she* wants it."

"You and Trinee?"

"That was over a while ago."

Deno threw a match on the soaked charcoal and watched as the fire went up two feet in the air with a whoosh. "Well, that girl looks like she got it goin' on. How'd you meet her?"

"She was working in one of the offices in the building where I used to do security. She's the one that hooked me up with this job I got now."

"Where she from?"

"Born in Brazil, moved to the ATL when she was five."

"Well, she seems like a nice girl, the type you really need to be with."

"So, tell me, unc." Lenny lowered his voice so that no one other than Deno could hear. "When you're in love with a girl, and she don't feel the same for you, how do you close the deal?"

Deno's chin elevated slightly, and his eyes turned upward. Lenny knew he was searching his memory for a story with a good moral lesson attached. Lenny folded his arms and waited.

"Man, I 'member back when I first met Marlie." The slight smile on Deno's face relayed the fondness of the memory. "Back in the eighties, things was still better than they was in the sixties, 'cept for Reaganomics, but a black man being with a white woman was still unusual. I thought she was the cutest woman I had ever met, and I knew I wanted to marry her. But man, she ain't feel that way about me at first."

"How did she feel?"

"Back then, Marlie was still young. She cared a lot about what other people thought. And in her circles, almost nobody approved of a white woman dating a black man. Almost lost her 'cause of that."

"How'd you hang on to her?"

"Thing is, it wasn't me. It was her decision. She decided I was the man for her, and she didn't care what everyone else thought. I couldn't change my skin color, so I had to be who I was—a young black man who loved the hell out of that white girl. Eventually, she saw I was worth it." Deno reached into the cooler and pulled out a beer. "Look, man, you can tell her how you feel, but that's it. You can't force her feelings. Only thing you can do is be yourself, and pray that she recognizes the value in you." Deno removed the cap of the beer with his teeth and flung it into a nearby wastebasket. "Besides, she in there talking with your aunt. As much as Etta wants to see you get married to somebody other than Trinee, your friend likely to come out of there ready to pick out a wedding dress."

Deno quickly turned away and started to greet some other relatives that had arrived. There was one word that Deno said that resonated with Lenny. *Pray.* He realized that who Summer dated was as much God's choice as it was hers.

Summer would be in the kitchen with Aunt Etta another hour, Lenny thought. That would give him enough time to go away somewhere, be alone, and ask God for a special blessing.

And he knew exactly where to go.

***

After Aunt Etta had coaxed Summer into her kitchen, it became clear that getting Summer to help with cooking was not her intention. When Summer saw Aunt Etta pull a big foil pan of baked beans out of the oven, she wondered what help was needed.

"I ain't call you in here to help me cook no beans, child," Aunt Etta confessed, setting the beans on the counter. "I been working on these since this mornin'." She pulled back the foil on the pan.

"Looks good," Summer said.

Etta pulled a small spoon from a drawer and handed it to Summer. "Have a taste."

Summer dipped the spoon in the beans, pulled away a small helping, blew on them for a moment, and then tasted, allowing the flavors of bacon, sugar, and molasses to massage her tongue. "Umm, these are delicious. Probably better than my mother's."

"Ain't no probably about it. They either is, or they ain't. I make mine from scratch. I don't do the canned beans like some folks do."

"Will you give me your recipe?"

"Lenny knows how to make 'em. You should ask him to make you some one day."

"Lenny told me he couldn't cook. Just breakfast."

"Don't let him fool you with that. He do alright. I don't see either him or Junior getting any skinnier." Etta moved over to a small folding table in the corner of the kitchen and sat down in one of the two chairs around it. She pointed Summer to the other. "Come sit down, sweetie."

Summer complied, expecting that Aunt Etta was about to reveal the reason that she was called to the kitchen.

"I want you to know that Lenny didn't ask me to do this, and he don't know I'm doing it," Etta said.

"Know what?"

"I wanted to talk about you and him."

Summer nodded.

"You know, I'm the closest thing he has to a mother. He was always like a son to me, even when him, his mom and dad, and me was living in Richmond."

"He told me how much you mean to him."

"Hmm. So, naturally, I want the best for him."

"So do I."

"So tell me, if you feel led to. How do you feel about my son?"

Summer hesitated.

"Don't worry. This is a private conversation. I ain't gonna tell him or nobody else anything you tell me. I ain't Catholic, but this kitchen is like my confessional."

Summer relaxed. "To be honest, I don't know. I like him a lot. I really do. But I'm sort of conflicted."

"There's another guy?"

"Lenny told you?"

"He told me you were seeing another guy, yes."

"Well, there's that. And then, he barely knows me. What if I fall for him, and he discovers something he doesn't like about me, and then I'm left with my heart broken?"

"You seem like a nice girl. What could he possibly find out?"

"I don't know." Summer stood up, collecting her thoughts. "I'm not exciting. I'm not interesting. I'm actually kind of boring. I'm not very outgoing. That's why I don't have many friends. I may be attractive physically, but I've never thought of myself as being attractive where it counts."

"Right there is your problem."

Summer turned to look at her. "What do you mean?"

"If someone does find you attractive where it counts, you reject them, because you're afraid they'll find out you're not *all that*."

"I just don't want to get hurt."

"That's fear. Girl, that'll paralyze you if you let it. I don't care how inadequate you think you are. God, in His time, will send you

the right people he wants to be in your life. But when he blesses you, you gotta be open to the blessing, 'cause it may not look like what you think it does."

"You think that Lenny is God's blessing?"

"I don't know, child. You gotta figure that out for yourself. You pray, tap into God's Spirit, and He will lead you in the right direction. But if you're scared, you always gonna go left when God wants you to go right."

"What if I go right, and find Xavier there?"

"Then that's the way you go. But I gotta tell you; I kinda doubt it."

"Why?"

"Now I'm saying this based on what Lenny has told me. But this Xavier guy. Is it true he dumped you to marry another woman?"

"Yes."

"And was having sex with this woman while he was with you?"

"Yes."

"And the woman he was seeing was having sex with some other guy?"

A more exasperated "yes" came out this time.

"Child, if that don't give you your answer, I don't know what does."

"But he's willing to change. He wants to go to church with me, and everything."

Aunt Etta stood to her feet to drive home her point. "Girl, do you know how many women done been hospitalized or wound up six feet under 'cause their man said those words? You're co-dependent, child. That man feeds a need in you, a need that should be fed by God, and no one else. Whether it's acceptance, love, or whatever, and you excuse all his crap because he gives you what you need. 'Scuse my words." When she saw that Summer had no response, she continued. "Now, Lenny ain't no shrinkin' violet. But I know he been workin' hard to get his life together, goin' to church, staying out of trouble. He even brought *you* to this picnic instead of that Jezebel Trinee."

Summer leaned against the counter. "I know. That was so sweet of

him."

"That's what I'm tryin' to say. You gotta stop and recognize when the Lord is bringin' good people in your life. If you don't, you gonna be one sad and lonely child."

Summer looked to the floor. *Already crossed that bridge*, she thought.

***

Along the shores of Herbert's Creek was a small tree-filled peninsula, the tip of which was 400 feet away from the other side of the creek. The tip of the peninsula was accessible by a short foot-worn trail, and the beginning of the trail was just a four-minute walk from Aunt Etta's front door. The view of the water was so romantic that local kids, hoping to get their dates in the mood for love, would go there occasionally to hang out. The teens dubbed it "Make Out Point." The trees were so dense that someone sitting among them could get a clear view of the water without being noticed from the other side. One of the local kids had the idea to steal a bench from a local playground and bring it to the tip and set it on the soil. When the bench started to sink in the soil after a few heavy rains, several enterprising teenagers decided to dig some holes, fill them with concrete, and mount the bench on the concrete slabs, where it remained.

Lenny remembered bringing Trinee here many years before. Now, whenever he was in town, Lenny used it for prayer. It was quiet, secluded, and he knew there wouldn't be many interruptions during the day, since the point was more heavily used at night. Lenny had told no one except Deno where he was going.

Lenny sat on the weather-beaten wood bench, which held several carved writings of teenagers declaring their love, and in some cases their conquests. He looked out over the water, tinted a greenish brown. A fisherman, his yellow lifejacket visible, sat across the creek on a pier, hoping that catfish were in the mood for bait.

Lenny sat watching the water for a while. He would have plenty of time to get back to the cookout, but for now, he needed his heart and mind clear. And the only thing that could do that was prayer.

His prayer was short and sweet, punctuated by the chirping of yellow warblers and the occasional slap of a wave against the banks of the creek.

Lord, you know how much I feel for Summer. But Lord, if she is not the woman for me, give me the wisdom, and the courage, and the strength, to make the right decision. Lord, if she is the woman for me, give her the same thing. In Jesus name.

Lenny looked at his watch. It was 3:30 p.m. Most of the family had surely arrived at the cookout by now. He planned to sit for another ten minutes, and then head back.

Suddenly, he heard a rustling in the trees and knew someone was approaching. Lenny wasn't startled, as it was not unusual for kids to duck into Make Out Point during the day just to throw rocks in the creek. But when he turned to see who was approaching, he saw the tall frame of Summer clearing the brush.

"Lenny?" she called. Seeing him, she walked through the moist soil over to the bench where he sat. "Hey, honey. You okay?"

"How'd you know I was here?' Lenny asked, looking across the river.

"Your Uncle Deno told me. He told me how to get here. He says that everyone's at the picnic now, except you."

"I just needed some time alone. I thought you were going to be talking to Aunt Etta for a while."

Summer walked over to the bench and perched herself on the arm of the bench closest to where he sat. She looked down at him. "Are you okay?"

"Yeah, just fine." Lenny quickly changed the subject before Summer got a chance to question him further. "So, you had a nice talk with my aunt Etta?"

"Yeah, we had a nice talk. Your aunt is very wise. I see where you get your wisdom from. You must have spent a lot of time at her feet."

"More like at her dinner table."

"Well, it shows. I could really benefit from spending some more time with her, with you, with Pastor Gillen, people who have spoken into my life." Summer drew a long breath, then let it out slowly. "Sometimes you pray, and when you don't get what you are praying for, you think God hasn't answered. But sometimes he answers in a way that you're not expecting. And meeting your aunt, and you, I realize that God has truly blessed me. Maybe not in the way I expected, but he has surrounded me with solid people my whole life, from my mom, and now you and your aunt. That's a great blessing."

"The scripture says, 'How much better is it to get wisdom than gold!'"

"And that excites me. Because it's God saying to me, 'Look. I have put people in your life that will add to you and not take away. I have given you friends that will bless you, not curse you. And they will not distract you from me, but will lead you to me.'"

"Hmm."

Summer got up from the edge of the bench, walked in front of him, and sat down next to him, so close that they were touching. She looked around, enjoying the serenity of the area. She thought about the night before last, when she was in Lenny's arms, enjoying the closeness of their bodies together, feeling his warmth and affection. She wanted to experience that again, momentarily pushing aside her feelings for Xavier. As much as she loved Xavier, he had never brought her back from the brink, or made her feel appreciated and valued, like Lenny did that night. "I'm glad you brought me here."

"I can't think of any other person who I rather would have invited."

Summer smiled, looked down, and gently lifted the cross pendant hanging from his neck. She toyed with it a second, then put her arm in his and leaned on him while looking out over the water. "I hear they call this the Make Out Point."

"Uncle Deno told you that, too, huh?"

"Actually, your aunt told me that. She said you used to bring girls

down here. All the kids in the neighborhood used to do it."

"Well, it wasn't a lot of girls. Just a couple, other than Trinee."

Realizing her question was personal, Summer decided to ask anyway. "What did you do down here with these girls?"

Lenny was almost embarrassed to answer the question, but knew if Summer asked, there was a reason for it. "Well, with Trinee, things got a little … uh … intense. But with the other girls, we just kissed mostly."

"Just kissed?"

"Uh huh." Lenny turned to her. "Just like I want to kiss you right now."

As soon as Lenny brought the words out of his mouth, he cringed. That was way too abrupt, way too inappropriate. He turned away. "I'm sorry. I shouldn't have—"

Summer placed her free hand under his chin and directed his face back to hers. "You're not sorry," she told him, moving her face closer to his. "You're not the least bit sorry. You want to kiss me. So, *kiss me*."

Lenny's heartbeat suddenly picked up pace. He didn't dare kiss her that day in her apartment, because he knew what would happen next. But now, with his affection for her growing by the hour, and with no danger of anything happening in broad daylight, he relented. He drew his face closer to hers, allowing their lips to touch, one, two, three, four times. On the fifth touch, they lingered a few seconds longer before parting. They said nothing after the kiss, but the thinness of their eyes as they looked into each other's told of the pleasure each had derived from the kiss.

Summer nuzzled her head into Lenny's shoulder while Lenny put his arm around her and pulled her to him.

"This is nice," Summer said quietly, staring out over the water.

"It is," Lenny agreed. "Especially with you here."

Summer broke a subsequent two-minute silence by feting Lenny with an impromptu song:

Sittin' on the dock of the bay

Watching the tide roll away
Sittin' on the dock of the bay
Wastin' time

Lenny looked at her and gently touched her cheek. "Never mind that this ain't exactly a dock, nor is this a bay."

Summer playfully slapped his knee. "Shut up. It's the only song I could think of. But I could waste time out here all day."

"Yeah?"

"Yeah. You know I'm a water girl. We lived only five miles from Ipanema Beach in Rio. I love the water."

"Maybe one day before the summer ends, I'll take you down to Virginia Beach. I hear they have a great jazz lounge down there."

Summer nuzzled into him again. "It's a date."

"We'd better get back."

"Just ten more minutes."

"Okay. Ten more minutes."

And again, their lips met.

CHAPTER TWELVE

A short time later, Summer and Lenny walked back arm-in-arm toward Aunt Etta's house. They could hear the familiar booming bass sounds of Junior Walker and the All-Stars' *Shotgun* surging in the air almost a block before they arrived at the house. When they reached the front yard, they could hear the jubilant sounds of the crowd in the backyard. The cookout was well underway.

Summer followed Lenny into the backyard as he started to hug, bump fists, and slap skin with cousins, aunts, uncles, nieces, nephews, and in-laws he hadn't seen since last year. He introduced them to Summer, referring to her as *my friend*, and feeling confident with whatever they interpreted that to mean. Many of the relatives cast awkward glances over at Trinee, as they knew she was the mother of his son and the woman on his arm at the last family picnic.

Trinee sat in the far corner, with Lenny Jr. on her lap nibbling from a plate of baked beans. She paid no attention to the elder Lenny, but glared at the statuesque beauty that followed him as he greeted his kinfolk. Jealousy hit her as suddenly as a passing odor.

Trinee's first cousin, a twentyish girl that for some odd reason everyone called Sweetie, followed Trinee's glare and saw her first opportunity to stir a boiling pot. "Girl, ain't that your man?" she said to Trinee.

"That's my baby daddy," Trinee answered, not looking away from Summer.

"Who he with?"

"Some trick he been seein'."

"I heard your Uncle Deno talking, and I hear they was down at the Make Out Point."

That drew Trinee's full attention. "You lyin'?"

"Naw uhn."

The words shot through her like fleeting nerve pain. Make Out Point was where Lenny had taken her after one of their first dates. It did not sit well with her that Lenny was there with Summer.

But that was just the sparks on the wick. The explosion came when Lenny Jr., who had just noticed his father's arrival, suddenly jumped off his mother's lap and ran over to Summer, yelling, "Hey, Miss Summer!" Trinee watched angrily as Summer knelt down and took Lenny Jr. into her arms.

Sweetie, ever the instigator, said to Trinee, "Why your son running over to her like she his mama?"

To Trinee, that was the operative question. It was one thing to have all of Lenny's kinfolk look at her like she was a bug brushed off someone's shirt. But it was another to have her son seemingly forget who his real mother was. Trinee had wanted to wait until an appropriate moment when she could pull Summer to the side and talk with her. But, her pride was so bruised, she had to take action. And now.

She stood and marched over to where Summer and Lenny were standing, and positioned herself between them, facing Lenny, her back to Summer. Summer, preoccupied with Lenny Jr., did not immediately notice her. Lenny started to greet Trinee. Trinee quickly interrupted.

"Why you got my son running to that trick?" Trinee said.

Lenny started to speak, but Summer had sent Lenny Jr. on his way and stood up just in time. She extended her hand to Trinee. "Hi. My name is Summer."

Trinee looked her up and down scornfully, then turned on one heel and said to Lenny, "You better get that bitch straight." She started to

walk back to her seat.

Summer had too much pride to let that go. "Excuse me, but who are you calling a bitch?" she said to Trinee.

Trinee stopped, turned, and headed back to Summer, stopping until she was just out of arm's reach. "I calling you a bitch, bitch!"

"You know what—" Summer suddenly decided it wasn't worth it. She waved Trinee off and turned back to Lenny, giving him a look that said *I told you so*.

Summer's brush-off was the perfect excuse to start a fight. Suddenly, Trinee flew into a rage. "Don't be tryin' to ignore me, bitch!" She stepped forward, grabbed a handful of Summer's hair, and yanked. Summer stumbled backward, lost her balance, and fell screaming, landing on her behind, with the soft grass breaking the fall. Trinee started to pounce on her, but Lenny quickly stepped in and pushed Trinee away before she could complete her assault. Sweetie busted out laughing in the corner.

"Back off, Trinee! Have you lost your mind?" Lenny yelled. Trinee ignored Lenny and tried to push around him to get to Summer.

By now, Deno had observed what was going on and abandoned the chicken on the grill to run over. "What's going on?" He glowered at Trinee, standing between her and Lenny.

Trinee started back to her seat. "Nothing." She knew Deno as a crazy ex-military guy and didn't want to challenge him.

Lenny reached down to help Summer to her feet. Etta rushed over to brush the grass away. "What is happening over here?"

Summer turned to Lenny. "I want to go."

Lenny's face sunk. "C'mon, Summer. We just got here."

"No. Take me home. Now!"

Lenny recognized that she was embarrassed and humiliated, and tried to pull her off to the side to talk to her, but Summer jerked away and marched toward the pathway leading to the front yard.

"You want me to talk to her?" Etta offered.

"No, thanks, Auntie. I'll do it."

Lenny shot a look of contempt at Trinee, then looked at his son.

Lenny was ashamed that his son had to see Trinee act like that. He headed out to the front yard. As he left, he heard Deno in his big voice tell Trinee and Sweetie to come into the house with him. That meant that Trinee was about to be shown the door. Deno had never tolerated any foolishness at his cookouts and wasn't about to start now.

Summer had already made it to the driveway and was getting in the passenger's seat when Lenny arrived. Lenny got in the driver's seat, switched on the ignition, and turned on the air conditioning so they would be comfortable while he pleaded with her.

"Summer. C'mon. You really don't want to go home, do you? After we traveled all this way?"

Summer glared ahead defiantly. "I don't want to talk about it. I just want to go home. And if you don't take me, I'll catch the bus, the train, or something. But I want to go home."

Lenny had never seen Summer so angry, and he didn't quite know how to appease her. "Of course I'll take you." He couldn't blame Summer for being upset, and he grew angrier at Trinee. But his anger would have to wait. Lenny Jr. was with Trinee, and if both Lenny and Trinee left the cookout, Lenny Jr. would be denied. Lenny dared not let that happen.

"Okay. Let me talk to Uncle Deno, then get us a couple of plates to go, and then we'll leave. Okay?"

Summer gave one quick, almost undetectable nod of her head.

Lenny left the ignition on, got out of the car, and headed toward the house. He gritted his teeth at the thought of asking Deno to allow Trinee to stay, but he wanted Lenny Jr. to have a good time, even if he and Summer could not.

***

Lenny and Summer traveled back to Richmond without saying a word to each other. For Summer, it was a long, tortuous trip, her anger visceral. She blamed Lenny for inviting her to the cookout when he

knew there was a possibility that Trinee would be jealous of her. This was the reason she didn't want to go in the first place.

And she blamed herself for being so enthralled by Lenny that she couldn't see clear to avoid a potential powder keg. She wanted badly to spend time with him, with his family, get to see him in his native environment. Now they were heading home after just a couple of hours, with the only salvageable memories being the kiss they shared on the shore of Herbert's Creek, and the conversation with Etta.

After ninety minutes of non-stop travel, Lenny pulled the car up to the gate at Summer's apartment complex. The gate attendant recognized Lenny and opened the gate without question. He drove inside and parked in Summer's designated parking space. He put the car in park, but left it running, hoping that Summer would not abruptly end their afternoon without speaking.

To his relief, Summer did not move, but looked straight ahead and said quietly, "Do you love her?"

Lenny answered immediately. "No." He turned to her. "I love you."

Summer turned, meeting his eyes, seeing the earnestness there. He meant it. It was genuine. He had the strongest of feelings for her. And she had feelings for him. But what were those feelings? Love? Lust? And Xavier still moved her. How could she reconcile the conflicts in her heart? She studied him for a few seconds before once again turning her gaze straight ahead.

Her response was a bit discouraging to Lenny. *'I love you too' would be a good thing to say here*, he thought. But maybe she couldn't say those words, because she was too conflicted. "Let me ask you a question," he said. "Do you still love Xavier?"

Lenny got his answer—or at least didn't get the answer he wanted—once Summer took too long to answer the question. After almost fifteen seconds of pondering, which seemed way longer to Lenny, Summer finally said, "I don't know."

Lenny nodded. The answer didn't surprise him, but heavily disappointed him. "Then, that's a problem."

"Why?" Summer asked.

"Because when you finally figure it out, I don't want to be left holding the short end of the stick. I don't want to be the rebound guy. I don't want to be his replacement. I want you to be with me because you want to be with *me*."

"I *do* want to be with you."

"Maybe so. But I also know you want to be with Xavier. You still love him. And that's not surprising. You've been with him a while. Just last week, you were ready to give up your body to him. That kind of devotion and affection doesn't go away overnight. You can't flick a switch and turn it off. It's there. It's in you. And it may be enough to drive you back to him."

"It won't."

"Then we gotta be sure. You're gonna need your space, get some time to heal."

"What are you saying?"

"You gotta get Xavier out of your system. It took me months to get Trinee out of mine, and I'm not sure I'm completely there. You need the same thing. And I can't be around you complicating things while you do that."

That statement drew Summer's attention enough to look at him. "So, are you saying you don't want to see me anymore?"

Lenny drew a breath. It literally caused an ache in his heart to say the words. "For right now. We need space. However long it takes, you need clarity of your feelings. You need to be in a place where Xavier no longer enters your mind and your dreams. And if I'm around, it'll just confuse that process."

Summer turned away. It pained her to hear Lenny say the words, but she knew they were true. She could never be devoted to Lenny as long as Xavier continued to be the center of her world. No matter how it ended, Summer needed to embark on that process of discovery.

"So, how do we do this?" Summer asked.

"I don't call you, you don't call me. We don't hang out anymore. If there's an emergency, then that's an exception; otherwise, we don't

have any contact."

"Isn't that a bit extreme? I mean, I don't have leprosy, or anything."

"We need to hear from God. As long as we are together, we are going to distract one another. We need to consecrate ourselves, so that we don't do something we're going to regret."

"For how long?" Summer's voice broke as if she was fighting back sobs.

"Until you get to the point where I ask you if you are still in love with Xavier, and you can tell me, without hesitation, no."

"No contact?"

"Not much. And I'd recommend no contact with him, either. We can speak to each other if we see each other in passing, but that's it. And I hope you use that time to really fall in love with Jesus and let Him guide your heart."

They sat there in silence, contemplating this new phase in their lives. Finally, when both of them had been drained of any more words to say, Summer grabbed her purse and got out of the car. She walked at a melancholy pace toward her apartment building, but then turned around and walked toward Lenny's car again. He rolled down the passenger side window as she approached.

"Can you promise me something?" Summer asked.

"What?" Lenny said.

"Promise me you won't date anyone else until things are clear for me."

Lenny thought for a moment, then said, "I can promise that I'll follow the Lord's will, whatever that is."

It wasn't the answer Summer wanted, but she knew that was probably the best commitment he could make. She nodded and said, "Bye, Lenny."

"See you later, Summer."

Lenny watched Summer walk into her apartment building. As she disappeared up the stairs, he clasped his hands in front of him and prayed to God that he hadn't made the wrong decision.

But at that moment, God did not answer him.

CHAPTER THIRTEEN

Twenty-nine days later

Summer walked in ten minutes late for the women's ministry Bible study at Heritage Church of Richmond.

Her decision to start attending Bible study was prompted by her need to once again reconnect with her faith. Two days after the July 4th debacle, Summer called Pastor Gillen to get him up to the minute, as she hadn't been to church in a while. Upon hearing the goings-on in Summer's life, Pastor Gillen referred her to his wife and the women's ministry, determining that she needed to be under the accountability of other women. Sister Gillen invited Summer to the weekly Bible study, and Summer had been attending for three weeks straight. This was her fourth meeting.

When she walked in, the ladies, twenty of them, were already in prayer, sitting in a circle in one of the church's classrooms. Summer quickly slipped into a seat, bowed her head, and joined in the prayer, led by Sister Gillen. Once they all said amen, they briefly looked around at each other before giving Sister Gillen their attention.

Sister Gillen wore wisdom like a royal robe; it oozed from her pores and seeped from her breath with every word she spoke. There

were several in the church who thought she should be the head pastor instead of her husband, but those people would never say so openly, and Sister Gillen would never entertain it, as she fully respected and honored her husband. Pastor Gillen felt the same for his wife, which was why he had no reservations in allowing her to be the chairwoman of the Women's Ministry, and other than hearing regular reports, rarely spoke into it, as he knew that Sister Gillen had things under control. She was young—only forty-five—but had the poise, the patience, and the maturity of someone twenty years her senior. There were rumors that she had been a college professor at one point, but Sister Gillen never addressed those rumors, especially since they were just rumors.

Sister Gillen welcomed everyone, introduced the newest member of the group and allowed a few minutes for the newbie to introduce herself. After the introduction, Sister Gillen opened her Bible. As if on cue, everyone else opened theirs.

"Let's turn to Matthew chapter five, verses 27 and 28." Sister Gillen waited for the ladies to find the scripture, and then continued. "'You have heard that it was said, 'You shall not commit adultery.' But I tell you that anyone who looks at a woman lustfully has already committed adultery with her in his heart.'" She looked around at her audience, seven of them married, one divorced, the others single. "I wanted to make three points about this scripture, and I hope to have some discussion about it. One, the scripture appears to be speaking only to men. But it would be a serious mistake to conclude that these instructions apply to men only. You see, when Jesus gave the Sermon on the Mount, he was speaking to his disciples, who were mostly men. I heard someone say that this scripture applies only to men because men are the ones with the greatest lust problems. I think men, in their role as pursuers, can get caught up in lust much more frequently than women, but I do not think that women are exempt from lust. Women are guilty of lust as well, and so this scripture applies to both sexes. If we did a study of all the mentions of sexual immorality in the Bible, of which lust is a major contributing factor, we will see that many of those scriptures do not exempt women.

"The second point I wanted to make is that this scripture answers questions I heard on a TV talk show one day. The questions on this talk show were, 'When is it considered cheating?' Is it considered cheating when sexual intercourse occurs, or is it when a man or woman starts to spend time with someone else? At what point can a man or woman say, 'my spouse has cheated'?"

A young woman, Pam, age thirty-five and married, cut in. "I can answer that question. It's just like the scripture said. He's cheating if he *looks* at a woman with lust. If I'm out to dinner at a restaurant with my man, and some hussy walks by with the skirt up to here and the neckline down to there, and he's checking her out, that's cheating."

"But that's not fair." Tatyana, the only divorcee in the group, spoke up. "Some of these women walk around these days with practically nothing on. Can we expect men not to look, to act like they're not there?"

"When you're with me, your eyes should be on *me*," Pam responded.

"What if he's not with you, and that same woman walks by?" Tatyana offered.

"Shouldn't matter. He shouldn't be looking at another woman when he's got one at home."

"But I think the point of the scripture is looking at a woman lustfully," Tatyana said. "Just because a man sees a beautiful woman, and he looks at her, doesn't mean he's lusting. If I pass by a gorgeous house, and I look at that house, but I know it's occupied, I'm not going to get out of my car and try to get that house. Why do we think when a man looks at a woman, he's lusting?"

"Now we know why you're divorced," Pam laughed. A couple of others laughed with her, but everyone else looked awkwardly, sympathetically, at Tatyana.

"Excuse me, I'm not divorced because of what my husband did," Tatyana shot back. "I'm divorced because of what *I* did."

Pam craned her head toward Tatyana. "What did you do?"

Sister Gillen jumped in. "What Sister Tatyana did or didn't do in

her marriage is not relevant here, unless she chooses to share it. But I think Pam's point is somewhat correct. A good definition of lust is sexual attraction that is functioning outside of God's purposes for it. Everything God created in us has a purpose, and sexual attraction was created by God for us for procreation, not recreation. It is to draw two single people together so that they can get married and enjoy intimacy in the confines of their marriage. When sexual attraction operates out-side of God's purpose and becomes merely a means to have fun or to feel good, it becomes lust."

"So, a man looking at a woman, or even a woman looking at a man, at what point does it become lust?" Summer asked.

"I think when a man, or a woman, looks at someone, becomes attracted, and is focused only on the physicality, I believe that's lust," Sister Gillen said. "In a lustful heart, the ultimate goal is to engage in a fleshly act. But for a single person who's operating in God's purpose, the sexual attraction becomes a motivator to get to know this person so that a long, loving, intimate relationship can develop."

Rosetta, one of the married women, said, "My mother once told me something about lust. Excuse me if this seems a little blunt, but she said that if you're having sex, and it is the greatest mind-blowing sex you've ever had, and two minutes after it is over, you're no longer interested in that man, that's a sure sign you're in lust. It's like, you're as close as you possibly can be with another human being, but after it's over, there's no kissing, no cuddling, no talking. Right after the act, you become distant."

"But even if there is kissing, cuddling, and talking, it can still be lust," Sister Gillen said. "Lust demands immediacy. It wants a physi-cal relationship, and quickly. A person wrapped up in lust will not wait until marriage. They'll have sex with that person, or if that is not pos-sible, with someone else."

Xavier immediately popped into Summer's mind. Was Xavier's love for her really lust? What about Lenny? If they didn't have to get back to the picnic, how far would they have gone at Make Out Point?

"Because for the lustful person, it's about physical pleasure, not

intimacy," Sister Gillen continued. "They want sex, but they don't want the closeness that comes with true relationship. Just like God wants a relationship with us where we are not just after God for what he can give us, but we are concerned about the things God is concerned about and how to please him."

Rosetta chimed in. "When I go into the bedroom to be with my husband, I'm focused on how to please him. And he's focused on how to please me. That's what relationship truly is."

"And lust has no interest in that," Sister Gillen added. "Lust says, 'How do I please *me*?' But to clarify, looking at a woman does not necessarily mean lust. Looking at a woman with lustful intent is the issue, and a man can look at a woman, note and acknowledge she's beautiful, without any lustful intent."

"I know a lot of sisters that will get mad if their man notices another woman's beauty," Tatyana said. "It's like a slap in the face."

"Men are that way, too," Summer interjected. "When I was out with my guy at a restaurant, I noticed this man, and he was fine. So, I told my guy about it, and do you know we argued about it the rest of the evening? It's like it's a taboo to acknowledge that someone else is handsome or beautiful."

"It's not," said Sister Gillen. "I tell married couples, and those about to be married, that they shouldn't think that because they marry their spouse, they are not going to find anyone else attractive except their spouse. That's not realistic. I love my husband, and I am devoted to him. But that doesn't mean I won't see a man every now and then that is amazingly good looking to me."

"Like Morris Chestnut!" one woman blurted out.

"No, no, girl. Idris Elba!" another said.

"Boris Kodjoe!"

"Denzel Washington!"

"Denzel?" Pam said. "Please. Denzel is played out."

"Still cute, though."

Sister Gillen quickly reclaimed her meeting. "But no matter how handsome they are, it is a sin to dwell on them in a sexual manner. The

Bible says it's adultery, whether or not you actually proceed to any physical act."

A young woman, about the age of twenty-six, piped up. "I got a question. At my old church, they taught that married women who committed adultery were stoned, but married men who committed adultery weren't. What's up with that?"

"That's how it was back in those days, girl," Pam answered. "Women were owned by men. We were their property. If a woman stepped out on her husband, she wound up with a rock upside her head. But men could have sixteen wives if they wanted to. It's jacked up. Glad we don't live in those days anymore."

"I know a lot of men who would like to get us back to those days," said another woman, laughing.

Sister Gillen interjected. "Yes, it's true that men in Bible times had more freedoms and rights than women had. But we have to consider one thing. Marriage has always been a type of Christ and his church. We are the bride of Christ. And just as God, who is a jealous God, doesn't want us giving ourselves to other gods, the wife shouldn't give herself to anyone else but her husband. It was so serious that married women who committed adultery were stoned."

"I have a question about that."

Summer's statement was so forceful and came so soon on the heels of Sister Gillen's response that it took some of the women by surprise.

"Like Pam just said, it seems like men dominated women back in those days. But we're supposed to obey the Bible, right?" Summer asked. "So, what do you say about all the stuff in the Bible that permits men to rule over women? Like the scripture 'wives, submit to your husbands'? And there's another that says, 'your desire shall be for your husband, and he shall rule over you.' Men have been using those scriptures for years to abuse women. So my question is, how can any woman have confidence in the word of God when it appears to give men a reason to dominate them? A woman gets stoned for adultery, but a man doesn't? A man can have many wives, but a woman can't have

many husbands? It's no wonder so many men quote the Bible before and after they beat the living crap out of you."

The question struck everyone silent. Most of them did not know where the question came from, except Sister Gillen. She knew Summer's history, but was a bit surprised that Summer did not raise this issue in a more private setting. But she understood—sometimes people ask the toughest questions in the safety of a group environment.

"Let me ask a question as I prepare to answer yours." Sister Gillen said, looking directly at Summer without the least bit of malice. "Why do you think that sixty-six percent of churchgoers are women? That seventy-five percent of Christian retail shoppers are women? That this Bible study is well-attended, but the men's Bible study is lucky to attract five or six men per week?"

"I've heard that it's because the church largely caters to the female aesthetic," Summer responded.

"And what is that?"

"Well, women like qualities such as love, compassion, relationship, nurturing, caring, sensitivity, and family, and the church places a big emphasis on those qualities."

"Yes, and I believe God created women to be that way. He created us to respond to those qualities. I also believe God created men with certain qualities as well; namely, the capability to love, to care, to provide for, to hunt, to conquer, to nurture, to lead."

"So, what's your point?"

"My point is, God created a symbiotic system, in which men are designed to lead in love, and women respond to that love through devotion and submission. Now the fact that men have often abused that privilege, and women have responded in kind, doesn't mean that the system has changed nor is it broken. I know a number of women who tell me they are very happy being in a relationship with their husbands in which they are under his leadership. That's the way God intended it to be in a loving relationship."

"Yeah, but don't you think that's kind of archaic, though," Pam said, speaking more to the group, as if she was trying to gain their

support and agreement. "I mean, that may have worked alright back in the days when women didn't have options. But now, we have women mayors, women governors, women pastors. We may even have a woman president one day. We lead, and are capable of leading. So, to say that God intends for only men to lead is like putting us back in the dark ages where we stayed in the house and worked our fingers to the bone. And for me, I can't see myself being subject to no man, not even my husband."

Sister Gillen decided to challenge her. "And why not?"

"Because I don't have to be. I have my own car, my own job, and my own house. My husband moved in with *me*." Pam paused amid the few snickers that came from the group. "Don't get me wrong. I love my husband, but I'm not gonna be obedient to his every command. Women can't sit around and wait for a man to make decisions. I have a mind of my own. I can make decisions. I think it works better for a marriage to be a partnership, where each person brings something to the table."

"And what makes you think that under God's plan, there's no partnership?"

"The husband gives the orders, and I have to obey. What kind of plan is that?"

Sister Gillen slammed her Bible shut and leaned forward. "First of all, let me correct you on a few things. First of all, as Christians, we should never take the position that when God says something, it's up for debate. If it is God's plan, then it is for our good, whether we like it or agree with it or not."

Sufficiently scolded, Pam reared back in her seat and folded her arms.

"Furthermore, anyone who wants to live in Christ must be submissive. It's our lifestyle. We have co-opted attitudes from the world that suggest that submission is weak, demeaning, and deprives us of power over ourselves. Well, it is no such thing. It is one of the strongest things you could do. It takes a strong faith to say to one another, 'you are greater than me, and I will bow myself to be in service to you if

you need me.' And that is what God calls us to do—serve one another. And we can't do that if we are looking at each other as if we are better than them."

Seeing she had their full attention, Sister Gillen continued. "I am a minister. Do you know what that means? The word minister comes from a Latin word that means 'less.' The minister was a person who was considered a servant to those greater than he. I am here to serve you. I am here to submit to you. And that is the beauty of my calling. Yes, God calls wives to submit to their husbands. But he also calls husbands to submit to God, children to submit to parents, and everyone to submit to leaders and those in authority, and us to submit to one another. It's God's plan, and it is how he designed us. And I can tell you from experience: if a woman has a man who submits to God, to leadership, loves her and cares for her, and is willing to give his life for her, she should have no problem with submitting herself to such a man. It happens all the time. A good woman will follow a Godly man anywhere. How often do you see women in church consistently without their husbands?"

Sister Gillen looked around for responses. Getting none, she said, "All the time. Women come to church every day, all the time, without their husbands. Now, let me flip that. How often do you see husbands in church without consistent attendance from their wives? Almost never. Studies show that a woman is more likely to follow a man to church, than a man to follow a woman to church. It's not in the nature of a man to follow a woman. It's the nature of a man to lead."

"So, what about all the women leaders?" Summer challenged. "Are they doing something that a man should do? What about women like Maggie L. Walker, Cathy Hughes, Condoleezza Rice? Is God saying to them, 'shut up and let a man take charge'?"

"Who's Maggie Walker?" Tatyana asked.

"Girl, you live in Richmond, and you don't know who Maggie Walker was?" Pam said.

"Probably grew up in Tuckahoe," another woman said, prompting a burst of laughter from the group.

Sister Gillen did not laugh, but calmed the din by raising and lowering her hand. "Maggie Walker was the first black woman to own a bank in the United States. Used to be down on St. James Street, I think." She turned to Summer. "You could also add women like Miriam and Deborah to your list. Both of them were prophets and leaders in Israel. When God needs something done, he can and will raise up women to do it. But that doesn't nullify God's direction for husbands and wives. In the household, the husband should lead."

Summer defiantly turned away.

Sister Gillen noticed it and said, "Summer, I know you've had some struggles in your life with regard to men. But don't let your past make you afraid of moving into the future with God's purpose in mind. Whatever man you decide to be with, you need to know his vision, his purpose. What's he here for? If he can't answer that, then you don't need to be with him, at least not until he finds out. A man without vision cannot lead, because he's going nowhere. If he can articulate that vision, and it is in accordance with the word of God, and it resonates with your spirit, then you'll have no problem submitting to that man, because you're both going in the same direction."

"What if he changes direction?" Summer asked. "What if he becomes abusive?"

"In no way does the scripture endorse abuse," Sister Gillen noted. "In fact the scripture says, 'Husbands, love your wives, even as Christ also love the church, and gave himself up for her … . In the same way, husbands ought to love their wives as their own bodies. He who loves his wife loves himself.' You can't love your wife and be abusive; it's impossible. A husband that abuses his wife, physically, verbally, or however, takes a power over her that is not scriptural. In such situations, I think it is perfectly acceptable for a wife to separate herself from her husband, because he is operating outside of scripture and placing his wife in danger. I know, based on what you've gone through, it is difficult for you to hear the word *submit*, because it has negative connotations for you. But hopefully, in time, you will come to recognize submission as a beautiful thing." Sister Gillen looked around

at all the ladies. "Hopefully, you all will."

And that was Summer's challenge. Whatever man she ended up with, she knew she was not ready to take a submissive role as a wife. That's what kept her from marrying Xavier. And she knew it would likely drive a wedge between her and Lenny. Almost twenty-nine years after she left her father behind in Brazil, Summer discovered she still had a lot of healing to do.

CHAPTER FOURTEEN

Six days later

Xavier hadn't heard from Summer in over a month, and he had resigned himself to the fact that he would never see her again. Having cut his ties with Jada Hardy, he threw himself into his work, staying at the office sometimes until he was too tired to keep his eyes open, then checking into the hotel across the street and sleeping there until the next morning. Some days he couldn't bear to look at his own apartment because of the memories of Summer that hung in the air like heavy humidity. There were moments he could sense her odor in the place, and yearned for her to be next to him. He would dream that she was there, and then wake up to an empty, lonesome darkness.

Once word spread around the office that both Jada and Summer were out of the picture, some women in the office started vying for his attention. In his not too distant past, Xavier would pick one, wine and dine her, and enjoy her as much as possible. He wouldn't care if all the woman wanted was his money and his lifestyle. He didn't care about his company's fraternization policies. He would live it up with her, even if it was only for a time, and then set his plans on the next woman.

Summer changed that. After going out with Summer a few times, he was convinced she was the woman he wanted to marry. She was a total lady, with enough class and sophistication to look good on his arm at parties, enough sexiness to keep him enchanted at night, and the right amount of demure southern charm to make him yearn for her company. Now, as he sat in his office, on a Monday morning, once again allowing his mind to fill with thoughts of her, he regretted ever allowing Jada to affect their relationship. The few moments of intimacy with Jada were not worth losing Summer.

He turned to his computer, which was set at a right angle to his desk, next to the glass window wall that gave him a bird's-eye view of downtown Richmond. He planned to answer a few emails before lunchtime.

After about fifteen minutes, Maureen, the customer service manager, walked through the open doorway of his office. Xavier's media relations team rarely had any direct interaction with the customer service division. But that didn't stop Maureen from visiting Xavier's office at least once per day after Xavier's break-up had spread through the rumor mill. Her visits were just to say hi, she would say. But it was more to show off her ample curves in whatever formfitting outfit she decided to squeeze into that day. Maureen was mere eye candy to Xavier most days; but now, loneliness ruled out over reason, and Maureen was looking especially good to him now.

"Hey, Mr. Williams," Maureen said, her voice high and flirty. "How you doin'?"

"Doing good, Maureen. How are you?"

"Just great." Maureen would usually hang around at the entrance just long enough for Xavier to get a good look at her. But this time, now that the rumors of Xavier's break-up with Jada had made their way down to the first floor, Maureen took the extra step of walking inside. "How was your weekend?"

Xavier stopped typing and turned to face her. "It was okay."

"What'd you do?"

"Just sat at home. Nothing exciting."

"Hmm. Man like you shouldn't sit at home by yourself."

"What makes you think I was by myself?"

"The way you said it. *It was nothing exciting.* If I was your woman, you would *not* be saying that."

Xavier was both shocked and titillated at her brash comment. He got up from his chair, walked past Maureen, and closed the door. Maureen checked him out as he walked. His Joseph Abboud tailored suit hung just right on him, his cologne sweet and fresh, a smell of princes, kingmakers, and high money. Maureen knew if she bagged this guy, she would never have to shop at Walmart again.

When Xavier returned to his seat, Maureen settled in the seat in front of his desk, making sure every bit of her thick legs were in full view. Before either of them got a chance to speak again, Xavier's phone rang.

"Excuse me," Xavier said to Maureen, checking the caller ID, and then picking up the phone. He listened for a few seconds, then said to the caller, "Thank you. I'll be right down." He hung up the phone, then stood again, looking at Maureen with an almost harried look. "I'm sorry, Maureen, but we are going to have to finish this conversation another time. One of our vendors is downstairs."

"Okay. I'll look forward to us talking again." Maureen got up and walked out, looking back at him with a seductive smile.

Xavier cursed. Just five more minutes, and he would have had her phone number. But this was a visitor he could not ignore. Xavier fastened the buttons on his suit jacket, then walked out to the hallway to make sure that Maureen was no longer around. He then walked back into his office and dialed the receptionist.

"Send her up to my office, please," he said to the receptionist, then sat down at his desk, faced forward, and waited.

Within minutes, Summer Maldonado appeared at his doorway. Xavier stood upon seeing her, and quickly took her in—her black ankle pants and perforated linen blouse made her look as if she were heading out for an afternoon of shopping. Xavier looked down and noticed that the Christian Louboutin shoes she wore were *not* the ones

he had bought her several months ago.

"Hi, X," Summer said, noticing that the weeks apart from her had not diminished his debonair style.

"Hey, Summer," Xavier said. "Good to see you." He waited for her to say the same. She did not. "Come on in."

Summer sauntered in while Xavier rushed behind her to close the door. He motioned Summer to a seat while he sat on the edge of his desk in front of her.

"How you been?" Xavier asked. "You look good."

"Thanks."

"I heard you lost your job."

"Yes, I did. They finally got around to firing me about two weeks after they suspended me."

"I was sorry to hear that. How've you been taking care of yourself?"

"My Mãe got a couple of churches in Atlanta to take up an offering for me. And she got the radio station to make an appeal over the air for me, so all together, they raised over $6,000 for me. So, that's good for now, until I find a job. How have *you* been?"

"Hanging in there. Missing you a lot."

Summer looked away. "Well, I'm sure Jada is keeping you occupied."

Xavier got up from the desk. "I broke up with Jada right after I got back from the Vineyard. And I cut my ties with Mark. You know she was the one who got you fired?"

"I'd heard something to that effect. But no worries. I've moved on with my life."

"Hmm." Xavier moved to the window and looked out over the city. "So, I guess you got yourself a new man."

Summer wasn't sure whether to tell the truth, or to evade the question, as she knew where the conversation would lead if she told the truth. Nonetheless, she told him. "No, I'm not dating anyone right now."

Xavier turned back to her and sat on the edge of the desk again.

"Well, you know I still love you. I always have."

Summer smiled. Xavier still had that charismatic persuasiveness about him.

"I've never been able to stop thinking about you," he continued. "Summer, as much as I screw up at times, I know you are the right woman for me."

Summer looked into his eyes and could see tears welling there. He had suffered the pain of loss as much as she had. His comely swagger made way for vulnerability and brokenness. Summer was emotionally struck. She stood and walked over to him.

Xavier's eyes brightened as Summer approached him. Summer was a much better catch than Maureen any day. And now, it looked like he had won back the woman of his dreams.

***

Nine months later

Lenny's work record had been so stellar that his supervisor transferred him to the weekday eight-to-four shift once the regular gate attendant transferred to another site. This was a major blessing for him, as it allowed him to see his son more often, and minimized his dependence on Trinee and her mother to babysit.

But with the great blessing that God had given him regarding his work hours, he also felt that God was ignoring his almost daily prayers to bring Summer back into his life. It had been ten months since he had a conversation with her, and other than seeing Summer occasionally coming and going to and from her apartment, he had no contact with her, and it seemed as if she was actually trying to avoid him. And it was bothering him immensely, especially since Summer, during the few times he saw her, seemed happy and preoccupied, as if she had moved on and found some other direction for her life. She also seemed

to have found a job. There were several times that he thought parting ways with her was the stupidest thing he could have done.

Maybe she's just not the girl for you was the thought that came into his mind more frequently than he desired. But if not her, then who? Lenny was thirty-five years old, not getting any younger, and the closest thing he had ever had to a wife was Trinee. Maybe, with all of Trinee's flaws, he should just settle for her and move on. Trinee was ready, willing and waiting. And she was the mother of his son.

He allowed these thoughts to consume him most of his days at work, but he resisted making any contact with Summer. It was up to her to make the next move. At this point, Lenny wasn't sure it was ever going to happen.

It was a late Wednesday afternoon in early May. The cloudless blue skies allowed enough sunlight to make it comfortably warm but not overbearingly hot. Lenny was preparing to end his shift, and had started to hand the reins over to Rod, the new night-shift gate attendant, when Rod studied him, trying to gauge whether he should or shouldn't say what he wanted to say.

Lenny noticed the attendant's eye-balling and said, "Is there something I can help you with?"

Rod was young, about twenty-nine, with biceps hard as marble and a smooth, boyish face straight out of *Tiger Beat*. He fancied himself a bit of a lothario, and had no problem with propositioning or seducing pretty girls while on duty. But Lenny had already warned him that Summer was off-limits, and thus far, Rod had respected Lenny's wishes.

"You know that girl you been trying to get next to?" Rod said.

"Yeah?" Lenny said, grabbing his car keys off the gate house desk and preparing to leave.

"She's getting married, man."

Unless someone had told Lenny that his son was hurt, nothing could have hit him harder. He stopped and looked sternly at Rod, hoping that he was joking. "Married?"

"Yeah. Saw the ring. I see a cute woman, there's two things I look

at first. One is the ring finger. Next is the body. 'Cause if the ring finger is naked, my goal is to get the rest of her naked.'"

"How do you know she's getting married?"

"She stopped by the gate house last night, said she just gotten a new car, and wanted, not one, but two parking passes. I saw the ring, and I asked her if she was married. She said no, she was engaged. So I wished her congratulations on the engagement, and she said thank you. Plus, she been keeping company with some dude."

"What does he look like?"

"Got some money, I can tell you that. Which ain't no surprise, 'cause your girl don't look like she come cheap. Light-skinned, maybe about your age. Good lookin' dude. Not that I notice stuff like that."

"Of course." He deflated. A reconciliation with Summer was no longer feasible, a done deal. Lenny almost wished he hadn't spoken to Rod. "Thanks, man." Lenny walked sullenly to his car.

Before Lenny was out of earshot, Rod said, "Man, don't sweat it. Them high-maintenance bitches do that kind of stuff."

Lenny turned and headed back to the gate house. His hangdog face became tense and smoldering. He came within inches of Rod and said, "I appreciate your advice, man, but if you ever call Summer a bitch again, we gonna have words, and maybe a little more."

Rod looked at him, sizing up the situation. Lenny was street-hardened and from Mosby Court. Rod grew up in Westover Hills and, despite his brawn, never had much of a fight in his life. He did the math. Lenny was the odds-on favorite. He quickly backed down.

"My apologies, man," Rod said. "Didn't mean no disrespect."

Lenny turned and headed back to his car. He got in and drove about half a mile away in bumper to bumper traffic before he came to a logical and sobering conclusion: Summer Maldonado would not be in his future. She had definitely moved on. And he was just a hair away from cursing himself and cursing God for letting Summer go. He had her. She was all his. And now she was gone.

He was on his way to Trinee's mother's house to pick up Lenny Jr. and take him home. Right about now, Trinee was looking awfully good

to him.

***

The next day

Lenny worked his eight-to-four shift, rushed home, and immediately started tidying up his apartment. He was not a slob; he normally kept his kitchen and bathroom pristine. But occasionally, clothes and shoes would find themselves in places other than the closet and drawers, and newspapers, magazines, and books would be scattered on furniture, kept company by Lenny Jr.'s toys and the occasional empty water bottle or two.

The day before, he had extended an invitation to Trinee to come over the next day, saying that he wanted to talk to her. He knew Trinee was not perfect, and that she would need a lot of work before she was ready to be a wife. But Lenny was hungry for female companionship, and a hungry person tended to eat what's being served rather than wait for a better meal.

Speaking of eating, he needed to make a quick call to Carl's carryout down the street and order some fried chicken and a couple of salads, then pick it up, return home, and put the final touches on his apartment before Trinee came over at six. Lenny Jr. would stay with Trinee's mom, allowing Lenny and Trinee some private time to visit.

Once he had picked up the food from Carl's, he returned to his apartment and put the food inside his oven to keep it warm. His living room was sparse, with a black leather sofa and love seat he had purchased from a local Goodwill; a large, wide square coffee table he caught on sale for $30 at Walmart; and a fifty-inch flat-screen TV that hung on the wall next to a balcony door with vertical blinds. There was no dining room table; he and his son typically had their meals at the coffee table in the living room. The only décor on the beige painted

walls was a large poster with the words of John 14:1–3 inscribed on it. The wood floor was fully carpeted, another $300 out of Lenny's pocket after a neighbor downstairs complained about the noise when Lenny played in the living room.

He switched on the TV, then checked himself in a mirror near the hallway. He did not want to seem as if he was trying to overly impress Trinee, or give her the impression that this was a date, so his khaki cargo pants and white T-shirt would have to do.

The knock on the door came early, but Lenny was ready. He put on some slippers and walked to the door. He unlocked the door, and opened it, ready to invite Trinee inside.

It was Summer Maldonado instead.

Lenny almost choked on his own spit. Once the shock subsided, Lenny nervously said, "Summer."

"Hi, Lenny."

Lenny stood there, unsure of what to do. Trinee would be over soon, and he did not want her to know that Summer was here. Yet, he was so curious as to why Summer was there that he couldn't send her away.

Summer's voice invaded his thoughts. "You gonna let me in?"

Uh, this is not a good time, Summer was what his logical mind was coaxing him to say. But this was the first time he had spoken to or seen Summer in months.

He opened the door wider to let Summer in, thinking that maybe he could call Trinee and delay her arrival. As Summer passed him, her jasmine scent caught his nose and drew his eyes to her. Her blue floral print dress and zinc-colored Jimmy Choo shoes were pretty, but it was the way she wore the dress, with a confidence and sexiness, that struck Lenny. Then he remembered. *She's getting married.*

Lenny shut the door, walked past, and spied the engagement ring on her finger. It was not a cheap cubic zirconia that someone had bought at a cut-rate jewelry counter. The ring was real, with a 14-karat gold band and a cluster of diamonds. Suddenly, he got his wits about him, and he walked into the living room ready to challenge Summer as

to why she was marrying a jerk like Xavier.

As Lenny moved to the couch, Summer stood in the center of the room, smiled, and said, "So, how have you been?"

"Hanging in there," Lenny said, his eyes focused on the TV.

Summer looked around. "Is this a bad time?"

"Depends on why you're here." He shot a confused frown at Summer. "How did you know where I lived anyway? I don't recall giving you my address."

"Your Aunt Etta."

"You called her?"

"Actually, she called me. We exchanged numbers at the cookout. She and I have been talking, on and off."

"She never told me that."

"That's one thing I like about her. She knows how to keep secrets."

"Speaking of secrets."

"What do you mean?"

"Your big event. When is it?"

"How did you know about that?"

"I'm not as dumb as I look."

"I never said you were."

"So, when is it?"

"This Saturday. It's what I came to talk to you about. And I didn't want to do it over the phone."

This Saturday, he thought. She probably was there to give him an invitation. Sure, invite me to your wedding, have me sit there in the church, as single as a dollar bill, and watch like a jilted lover as you give yourself to a man who cheated on you. Twice. No thank you, darling.

"Well, if you're inviting me, I respectfully decline."

"Why?" Summer moved closer to him, unintentionally blocking his view of the TV. "The pastor who's officiating over the ceremony asked me to—"

Lenny interrupted Summer. "I appreciate the invitation, but I don't

think it's a good idea for me to come."

Summer sensed a hostility that seemed strange and misplaced. "Are you angry with me about something?"

Other than kicking me to the curb to marry the guy that cheated on you?

Instead, Lenny asked, "Are you serious?"

"Yes. Have I upset you?"

I sent you away to find God, not to find Xavier.

"I just can't come."

"Why?"

"You know that part where the pastor asks if anybody has just cause for these two not to be married, then let them speak now, or forever hold their peace?" Lenny said. "I'd probably have to say something, so it's best that I not attend."

"Lenny, what are you talking about?"

"I'm not gonna attend your wedding, Summer. Point blank."

"What wedding? You think I'm getting married?"

"Well, aren't you?"

"No! What gave you that idea?"

"That ring on your finger, for one."

Summer held up her hand, looked briefly at the ring, and laughed. "No, this is—" She interrupted herself with another laugh, then motioned to the loveseat. "Can I sit?"

"Sure," Lenny said, his eyebrows furrowed. "Pardon my manners."

"Not a problem." Summer moved to the loveseat and sat. "This ring is actually my Mãe's engagement ring. Let me explain. I've been involved quite a bit in the church over the past few months. Pastor Gillen's wife heads the women's ministry, and I became a part of that. About four months ago, Sister Gillen asked all the single ladies to bring an engagement ring to church. She said it didn't matter what type. It could be cheap. It could come out of a Cracker Jack box. As long as it was an engagement ring. So, my Mãe lent me hers, and I brought it to church. So, Sister Gillen said that for the next few

months, to wear your engagement ring as a sign of your engagement to Jesus. She said that this is the time of our consecration. We were not to date or have any other men during that period, but focus on prayer and our commitment to Jesus. So, that's what I've been doing, and that's why I'm wearing this ring."

Lenny laughed, ashamed that he had been so misled. "I'm sorry. I thought you and Xavier were—"

"X and I are history. I'm engaged to Jesus now."

"You really left him?"

"It wasn't easy. But nine months ago, I did it."

Nine months earlier in Xavier's office

"I've never been able to stop thinking about you," Xavier said. "Summer, as much as I screw up at times, I know you are the right woman for me."

Summer stood and walked over to him. Xavier's eyes brightened as she approached. He was hoping their lips would touch for the first time in over a year. But instead of presenting her lips, she presented her hands, outstretched, palms up.

Xavier look confused.

"Give me your hands," Summer clarified. "I want to pray with you."

Xavier frowned. "I got other things I want to do with you."

Summer withdrew her hands. "I'm not the girl for that. I can be your friend. I can pray for you. But that's it."

"So, you came here in person to tell me you wanted to pray for me? You could have done that over the phone."

"I wanted to close the boyfriend–girlfriend chapter in our lives, X. I couldn't do that over the phone. You will always have a place in my heart and in my prayers, X."

"I thought it was closed!" Xavier's voice escalated slightly. "I was ready to move without you. Now, all of a sudden, you show up and just

confuse the situation again."

"You were ready to move on, yet you were still thinking about me?"

Xavier stood. "When a man loses something precious, he may face the reality that he's lost it. But that doesn't mean he won't regret it, that he won't think constantly about how good he had it."

Summer nodded, completely understanding the point. "I'm sorry it worked out this way."

"Well, if it was meant to be, it would have happened." Xavier turned and walked to the window. He stood there, staring out at nothing in particular.

Guessing that Xavier no longer wanted to talk, Summer turned and headed for the door. As she opened it, Xavier said, "Summer?"

"Yes?" Summer said, turning.

"Make sure your next man knows just how incredible a woman you are."

Summer nodded and left Xavier's office. As she headed for the elevator, she thought about Xavier's last comment.

Incredible woman.

She felt blessed that she no longer needed Xavier to make her feel that way.

***

"So, what's happening on Saturday?" Lenny asked.

"Well—" Summer perked up with excitement. "—I'm preaching my trial sermon!"

Lenny quickly grabbed the remote and switched off the TV. He wanted to hear every word of this, with no distractions. "Your trial sermon? Are you gonna be a preacher?"

"An evangelist."

Pride washed over Lenny's face. "That's wonderful. That's a great calling."

"Yep. I've been feeling the call for a while now. Finally decided to answer. Anyway, my pastor said that I should invite three people who are most important in my life. So, of course I picked my Mãe. And then, there's you and Lenny Jr."

Lenny lowered his head in humility.

"So, if you—"

Summer was interrupted by a knock on the door. She held her thought and looked at Lenny, who seemed to cringe when the knocking started.

Lenny never thought a moment of delight could be followed so closely by a moment of dread. He got up from the couch. "Excuse me," he said to Summer as he headed to the door.

The moment Lenny opened the door, Trinee rushed inside, touting a royal blue bottle of Moscato. "I know you don't drink, but you—"

Trinee stopped both talking and walking when she saw Summer in the living room looking at her with the most awkward of expressions. She glared at Summer for a few seconds, then turned to Lenny. "Why you invite me here when you got her up in here?"

Lenny touched Trinee on her back and tried to gently goad her toward the door. "Lemme talk to you in the hallway for a minute."

Trinee looked again at Summer, and then, to send the message that she would be back, set the Moscato forcefully on the coffee table. Then, she walked ahead of Lenny out the front door.

Lenny led her further down the hallway a few feet from his door, close to the stairway. "Listen, I didn't know she was gonna be here today," he said quietly.

"I thought you said she was out of your life," Trinee said, not so quietly.

"I thought she was. She just came over to invite me to a special church event she's a part of."

"So, she just shows up out of the blue like that?"

"Yeah, she did."

"You must think I'm—"

They both heard Lenny's front door open. Summer stepped out

into the hallway and walked to them. "Look, I didn't mean to cause any friction, so I'm going to leave," Summer said. "Lenny, I left the name, address, and service time on a card on your coffee table. Bye." She disappeared down the stairway.

Lenny looked at Trinee, glad that Summer had confirmed what he just said. Trinee turned and headed back into the apartment, with Lenny following close behind.

"She should be glad I was in a good mood, or I would've whipped that trick's ass." Trinee headed into the kitchen and opened a cabinet door, peering inside. "You don't have any wine glasses?"

"Why would I have wine glasses? I don't drink."

"For guests." Trinee grabbed a drinking glass, set it on the counter, then peered in the oven and took a whiff. "Hmm. Smells good. You get this from Carl's?"

Lenny ignored the question. "Why do you call her a trick? She's not a trick. In fact, she's never been with a man."

"Who told you that? Her?"

"Yeah."

Trinee scoffed. "You got a lot to learn about women." She removed the food from the oven and grabbed two plates from the cabinet. "A girl that looks like that, with all that body and that face, ain't no way she made it past thirty without some dude smashin' that. All men are dogs. With all y'all barking up her tree, she bound to come down for one of y'all. That's all I'm sayin'. I wouldn't be surprised if that someone was you."

"So, you think I'm a dog?"

"Put it this way. If you was my man, I wouldn't trust you around that trick if my life depended on it."

"I don't appreciate you calling her a trick," Lenny said sternly.

Trinee stopped what she was doing and swung her head toward him with major attitude. "Why you invite me over here anyway?"

"I'm beginning to wonder." Lenny returned to the living room and sat on the couch. Trinee followed and stood in the same spot that Summer had stood earlier.

"You still in love with her, ain't you?" Trinee had her hand on her hip, posturing as if to dare him to lie to her.

Lenny hesitated, like one might hesitate before jumping into freezing water. "Yeah," he answered. "And it wouldn't have made a difference if she came over, or if she didn't."

"How can you be in love with somebody you haven't seen in almost a year?"

Trinee had asked a good question. Lenny wasn't sure how to answer it. "I don't know. It's as if God is keeping her in my heart, and I can't get her out. Not that I'm trying much."

Trinee moved over to the loveseat. Her strategy with Lenny had been to win him over with her body. But given what he had just said, she knew she would never be able to win his heart. And that was not enough for her. And that gave her no reason to continue to be in his apartment.

Trinee stood and walked toward the front door. Before she left, she turned to Lenny and said, "You need to come and get your son." Then she walked out, slamming the door behind her.

Come and get your son. Lenny thought about this statement, which seemed a normal thing for a mother to say to a father. But Lenny knew Trinee well, and there was more in those words than met the ear. That was Trinee's indirect, off-handed way of saying that she was going to hang out tonight, and was not going to babysit his son. Trinee often tried to make Lenny jealous by telling him she was going to a party, or a club, or some other place where she would likely meet and/or be propositioned by men. It never worked. But that didn't stop Trinee from trying it anyway.

Lenny looked down at the card that Summer had left on his coffee table. There was no way he was going to miss Summer's trial sermon. And since Trinee had suddenly and unwittingly blessed him with Lenny Jr. for at least 48 hours, his son would be able to go with him.

CHAPTER FIFTEEN

The Heritage Church of Richmond's pastor, Jim Gillen, had always bristled at the idea of his church being called a megachurch, so despite the fact that his church on Hungary Spring Road had barely enough room to hold his swelling congregation, he choose to remain there. The T-shaped church, with brick veneer, traditional stained glass windows, and a white steeple at the foot of the T, was purchased ten years before, and already he was having multiple services on Sunday to accommodate his growing crowd.

Pastor Gillen added a Saturday service to siphon off some worshippers who would otherwise come on Sundays. To him, God didn't care which day you worshipped, as long as you worshipped. In addition, he had read a statistic somewhere that said that twenty-seven percent of Christians work on Sundays and cannot make it to a Sunday service. The Saturday service seemed like not only a good idea for those saints, but also to allow his ministry team to exercise their preaching muscles so that he could focus on the Sunday service.

The Saturday service was the perfect opportunity to allow his pupil, Summer, to give her trial sermon. The service was often well-attended, consisting of mostly church members and friends. If Summer did not do well with the sermon, she was among family, with a minimal amount of visitors to impact their impression of his church.

The 300-seat sanctuary was half-full, with more people arriving. The musicians had already started to file into the sanctuary, heading to their instruments, starting to warm up. Lenny sat outside in his car in the parking lot, watching people go inside. He was nervous, even though he was doing absolutely nothing but attending a service. But he knew Summer's mother would be there, and he definitely wanted to make a good impression on her. It was eighty-five degrees outside, but Lenny would not shirk on his attire. He brushed lint off his black suit, purchased just the day before on a shopping trip to the mall. He finished it off with a purple silk tie and black leather oxfords. Lenny Jr., who sat in the back seat, coaxed his father into allowing him to wear blue jeans and a striped short-sleeved T-shirt. Since it was not Sunday and it was getting hot outside, Lenny acquiesced.

When it was almost five minutes to the service time, Lenny and his son walked in. Lenny was prepared to sit near the back of the church, but when he got to the entrance of the sanctuary, a silver-haired usher asked his name.

"Lenny Yates," he said.

The usher handed him a program, and said, "We have a special seat for you, Mr. Yates. Would you like your son to participate in the children's service?"

Lenny looked down at Lenny Jr., who was smiling his approval.

Lenny looked up at the usher and nodded. Another woman stepped forward and led Lenny and his son to a large room near the rear of the sanctuary, where there were already twelve children Lenny Jr.'s age. Once he was certain that Lenny Jr. was situated, he walked back to the sanctuary. The usher led him past several full pews to a half empty one in the second row. Orange sheets of paper labeled "Reserved" lined the pew. The usher took one away, and invited Lenny to sit. She then hurried back to the sanctuary entrance.

Lenny looked around the church and noticed its racial variety. There were more blacks than whites, but there were also a few Hispanics and one Asian. The worship team also reflected the diversity of the church, its music eclectic and designed to appeal to a broad spectrum

of worshippers. As the service started, Lenny got caught up in the worship songs, smooth and reverent, with lyrics born out of desire to shower God with adoration and appreciation. This was not a time to think about problems; it was a time to bless God for who He was, and not for what He could do. Lenny closed his eyes and lifted his hands, enjoying the full sound as it filled the room with joyous refrain, and offering to God his own whispers of praise.

When the praise and worship time was done and Lenny re-acclimated himself to the crowd around him, he noticed that a few more people had been seated in his row. One of them was an older woman who bore a striking resemblance to Summer. *Must be Summer's mother*. The resemblance was just too canny. Two people sat between Susan and him, so he couldn't slide over and introduce himself. He knew he would have an opportunity to meet her after the service.

Summer and a few clergy came out to the platform and sat in tall pulpit chairs that looked as uncomfortable as they actually were. From the moment Lenny noticed her, he couldn't take his eyes off her. Her purple sleeveless dress was a bit formfitting, Lenny thought, but still very tasteful. Her high-heeled purple pumps looked to be made of patent leather or some other type of smooth material. Her Bible was in her lap, and she clutched it tightly. Lenny could tell she was nervous. He hoped no one could tell he was just as much so.

Pastor Gillen took to the pulpit after the singing was done. He was a man who didn't believe in wasting time or dragging things out. He was grateful that so many people came out to church on a Saturday, and he did not want to abuse the privilege by keeping them longer than was necessary. After a scripture reading, announcements, a few remarks, and the offering, Pastor Gillen proudly set out to introduce his new charge.

"Over the course of my ten years in the ministry, God has privileged me to oversee and shepherd the callings of many people, to the point where I sometimes feel that my only calling on earth is to help others realize theirs. If that is the case, I have no apologies nor regrets, especially when God brings people into my circle like Sister Sum-

mer. I met her under unfortunate circumstances, which, if God leads her, she will share with you. But I knew when I met her that she had a special calling from God, though I'm sure she would have denied it at the time. But you know, you can run from your calling a little while, but eventually, God catches up to you."

Several *amens* came from the crowd.

"My wife and I have known her for a little over a year, and I can tell you with all confidence, in that short period of time she has come a long way. And this morning, she is ready to take the next step, and very important step, toward realizing what God has planned for her life. Speaking from the subject, 'God Won't Hang You Out To Dry,' saints, let's welcome and receive our woman of God for the hour, Sister Summer Maldonado!"

In respect, everyone in the crowd stood and clapped, with Lenny and the woman on his left being the first to stand. Another young woman on the platform took Summer's Bible and notes and set them on the pulpit, while Summer stood, stepped over to Pastor Gillen, and embraced him. Summer took to the pulpit, switched on the wireless mic attached to her collar, and cast a gaze over the standing, clapping congregation. To Summer, it felt good to be honored this way, but it was also a little discomforting, as she was not used to speaking to this many people. Summer knew only one way to deal with it, to deflect the adoration from her and redirect it toward God.

"I want you to keep clapping and keep standing, but I want you to praise the King of Kings, and the Lord of Lords!" Summer declared. This time, voices of praise and exultation chimed in with the applause almost like the roar of a motorcycle. In the midst of praise, Summer's nervousness died down a bit, and she knew she would have no problem finding her sea legs once it was time for her to speak.

A couple of minutes later, the praise faded out, and Summer motioned everyone to sit. She surveyed the crowd, saw her mother in the second row smiling up at her. The look of good pride on Susan's face brought Summer to tears. The crowd supported her with affirmation, understanding her emotion. The young woman brought her a tissue,

and Summer used it to dab at her eyes, grateful she didn't wear or need to wear makeup.

"This is a great day for me," Summer said, clutching the tissue as if it was a source of comfort. "When I look in my mother's eyes, I see her pride at the fulfillment of her dreams for me. Some people may be surprised that I'm standing up here about to preach, but my mother was not surprised. She'd wished for this since before the day I was born in Brazil."

Susan looked up her, smiling and nodding.

"She went through so much for me. It wasn't easy for her. My mother never had much money, and her husband—my father—was abusive. But despite that, she kept me focused, and gave me a good foundation in the church. She is the reason I'm here today, and I'd like to honor her for never giving up on me. Her name is Susan, and she's here today. Mãe, would you stand."

Susan reluctantly came to her feet and smiled as the crowd stood and clapped for her like they did for Summer. But Susan, who, like her daughter, was a little uncomfortable with such praise, nodded her thanks and quickly took her seat.

Summer looked to her left and saw Lenny, smiling at her, looking handsome as ever in his black suit, the same pride on his face. She adored the purple tie. She figured he wore it because he knew that purple was her favorite color. "There's another guest I would like to acknowledge," Summer said, looking directly at him. "He was working in my building back when I was employed with Visual Notions. I helped him get a better job about a year ago. After that, we became friends. But as it turns out, he has helped me more than I have helped him. And I'm so grateful for that, and I'm so glad he could be here today. Lenny Yates, would you also stand?"

Lenny stood. Once again, the crowd clapped, but did not stand. Lenny was not the least bit offended. Mothers of preachers always received more honor than friends, and given what Susan did for Summer, it was only fitting. As he received his applause, he looked over at Susan, who was clapping and smiling. As he sat, he noticed one of the

deacons in the front row looking back at him with scorn.

Summer arranged her notes on the pulpit and took a deep breath. "My being up here is controversial for several reasons," Summer said, focusing on a wall at the far end of the sanctuary as she collected her thoughts. "One of the reasons is because these days, people want their preachers to be perfect. They may acknowledge that no man is perfect, but when it comes to preachers, people are ready to hang them out to dry the moment they make a mistake."

Some *amens* came from the crowd.

"And it doesn't matter if the mistake is past or present. Even though we have a long history of prisoners becoming preachers, former drug addicts becoming preachers, prostitutes becoming preachers, porn stars becoming preachers, some people tend to think that those who are involved in these vices have a permanent stain on their character, that they can never be anything other than what they were, and that makes them unworthy of serving God in any office." Summer paused for effect, hearing a few *umm hmms* in the crowd. "Well, I was never a prostitute. I was never a drug addict. I was not a prisoner, at least not in a *physical* jail."

The congregation appreciated her distinction, and several in the crowd rewarded her with "amen" and "come on, now."

"I was never a porn star. But a little over a year ago, I was dating a successful and handsome man. You know, single ladies, the same kind of man you are hoping God sends you. And some of you married ones, too."

The congregation broke out in laughter.

"But what looks good isn't always good, and this man cheated on me with one of my co-workers, then broke up with me. I lost my job because I threw a drink in the other woman's face, and the woman was my boss's assistant. But I was so obsessed with my man, I tried to get him back. When I couldn't, I went to a bar and drank until I was sloppy drunk. Then, I got into my car, ran a red light, flipped my car and almost killed myself."

Groans came from the congregation.

"Looking back, that's likely what I wanted to do. Later, I extorted $15,000 from my former supervisor. I won't go into details about how I did it, since this is a family service." Summer paused to allow the few snickers that came forth. "I also tried to get my man back by inviting him to Martha's Vineyard, where I was covering a story. Eventually I gave the money back, but it cost me my second job as a TV reporter. And I found out my man was still sleeping with the woman that he dumped me for. So, I found myself without my idol man and without my idol job."

Summer had pushed her notes to the side and was talking from her heart now. She stepped away from the pulpit and sauntered in a straight line in front of the platform, her tall frame in full view, to the delight of some of the men in the congregation.

Lenny cut his eyes over to the deacon who had eyed him earlier. As Summer stepped from behind the pulpit, the deacon's eyes, still firmly fixed on Summer, went south. This discouraged Lenny. Summer had told him that Xavier was history, but given the way that this deacon was ogling her, it was clear that this man wanted to be in Summer's future. He even resembled Xavier a bit. Lenny wondered if he was the guy that the 4 p.m. shift gate attendant had seen with Summer.

Take captive every thought to make it obedient to Christ. The scripture rang clear in his head. Lenny cleared his thoughts of the deacon. He couldn't go there now. If he did, he would spend the rest of the service in a foul mood. No, he was there to worship God and to support Summer.

"You know, I've talked with people who say they can't understand why people would want to commit suicide," Summer continued. "I used to be that way, until I found myself in so much emotional pain, I couldn't take it anymore. Once I lost my job, I lost my will to live. I started drinking again. I thought about starving myself to death, the pain was so deep. I had come from having a $95,000 a year executive job and a trophy man, to having no one and nothing. I was flat broke, and I was almost homeless. But thank God, Lenny Yates was there for me. Whenever you're in need, God has a way of sending the right

people at the right time."

After a chorus of *amens*, Summer continued. "He ministered me out of my depression. And it was shortly after that when I committed myself to Jesus again."

Polite applause followed. Lenny looked over at the deacon and noticed that he had started looking down toward his shoes.

"Now, I stand here only one year removed from the most painful and challenging time of my life. And there are many people in the Christian community, including in this church, who would try to step into God's shoes and make judgment as to whether a person is worthy enough to move into their calling. But if it was up to people, I would not be worthy of my calling, at least not now. But fortunately, it is not up to people. It is up to God."

The crowd roared their approval. Summer, now fully warmed up, was in her zone.

"So, for those who think that I'm too new to be under review, who think that I'm too wounded to preach healing, who think that what I went through is a reflection of where I am going, I submit to you the words of Philippians chapter one, verse six, which is my text today—," she recited the text from memory, "—'Being confident of this very thing, that he which hath begun a good work in you will perform it until the day of Jesus Christ.'"

Now even the ministers seated in the hard chairs behind her were cheering her on. That let her know she was right on target.

Her voice was elevated and sharp, with a passion that she was trained to keep absent from her objective journalistic reporting. "I am here because of the vision my mother had before I was even formed in the womb. And though the devil tried to keep me down, tried to take me out before I had reached my destiny, for every 'no' that the devil had for me, God had a 'yes.' And I want to encourage those of you who are contemplating suicide, those of you who are in a broken home, those of you who are sleeping with a man you know you shouldn't be sleeping with because you think you can't find anyone better. God has not put you on this earth for nothing. I don't care how

you got here, when you came, or how or when you are going out. God has you here for a purpose, and you will find peace and joy in Him when you are in the place where God has designed you to be."

Summer was on fire now, bolstered by the response from the congregation. "I know they call this a trial sermon, and I'm not mocking this process, because I know that there has to be a process to determine whether a person is fit for an office in a church. I understand that. But I've already had my trials."

"Amen" went the crowd.

"And I'm not done with them. Stepping into the office of an evangelist means that I will have new trials. You are not going to do anything impactful for God without some trials along the way. But the hope and faith that we have is that God is faithful. He is not the contractor that takes all your money and only finishes half the job. He is not the bride who arrives at the wedding chapel and can't say 'I do.' God will not hang us out to dry. If he started it in us, He will finish it!"

By now, all of the ministers, as well as several people in the congregation, were standing. It was their way of showing Summer that her words resonated with them, touched them, the Spirit moving in them so much they could no longer sit.

"You see, I left God, but God never left me. Oh, yes, I was a Christian. But I was a safe Christian. I didn't want to go into the danger zone of Christianity, where your allegiance to Jesus requires you to give up something precious, to face fears, to confront issues, to change your way of doing things. I picked those aspects of faith that were safe, that allowed me to maintain some connection to Jesus without being fully devoted. So, what was it for me? I never went to church. I rarely picked up a Bible. But I tried to be a good person. I tried to keep my body pure. For me, that was the extent of my devotion. For others, it may be different. Some may go to church every Sunday, and that's it. They think that act helps them maintain a link to Jesus without being fully sold out for Him. Of course, they live like they want the other days of the week. There's a radio station in Richmond that plays the vilest music twenty-four hours a day, six days a week. On Sunday, they

play the vilest music twenty-one hours. The other three hours, in the morning, they play gospel. It's like they are saying that they are going to take three hours of programming time to do this Jesus thing, and then they'll get right back to their regular programming. But what they don't realize, and I didn't realize, is that God doesn't just want part of us. He wants ALL of us. He wants us completely and totally devoted to Him. God will not settle for anything less. And I declare, this day, that God will not just have my deeds or my lady parts. He will have all of me, my heart, my mind, and my soul."

As the congregation responded with jubilant applause, Lenny watched Summer in awe. Just nine months before, he held her in his arms, when she was reeking of vodka, broken and ready to check out. Then, he would never have thought he would see this moment. But as he joined the audience in applauding, he was not clapping because of the insightfulness of her words. He was clapping because of the faith-fulness of God, who had done something in Summer that neither he, nor anyone else, could have done. They had not been in contact for almost a year, and now Lenny was convinced it was a good idea. In fact, it was brilliant. He had let her go, so that God could have her.

***

Once the service was over, Summer had so many people gathered around her that Lenny knew it would be a while before he got to extend his own congratulations. He looked around for Summer's mom, but she was nowhere to be found. Lenny thought he would wait in his car for most of the crowd to leave, after which he would head back into the church and touch base with Summer. But as he was heading back to the children's church room, the young woman who had been attending Summer on the platform caught up to him and tapped him on the shoulder from behind. Expecting it to be Summer, he turned quickly, then tried to hide his disappointment.

"Sir, I have a request from Sister Maldonado," the woman said.

"She would like you to join her back in the assistant pastor's office. Shall I show you the way?"

"Yeah, but I need to get my son first," Lenny explained.

"Not a problem. You can come with me to the office, and I'll see your son is escorted back to you," the woman said.

"Of course."

Lenny followed the young woman toward the sanctuary doors. Just before he exited, he looked back and saw that Summer was still at the front of the church surrounded by at least ten people. One of them was the deacon who was ogling Summer through most of the sermon.

Lenny followed the woman down a long corridor and through a door. He found himself inside an office, but it looked more like a lounge, with plush couches and chairs surrounding a big square glass table, a porcelain coffee service and refrigerator nearby, and a small desk in a corner which held nothing but a few files and a Bible. There were two additional doors, one that looked like a closet, and the other leading to the outside parking lot.

"Sister Maldonado will be with you shortly," the woman said. "Can I get you anything?"

"No, honey. I'm fine," Lenny said.

The woman gave him a final quick smile, and then left the office.

Lenny moved to the couch. As he sat, he heard water running from behind a door along one wall of the office. He had believed it to be a closet, but now surmised it was a bathroom. About a minute later, the door opened, and Susan stepped out. Lenny quickly returned to his feet.

"Lenny, right?" Susan moved over to the couch.

"Yes, ma'am. You must be Summer's mother."

"Sure am." Susan's smile was just a bit shy of laughter. She walked over and embraced Lenny. "So glad to meet you."

"Glad to meet you, too."

They both settled on the couch.

"Summer's told me so much about you," Susan said. "You've made quite an impression on her."

"Well, she's a precious young lady." Lenny almost slipped and said *girl*, but he found that term unsuitable for a budding evangelist.

"How did you enjoy the message?"

"I liked it a lot. She's a good preacher. Her style is a little more reserved than I'm used to, but I've learned long ago that the style isn't as important as the message."

"That's right. And Summer will likely never be one of those whoopin' and hollerin' preachers anyhow. That's not her."

"Well, I really enjoyed her today. And thank you for raising such a wonderful daughter."

"Oh, you're so sweet." Susan stood up and grabbed her purse from the table. "I have to get some groceries for dinner tonight. I'm sure I'll see you again." She headed for the parking lot exit.

Lenny stood as well. "I'll look forward to it."

Once Susan had left and Lenny found himself in the office alone, he entertained himself by reading the plaques on the walls and looking out the window at the congregants leaving church. About fifteen minutes later, Lenny heard the office door open, and in walked Summer. Lenny noticed she had ditched the high heels for a pair of flats. They embraced, then moved to the couch.

"I'm so glad you came," Summer said, the smile on her face displaying her delight.

"You kidding? I wouldn't have missed this," Lenny said. "You were great."

"Really?"

"Yeah. The content was great. You were inspiring. I could have listened to you for another hour. And trust me, I don't say that about many preachers."

"Thanks. That means a lot coming from you."

"And you're one of the foxiest preachers I've seen in a while. Even the deacon in the front row couldn't keep his eyes off you."

Summer rolled her eyes. "Deacon Staples."

"When you called me out in the service, he gave me the stink eye something awful. What's up with that?"

"Deacon Staples kinda likes me."

"Yeah? You going out with him?"

"He's driven me home from church a few times."

"Hmm." Not a direct answer to his question, but Lenny was in no mood to dig deeper.

Summer eagerly skipped the subject. "What are you doing later today?"

Lenny could think of several things he had to do, but answered, "Nothing really."

"Would you like to have dinner with me and my mother?"

Lenny answered immediately. "Sure."

"There's just one catch."

"What?"

"You have to drive about an hour and a half away from here."

"Don't tell me you moved."

"No. My mother and I are spending the weekend at Stingray Point. Ever heard of it?"

"No."

"It's right on the shore of the Chesapeake Bay. Pastor Gillen knows a couple that have a weekend home there. But the couple are out of town, and they wanted to bless someone with a mini-vacation, so Pastor Gillen nominated me. So, we're there for the rest of the weekend."

"Sounds nice."

"So, you'll come?"

"Dinner at the Bay? Are you kidding? I'm there."

"Cool." Summer walked over to the desk, removed a piece of paper from one of the files, took a pen, and began writing. She walked back over to the couch and gave the paper to Lenny. "That's the address and directions. We'll have dinner at six, but you can come early, if you want."

"I look forward to it."

"Where's your son?"

"Still in the children's church room. They're supposed to bring

him to me."

"Bring him along, too."

"Can't. Gotta take him back to his mother. This is her weekend with him."

"Oh, shame." Summer stood. "Well, I gotta go. Pastor and First Lady Gillen have invited me to lunch. They probably want to debrief me on my sermon."

"Looks like they enjoyed it, too, so I wouldn't worry too much." Lenny stood.

"So, I'll see you tonight."

"You bet."

"I'll stop by children's church and say hello to Lenny Jr."

"He'd like that."

They embraced again before Summer pointed to the parking lot door and said, "That leads to your car." She then hurried out of the room.

Lenny stood in the middle of the room, engaged in thought. He wished Summer hadn't seen Trinee the day before, as Summer seemed distracted and distant. He guessed he would have to clarify things at dinner, just like he would want Summer to clarify her relationship with Deacon Staples. Based on Deacon Staples's response to him, and Summer's willingness to quickly skip the subject, Lenny would have some serious questions at dinner.

CHAPTER SIXTEEN

Lenny followed Summer's directions precisely and found himself at the end of a state maintained road. A few yards ahead of him, beyond a few white siding cottages, was the blue-gray expanse of the Chesapeake Bay, punctuated periodically by the foamy whitecaps of waves. To his left was a dirt road, extending a few yards until it merged into grass. Lenny turned left, following the road past a small grove of trees, and found the house on the right. It was a simple, white siding one-story rambler, with a gabled roof almost half the height of the entire house. A large backyard extended out to the shore, where there was a wooden dock and a small motorboat parked near the slip leading out to the Bay.

Lenny parked and got out of the car. He took a deep breath, inhaling the fresh, salty air, mixed with the odor of burning wood and charcoal. He heard nothing except the waves crashing against the shore, a few birds, and the occasional seagull.

He looked down at himself, wondering if he had made the correct choice of attire. Once he got home from church, and after he had taken a shower, he debated whether he would wear picnic casual, or around-the-corner casual, or casual-Friday casual. He eventually settled on a pair of dark blue jeans and a white polo shirt. He completed the outfit with a pair of tan boat shoes. He hadn't worn them for a while, after a

friend told him they were only for white preppy types. But in this case, he figured they would be appropriate.

He saw smoke wafting up from the behind the house, and he walked in its direction. As he cleared the side of the house, he saw Summer in the middle of the yard, tending to a self-made stone and brick grill, wearing a short pink dress and an apron. When she heard his feet swishing on the grass, she turned.

"Hey! You made it."

"Wasn't gonna miss it. Those were great directions you gave." He looked out at the water and saw a schooner in the distance. "It's beautiful out here."

"I know. Me and Mãe have been here since Friday. It's going to be hard for me to leave. And Mãe loves it, too. There's hardly an inch of this beach she hasn't stepped on barefoot."

Lenny pulled up next to her. "What you cooking?"

"Rockfish, straight from the Bay." Summer flipped one of the fish halves, stood back as the flames licked up around it, then grabbed a lemon and began squeezing it on the fish. Lenny's mouth began watering already.

When the fish was ready a few minutes later, Summer and Lenny joined Susan inside the house. The home was very open in design, with no walls separating the living room, the dining area, and the kitchen. Large floor-to-ceiling windows occupied one wall facing the Bay, providing the trio with a gorgeous view as they sat down to eat. In addition to the grilled rockfish, Summer brought to the table a vegetable medley of squash, zucchini and onions, fried plantains, and herb-roasted potatoes. As they ate, they made light conversation about Summer's sermon, life in Brazil, and current events. Lenny ate until he was full, leaving no course untouched. By the time he was done, he felt as if he had packed on twenty pounds.

Once everyone had finished, Susan rose, collected the dishes, placed them inside the dishwasher, and then announced she was going out to a movie. She grabbed her car keys, gave both Lenny and Summer a sly smile, and then made her exit.

There was an awkward silence once Susan had left. Summer quickly broke it by saying, "You want some dessert?"

Lenny shook his head and patted his belly, which had developed a noticeable curve. "Not right now, thanks."

"You look like you need some exercise. Wanna take a walk with me to the dock?"

"Sure."

They walked out the dining room patio door and strolled across the grass to the edge of the shore, which was lined by a seawall of large stones. They walked across the dock and down the stairs to a golden sand private beach. They stood on the beach for a few minutes, watching the sun drown in the sea, making way for dusk that transformed the bay to a mirror-like sheen. While the melding of sun and sea made for a compelling and beautiful vision, Summer found the man standing next to her even more compelling. She turned to him, dying to say the words she had held back for many months.

"Lenny?"

"Yes?"

"That question you asked me right after you brought me home from your family's July 4th cookout?"

"Yes?"

"Ask it again."

"No."

"Why not?"

"Because I don't like to ask questions I already know the answer to."

"So, you got me figured out, huh?" Summer said with a smile.

"Well, you already told me that Xavier was history, and you invited me out here to this very beautiful—and kinda romantic—waterfront, and cooked me a wonderful dinner, and conveniently arranged for your mother to disappear—"

Summer laughed.

"—and you're wearing this alluring pink dress, yeah, I think I got you figured out."

Summer drew within inches of him. "I missed you so much."

"Really? Why didn't you call me?"

Summer sighed. "I wanted to. But I couldn't. I wasn't ready. Sister Gillen said not to call you unless I knew for sure I was ready to enter into a serious relationship. She said I didn't want to lead you on and then disappoint you. If you were the man for me, God would keep you until I was ready."

"Well, you made it to my apartment just in time. I was about to start talking to Trinee again."

Summer threw him a concerned look. "You and Trinee are—"

"Just friends," Lenny completed her sentence. "She left my apartment last night soon after you did, after I told her I was still in love with you."

"Do you love her?"

"No. Never did. Trinee was the woman I turned to when I was afraid I would spend the rest of my life alone. She was my safety net when my faith was weak. But I have loved you since the day you came to my church."

"The day you called me *fine* in front of 150 people."

"Yep. And I'd do it again."

Summer quietly laughed and gave him a flirty look.

"So, X is history, huh?"

"Yep. Back in August, I went to see him. He tried to convince me to come back to him, but I told him I couldn't. Since I've been participating in the sisters group at church, I learned that I wasn't really in love with X. I was in love with the *idea* of X."

Lenny was intrigued. "Explain that to me."

"X was the handsome guy. The suave dresser. The fat pockets. The man who could wine and dine me, sweep me off my feet, whisk me off to a weekend getaway on a whim. The man every girl dreams of. The man who treated me like I was a queen. The problem is that when the real man surfaced, I still wanted to cling to the ideal. I never fell in love with the real X. The real Xavier is a controlling man whom I have no expectations of actually being faithful to me more than five

minutes. The real X has no faith, no God that he answers to. And that bothered me. But again, I wanted to project my ideal onto him."

"How do I know you're not doing the same thing with me?"

The question caught Summer off guard. "Excuse me?"

"How do I know you're in love with me, and not the idea of me? Just because I go to church and love the Lord doesn't mean I'm the right man for you."

"Because there's a saying that goes, 'If you love something, set it free. If it comes back to you, it's yours. If it doesn't, it was never yours to begin with.' I spent almost a year not contacting you because I needed to know that my devotion to God was more important than my desire for you. I had to work on my own self-esteem so that I wasn't co-dependent on a man. I had to risk losing you. Sort of like when Abraham was willing to sacrifice his son in order to prove his faithfulness to God. I had to trust that if you were the one for me, God would keep you for me."

Lenny smiled. "You sound so much like a preacher now."

Summer shortened the distance between them by a couple of inches. "Is that a good thing?"

"That's a real good thing."

"The thing is, I didn't want to be in lust. I wanted to love you. I heard a preacher say once that lust is when you want something so bad, you can't be happy without it. That was me and X. And it wasn't just about sex. A woman can lust after a man's money, his power, his fame, everything good thing that he has that she doesn't."

"Let me ask you a question." Lenny held Summer's hand and led her further away from the dock, closer to the water's edge. "I've seen couples come together in lust, but they eventually had wholesome and fruitful relationships. So, can we truly say lust is a bad thing when it results in people coming together in real relationships?"

Summer thought for a moment, then said, "I don't think the end justifies the means. I mean, there are some preachers who cite being in jail as the reason why they turned their life around and became preachers, but that doesn't mean that we should go to jail. I believe that God

can turn any situation around, but that doesn't mean we should get in that situation in the first place. That's why I wanted things to be right with us. I had to learn to be happy without you in order for God to give you to me. Does that sound strange?"

"No. It sounds like wisdom to me."

"So—" Summer laid her arms on Lenny's shoulders. "—you did the right thing kicking me out of your life."

"I didn't kick you out of my life."

"Felt that way."

"Sorry you felt that way."

"It's okay, because I'm yours now." Summer drew close and placed her lips on his, giving him three short, sweet kisses. "But I do have some ground rules."

Lenny nodded. "Why doesn't that surprise me?"

"The first one is, no matter how romantic this is, and whether or not you stay over tonight, you are not going to be smashing this. Not until we get married."

Even though the statement did not surprise him, and he had no plans to be intimate with her, it still struck him as harsh for some reason. He would later learn it was his flesh reacting, not his spirit. "I wouldn't have expected anything else. I'm totally okay with that."

"Are you?"

"Yeah."

"I mean, what if you're tempted, or something?"

"Been 'cross that bridge."

"When?"

Right now, with you kissing me, wearing this sexy dress. Instead, Lenny said, "That night in your apartment."

Summer's eyes rolled back as she remembered. "Oh, yeah. That could have been a problem."

"And that time at Makeout Point."

"Yeah. I understand that."

"And *now*."

"You're tempted now?"

"Every time you kiss me."

"Maybe we should stop."

Maybe we shouldn't.

"Maybe we should."

"I'd be okay with that." Summer twisted her lip. "Kinda."

"We'll be okay. What about your other rules?"

"Be totally honest with me, even when it hurts."

"You got it. What else?"

"Always stay close to Jesus. Never give him up, not even for me."

"Hmm." Lenny looked at Summer proudly. "Well, I think that's the most important rule."

"Any rules for me?"

Yeah. Wear a burqa and a burlap bag until we get married.

"In addition to all those you just mentioned, just love me. Because I definitely love you."

"That's what's up." Summer wrapped an arm around his waist and snuggled against his shoulder while watching the seemingly infinite expanse of the Bay, knowing that her life contained as many possibilities as the waves, and harbored as many unknowns as the deep. Yet, she looked forward to facing them, with glee, knowing that the man she was meant to spend the rest of her life with was right by her side.